IN THE SHADOW OF THE KINGS

The Fabled Quest Chronicles

Book Two

AUSTIN DRAGON

Published by Well-Tailored Books, California

In the Shadow of the Kings
(Fabled Quest Chronicles, Book 2)
978-1-946590-82-4 (paperback)
978-1-946590-00-8 (ebook)

http://www.austindragon.com

Book cover design by Humbert Glaffo

Printed in the United States of America

CONTENTS

FÄE-LAND MINOR

The Lands of Fairies, Sprites, and Giants

CHAPTER ONE

Beyond the Threshold

"I will see you all in a week—a fae week, which in this realm may be a week or three."

That was what their caravan master had said to them before mounting his shape-shifting dog as the animal transformed into a giant white hawk with multicolored wings like a peacock, colored plumed feathers sprouting from its head, and eyes the brightest blue they had ever seen. Its fanciful form was that of the true fauna, flora, and lands of this magical region. Then, man and animal flew high into the perfect blue sky and disappeared into massive billowing white clouds. The sun sparkled with a rainbow hue.

That was three days ago.

They had reached the other side of the Mirage Plains' magical barrier. Lady Aylen occasionally pinched herself to prove she was not dreaming. They had suffered through many obstacles and setbacks but had made it to the magical lands, thanks to their able guide and trailmaster, the man called Traveler.

The first and second day of their camp respite was quiet and uneventful, save for the endless stories the men told each other to pass the time in anticipation of the journey ahead. Undoubtedly, they would encounter danger, have fearful days, maybe days of battle, and maybe bury men killed along the way. But for now they were in awe of the land, which twinkled with enchantment, bold and bright colors, and they could not wait until they saw their first flying horse, unicorn, fairy, or gnome.

This was the third day. Lady Aylen looked out across their five-thousand-man-strong camp, and saw why Traveler had left them there. Most of the men were asleep, but it was more than napping. They were in such a deep state of sleep, nothing could arouse them. She tried to wake their steward, Hobbs, who as a noble, had been trained to be the first man to rise and the last man to bed, but he lay upon the grass, immune to all her attempts. There was a peacefulness to his state, as there was with all the others who slept; some even had smiles on their face as if in some faraway dream. However, her own maidservant, Gwyness, was not as fortunate. She, too, slept but tossed and turned from within their tent as if gripped by a nightmare. Nothing could be done to rouse her either.

Lady Aylen watched the men who were not sleeping. Some appeared to be sleep walking, their eyes closed, wandering aimlessly from side to side or in circles. Others seemed mad, laughing uncontrollably to themselves. When she looked into their eyes, their gaze was someplace else. Only one other was awake as she was, but unlike her, he was also under the spell of the land.

"Mr. Pangolin." She slowly approached their berserker master-at-arms. He sat on the ground, facing away from the camp. As she walked around him to see his face, she noticed that his hands were locked together, fingers contorted like claws. "Are you well?"

He did not answer; his face bore a blank stare. He was awake but not there. Thick cobwebs clung to his magical armor. Suddenly, the berserker startled her, yelling out and clawing at the cobwebs. "No! I will not be entombed!"

"Mr. Pangolin, what is happening?"

He did not hear her. His gaze remained fixed into the distance. He would have continuous outbreaks, and she could do nothing to help him. The princess slowly returned to the main camp.

King Aereth lay in his royal tent so still that he seemed without life. The princess pressed her hand against his chest, and his heart beat normally, but he too was under the same magical sleep as were most of the men.

Lady Aylen again returned to the women's tent. Gwyness's state hadn't changed. Occasionally, she talked in her slumber, but the words were gibberish.

"What madness have you left me to watch over, Mr. Traveler?" Lady Aylen asked the question, but there was no one to hear her. All she could do was sit quietly by herself and continue with her vigil. She could not help but feel uneasy about the complete helplessness of the camp.

Traveler's words of a fae week weighed on her heavily. Had three human days passed or three fae days? Was there such a difference? Regardless of the answer, she did not wish to spend another day alone such as this.

◆◆◆

Lady Aylen opened her eyes and stared up at the tent from her trussing-bed. It was not the large, extravagant bed she was accustomed to in her royal court, but it was not a cot, and it was more than comfortable and elevated a foot off the ground. She turned her head and saw Gwyness fast asleep. Her maidservant looked content and finally free from the nightmares that had plagued her. The princess looked around their women's tent: provisions against one side, wide bowls of water on collapsible tables in the center, and weapons closest to them. She felt strange somehow. How long had she been asleep? At first she was sure she had slept straight through the night, but now she wondered if she may have slept much longer.

She leapt from her bed. After she cleaned her face in the wash basin of water, groomed herself, and dressed properly befitting the princess of Sirnegate that she was, she stepped out of the tent. Her mouth dropped open, aghast.

Hobbs was covered in an assortment of rainbow-colored flowers growing from his hair, ears, and clothes. Other men were covered in the same, or mushrooms, or a single variety of flowers such as tulips, daisies, lilies, daffodils, or sunflowers. Thick dewy cobwebs covered other men, while others still were covered with grass so thick that no natural part of the man was visible.

She stepped back into the women's tent to look again at Gwyness. Her maidservant's hair, face, and neck were free, but her blanket was like a miniature forest of trees and plants she had never seen before. Gwyness exhaled, and from her mouth came an eruption of white seeds as if she were a dandelion. The air carried the seeds out of the tent and into the sky.

Lady Aylen found herself trying not to laugh. Then she remembered. She dashed from the tent and through all the sleeping men. Pangolin sat alone, facing away from the camp. He was coated in thick reddish soil over all his magical armor. The soil had also formed a mound up to his chest. She walked around to see his face; he was awake. His blank gaze was fixed far off in the distance, and his eyes were red, as if from crying.

"Are you awake, Mr. Pangolin?" she asked.

"I am, princess."

"What is happening to you? Are you in pain?"

"No pain. The worst of it is over. I can feel it ending, this magic."

"Is there anything I can do? Do you need any water?"

"No. I must let the magic pass through me."

"We will all see this through, Mr. Pangolin."

"You are unaffected, princess?"

"Yes, it would appear so."

"You were unaffected by the king's teleportation spell too. Are you immune to magic?"

"No, Mr. Pangolin. I am definitely not. When Mr. Traveler returns, I am sure he can tell us what my special uniqueness is."

"Yes, I hope he returns soon."

"You should try to sleep, Mr. Pangolin. All the men are asleep, and so is my maidservant. I have been standing watch over the camp, just as you would, and Mr. Traveler said we are safe here."

"Yes, I should sleep." The berserker warrior drifted off into a deep sleep at the very moment he closed his eyes.

Lady Aylen sighed. Her patience was growing thin, but she hoped Mr. Pangolin's words were true: the magic's effect on them was ending.

♦♦♦

Mr. Traveler told them not to leave the circle. Lady Aylen knelt on the ground to study it closer. At first glance it appeared to be a thick line created by paintbrush, but it wasn't white as she first thought. It seemed to be made of light itself. It was not solid or physically etched on the ground. The light circle actually floated above it.

"Is this of magic too?" she asked. With everyone asleep, she found that she had been doing quite a bit of talking to herself the past few days.

"Good day, m'lady."

Lady Aylen turned. A man, still half-asleep, approached, barely able to stand.

"Good man, you should return to your sleeping before you fall where you stand."

"Yes, m'lady. I—I do feel a bit—" The man collapsed.

Lady Aylen checked him, but he hadn't injured himself. He was, however, fast asleep again, smiling, off into a dream.

◆ ◆ ◆

Am I sleeping?

Often, Lady Aylen wondered if she, too, might be sleepwalking. It was merely a feeling, but sometimes she felt that the reality of things around her was distorted. Something disturbed the silence of the camp, and she reacted—but very slowly, as if waking from a sleep state. She thought she had seen a figure moving quickly through the men, but as she scanned the camp with her full wits regained, there was nothing to be seen.

She didn't know how much later it was, but she had the same feeling of a presence.

"What is that? Is someone there?" Near the women's tent was a new tent, one not there before. Light glimmered from inside it. "Ha!" She ran to the tent.

At the entrance to the new tent was the dog.

"Miserable animal, you are back!" she said with a smile. The dog snarled. "Where is your master?"

She reached the tent. "Princess, you should not smile so in front of him." Mr. Traveler, their guide and trailmaster, had returned.

"Mr. Traveler." She could barely contain her glee. "You and your companion crept into the camp like thieves."

"Crept, princess? We flew in a day ago as brashly as when we departed. You were as deep in sleep as the men."

"A day ago, Mr. Traveler? A human day or a magical day?"

Traveler laughed. "You took me too seriously, princess. Now that we are in Faë-Land, it might be best not to make continual comparisons to the Lands of Man. I thought you were the one most eager to put those days behind us."

"I was, and am. Was I truly asleep for a day, or are you not being serious again?"

"You were. However, do not be concerned that you did not look your noble best. Also, should you be wondering, all the men, including the king, are in perfect form. They will rise from their enchanted sleep fully recovered."

"When will this magic upon the camp leave us be so we can continue our journey, Mr. Traveler? I do not want to remain here forever."

"We can wake the men tomorrow. They will all be famished, so days of sleep will be replaced by days of eating and drinking."

"As long as we are on our way at the earliest possible time, Mr. Traveler. Then we will determine how able a guide you truly are."

Traveler grinned. "Yes, princess."

"Good morning, sir," Hobbs said, his eyes heavy. Still, he managed to stay on his feet. "Or, I think it is morning."

"Well, Mr. Hobbs," Traveler said, as he prepared a broth in not one but three large pots over a large campfire at the center of the camp, "it is a good morning somewhere on Pan-Earth."

"Sir, I can attend to the meal for the men," Hobbs said, reaching out to take the extremely large wooden spoon from Traveler to stir the pots. "Did we have that spoon before, sir?"

"The dog and I stopped by a fae town and purchased some new supplies and provisions. The men must get accustomed to eating the foods of the region."

Hobbs drew closer to the pots resting on the metal grill over the fire and peeked in. "What are we eating, sir?" He looked up, smiling. "Fae food, sir? Is there such a term?"

"Fae food." Traveler chuckled. "Yes, Mr. Hobbs, we humans will be an endless source of amusement to the fae in this region."

"Oh, good morning, m'lady," Hobbs greeted.

Lady Aylen appeared. "Good morning, Mr. Hobbs. We are glad to have you back among the wide-awake. What are you having our Mr. Traveler serve us this morning?"

"Fae food, m'lady."

Lady Aylen laughed. "Fae food? Pray tell, what is fae food?"

A scream erupted from the women's tent. Hobbs started to it, but the princess held up a hand. "No, Mr. Hobbs. I can tell the different types of screams from my maidservant. That was one of annoyance. There is no cause for concern. She is fine."

"Mr. Hobbs," Traveler said as he handed the large spoon to the steward, "I will leave this to you while I start more campfires."

"Our guide and trailmaster is also a cook," Lady Aylen remarked. "What can you not do, Mr. Traveler? Healer, swordsman, miserable dog tamer. This is far too much for me to keep track of."

"I am sure you will manage, princess."

"Sir, have the men help you. I see more than a few awake. Mr. Quillen! Get up from your sleeping. Mr. Sutton, I see you. Get up! Get the men up and attend to the morning meals. Our caravan master is not the cook too."

Lady Aylen laughed.

Gwyness yelled out again, seated on her bed. She looked at the second long flower that she had pulled from her ear. "How did you get in there?" She threw it to the ground and vigorously passed her fingers through her hair. "Why are plants growing on me?!"

"Gwyness!" She heard Lady Aylen's voice from outside the tent. "The entire camp can hear you throwing a fit."

"I have plants growing on me, m'lady!"

"I have stories of you from when you slept."

"What do you mean, m'lady? What stories?"

Hobbs was content as he walked through the camp. Order had finally been restored. Those with duties were busy at work—cleaning up after the meals or setting up the full camp. For most others, they sat in smaller groups talking, smoking pipes, telling stories, and laughing at jokes. Horseplay was kept to a minimum. He reached the leadership all seated around the fire near the royal tents and Traveler's.

"Are you happy, Mr. Hobbs?" Traveler asked.

"I am, sir. Titan's Caravan is back to its routine." Hobbs took his place around the fire, sitting on a stool from the Kings Elder he was growing very fond of.

Hobbs thought to himself, that it was the first time he had seen King Aereth without his crown, but he wore a very regal tunic over his trousers.

"Mr. Traveler, are we past the effects of this land? I take it this befalls all who enter it for the first time," the king said.

"Yes, sire. It happened to me, as well, when I first came here as a boy."

"Is it ever dangerous, Mr. Traveler?" Gwyness asked.

Traveler shook his head. "Never."

"So, Mr. Traveler," Lady Aylen asked, "what is our course of action moving forward?"

"We will endeavor to make our caravan less human and more fae, princess. It will not take long, but it will take time. I have already sold our horses and donkeys."

"Yes, I was about to ask," she said. "We do not want to vex any centaurs or provide meals for hippogriffs and griffins."

Traveler held back a grin. "I know how fond royals are of their steeds, so you will have new steeds."

"New steeds?" Quillen's eyes lit up. "What kind, Mr. Traveler?"

Traveler looked at the lad. "What kind should we get, Mr. Quillen, since you are our resident magical beast chronicler?"

The lad thought for a moment. Estus and Pangolin began to laugh. "Hippogriffs and griffins are too...commonplace for us now."

"Commonplace?" Lady Aylen asked. "How quickly have our standards inflated?"

"Flying horses, Mr. Traveler," he declared.

"Interesting choice, Mr. Quillen, but we should have our steeds land-bound like ourselves—easier to maintain and drawing less attention. I am already at work on the matter, but it will be the last thing we attain before we set out from our first fae city."

"Can I have a steed, Mr. Traveler?"

Hobbs scoffed at the lad. "Mr. Quillen, no."

"Unfortunately, I must agree with Mr. Hobbs. The king and the princess and Maiden Gwyness. The steeds will be for ceremonial purposes mostly, though such ceremonial courtesies are of extreme importance. But the ones I have in mind will be intelligent enough to also protect our caravan."

"Ceremonial? How do you mean, Mr. Traveler?" King Aereth asked.

"Once we cross into Faë-Land Major, sire, leaders of caravans or any party only speak to one another from mounted steeds, royal to royal only. It is a role you and Lady Aylen will excel at. But we are getting ahead of ourselves. We have not even started across Faë-Land Minor."

"What is the difference between the lands, Mr. Traveler?" Lady Aylen asked.

"Simply put, princess, Faë-Land Minor is the land of the fairies and sprites. Faë-Land Major is the land of the elves."

"What of goblins and the like, Mr. Traveler?" Quillen asked.

"All dark fae also inhabit Faë-Land Major, the farthest reaches from where we will journey. Goblins, hobgoblins, orcs, and the like."

"Trolls?" the lad asked.

"They can be found anywhere in Faë-Land."

"What of witches, warlocks, and undead creatures?" Gwyness asked.

"They inhabit another land—the Dark Lands, or a region called Necropolis. But you need not worry yourself about either. They are nowhere near our journey along Titan's Trail."

♦♦♦

They learned that where they made camp was called Beyond the Threshold. The threshold being the Mirage Plains, which marked the end of the Lands Between. Though the magical effects of the land had passed, it still retained an enchanted feel. The men said even breathing the air was like drinking a medical tonic that aroused a happy, carefree state of mind. They also noticed the nights were more like dusk—the trees, grass, brush, the land were always giving off a sort of illumination.

"You must be thinking the same thing I am, Lady Aylen." King Aereth and the princess were the last two at the campfire, enjoying the quiet as the men of the camp settled in to sleep.

"What might that be, sire?"

"That one might be content with staying here in this land between the Lands Between and Faë-Land and decide not to move on farther."

"Tempting, sire. But we cannot attain riches for our kingdoms by remaining here."

Lady Aylen watched her maidservant speaking with Traveler. When he dismissed Hobbs and the rest of the men, he gestured to Gwyness. They had been talking for a while now, though their voices were hushed. Still, she normally would have been able to hear them from the distance she sat, but something in the air was preventing it— something like a low hum. Was it the dog? She did not see him. With the growing night, she also could not see their faces. It was clear her maidservant was upset. King Aereth had also taken notice of them.

Gwyness walked back to the women's tent.

"Is everything fine, Gwyness?" Lady Aylen asked as she passed.

"Yes, m'lady." She glanced at her only for a moment.

Lady Aylen looked up, but Traveler was already gone. She noticed him again strolling through the camp, the dog at his side.

"Well, Lady Aylen, I will bid you a good night," King Aereth said as stood from the fire.

"Yes, sire. I should do the same. We should have a productive day tomorrow."

Lady Aylen emerged from the women's tent early in the morning with a perplexed look. Gwyness sat at the campfire with King Aereth eating their morning meal. Estus always ate with the men he camped with, and Pangolin ate exclusively with his Cut-Throats. Hobbs used the time to mingle among the men and ate his meal on the move. The princess noticed the camp was very quiet.

"Are we missing some men?" she asked.

"We are, Lady Aylen," King Aereth answered, drinking from his cup. "Our Mr. Traveler led a thousand of the men away before dawn. No one knows where, but they are supposed to return by noon, or thereabouts."

Lady Aylen sat beside her maidservant. "We have no idea where?"

"None, m'lady."

Lady Aylen looked up and there was Hobbs, rapidly approaching. "M'lady, your morning meal will be served quickly."

She laughed. "How do you stewards do it? Have you been watching for me all this time? Mr. Hobbs, I can pour my own tea."

Hobbs directed a camp lad to serve her morning meal. "No need, m'lady. A caravan is a community, and everyone has their own tasks. Please do not interfere in the order of things."

The royals laughed. "Lady Aylen, you have been reprimanded," Aereth said.

"Yes, I have, sire." The lad handed her a cup and plate of food. "Thank you, young lad." She settled the plate on her lap and turned to her maidservant. "So, Gwyness."

"M'lady, I will save you the time."

"You do not know what I was about to ask."

"I do, and it was nothing at all, m'lady." Gwyness had finished and rose from her seat. The royals watched as she returned to the women's tent.

"Sorry for that, sire. My maidservant seems not to be in a particularly gracious mood today."

"I am sure we will all have many days of similar behavior. This is a long journey."

"A journey, sire, that we have barely begun. Where did Mr. Traveler take our men off to?"

"Lady Aylen, what are your thoughts and feelings of what occurred in the Mirage Plains?"

She was quiet for a moment before answering. "Sire, it is as if, all of it, was…a dream."

"Yes, exactly."

"It is this place we rest in."

"I normally do not move on so lightly and quickly from the murder of anyone, let alone almost five thousand men."

"And that evil sorceress, sire. I do hope it, too, is behind us. I would ask our guide and trailmaster, but he is not the most optimistic of storytellers, is he?"

"No, he is not, but he speaks the truth and does not give any unrealistic expectations. Somehow I think that is more important here than was the case in Avalonia."

"I wonder, sire, how things stand in your kingdoms."

"I have full confidence in my fellow kings, our sorcerers, and our men. I know we have already triumphed in that illegal war, or will soon do so."

"Yes, sire."

"Let us pray we do not have to face any here."

♦♦♦

"The men return!"

The camp came alive. Men stood from where they ate their noon meal to watch Traveler lead their thousand comrades back to camp, his dog at his side.

"What are they carrying?" Lady Aylen asked.

King Aereth and Gwyness sat near her, but they could not see the men at that distance.

"You have the eyes of a falcon, Lady Aylen." King Aereth stood to get a better look. The camp gathered around them as Traveler moved past, headed to his tent with the dog.

"Mr. Traveler," the king greeted. "Any trouble?"

"None at all, sire. The men will settle back in."

"What are those men carrying, Mr. Traveler?" Lady Aylen asked.

He smiled as he passed. "Princess, you three should join the men and see."

"Ladies, let us see what there is to see." The king led them to the gathering men.

The chatter had grown quite loud. Men parted to let the royals and Gwyness move closer. Gwyness stopped, but the royals continued.

"Are those...eggs?" Lady Aylen asked.

"Yes, m'lady," one of the men replied. He held a large, brown, leathery egg with both arms.

"That egg is half your size. What is it?"

"M'lady, they are lizards."

The royals looked at all the men who had returned with Traveler. Each one of them held a similar leather egg. "Lizards," Lady Aylen remarked. "Why do we have lizards? I hate lizards. Mr. Traveler!"

Hobbs gathered the men in front of the royal tent. The leadership stood facing the men. The men with the new lizard eggs stood to one side.

"Men, we are in the Magical Lands, but our journey through Titan's Trail has not really begun. All we have done is left our own homeland. However, before we can begin our true journey, we must prepare ourselves." Traveler's voice carried loudly across the camp.

"We are in a land of magic, but we are not magical beings. First, you had to rest so your thoughts and bodies can grow accustomed to these new lands and its magic. Earlier today, I took some of your colleagues on a brief trek to acquire the newest fae members of the caravan— giant lizards."

Men laughed and looked at those holding the lizard eggs.

"When the eggs hatch, these lizards will be of every color of the rainbow. They will be the size of a small pup at first, but when fully grown, will become many times larger than a horse."

Everyone looked at each other with smiles and surprise.

"These lizards will protect our flanks, and the men who mind them will no longer be servants, but will be part of our caravan's defense. They will remain under Mr. Hobbs's stewardship though."

"What shall we call them, sir? We have the Cut-Throats. Should they be called the Lizard Men?" The man got the laughter he expected.

"They will be our lizard minders," Traveler answered. "Each man will manage one lizard. These lizards will protect all of our lives. As they grow, you will see their abilities."

"Protect us from what, sir?" another man asked.

"Everything. Before I can be your caravan master, I must ensure that you all cease to be a human caravan but become a fae caravan. This is only the first step.

"I will work with Mr. Hobbs for the remainder of the day, instructing him on the dress and customs to be found in Faë-Land. You will not be humans from the Lands of Man. You will be humans at home and knowledgeable in the ways of Faë-Land.

"There will be many rules for you to know as we travel our yearlong trek through Titan's Trail, but there are three above all others. One, never go anywhere alone, even within the camp. Two, never leave the circle—never, unless given permission and you are not alone. Three, never leave the circle without your charms."

"Charms?" "Charms, sir?" Many men asked the question at the same time.

"Mr. Hobbs will show you. We are humans. We are in the lands of fairies and sprites. Without those charms, a fairy could fly up to your ear, completely invisible to your eyes, whisper, and you would run into the nearest river and drown. Or an imp could look into your eyes, mesmerize you, and command you to stab yourself out of simple malicious glee. That is not to mention what dark fae can make you do, and some of those fae are carnivorous."

Traveler's words made everyone nervous.

"Three rules!" he shouted. "And Mr. Hobbs will drill you on them daily, so be prepared. Another thing. If any of you have any dreams that seem strange to you in any way, you must tell Mr. Hobbs immediately. We may be humans and not of magic, but who may know if one of your ancestors was fae and you possess an ability or two that will become active in these lands?"

Everyone looked at each other again.

"Tomorrow, I will take another thousand men out to get them their own lizards."

"More lizards, Mr. Traveler!" Lady Aylen cried out. Men laughed.

Pangolin raised a hand. Traveler nodded. "Mr. Traveler, we have five thousand, maybe six thousand men. You are turning two thousand of them into warriors, correct?"

"Yes, Mr. Pangolin, that will be their primary function moving forward. Those men will be the caravan's defense under Mr. Hobbs. Your two thousand will be the caravan's battle offense when needed. And I will assign almost a thousand others to Mr. Estus."

"Me, sir?" Estus was surprised.

"Yes, Mr. Estus. Our new lizard and warriors will need to be properly armored."

Estus slapped his forehead. "Of course."

"They will be your metalworkers and armorers."

"Mr. Traveler, that will leave precious few for domestic and laborer work, not to mention we will have no bearers at all," the king said.

"Very true, sire, which is why we will be adding many more fae members to our caravan. And not lizards."

King Aereth grinned. "The human-like variety, I imagine. Will we also be adding a healer to our caravan, Mr. Traveler? As gifted as you are, guide and trailmaster should be your only functions."

"Yes, sire, we will. We will also acquire fae warriors—"

"Fae warriors?" Pangolin asked. "Good."

"Yes, Mr. Pangolin. Without them, our caravan would not survive in a real battle."

"You, me, and the dog cannot do all the real fighting."

"Gentlemen, I am capable of battle too," Lady Aylen snapped. "Quite effectively, I might add."

"And so are we, Mr. Pangolin!" one of the Cut-Throats added.

"Mr. Pangolin, seems like you stirred up a bit of controversy by your comments," Traveler said.

"They will get over it. What fae warriors? Will they be under my command?"

"Yes, Mr. Pangolin, but you will need to earn their respect."

"That will be no problem."

"I know. Tomorrow, the rest of the lizards. The next day, you and I set out to acquire those fae warriors." Traveler looked at the royals. "The day after that, we will take a small party to a fae town and see what supplies we can attain, maybe also acquire some men."

"Mr. Traveler," Gwyness spoke up. "What of sorcerers?"

"Yes." Traveler's face seemed troubled. "It will not be easy to find a suitable one, and we must have at least one in our caravan, or we cannot move forward."

"You are starting to worry me again, Mr. Traveler," Lady Aylen said.

"The deeper we move into Faë-Land, the more the people and animals of the land will not only be more magical, but will be able to work magic against us. We need at least one sorcerer. In the Lands of Man, the caravan chose who they accepted into their group. Here, it is the reverse; the fae choose the caravan they wish to join and serve."

"Mr. Traveler, is being human a black mark against us?" King Aereth asked.

"It is, and it is not," Traveler answered. "We must show the fae that we are powerful enough to make the journey through Titan's Trail to Atlantea. If we can, they will join us because we have something they do not."

"The Atlanteans like humans," Lady Aylen said.

"Yes."

"So that was not a jest?"

"Not completely. The truth is we humans are the only race that has not made war against Atlantea in the past. For that reason alone, we would be welcome. Any others would need to be under our auspices to be allowed in."

"Is Atlantea a good kingdom, Mr. Traveler?" Gwyness asked.

"A strange question to ask this late into the journey."

"It is a fair question, Mr. Traveler," Lady Aylen said. "You did say you lived there."

"I did, and it is a good kingdom. The people, like in every other kingdom, run the gamut from beautiful to wretched. When we arrive, we will learn which sits on the throne."

"Now, I am worried," Lady Aylen said wryly.

"Princess, we will have so many other things to worry about along the way that, by the time we reach there, if we reach there—"

"When we reach there," she corrected.

"When we reach there, you will have long forgotten this conversation and any worry you had about the destination."

Traveler took the second group of men out of camp before dawn, but most were already awake, even before Hobbs. Quillen walked through the first group of men with their lizard eggs, notebook in hand, filled with questions.

"How do you care for the eggs?" he asked.

"We carry them with us during the day, and at night, we must bury them and sleep on top of the ground."

"Sleep on top of them? What if they hatch?"

The man didn't answer. He had a frightened look. "I would rather not think about it."

The men returned. Another thousand men carried leather fae lizard eggs. Traveler let them settle in as the camp gathered around them to gawk at and touch the eggs. Hobbs walked with him back to the leadership tents. He glanced at the dog. It was different somehow, but he could not place it.

"Sir, can the men truly manage lizards larger than horses?"

"There is no danger, Mr. Hobbs. The lizards bond with and protect those who care for them. The caravan is their home, and they will protect it."

"Sir, the lizards...how do they fight an enemy?"

"The lizards are pack animals, like many in the magical lands. They watch as a pack. They fight as a pack. It is quite something to behold when you do. Once Mr. Estus equips them with armor, they will become almost like a living wall."

Hobbs nodded. "Tomorrow, you leave with Mr. Pangolin?"

"Yes, that is the plan."

They entered Traveler's tent. The dog barked. They turned. Nirgund, the berserker, was following them. "Mr. Traveler, can I speak with you privately? I can return."

"No, not at all, Mr. Nirgund," Hobbs said. "Sir, I will see to the men's duties."

As Hobbs left, Nirgund entered. The dog watched him. The berserker smiled at him sheepishly.

"Yes, Mr. Nirgund."

"Well, sir. I—I—"

"Mr. Nirgund, I am surprised that a fearsome warrior such as yourself cannot come right out and say what is on his mind."

"Sir, I want an animal."

"What?"

"The men have fae animals. I would like one too. I had a beautiful wolf when I was a boy. We were inseparable. He was killed in a battle, and still I miss him. I am a natural with animals, and I would not mind caring for one and training it."

"Mr. Nirgund, you are one of the Cut-Throats. Are you not Mr. Pangolin's second-in-command?"

"I am, but, sir, this is a once-in-a-lifetime opportunity."

"I do plan to get the Cut-Throats animals too."

"Oh, very good, sir."

"But it sounds as if you have something else in mind."

"Well, sir, I'm aware that I am known as an eccentric berserker, but I was once the guardsman for our king. It was short-lived, as he was killed in battle too. I was not present at the time."

"Good to know, Mr. Nirgund."

"I feel I can do more. Our royals do not have a proper royal guard, and they should. I could fill that role. King's guardsman with my own animal, as you have, sir."

"Well, Mr. Nirgund, I must say I am surprised by your request, pleasantly, that is."

"I know, sir. Berserker and all. We are known for warring but not much else. But I can do much more. The king is without his own king's guards, and so is Lady Aylen. I could protect both of them so that you would not have to."

"With the proper animal."

"Yes, sir."

"I will see to it then, but it will not be for a while."

"Yes, sir. That is more than acceptable."

"Then it is settled."

Nirgund smiled. With so many men in the caravan, it was the first time that the caravan master had gotten to take in the berserker's facial tattoos, and the fact that he was missing quite a few teeth.

♦ ♦ ♦

Hobbs rose before dawn and started his morning routine as he always did, which included getting into his clothes for the day, washing his face, and then making the rounds through the camp to wake up any laze-abouts.

Ever since they entered the magical lands, they had all noticed how hospitable the weather was, even at night. By day, there was an ever-blowing cool breeze. By night, the air had a warm comfort. The royals and Traveler had tents, but all the other men slept under the stars, which most preferred. Most would not want a tent even if it was offered. It was the expected life of a caravan.

"Mr. Hobbs." Traveler had appeared on his rounds before the steward had barely started.

"Yes, sir."

"Change of plans. I am postponing my outing with Mr. Pangolin for the moment. Instead, get the men ready to head out. We will still do our training of the charms, though."

"Yes, but head out, sir?"

"Yes, we leave this area and step into Faë-Land Minor, the land of fairies and sprites. Prepare the men."

"Yes, sir. The change of plans is not a bad omen is it, sir?"

"Not at all. Nothing of concern. Simply an event I became aware of, that Mr. Pangolin and I can take advantage of to benefit the caravan. I will notify the royals. We will set out after the lizards hatch."

"Hatch, sir." Hobbs half-laughed.

"Any day now."

"Sir, will we have a specific destination? You mentioned visiting our first fae town days ago."

"Yes. It is very similar to when we were in Avalonia. Before Hopeshire, there were the Grass Lands. Here, there is also a loose network of fae villages that we will visit. They are called the Enchanted Glens. Then we will acquire what we need before we dare move on to our first fae city. The cities here are of a magnitude that none of you can imagine, not to mention the danger. But that is much later on, so no need to concern yourself."

"The men are going to ask, sir. What manner of people will they see in these villages?"

"Fae, of course, Mr. Hobbs. Sprites, fairies, gnomes, and more. However, it is not quite the childhood fairytale."

"How so, sir?"

"They are people, Hobbs. Good and bad, just like humans."

CHAPTER TWO

The Enchanted Glens

"No!" The man's scream rang through the camp.

Traveler bolted out of his tent towards the scream with his large sword sheathed, and the dog running behind him. He drew near the commotion and stopped with a look of annoyance.

The man grimaced in fear, holding a large orange lizard in his hands.

"Why are you screaming, man? I told you the lizards are not carnivorous."

"But, sir, what is it trying to do?"

"Well, it is not trying to eat you. Let it go, and you will see."

The man reluctantly set it down on the ground, and it instantly jumped on the man and ran under his tunic. "Ah!" the man screamed and set off laughter among the men.

"Lizards are cold-blooded. That is to say, as living things, their blood is cold and ours is warm, so it is seeking out heat. That means your body heat. Stop screaming. It is not dignified for a large man like you to be screaming."

"Sorry, sir."

They heard another man screaming. His lizard's leather egg had hatched too. A yellow lizard's head popped out. Men looked around. The eggs seemed to be hatching all at once.

Traveler turned to Hobbs, who stood next to him. "Instruct the men to do as we prepared for."

"Yes, sir."

"Bundle up the lizards in a blanket and have the men tuck them under an arm to give the lizard the most heat possible. Then have those men without lizards prepare the pouches of food for each man. The lizards will be constantly eating, so the men might as well get accustomed to their new daily duties."

"Will it be the same when the lizards grow, sir?"

"Then it will be different. We will simply set them in front of their food, but usually they will eat only once per day. It becomes easier to manage, but that is when they are twice the size of a horse."

"Sir, twice as large as a horse?"

Traveler smiled. "Ask me again and I will tell you that the lizards will be three times the size of a horse."

"How large will these lizards become, sir?"

"You will see, Hobbs."

"Oh dear. That means at least five times the size of a horse."

"I did say they would be like a living, breathing wall for the caravan."

"You did, sir."

More men cried out.

"Hobbs, take charge of these men. No more screaming. This is the fearsome Titan's Caravan. It is embarrassing."

The men without lizards stood in columns at attention as Hobbs walked from man to man for inspection. Each man showed him double necklaces of herbs and crystals around their necks—the charms.

"Mr. Hobbs, these seem to be nothing more than leaves and rocks strung together," one man said.

"They are far more than that, man. Keep them tucked under your top, and make sure they never leave you."

"Yes, sir."

Hobbs's inspection took some time as he was very thorough. Many of the men didn't believe the "charms" had any magical properties at all, but he sternly rebuked them.

He returned to the front of the column where Traveler, his dog, and the leadership waited.

"All inspected, sir," Hobbs said. "Though, I must inform you that not all the men take the seriousness of the charms to heart."

"That is fine, Hobbs. As long as they never remove them from around their necks, I do not care."

"That is not very charitable, Mr. Traveler," Lady Aylen said to him. "The men should believe in what they are doing."

"No, they need to simply follow Mr. Hobbs's orders. Often on this journey they will be asked to take a certain action, and it will not always make sense, but we won't have time to give them a lengthy explanation. They must do it out of trust."

"Yes, indeed, Mr. Traveler," the king said. "Loyalty and trust. The foundation of any successful group of men under command."

"Yes, sire." Traveler made sure all the leadership were listening. "The lizard minders—"

"We must find a better name for them than lizard minders, Mr. Traveler," Lady Aylen remarked.

"I am sure we will, princess. They will remain within the camp. Mr. Hobbs, you will command the camp in our absence."

"Yes, sir."

"Mr. Estus, you will also be busy at work in the camp."

"Yes, Mr. Traveler. Fashioning leashes for every one of our colored fae lizards for the minders. And adjusting them as the beasties grow. Seems my work will never be done, because then Mr. Traveler tells me that I will be tasked with turning the whole lot—lizard and minder—into battle-armored fighting teams."

"Job security, Mr. Estus. Mr. Pangolin will accompany the royals and Maiden Gwyness with a contingent of his Cut-Throats."

"Mr. Traveler, can I come?" Quillen asked. "Please?"

Hobbs looked at the lad and shook his head. "How can you be my second if you run off all the time?"

"Mr. Hobbs, it is my first fae village. I must be there."

Traveler smiled. "If Mr. Hobbs agrees, I have no issue with it."

"Go," Hobbs said.

"Thank you, Mr. Hobbs."

"Don't thank him yet, Mr. Quillen. It simply means you will act in his stead on this trip."

"Yes, Mr. Traveler." The lad barely could contain his anticipation; he smiled and clapped his hands.

"Mr. Hobbs," Traveler began, "under no circumstances is any man to leave the circle of the camp."

"Yes, sir."

"No, you do not understand. I have no doubt you will be besieged by all manner of fae trying to get you or any of the men to come out of the circle. You must guard against this. In fact, keep the men close to the center and away from the perimeter. Men without lizards will stand as sentries around them."

"What would happen if they left the circle, Mr. Traveler?" Quillen asked. "The charms would protect us."

"Mr. Quillen, the charms protect against enchantment, not a blow to the face, or someone or something snatching the charms from around your neck to steal the boots from your feet."

"Thievery, Mr. Traveler?" Lady Aylen was as surprised by Traveler's answer as the others.

"Fae mischief, princess. Let us set out. Mr. Hobbs, tell all the men who must remain behind that I will lead a special trip to the fae villages for them later."

"Oh, thank you, sir. They will be very glad to hear that."

The full caravan had moved out of the area beyond the Mirage Plains threshold, an hour's march into Faë-Land Minor, where they set up the new camp with a quaint vibrant-green wooded area to one side. The towering green moss-covered mammoth trees of where they had camped before, were far behind them.

They watched Traveler and Pangolin lead the royals and five hundred men off to the first fae village in the Enchanted Glens. Hobbs wished he was with them, but he was in charge of the camp. With Quillen gone too, Hobbs assigned two men to act as his own guards.

"Maybe we will get to see a fairy or two, Mr. Hobbs," one guard joked.

"Yes, maybe."

"Just remember what Mr. Traveler said," the other guard began. "Don't step out of the circle."

Hobbs did not envy Mr. Estus. Their weaponsmaster and forge had begun the laborious work of fitting each lizard with a leash. It was a thick leather collar with a long thin chain. The lizard minders were still a source of amusement in the camp. The lizards, in addition to being fond of running under tunics, liked to perch themselves on the men's shoulders and heads. Also, as Traveler warned them ahead of time, the lizards were forever wanting food. The men fed them a mix of what looked like grain, roots, and seeds.

"What if a man were to eat this, Mr. Hobbs?" a man asked.

"Do not eat your lizard's food," Hobbs scolded. "You have your food."

"But they eat my food, too."

"Then don't let them."

"Mr. Hobbs!" someone called from within the camp.

As he turned, Hobbs saw them immediately. A group of hooded-cloaked people approached the circle from a wooded area. His guards followed as Hobbs neared them from within the camp. There were five of them—a woman in the lead and four men.

When the woman came into clear view, Hobbs was immediately taken by her. She had striking features, and her skin appeared to glow. They all looked to be human. Having fitted many a royal, Hobbs knew his fabrics well. Their hooded cloaks were made of a material that seemed to be nothing more than blue butterfly wings weaved together.

"Good day, kind sir," the woman greeted.

"Good day, mistress," Hobbs responded.

"We are so fortunate to have come across you. Our journey has been long and perilous. May we ask for kind assistance?"

"How may we be of service, mistress?"

"We seek shelter to rest our tired bones. May we rest within your camp until morning? We are happy to pay a recompense for the privilege."

"That is most kind, mistress. My master is elsewhere, but he will return soon. Rest yourself nearby; we can bring your request to him upon his return."

Fear came over the woman's face as she looked behind her. All her male companions were equally frightened. "But, sir, we are in danger."

"Danger, mistress? From what?"

"We are in grave danger outside your circle. Bogeymen and bugbears are stalking us. Can we not wait within?" The woman reached into a cloak pocket, and her hand reappeared with glittering red and blue gems.

Hobbs looked back at her face. "Mistress, I must tell you and your colleagues something."

"Yes, kind sir, by all means."

"Under no circumstances will I let you cross the circle into our camp. My master warned us that fae would try to do so. You may be completely innocent of trickery, but I am a stranger to this land. He is not. You can produce whatever riches you may. You can tell me any stories of hardship and danger you must. However, until his return, we will stay on this side of the circle, and you will stay outside it. I am the kind of human trained to speak plainly and forthrightly."

"Do your companions feel the same?" she asked.

Hobbs glanced at his two guards. "Yes, they do, mistress—"

"Mr. Hobbs." One of the guard's eyes widened.

Hobbs returned his attention to the strangers. The woman and her male companions were gone, but five green foxes with large antennae sprouting from their heads ran off, back into the wooded area around the camp.

"Mr. Hobbs, I never—" one guard began.

"Neither have I," Hobbs finished.

"Never step out of the circle," the other said.

"Never let any stranger step in," the first guard added.

"Beautiful lass with riches in her hands. Either one alone would have been enough to tempt me, but both? We would have been done in for sure. We are well glad you are in charge, Mr. Hobbs."

"What do you suppose they would have done if we had let them in?" Hobbs asked.

◆◆◆

Pangolin walked alongside Traveler as they led the party down a simple dirt path. On either side were woods, but the greens of the foliage and trees were of an intensity he had never seen. The sights were normal enough, but not the sounds. Birdsong surrounded them—a harmonic frenzy of countless animals, but not a bird was to be seen.

"I see no animals of any kind, Mr. Traveler."

"They are there, watching us. Fae animals can also make themselves invisible."

"How do I obtain that magical property?" the berserker asked.

Traveler grinned. "With the right amount of money, we can see what we can arrange." He looked back at the royals and Gwyness. "We near our first fae village."

"Good," Lady Aylen said. "I hope they have taverns where one can get a proper meal." She saw their caravan master's face change. "What is it now, Mr. Traveler?"

"It is best that you do not drink or eat anything outside my presence."

"Why is that?"

"Mischievous fae, princess. They could give you something to eat that could shrink you to the size of a mouse or give you something to drink to make you ten times the size of Mr. Pangolin."

"My goodness, Mr. Traveler. We cannot have a simple meal?"

"I will check the eatery first, before you eat or drink anything."

"Who might that be, Mr. Traveler?" Gwyness asked with a smile. "Is that a gnome?"

Traveler turned his attention back to the road. His dog had stopped to stare at a tiny man in a red cap strolling up to them. He was half the size of a normal man, and he had a large head and facial features. He smiled as Traveler neared him.

"Ah, visitors from the world of men. How can Durki Goodhelper be of assistance? Do you need a guide through the villages?"

Traveler reached into his cloak and threw a handful of dust at him. The little man's face contorted in rage, his eyes turned black and a puff of smoke exploded around him. There stood a smaller gray humanoid creature with bat-like wings, big ears, and tiny horns poking through his skin above his eyebrows.

"Go pester another," Traveler yelled. "And I will find the real Durki Goodhelper and tell him you are impersonating him."

The creature huffed and threw a ball of fire at Traveler. The caravan master effortlessly smacked it away with the back of his hand. The creature's eyes widened when Traveler reached for his sword, and it quickly flew away into the woods.

The party was enraptured by what they saw.

"What was that, Mr. Traveler?" Quillen beat Lady Aylen to the question, having left his post to stand next to Traveler.

"That, Mr. Quillen, was an imp. Mr. Quillen, will you be joining Mr. Pangolin and me at the front of the column?"

Quillen laughed. "No, sir. Sorry, sir. I could not see from where I was."

"Was it dangerous?" Pangolin asked.

"Not at all," Traveler answered. "However, its purpose was to befriend us and get into our camp. Then we would have learned the full uncontrollable frenzy that an imp can inflict. Any supplies, they would destroy. Any animals, they would run off. Anything of value, they would take or discard in the woods."

"It looked like a demon," Lady Aylen said.

"It looked like a tiny gargoyle," Quillen said. "Are they related?"

"Very good, Mr. Quillen. They actually are. Since the spectacle is over, and we have given Mr. Quillen some more to write in his book, may we proceed?"

"Mr. Traveler, we are so fortunate to have you here. None of us would have known," King Aereth said with relief.

"Which is worse, Mr. Traveler," Quillen began, as he returned to his place behind the royals at the front of the column, "imps or pixies?"

"They are equally destructive to the unsuspecting."

"What did you throw at him, Mr. Traveler?"

Traveler looked at them with his own mischievous grin. "Pixie dust."

Of course, everyone wanted to have their own supply of pixie dust, but Pangolin noticed the change in Traveler's demeanor as they neared the first sign of fae society. The levity of the encounter with the imp would occupy the men and be the talk of the night, but the day was still young. Pangolin wanted to see animals, but now he wasn't so convinced. Above them were birds galore, and all of them were watching the party. The fae birds were quite different from those in the Lands of Man—all different sizes, from no bigger than a fly to almost the size of a man. They represented every color of the rainbow. Some had feathers, others fur, others scales. Most of them were not birds but hybrids—some with the heads of squirrels or fish, while others were more insect than bird. Pangolin saw a flying cat, rabbit hybrids, and flying toads.

The village before them was a tiny hamlet of only a few dwellings. The dwellings filled the entire wooded area—one to six levels high, most were on the ground, but some were in the trees. Some *were* the trees themselves, complete with doors and windows. In front of each dwelling, standing in doorways, hanging out windows, sitting on roofs, and suspended on the sides of the houses or trees were the fae residents themselves.

"There is no reason to be alarmed," Traveler announced to the party. "We will move through to a clearing and settle there. They are as curious of you as you are of them."

In their minds' eyes, they'd had images of fairies and gnomes, but now they realized fae-folk had so many other species that it was truly overwhelming. Traveler led them down the dirt road intersecting the fae villages. The people were more fantastic than the "birds" above their heads. Some looked like gnomes, bearded little men with pointy caps. Most had oversized noses, eyes, mouths, and hands. They saw fae who looked like insects with bulbous eyes, and others with antennae, moth or butterfly wings, or translucent wings. Some fae looked like humanoid fish or amphibians. Most wore clothes similar to those that the caravan members wore, but others wore only trousers or tunics of some sort.

As they passed by, they heard many languages. None were intelligible. Some of the fae made sounds of animals. Others made no sound at all. Traveler was right: the fae were as amazed at seeing humans as the reverse. Very few of the fae were larger than the average man; the majority were half their size.

Traveler pointed. "There is a clearing where we can set up camp."

"I will stand guard," Pangolin said.

"My dog will join you."

"What is our purpose here, Mr. Traveler?" Lady Aylen asked.

"Supplies, Mr. Traveler?" King Aereth asked.

"Our purpose is two-fold. Acquire supplies: food, seed, herbs, spices, the like, fabric, torches, and caravan furniture, including new bedding supplies. The second is to be seen."

"Be seen?" Lady Aylen asked.

"When the people of the land can see us up close for themselves, learn what we require, those resources will seek us out. Remember, we cannot succeed in our journey without fae." Traveler gestured to Mr. Quillen, who stared at the fae in a stupor of excitement.

"Mr. Quillen, I have a list and a task for you."

The lad ran to him. "Yes, sir." He took the parchment and looked at it.

"Take a team of men with you, and secure all the items on the list and the quantities designated. The fae will bring it to the camp. I will inspect it and then pay them."

"I cannot read this, sir."

"Because the list is for fae and not nosy human lads."

Quillen laughed. "Sir, you can write fae? I mean, there's a fae language?"

"Mr. Quillen, there are hundreds of thousands of fae languages and hundreds of thousands of fae dialects within them. I gave you the task because I thought you best suited for it, as you would be required to talk to actual fae. However, if you wish to remain here and ask me never-ending questions, I can assign the task to another."

Quillen ran off to the crowds of fae.

"Mr. Quillen!"

"Sorry, Mr. Traveler. I am getting my team of men."

"Rule number one!"

"Yes, Mr. Traveler. Never go anywhere alone."

Quillen returned to the camp and found a sea of raised hands wanting to accompany him.

"Sire, princess, maiden," Traveler said. "Feel free to stroll through the village and strike up conversation with the local populace."

They looked at each other. "There is no danger, Mr. Traveler?" Gwyness asked.

"No. I will wait in camp with Mr. Pangolin and keep watch. You can explore."

The royals and Gwyness smiled.

"Ladies, shall we stroll?" King Aereth asked. They walked to the crowds of watching fae.

CHAPTER THREE

Humans of Fae

Pangolin watched with amusement as the supplies stacked up higher and higher next to their small camp. Quillen was very diligent in his work and relished interacting with fae. A team of six-armed humanoid fae brought in more supplies in large baskets.

"Mr. Traveler," the berserker began.

"One moment, Mr. Pangolin." Traveler stood before the men in the camp. "Divide up into groups of ten, and two groups at a time can explore the village. However, you cannot travel out of sight of the camp."

It took no time at all for the men to form their groups, and two headed out in different directions.

"I do believe, Mr. Traveler, that you will be the most popular caravan master in history."

"Thank you, Mr. Pangolin. What was the question you were about to ask?"

"I was intrigued by your second reason for us being here."

"Yes, it is extremely important. We are humans and strangers to this land. We cannot find the fae we need on our own. They must come to us or allow us to find them," Traveler informed him.

Pangolin gazed out across the camp. "Still, we have a major deficiency without decent archers. Bard took the able ones with him. So we will have fae archers?"

"Yes, and truthfully, if we had retained our human archers, I would have eventually reassigned them. Human archers cannot match fae archers."

"The myth is that elves are the best."

"Elves and centaurs. However, many other fae races are equally gifted."

"Archers, bearers, sorcerers."

"And guardians, warriors, and night guards. Oh, and a healer."

"Night guards and guardians are separate things?"

"Guardians will protect our weapons and key supplies at all times," Traveler said, "both physically and magically. We can hire some fae races for that purpose alone. Our night guard must also be fae. Those who can see into the night and defend against any of the many creatures we may encounter. The circle will protect us from most attacks, day or night, but we still need them. Circles can be penetrated or even shattered with the right magic."

"The fae steeds and animals will be the last step before we move on?"

"Yes, and we take on other parties along the way."

"Titan's Caravan at last." Pangolin smiled.

"Titan's Caravan. Much better than Traveler's Caravan."

"I know you miss our old name. Do you think this is how the late King Oughtred created his Kings' Caravan?"

"No. I do not believe it for a moment, though it may have started benevolently. Why do you ask? He too is behind us, and permanently. The spell cast in the Mirage Plains survived his death. It is not an indication that he lives."

"I hope you are right."

"You will feel much more confident when we set out for our trip."

"Yes. You did not say why you postponed it."

"It was for a good cause that you will welcome."

"I am intrigued."

"We have visitors."

The group of men who slowly approached them were human, most middle-aged and some elderly. They wore the bright colors of fae society, but their faces were not joyous. A deep sadness came through, despite the smiles they forced as they neared Traveler and Pangolin.

"Good day, sirs." A large balding man in a bright-orange tunic spoke.

"Good day," Traveler answered.

"We are sorry to bother you, sir."

"No bother."

"You are from the Lands of Man, sir?"

"We are."

They looked at each other with genuine happiness.

"However, we are not returning home," Traveler cautioned. The men's brief joy was gone.

"You are not returning?"

"We travel the opposite direction. Through Titan's Trail, through Faë-Land clear to Atlantea. We may not return to our lands for two years or more."

A dark cloud of silence descended on the men. Some closed their eyes in distress. Others cast their eyes downward.

"I am truly sorry," Traveler said. "If you would like, I can provide a map and you can risk the journey back if you desire."

The spokesman for the group looked up. "No, sir, but it is very kind of you to offer. Our daring, swashbuckling days are long behind us."

"Sailors?"

"I was once, sir. Long time ago."

"Sorry we cannot help you."

"You are a party of a few thousand, sir?" another man asked. He was older, but his shoulder-length hair remained mostly black.

"Yes."

"Would you…are you taking on any more men for your party, sir?" asked the large man in the orange tunic.

"But we are not going home."

"Yes, sir. I wonder if we would even recognize our lands if we were ever blessed to return. If the Fates will not allow it, we would be content with being with our own kind."

"You seem settled in here nicely."

"It is adequate, sir. But we would prefer to be with other humans. We can still put in a solid day of work."

"What are your skills?"

"Any task you require, sir," said the elderly man with black hair. "We have done them all. Cook, fire-lighter, tentmaker, water fetcher, bearer, wagonmaster, sentry, guard, any."

Traveler glanced at Pangolin, who nodded. "We are short on laborers."

Smiles returned to the men's faces. "We can fill those roles for your party, sir," the large man said.

"And it would be nice for there to be more than one person in our caravan who personally knows the Lands of Fae, its people, customs, and ways."

"Yes, sir. That we do."

"Is this all your men?"

"Yes, sir."

"Men, line up shoulder to shoulder in front of me and hold out your hands."

The men quickly formed up. Traveler examined each man's hands.

"What do you look for, sir?" the elderly man asked. Just as he did, one of the men laughed out loud and, with a flash, turned into a pixie.

They watched the tiny, giggling sprite, with its large, child-like head and big eyes, fly away on its four translucent, fly-like wings.

"That," Traveler answered.

"Pixies, imps, and trolls in the night. Terrors to every human in the land," one of the men said.

◆◆◆

Pangolin led the party back to camp. They had acquired so many supplies that every man pulled a borrowed wagon stacked high. It was good that they were in a land of magic with magical carts, as their walk back would have been impossible.

He saw the animals. Maybe they had been hiding or invisible before, but now the animals didn't mind him staring at them as they passed. He wished he could say what they were, but like the "birds," these looked like deer, squirrels, and frogs, but they weren't. Different colors and hybrid animals, all of them. A pair of bright-yellow and green squirrels scurried up to him to have a better look. He noticed their hands and feet were like those of tree toads. With a wave of his hand, they disappeared into the woods.

The party arrived back at camp without incident, and immediately their steward, Hobbs appeared with a man on either side.

"Any problems, Mr. Quillen?"

"None, Mr. Hobbs. Look at all the supplies we got."

"Yes, bring them all in."

Their party crossed the threshold of the circle as Hobbs approached Traveler and the royals.

"Mr. Hobbs, what of you? Any problems?" King Aereth asked.

"None at all, sire. Though, we did have some visitors."

"Did you let them into the circle?" Traveler asked.

"No, sir."

Their caravan master smiled. "Then it is not important. You can tell us all about it at the night meal. I want to introduce you to the newest additions to our party. This is Tyfer and Oeric." The large man in orange and the older man with long black hair nodded. "Gentlemen, this is Mr. Hobbs, the steward of the caravan. He oversees the daily running of the camp and all its non-warriors. Mr. Hobbs, these men will be joining as domestics and laborers."

"Whatever is needed, Mr. Hobbs," Tyfer added.

"Very good. I will get you and your men settled in. How many in your group?"

"We are an even 102 of us, Mr. Hobbs," Oeric replied. "All able men."

"Once you get the new men settled, Mr. Hobbs, see to the supplies," Traveler said.

"Yes, sir."

Traveler walked past them with the royals, Gwyness, and Pangolin.

"I will see to my men," Pangolin said and left them.

"Mr. Traveler, I must say that Lady Aylen and I very much appreciated the visit to the fae village. A very gracious and amiable people. They were so eager to learn all about our lands and people."

"The king and I could have spent days speaking with them in interesting conversation," Lady Aylen said.

"I am glad," Traveler said to them. "The Enchanted Glens are like this to all benevolent people. Eager to share stories and learn of others."

"Is this region different from other parts of Faë-Land?" Lady Aylen asked.

"It is like many. But not all lands here welcome humans, or anyone else for that matter. Be forewarned that our first visit to a fae city will likely be an unpleasant one."

"That is unfortunate," King Aereth lamented.

"Enjoy everything you can, sire. You must all do that. Ignore what is unpleasant, as it is the way of life, and enjoy what is to be enjoyed. Tonight, I will take Mr. Hobbs back into the villages to see about hires. We will leave after the night meal."

"Is the night dangerous at all here in the Enchanted Glens, Mr. Traveler?" Gwyness asked.

"Not at all. We should have no incidents."

In the center of the camp, Quillen held court, recounting his visit to the fae villages to all those who had remained behind. The lad had an uncanny knack for describing every nuance of the village, its fanciful inhabitants, and all the animals around it. It was as if he were performing a play, re-enacting all his encounters as he obtained their supplies.

Though not as lively, Pangolin ate his night meal with the Cut-Throats so he could tell his tales. Berserkers and warriors had their own way of storytelling. Their master-at-arms gave details of his observations from the time he left the camp. He spoke more of the feel of the air, smells, sounds, the disposition of the people, and the defensive and offensive nature of the dwellings. Fighters wanted to know about potential dangers, possible enemies or potential allies, and sources of food and water. Their storytellers told plenty of jokes with gross exaggerations to send the men into roaring laughter. Pangolin did not need to lie as his physical descriptions of the people were funny to the men, but still true and on the mark.

Hobbs and Estus ate with Gwyness and the royals. They held their own private conversation about the visit.

"We will have stories for days, from just one visit," Gwyness remarked.

"What troubles you, Mr. Hobbs?" Traveler asked. His dog lay on his stomach at Traveler's side.

"Not so much troubling, sir. The new men. There is a deep sadness about them. I asked Mr. Tyfer how long he had been in Faë-Land, and he was almost brought to tears. He said a long time, as did Mr. Oeric. He later told me that he had first arrived as a boy. He must be nearly sixty."

"Mr. Hobbs, humans have been stumbling into Faë-Land for centuries. Not all have had happy endings. Some men have come and been unable to leave, unable to find their way back home. The new men probably have been trapped here, longing to go home, for many years. It has happened to many."

"Mr. Traveler, you once said that time does not work the same here," Gwyness said.

"Yes, that is true. Because they have been here so long, they could return home and find that a hundred years have passed."

"No," Lady Aylen said. "That cannot be."

"Or they could cross back into our lands, go to sleep, turn old and gray, and die. Different men are affected differently by the magic of these lands. When I was here as a young man, I met a man that I realized had left for the magical lands when my grandfather was a boy. I did not have the heart to tell him that all he knew back in the Lands of Man was gone."

"These men could return and die from old age? Do they know that?" Gwyness asked.

"They know."

"But if that is their fate, they wish to die in the lands of their birth," King Aereth said.

"Correct, sire. They would gladly die there and be at peace."

"That is so sad," Gwyness said.

"Mr. Hobbs, let the new men fully contribute to the camp."

"Yes, sir. They do seem quite eager."

"They have much knowledge amongst them. They probably could teach us a thing or two."

"I will see to it tomorrow, sir. Yes, I feel they will be valuable additions to the caravan."

♦♦♦

Hobbs made his final rounds through the camp. The men had grown to expect it before sleeping—that final pass through of their steward. Tonight, he would make his final stop at the spot where the new men had settled. He did not have to instruct them in any way on how to set up their personal camp. They set up their campfire in a ring, each with groups of ten to twelve around it. In each camp, a man sat awake, while others in the smaller groups lay down to sleep.

"Hello, Mr. Hobbs." It was Tyfer who was one of the men sitting awake.

"How have you all settled in, Mr. Tyfer?"

"Very well, sir. Thank you."

"You can all go to sleep now. We have sentries and Mr. Pangolin has a patrol walk through camp at scheduled intervals."

"Yes, sir. This is a well-run camp and well organized. We have been in many that were not. You must be a seasoned caravan steward, Mr. Hobbs."

"Not at all, but I do have previous experience. For most of my life, I was the steward of a king's palace staff. I would like to think I have adequately transferred those skills to the caravan in instilling order and routine."

"You have, Mr. Hobbs. It is a welcome state of affairs for us. We are glad to be back among our own kind, and able ones at that. Mr. Hobbs, do know you can count on us."

Hobbs could see in his eyes that distant sadness again.

"I do, sir. We will discuss your new duties in the morning."

"Thank you, Mr. Hobbs. Thank your master again for giving us this opportunity to serve."

"Yes. Good night, sir."

"Good night, Mr. Hobbs."

CHAPTER FOUR
The Väki

Hobbs was glad to forego sleep and be whisked away for a night outing to the fae villages. The dog had transformed into a gigantic horse-like creature with cat paws instead of hooves. It galloped into the moonlit Enchanted Glens with Traveler and Hobbs on its back. Upon arrival, they were immediately greeted by fae gathered around swarms of fireflies for illumination. Clearly, everyone in the Glens knew who they were. From their smiles and pats on the body, they were happy to have humans among them.

Traveler spoke to them in a tongue Hobbs did not understand. The fae, some humanoid, others more insect-like, pointed at a dwelling down the path. Traveler led Hobbs down the faintly glowing path, then Hobbs realized that they had passed into a pocket-realm. Inside was a bustling nighttime square filled with music, laughter, and dancing, with fae drinking and conversing outside taverns. The steward smiled; fae-folk rollicked just as humans did.

He followed Traveler down a dark alley between a pair of taverns. The dog grew a long cat-like tail with a luminous tip. They saw not another soul in the alley, as they went through a side door.

At first, Hobbs thought they had stepped back outside because he almost stumbled over the roots of a large tree. It was indeed a tavern, but inside was unlike anything he had seen before. Branches and tree roots formed the landlord's counter, tables, chairs, benches, and stools. The walls were indistinguishable from a thickly wooded field, and foliage hung from every inch of the ceiling. However, that was not what Hobbs found unusual. The tavern was filled with seated, frowning gnome-like men dressed in clothing of every color and wearing every kind of hat. In one hand, each sprite held an open book, and in the other, a large mug, but not one was engaged in conversation. They all stared at Traveler and Hobbs with squinting eyes.

"No dogs of humans allowed!" one yelled, pointing at the animal.

Hobbs looked down in time to see the dog "grow" bird wings. The gnomoids were less than pleased but said nothing more.

Traveler walked to the counter, where a large man stood wearing a white apron. Well, Hobbs thought it was a man until he looked again and saw that the man had no nose at all and an unusually small mouth. Traveler showed him a piece of paper, and the man pointed up with fingers as long as his forearm.

They climbed a spiral staircase, carved out of another tree, to the upper floors. Hobbs stopped counting once they passed the tenth level and decided to take in the sights as they went. Quiet, grumpy-looking, gnome-like men filled each level.

"Sir, are these gnomes?"

"No, gnomes are a good-natured and sociable people. These are a different fae."

"Dour and solitary."

"Very, to outsiders. They act this way because we are here. They knew we were coming before we entered the establishment."

Traveler finally stepped out on one of the levels; Hobbs felt a bit dizzy. The floor looked almost the same as the ground level, but the gnomoids wore dark-green clothes and light-green pointed hats.

Hobbs followed Traveler to a large oval table near the back, where a group of gnomoids sat with books, parchments, and drinks scattered over the top. Their eyes fixed on Traveler and Hobbs; some of them sneered.

"Good night, fine gentlemen," Traveler greeted them.

"Why are you here, human?" one snapped.

"We are in need of guardians for our caravan."

"Yes, yes. We know all about you, human. You will find no guardians here."

"Yes, I know. I am seeking an introduction to those who may provide such services."

"Why are you wasting our time, human? Your caravan will not make it past the lands of the fairies. Go back where you came from."

"We will make it to Atlantea."

"How?"

"Rather than debate the issue with you, those who are not guardians, I would prefer to debate it with those who are guardians and seeking service."

"No, human. Go away and stop wasting our time. We are working."

"I will pay you for your time and introduction."

"We do not take human coins."

"What money do you accept?"

"None that you would possess."

Traveler tossed a sparkling jewel on the table. To Hobbs's eyes, the thumb-sized jewel looked like a ruby of yellow, blue, and green fragments. The little men watched it.

"Where did you steal that from, human?"

"I did not steal it."

"We don't believe you."

"You are very disagreeable men. How long must I subject myself to your perpetual dark moods? I seek an introduction to a true *haltija*. I am only here because I was told I need to speak to you. If I was misinformed, tell me who I must speak with."

"You will never get past the fairies."

"I will."

"How?"

"This is not my first journey into Faë-Land. I know how to deal with fairies."

"How will you get past the elfin lands? They don't listen to human talk."

"My caravan has an elfin princess."

"None have seen an elfin princess in your group."

"Nevertheless, she is there."

"How will you pass through the monsters along the way?"

Hobbs did not realize that Traveler's sword was already unsheathed until Traveler suddenly drove it into the center of their table. The gnomoids were not startled in the least, though Hobbs was. The men stared at the sword for a while.

"What steel is that? That is not human steel."

"It is not."

"We do not know what steel it is."

"It is the steel that can cut elfin, goblin, and even dwarvin blades," Traveler said.

"Impossible."

The dog jumped on the table, snarling at them. Its eyes turned to a shimmering black, and its teeth lengthened into razor-sharp metallic fangs.

"He can cut elves, goblins, and dwarves, too."

The gnomoids stared at the animal. "That shape-shifter is not from your lands."

"My shape-shifter is not from this world."

They studied him for a moment.

"We don't like you," one finally said. "But we will take your request to the haltija, and you can waste their time. I doubt you will find any *väki* to take on your contract."

"Thank you. When will I know?"

"We will send him to your camp. We know where you are. Take your gem, and pull your sword from our table, and go away. Take your shape-shifter too."

"Thank you again."

"You humans smell. It will take days for the smell to leave our place. Go away now, and don't come back."

They were back in the dark alleyway. Hobbs was still laughing.

"What a morose group, sir. What are they called?"

"You would not be able to pronounce it. It is easier to call them gnomoids. There are so many races that are similar to gnomes. If they are a happy lot, they are gnomes. Otherwise, gnomoids. Whether or not they have beards, they always wear hats, though the hats don't have to be pointy or red."

"This other group you seek, sir, please tell me they do not have the same sour disposition."

Traveler smiled. "I could tell you that, Hobbs, but that would not be truthful."

"Oh, no."

Lady Aylen and Gwyness took another bite of their morning meal and looked at each other.

"This is heavenly," Lady Aylen exclaimed.

King Aereth laughed as the new man Tyfer blushed. "Thank you, m'lady."

"This is the most wonderful food to greet our morning. King Aereth, with these new men in the caravan, all of us will be eating like kings."

"I do not even know what it is," Gwyness said.

"No, Gwyness, do not spoil it. It is too good to worry about details. Keep up the good work, man."

Tyfer nodded. "Yes, m'lady." He moved on from the royals.

Hobbs had gotten up before dawn as usual and had finished his morning rounds. He had already gotten his breakfast and walked to join the royals and Gwyness.

"Mr. Hobbs, please sit," Lady Aylen said. "We are to keep these new men from the fae villages. Their food is magic, I tell you."

"It is quite good, m'lady."

"It is better than good. It is fit for kings and queens."

"The new men are fitting in well," King Aereth said.

"Yes, sire, they are."

"Good."

"We heard that you accompanied Mr. Traveler into the fae villages in the dark hours of the night."

"Not too late, m'lady."

"Any new additions to the camp, Mr. Hobbs?"

"I am not sure, m'lady. It was a most interesting meeting. I am actually still laughing about it."

"Why?"

"We met with these gnome-like men, and they were the grumpiest lot you could imagine."

As Hobbs recounted his experiences, Quillen ran up to him and pointed. They all looked. A frowning little man stood outside the circle of the camp.

"May I help you, sir?" Hobbs asked as the little man neared him.

He was dressed plainly in brown clothes. A pointed cap with a sagging tip sat on his head. "Where is the human called Traveler?"

"Oh, so you know his name?"

"We know all your names, Hobbs."

Hobbs smiled. "How do you know my name?"

"You humans talk so loud, and you are always talking. Every animal and plant for miles around can hear you talking."

"I am Traveler." The caravan master stood next to Hobbs.

"What do you want?" the gnomoid asked.

"I want an audience with your väki leader."

"No. We are not interested."

"What väki would be?"

The gnomoid made a sound. "I do not know. Why are you bothering me?"

"Take me to all the väki seeking contracts now. You are right. I should not bother you. I will bother those who want to be bothered for a contract and compensation."

"You will not convince any of them."

"Take me to all of them."

"Yes, yes, human. Follow me now, and don't complain that you will be talking to väki all day. Also, don't complain when none of them accept your contract."

The gnomoid had already begun walking away; Traveler followed with a smirk. The dog rushed after his master. Hobbs watched, trying not to laugh.

♦♦♦

Ever since entering the magical lands, Pangolin had not drilled his men. While Hobbs kept the work routine for his men, the warriors lay about idly telling tales and sleeping. Nirgund stood from his campfire and approached their master-at-arms.

"Pangolin, you're brooding again."

Pangolin sat alone at his campfire, quiet and deep in thought, watching his surroundings.

"Though our warriors are content with being lazy all day, do you not think it best for the Cut-Throats to get back to battle drills?"

"We're being watched."

Nirgund looked around and crouched beside him. "By whom?"

"Everything. The birds, animals, insects."

"That is ridiculous."

"Watch for yourself and you will see. That is why I have not begun the battle drills again. I am going to ask Mr. Traveler if we can use the magic pocket for ourselves on a daily basis. I much prefer that so we are away from all the eyes in this land."

"I see what you mean. The birds, even. They watch but do not sing."

"Yes, the same with all the animals. The insects are even more devious. They watch, but you cannot see their beady eyes."

"Is there an intelligence to them?"

"Yes, all of them. They speak to each other and across other species."

"I see why you have been brooding. We have no privacy at all."

"At the night meal, Mr. Hobbs said that when he went into the fae village with Mr. Traveler every last fae knew of us, all about us, in fact."

"Well, they are a friendly people."

"But there are those who are not in these lands. We were in our lands and encountered hippogriffs, ogres, and wizards. We are now in their domain."

"Mr. Traveler has not failed us yet."

"No, he has not. I see in him a man who is determined to not have the horrors he encountered in these lands as a boy befall any of us today."

"Our Mr. Traveler lived here? Incredible. And the new men, have you spoken with them? They are so glad to be with humans again. They are a lot who seems to have suffered here. What...is it raining?"

The warriors looked up. Droplets were falling.

Hobbs ran through the camp. "Men! Cover up anything you do not want wet."

"Mr. Hobbs," a man said, pointing. "Mr. Traveler returns."

Hobbs smiled and turned. Traveler was running back to the camp with tremendous speed, the dog at his side. Hobbs worried as he watched their caravan master run into the camp and to his tent.

"Sir?" Hobbs spoke, but he was too far for Traveler to hear. He quickened his pace, but stopped when Traveler reappeared with the cloak he recognized.

Traveler ran to the center of the camp.

"Mr. Traveler?" Lady Aylen called out, but he ignored her.

Traveler threw the cloak, and it took the form of a black hole. He disappeared into it. Everyone watched as the oval hole changed into a larger opening, like that of a large dark cave. Traveler reappeared.

"Mr. Hobbs! Mr. Pangolin! Get all the men into the pocket now! King Aereth! Lady Aylen!"

The men had learned to watch Traveler's expressions closely. If he was confident in a situation, they were. If he was worried, they were scared.

Hobbs got the lizard minders into the pocket first. Everyone else followed; Pangolin and his warriors entered last. As they once again set up the camp within the pocket-realm, Traveler stood at the magical entrance. The royals and Gwyness watched with amazement. The water had already reached more than two feet.

"We just entered," Lady Aylen noted.

"How high will this rise, Mr. Traveler?" King Aereth asked.

"No way to know for sure, sire, but I suspect that it will reach well past the top of this entrance."

"That cannot be correct, Mr. Traveler," Lady Aylen challenged. "That is a flood. It will wash away everything, all the fae villages."

"The fae village is fine. They are already in their own pocket-realms, and all the animals of the land are more than safe, too. The rains are commonplace for them. When I traveled here, many years ago, the caravan I was in the employ of called them Death Rains."

"Death Rains?" Pangolin and a contingent of his warriors had joined them.

"They were harmless to fae but deadly to us. That is what we called them, but I do not agree. It is fae nature at work. It looks like the waters will cover the entire entrance. Where is Mr. Hobbs?"

"Here, sir."

The steward ran to them. "Hobbs, spread the word among the men, especially our Mr. Quillen. They might want to start setting up sitting places in front of the entrance."

"For what, Mr. Traveler?" Lady Aereth asked.

"For that, princess."

A school of multicolored fish swam past the entrance.

Quillen had first sat as close to the entrance as possible but quickly realized that he did not have a full view. Now, he sat with a writing instrument and a book on his lap, a few yards back in the center to get the most panoramic view.

Men huddled all around, watching with eyes of wonder as such an array of fish, of all sizes and colors, swam to and fro in front of the threshold of the entrance. The lizard minders stood on either side with their individual lizards on leashes. Strangely, the fae reptiles appeared as entranced as the men at the sights passing by their magical opening and remained as still as statues.

The pocket-realm rang out with astonishment as men took to their feet. "What? What happened?" Quillen asked, lifting his head from his book. "Oh, my word!" He ran in front of the crowd to the entrance. He tripped over his own feet and would have fallen out if Pangolin had not grabbed him.

"Okay, Mr. Quillen, no need to jump out and propose yet."

The men who heard him laughed. Quillen looked out at the mermaids. Their skin was an almost luminescent light blue. Their long, flowing hair was a blue-green, and their eyes were like fish's. Their only clothing was a type of brassiere, more like cloth wrapped around their breast area several times. Dozens of them swam around in a circle, before they moved past and disappeared. Every man was speechless.

"Seems like our charms are no longer working for the men," Lady Aylen whispered to Gwyness.

The men's bliss was abruptly broken by the appearance of another being that darted by the entrance. It looked like a brown fish but with the head of a man—blue-green hair, unsightly teeth, and slits for eyes.

"What was that ugly thing?" Quillen asked Traveler, who stood to the side of the entrance watching.

"That, Mr. Quillen, was a merman."

"Merman? Why so ugly?"

"In their race, the women are beautiful, while the men are ugly."

Quillen frowned. "That does not seem fair." Men chuckled.

"Which is why mermaids do not mate with mermen."

"Mr. Quillen, now you can find them and propose," Pangolin said with a smirk.

"I will stay here, Mr. Pangolin. That merman after them had sharp, ugly teeth. He can swim, but I cannot."

Quillen almost fell back onto his feet. The men stood again to see gigantic fish slowly swim by.

"A white octopus!" Quillen said, pointing.

Traveler grinned and looked at Hobbs. The steward nodded and pointed behind the crowd. The new humans of fae were busy preparing meals for the men.

No one budged from their places in front of the magical entrance of their pocket-realm as meals were served. The aquatic animals that swam by were endless. Even, as the night fell, they would not leave, as the fae sea animals that swam before them glowed in the dark.

"Mr. Hobbs," Traveler whispered. "It is fine to let all the men sleep in later tomorrow."

"Yes, sir."

"Including you."

"Very good, sir."

Dawn arrived with the men still fast asleep. Many had gone to bed only a couple hours earlier. Traveler came out of his tent and walked to the entrance with his dog. Two of the warriors were on guard.

"Good morning, Mr. Traveler," they said.

"Good morning, men."

The waters were receding, and unlike the day and night before, there was nothing to be seen. The waters were no longer clear but cloudy and filled with dirt and debris.

"The water is flowing away so quickly, sir."

"Who are they?" the other warrior asked. Both guards were startled.

Traveler smiled. In front of the entrance were dozens of frowning, full-bearded little men with pointy hats, all in charred dark brown and orange fabric.

"Their race is known as the haltijas. A clan is called a väki. There are many different clans in Faë-Land. They are *tulen väki*. Haltijas of fire."

One of the grumpy little men adjusted his groin area, and another spat out a chunky spittle that oozed over the ground when it hit. The two warrior sentries looked at Traveler in disgust and dismay.

CHAPTER FIVE

Elman and the Forsaken

"Impressive," Hobbs remarked, standing over the lad's shoulder.

Quillen sat in an area of the camp away from most, busy sketching the fae and fish they had all seen the day before. His rendering of the mermaids was especially detailed.

"You have the eye, Mr. Quillen," Hobbs said.

"I thought I had enough notebooks, but I have filled one completely from just the observations of yesterday. This is a year-long journey. I will need my own wagon or two just for my notebooks."

"Ah, here comes Mr. Traveler for you."

Quillen looked up and turned. "Me?"

Their caravan master approached with a large leather book in his hand. "Mr. Quillen, are you drawing or working?"

Quillen jumped up from the ground. "Uh—"

"He did his morning work early, sir, and asked permission to take his break early. I granted it, of course. Look at his work. Very impressive."

"Oh, I have seen his work. I saw his drawings of the hippogriffs, griffins, and ogres we encountered. Here, Mr. Quillen." Traveler handed the lad the large leather book. "How ever many books you purchased will undoubtedly not be enough, and I am not going to have any bearers assigned to the task of carrying weighty book collections for you. We are in the magical lands and have a recorder for observations of a magical nature. Well, now you have a magical book."

"Magic, sir?" Quillen dropped his own books to the ground and took the leather book. He opened it to see its blank, sturdy pages.

"Every time you fill the last page with your writings or drawings, a new blank page appears."

Quillen smiled. "Truly, sir?"

"Yes."

"Thank you, Mr. Traveler! This is what I needed."

"As for the notebooks you have already filled—take each page, turn it over to touch a page in the magic book, and vigorously rub the back of the page. The words and images will move onto that magical page."

Quillen's mouth hung open in joy. "Truly, sir?"

"Go and work, Mr. Quillen."

"Thank you. Thank you, Mr. Traveler."

Hobbs laughed. "Go on, lad, before our caravan master changes his mind."

Quillen grabbed his notebooks and ran off.

Traveler stood before Pangolin and the Cut-Throats for an early morning meeting. Warriors, berserker or otherwise, did not do well with idleness.

"You did admonish us about bringing dogs from our lands here, but what of fae dogs of some kind?" one of the warriors asked.

"I am concerned by all the many eyes on our camp," Pangolin added.

"Many eyes have been on us from the time we crossed the threshold into these magical lands," Traveler said. "As for animals, I will continue to secure additional ones for our caravan. The nonwarriors are partnered with their animals; the Cut-Throats will have theirs."

The warriors applauded at the announcement.

"Please, Mr. Traveler, not more lizards," one of the berserkers pleaded.

"No. They will be animals as fierce as you, that can fight by your side."

"What animals will these be, Mr. Traveler?"

"Chamroshes."

"What, pray tell, are they?" a warrior asked.

"A particular fae hound." Traveler was no longer looking at them but past the perimeter. Hobbs was approaching, but stopped, seeing that his master already saw the visitor. "I will return shortly."

A male human, dressed in a white collared robe, neared the camp from the direction of the fae villages. He was balding but had thick graying hair at the sides. In his right hand was a long oak staff reaching just above his head. He tapped the ground with it as he walked.

Traveler watched him cautiously, as did the dog. A sorcerer?

"Good day," he said with a smile. He was not threatening in any way.

"Good day, sir. May we help you?"

"My name is Tane, sir. May I approach?"

"A sorcerer?"

He chuckled. "I was once. Those times are well behind me. I am a teacher and guide. You do look familiar, sir."

"I was about to say the same," Traveler responded as the man stopped before him. "Teacher of what and guide to whom?"

"Teacher of life and guide to my charges."

Traveler saw a group of youths exiting the nearby woods to approach them. There were both young men and women, all dressed simply and commonly. The hair on their heads looked disheveled—by design.

"The youths are in my care," Tane said. "Word has traveled far about your party."

"I am sure."

"Traveling parties led by humans are a rare thing."

"Is there not the Kings' Caravan?"

"That is a traveling army, sir. Not my place to comment on them, though, if I could, it would not be anything nice. No, I see your appearance in our magical lands as a good omen. I would like to have you take on my charges. They are intelligent, obedient, well-skilled in many things, good workers, and dependable."

"Do you know where our party travels to?"

"Everyone knows that, sir. Atlantea for treasure and wonder."

"It is a perilous journey, and any on such a journey may not be seen again for years, if ever."

"Oh, yes. I am well aware. Time has come for them to become adults and take their place in the world. There is nothing more for me to teach them. Another must be their guide."

Traveler watched the young people more closely. They stood in three rows, seven young women and eleven men, their eyes cast down to the ground. Not one of them made eye contact.

"Sir, I will compensate you."

"Compensate me to take on these youths? Why would you turn them over to strangers, especially mere humans?"

"Sir, you are far more than a mere human. Your party is as well. I see you acquiring the supplies and animals you will need. You have begun to bring on the fae you need, and more will come. Besides, we are not strangers."

"So, you have remembered where we met?"

"We met when you were much younger. You were with a caravan of humans and elves. You were their healer. I see you have been promoted to swordsman."

"I am the guide and trailmaster."

"A full caravan master. Very good."

"I do not remember you, though. I cannot place you."

"You will not. When you saw me, I had another appearance. I was a sorcerer back then."

"Why would you have another appearance?"

"Why would your dog?"

"He is a shape-shifter. Are you?"

"I took another appearance because I did not wish to be recognized by those within the city we met. You were quite distressed at the time. A vicious battle. Your party had lost many men. I believe it was an attack by goblins and kobolds."

"The mines. Ah, yes. Your appearance was quite different. Our conversation was welcome, but not particularly memorable or worthy of being remembered after so many years."

"I remember everything, sir—from the moment of my birth—with crystal clarity. Gift or curse. Who is to say? Can my young charges join your party? I promise they will be of value, and I am willing to pay."

Traveler thought to himself, trying to come up with a reason to reject them.

"Of course, I'm sure you're aware that the more residents of Faë-Land within your main caravan, the more your chances of success increase."

"True. Besides, if we are not pleased with their work, there are many towns and cities where we can leave them."

"You will be very pleased with them, sir. All they require is strong guidance and leadership. Then they will prove themselves."

"Will you not be joining them, sir?"

"Oh, no. My guidance ends here. You will be that other who will continue them on the path."

"Such a dangerous path, though?"

"Life can be dangerous, sir. The path is immaterial." The man, Tane, revealed a pouch of coins in his other hand. "This should be acceptable."

Traveler reluctantly took the purse and looked at it. The coins were of the highest elfin denomination, worth more than many wagons of human gold.

"Please take care of them, sir," Tane said. "And most important of all, be patient with them. Not everyone is as independent as you or I. Others need more time to overcome their self-doubt."

"Yes, sir. I will accept them. If they prove themselves to the men, they will be welcome. And we do have a princess in the camp, so it would be good to have her own female attendants. I had not thought of that before."

"Oh, very good. Thank you, sir."

Tane reached out his hand, and Traveler shook it. Traveler looked at the young people and was immediately struck by their expressions. There were tears in their eyes. Traveler looked back at the man and was shocked.

Tane knelt on the ground with his eyes closed. The man wasted away before them. His staff shrank into nothingness. What remained was a thin, almost mummified corpse. It fell forward, but Traveler lunged at it. The dog barked, and Traveler was startled again.

A tall, thin elf appeared out of thin air, wearing a dark-green robe. Two others in similar hooded cloaks followed. The elf looked sadly at Tane and reached down to take the corpse from Traveler.

"How long was he dead?" Traveler asked as the elf picked Tane's corpse up into his arms.

"He waited quite some time to pass on the burden he had taken onto himself."

Traveler saw the youths crying and was deeply saddened. His memory of the man was distant, but he recalled Tane as gracious and kind to him. Traveler now remembered it wasn't a short encounter; the sorcerer had helped him care for the dying men of his party.

"Did he suffer?" Traveler asked.

"No, he used all his magic to sustain himself."

"Sad."

"We heard your conversation."

"Yes?"

"If you do see fit to leave them behind, do so when you return to your own lands."

"Why is that?"

"We do not want them here."

"Are they not of these lands?"

"No, they are not."

Traveler watched the elf with growing disdain. "I understand why he waited then."

"Tane was a respected friend, a blood brother, long before you were born, human. He will be buried with noble honor here in these lands. However, no other humans will be buried in our lands. See to it that you take them away. It can be anywhere but here. Far too many humans are in this land and too many elves in yours. We have come to forcibly believe that we all should stay in our own lands without exception. Goodbye, Traveler."

The elf, even before he had turned with Tane's body in his arms, began disappearing from Traveler's sight. The two other elves also walked into invisibility.

Traveler sighed as he stared at the half-elf youths, wiping the tears from their eyes, and quieting their sobs. Now, their eyes were on his.

Traveler led the youths into the camp. Hobbs stood at the circle, waiting. Almost everyone had been watching.

"Hobbs, have our newest members settled in."

"Yes, sir."

"Give them space to themselves for today to mourn their loss."

"I will give them the time, sir. And I will see to their meals."

Traveler turned to them. "Hobbs is the caravan's steward and sees to the proper running of the camp. He will see to you, and we will also talk later."

They followed Hobbs, as the men watched. Estus approached.

"Mr. Traveler, those three elves looked similar to that elfin witch we encountered."

"Different clan."

"That magic they do—disappearing from sight. Are they passing through a portal?"

"No, they become invisible."

"Invisible? That is worse. So they can still see us?"

"Yes, they can."

"Are there other invisible fae around?"

"All around us, Mr. Estus, all around us. Just stay within the circle."

♦♦♦

The lizard minders had a new daily routine—walking their lizards around the perimeter three times a day, circling the camp multiple times each session. Traveler told Hobbs, and Hobbs told them. The fae lizards had to be trained to walk with their masters and, more importantly, as a group.

It was the next morning, and the lizards were being walked around the perimeter for their first session of the day. They would do so seven times before they could stop. The men without lizards found this most amusing.

Hobbs arrived at Traveler's tent with news. Their caravan master sat at his desk, examining several maps. The dog sat on guard at the entrance.

"Good morning, sir."

"Good morning, Hobbs. How are they?"

"Our new young people? Not good, sir. They have remained in their small group since yesterday. They won't eat. They won't even acknowledge me. Was the man their guardian?"

"Yes, I am certain he cared for and protected them all their lives. He may have raised most of them too."

"It is still a shock for them, sir."

"Yes, it is, but we do not have the option of giving them more time to mourn. We have too much to do, and we must get done it so we can leave at our earliest opportunity. I am becoming more of the same mind as Lady Aylen and Mr. Pangolin."

"Yes, they are eager."

"Yes, and they are right. I will speak to the youths now."

"Sir, are they humans, too, like Mr. Tyfer and Oeric's group?"

"No, they are half-elves."

"I assumed the elves wanted them with us because they were human."

"They want them with us because they do not want any half-elves in these lands."

It was as Hobbs said. The youths sat in their own separate part of the camp, clustered together. They were awake and alert but completely silent.

As Traveler neared them, they barely acknowledged his presence. They were as surly a group as the väki, but for the sprites, it was their nature. The insolence of the half-elfin youth angered Traveler.

"I was about to greet you with the common courtesy of a 'good morning,' but we can forego that. I am not going to pretend to know your feelings, but frankly, I do not care. Many things happen in a caravan that are not deserved, but they happen just the same. Your guardian, Mr. Tane, put you in my care. I had every intention of honoring that commitment, but if this is going to be your position, then I withdraw. None of you are slaves. I will take you this instant to the nearest fae city, and you all can make your way from there. I cannot take on this burden. We are set to leave soon, and I will not have your disruption within this camp. I will tell Mr. Hobbs to try again to give you a morning meal, then we will go."

"So," one of them began, holding back his anger, "you wish to forsake the forsaken."

"Forsaken? Why are you forsaken?"

One of the half-elves uttered a word.

"That means…cursed, no, undesirable."

"Forsaken," one repeated.

"I am not an elf. I know nothing about you or your past. I do not care that you are half-elves, and neither does anyone else in this camp. Every man, or woman, is judged by their own character and actions within this camp. We have humans, väki, and before we officially set out, we will have many more fae races among us. Everyone will be judged the same. If you do not want to be here, or you want to feel sorry for yourselves, or be angry at everyone, including those who never met you before, that is your decision. But not in this caravan. Be forsaken someplace else, not here. This is not a journey for children. It is far too long and dangerous for that. My patience with you is at an end. You will have to find another who can give you the patience you need. It is not me. We are just passing through."

Traveler turned from them, marching back to his tent, his dog following.

"Ah, Mr. Traveler," King Aereth said, waiting with Lady Aylen.

"Let me guess, sire."

"When are we leaving, Mr. Traveler?" Lady Aylen asked.

"Three days, princess."

"Three days? Is that a number you snatched out of the air, Mr. Traveler?" the princess asked.

"No, princess. In three days, the lizards should be large enough for our purposes and I will have completed my other tasks. Then we set out to Fae-Wick."

"Fae-Wick?"

"Our first fae city, sire."

The royals smiled.

"Also, at tonight's meal, sire, I will give you a special task."

"Oh, what task would that be, Mr. Traveler?"

"Royal protocol. We may be in Faë-Land Minor, but afterward we will be in the land of the elves. They are a people of royal protocol and noble customs. You will not only know everything I know, you will learn more than I know."

"A task I am well suited for, Mr. Traveler."

"And myself, Mr. Traveler?" asked Lady Aylen.

"I do have a special task for you, as well, princess. We will talk about it tonight."

She smiled. "I cannot wait."

"Sir." Hobbs was at Traveler's tent, peeking in. He did not mind the dog, and the dog did not mind him.

"Yes, Mr. Hobbs."

"I have a visitor for you, sir."

Traveler looked up from his table of maps. Hobbs gestured and one of the half-elves entered. He was the largest of them and probably the oldest.

"This is Mr. Elman, sir."

"What is it, Mr. Elman?"

The young man swallowed as he collected himself. "Sir—I am—I apologize. We apologize."

"No need for apologies. All will be right by setting you and your colleagues on your own path."

"No, sir. Master Tane wanted us to be here."

"Master Tane waited until the first capable human party passed by."

"No, sir. He wanted us to be with a good party of men, not simply human."

"You do not want to be here, Mr. Elman."

"We are sorry, sir. We misbehaved. You only showed us compassion and respect. We are sorry for how we behaved. Give us another chance and we will prove to you that our master was truthful in what he said about us."

"I am not sure, Mr. Elman."

"One more chance, sir. As you said, you can leave us in any town or city along the way."

"Yes, Mr. Elman, that is very true. Very well, we will see how you do. Mr. Hobbs will report to me daily."

"You will have no ill reports about us, sir."

"Mr. Hobbs, assign our new members regular duties."

"Yes, sir," Hobbs responded.

"Thank you, sir." Elman nodded and followed Hobbs from the tent.

As night fell, Hobbs had the last meal of the day served to the leadership gathered around a large campfire. The cooks and servers were all members of the new fae humans. Lady Aylen insisted they be the official cooks of the caravan going forward.

"Mr. Traveler," Estus asked as a server filled his mug, "are these väki under my charge?"

"No, they are really under no one's charge, even mine. The caravan has hired them for a specific task: to protect our hoard of weapons."

"The weapons from Ironwood?" Pangolin asked.

"Yes."

"We thought you and the dog buried them somewhere."

"No. Mr. Estus has had them in his care all this time."

"Another pocket, Mr. Traveler?"

"Yes, sire. It is where the weapons are stored and Mr. Estus does his work. Only he and his men are allowed in there."

"Should the men not have these weapons?" Pangolin asked.

"Before we set out, we will replace all our weapons with the magical weapons of our hoard."

"Mr. Traveler, these väki are—"

"Yes, Mr. Estus."

"They are not the friendliest of folk."

Traveler laughed. "No, they are not, but we did not hire them for conversation or their disposition. They will protect our weapons and supplies from any thieves or magic. Without them, one day we would walk into that pocket-realm and find ourselves without a single weapon, piece of food, or container of water. We will be in many regions where there is not a single civilization nearby to resupply. But no fear, Mr. Estus. Väki are nocturnal folk. You work in the day. They work at night."

"That suits me best. All I get from them are cross looks and snarling frowns. Do these väki have womenfolk? I cannot for the life of me see any woman, even fae, taking to the likes of them."

"Mr. Estus, their women are…let us simply say they are equally matched."

The leadership laughed. "What does that mean, Mr. Traveler?" Lady Aylen asked. "They have beards and frown too?"

"Something like that."

The laughter was briefly interrupted by an approaching figure just outside the light of their fire.

"Yes, Mr. Elman," Traveler said. Some of them turned to see him draw nearer.

"Sorry to bother you, sir."

"Out with it, Mr. Elman," Hobbs told him.

"You will be receiving visitors," he said.

"What visitors?" Hobbs asked. "How do you know, Mr. Elman?"

"We can see them from our place in the camp, sir. We can hear them too."

"Who are they?" Traveler asked.

"Friendly people, sir. Fae-folk eager to converse with humans. They wish to know and see for themselves what is true and not true from their fables of the lands of humans—I mean—Lands of Man."

"Fae have fables about us?" Quillen asked.

"You did not think that we were the only people with fairy tales of other lands and realms, did you, Mr. Quillen?" Traveler asked. "Well, Mr. Hobbs. We should prepare for our guests. Thank you, Mr. Elman."

Pangolin and the Cut-Throats began taking positions at the perimeter, but when they saw the approaching fae, the master-at-arms gestured for them to move back. The men were treated to another visual spectacle, and it would be right in their camp.

Crowds of little people, knee-high, strolled to them, bright-green pointy hats as long as their bodies, and wide smiles on their faces. They were both men and women. The bearded men wore standard dark tunics and trousers. The women were in lighter-colored dresses with their blond hair braided behind them.

"Hello," Traveler greeted.

Each greeted the caravan master, enthusiastically shaking his hand, both men and women gathering around his legs. He gestured to the main campfire, where the leadership sat, and they moved past him. They gave the same greeting to King Aereth, Lady Aylen, Gwyness, Estus, Quillen, and Hobbs. Their smiles and giggles were infectious.

Then came the tree people, who were of normal human male height. They were truly humanoid trees with bark for skin and wide eyes. Their hair was loosely foliated branches, and it was not clear if they wore clothes that blended into their appearance or not. The lead tree shook Traveler's hand as he nodded.

"Browncrown," he said.

"A pleasure." Traveler nodded and gestured him in.

The tree king sat closest to them near the fire. His dozen and a half people sat together behind him. The leadership sat around the fire in their usual positions, only allowing more space for their new tree-person guest. The little people swarmed around them, sitting and standing.

"These little folk are commonly called nisse, very similar to gnomes and brownies. Very friendly and gregarious people. Browncrown and his people are simply known as tree-folk and are often advisors and arbitrators to sprites and fairies."

"Who are your royal humans?" Browncrown asked.

Traveler looked at the king and gestured for him to reply.

"I am King Aereth the Wise of the kingdom of Helm Earldom. My kingdom is part of a three-kingdom alliance called the Kings Elder in the empire of Avalonia."

Traveler gestured to the princess. "I am Lady Aylen of the kingdom of Sirnegate, also in the empire lands of Avalonia. I am a princess of the king's court second in succession to its throne. This is my maidservant and counsel, Maiden Gwyness."

Traveler pointed. "Oh, I am Estus of the Baltica Empire by birth. I am this caravan's forge and weaponsmaster."

"I am Hobbs, the steward of the caravan. Originally, the steward for the royal family for the kingdom of Theogar. This is—"

"No, I can say, Mr. Hobbs. I am Quillen the Scribe of a small town called Forestford. I am also the caravan's chronicler of the fantastic beasts and people of the magical lands!"

The nisse giggled as a group and whispered to each other with excitement.

"You are the one called Traveler," Browncrown said.

"I am. The caravan master, both guide and trailmaster for our journey."

"Your dog is the shape-shifter."

"He is."

"Not of this world."

"No."

The nisse feverishly whispered to each other again.

"You travel all the way to Atlantea?"

"We do."

"We have never been outside our own region and have no desire to change."

"Tree-folk are known for that."

"You have haltija amongst you."

The nisse expressions changed to disgust. Traveler laughed. "Yes, the väki. They are guardians of our weapons and such."

"Yes, they are powerful guardians, but they are such a repulsive people. Only elves and humans will hire them."

"Yes, my own people have questioned my sanity."

Browncrown uttered a slow and rolling laugh, then all his people behind him laughed in the same manner as a group, as if on cue.

"Since we are pleased to have your company, may I ask a delicate question?" Traveler asked.

The tree-folk's leader paused, thinking deeply. "On one condition."

Traveler grinned. "Fae are fond of bargaining."

"I will answer your question, but you must tell us a story."

The nisse jumped to their feet, giggling.

"A story?" Traveler asked.

"Yes, Mr. Traveler," Lady Aylen said. "You have yet to tell us these great stories you have promised from your youthful days in Faë-Land."

"We are told that you lived in Atlantea a time ago," Browncrown said.

"Yes, I did."

The nisse began jumping up and down, holding up two fingers.

"What does that mean?"

"They want you to tell us two stories."

"Oh, please, no. Will I be able to ask two questions then?"

"You will, and I will answer. However, you can ask and I will answer both after you tell your stories."

"What are the two stories you wish to hear?"

"How you got to Atlantea. And how you came upon your sword and shape-shifter afterward."

"Those are three long stories. The adventure of my sword and my animal companion are two separate adventures. I will tell you of Atlantea and my animal companion. Both are longer and more exciting."

The nisse applauded. "Romance too?" they asked, giggling. "Comedy too?" They laughed.

"What is all this? Am I telling these stories, or you?"

Browncrown smiled. "You, and we like long, exciting stories."

It was not only the tree-folk, nisse, and leadership that were enraptured by Traveler's retelling of his first journey as a boy to Atlantea. The entire camp listened quietly from where they sat or lay in the camp. No one stirred or made a sound.

Elman and the half-elves listened intently too.

We must tell him, one of the young female elves said in Elman's mind.

Maybe he suspects and will ask the tree-man in his two questions, a male elf said without speaking.

Elman found himself able to imagine the very road that Traveler spoke of where their caravan master, as a young healer, had met his caravan of humans and elves.

Traveler's story was more than captivating, but the leadership knew there was much more. It would not be until they marched along Titan's Trail deep into the Great Forest that they would receive fuller accounts of Traveler's first and early years within Fae-Land. As their tree-people and nisse guests and the caravan sat for hours listening, living out Traveler's stories with all the emotions of surprise, sadness, exhilaration, and joy, there was something poignant that the leadership learned. Their caravan master let it slip briefly, but he quickly put the smile back on his face and bellowed out his encounters with great theatrics. Traveler did not become the great storyteller that he was to entertain human and fae alike at campfires. There was a more dire origin of his talent. He learned to tell stories so well because, in his days as a young healer, that was how he comforted the men in his care, those recovering and those dying. It was how he passed the hard times in the healing tent, or as it was so often known, the death tent.

CHAPTER SIX

The Erymanthian Games at the Giant City of Khury

"**M**r. Traveler," young Quillen said as he jumped up to catch their caravan master in midstride. "I wanted to thank you for last night's stories."

"You are quite welcome, Mr. Quillen."

"I am wondering if, in addition to recording the fantastic beasts and races of this land, I might also write the biographical accounts of your younger years."

Traveler laughed. "That, Mr. Quillen, must wait for another time. You will be more than occupied with compiling your own firsthand accounts. There will be no time for another bold undertaking."

"Then, sir, you must write down notes so you do not forget them."

"Mr. Quillen, I will never forget my early years in these lands—never. Do not worry."

"When we reach Atlantea, I will ask again and try to convince you."

"You do that, Mr. Quillen." Traveler continued his brisk pace into the camp.

The half-elves were standing, waiting for him in their part of the camp.

"Women, follow me," he said.

They all looked at each other, but the seven young women followed him. He marched them back to the royal tents and into the women's quarters.

"Mr. Traveler, it is not proper to enter a woman's tent or that of a royal without announcement." Lady Aylen stood with her maidservant at a table of food and drink.

"Yes, princess, what will we do about my roguish manners?" Gwyness stifled a laugh. "Princess, these are the new additions to the party. These young women will be assigned to you."

"Assigned to me, Mr. Traveler? I do not need any servants. Gwyness is all I need. I am not one of those royals who needs an army of servants to dress her and fuss over her."

"Yes, princess, you are too independent and strong-willed for that. But they are not to be your servants. They will be your royal guard."

"Royal guard?"

"Yes. King Aereth will have a king's guard. You will have a royal guard. That will be their primary role, and any other, as needed, they can fulfill as well."

"A royal guard of women? Interesting, Mr. Traveler. Can you all fight?" she asked the young women.

They all nodded.

"Very good. Yes, Mr. Traveler, a good idea indeed."

"Then it is settled. Maiden Gwyness can take charge."

Traveler looked at the women. "Later, I will take you to see our weaponsmaster, Mr. Estus, who will fit you with elfin armor—"

"Sir, may we have another type of armor?" a half-elfess asked.

"No. You will all be fitted with elfin armor because it is both the strongest and lightest. We talked about this earlier. I do not have time to indulge your bias against all things elfin. As for your hand weapons, you can choose what you like, but again, elfin will be your best choice. I cannot see any of you wielding a bulky dwarvin weapon or even touching a goblin one. Can any of you shoot a bow?"

None of the women responded. "They would not allow us to learn," one of them finally answered.

"A shame. Well, I want you all to at least practice with crossbows and become proficient. If you are to be the royal guard to Lady Aylen, I want you to deal with the threat before it is close enough for you to feel its breath."

Traveler pointed to the entrance. "Work it out amongst yourselves, and make it part of your routine. The entrance to the women's tent will have two sentries at all times. At night, the entrance will be closed when you all turn in for bed. Understood?" he asked them, and they nodded.

"Very orderly, Mr. Traveler. Are you going someplace?"

"Yes, princess. I should see to the rest of my tasks." He left the tent and the women behind.

They stood silently with their eyes cast downward.

Gwyness stepped forward to one of them. "Everything will be fine. I have known the princess all my life, and I can attest that she is a fine leader." Gwyness touched the young woman's hair. "We must do something about this mess of hair, all of you. We must all be presentable, as representatives of both her and the kingdom of Sirnegate." Gwyness saw the pointed tip of the young woman's ear but, more importantly, her deep discomfort and near-panic. Gwyness let her be. "We shall sort everything out to everyone's satisfaction."

"Come now, no long faces. Gwyness, settle them in. While we remain idle in this camp, we can at least amuse ourselves with conversation and games. And you will tell me each of your names."

The half-elfin women were showing Lady Aylen and Gwyness a card game, with all sitting on the ground, when Hobbs appeared at the entrance.

"Maiden Gwyness, may I speak with you for a moment?"

"Where are you kidnapping my maidservant off to, Mr. Hobbs?"

"Not far, m'lady."

Gwyness got up and followed Hobbs. Lady Aylen continued her lessons in fae card games with the far more relaxed female half-elves.

A few moments later, Traveler returned to the entrance.

"Princess," he called out.

"Mr. Traveler." She got up from where she sat and walked out of the tent.

"Follow me," he said calmly.

"Follow you?"

He led her to another tent.

"Was this set up for me, Mr. Traveler?"

When she entered, she was immediately surprised, as the tent was much larger inside than it appeared from outside. Dim light came from a single candle from a stand in the corner. There, on a stool, sat Gwyness, whose eyes darted around to avoid direct eye contact.

"What is happening?" the princess asked.

"Please sit." Traveler gestured her to a seat across from Gwyness. He sat next to Gwyness.

"What is happening? Gwyness?"

Traveler leaned forward with a somber expression. Lady Aylen was frightened. "What is happening? Why won't anyone tell me?"

"Princess, when we first crossed the threshold, I was not sure if I should tell you then or wait, so I asked Gwyness for guidance. She knows you better than anyone else."

Lady Aylen glanced at her maidservant. Gwyness sat quietly.

"She told me to wait as long as I could. I did so. Princess, you were of the impression that you were immune to the enchantment of the land, that only the men had to endure the effects of this magical land and allow their bodies to become accustomed to it. That is not true.

"The same is happening to you and has been ever since we crossed the threshold of the Mirage Plains. Princess, elves are magical beings. You have hidden it all your life, but you are an elf. However, you have the body of a human. When the magic of the land saturates your physical form, you will have a reaction far more serious than the men experienced. It may even be violent."

"Violent?" Lady Aylen was truly frightened. "Why?"

"I speak to you as a healer. If you had remained in the Lands of Man, it would not have mattered. You would have lived and died as a human, though you would have been extremely long-lived. But you returned. You returned as an adult female. You should have returned as a child.

"How can I explain it? Your body has been deprived of the magic it should have had as you grew and matured. Without that magic, your body is that of an elfin child."

"Child!" Lady Aylen jumped from her seat. "I am no child."

Traveler remained quiet. Lady Aylen calmed her anger and sat back down.

"When the magic rises within you to a certain point, you will change. You will change from a human to a true elf. The danger lies in that your body will go from human to elfin child to elfin adult in a relatively short period of time. It is not natural for it to happen this way." He swallowed as he paused. "The physical stress and shock on your body will be incredible. Lady Aylen, you could die."

The princess's face froze with an expression of shock. She began blinking rapidly to try to keep her eyes from welling up with tears. Her eyes connected with Gwyness, and her maidservant was crying.

"No, I will not accept this. I will not be stopped now. I am here in Faë-Land, and nothing will keep me from our Titan's Caravan and its ultimate arrival at Atlantea."

She noticed the slight smile on Traveler's face. He took her hand. "That, princess, is what I needed to hear. If you can hold onto that determination through it all, you can survive."

He squeezed her hand and let it rest back on her lap. "Gwyness and the half-elves will watch you at all times. When it will happen, I do not know. It will be either a state of collapse or a violent fit. You are to go nowhere alone for any reason.

"I will keep you segregated from the camp, but you will be in my care until you pass through the effects. Most of the physical changes you can guess. Your eyesight and hearing will increase dramatically. Your ears will grow out and drop to their correct position. No more hiding them in your hair. Elfin ears have a mind of their own and do not take to cover. Also, you are already stronger and faster than most men. Both will also increase dramatically. Not to be indelicate, but you will go through puberty again."

"But there is more. There is always more. Something more terrible."

"Your mental state, princess. That is what I must monitor most of all. I do not think we have the word in our language. How would I translate it? We would call it 'two-ness.' You are one thing, but you see something else when you look in the mirror. You must accept your transformation into your true self."

"If I am unable?"

"Those who are unable have...destroyed themselves or gone mad."

Lady Aylen grasped the sides of her head and closed her eyes. "Oh, no."

"I am sorry."

She opened her eyes. "You knew this would happen when we were back in Last Keep. No, even before that."

"I knew it might be an eventuality, but if you recall, I did not even know we would make it out of the Lands of Man. I am a person who likes to deal with the situation in front of him, rather than the situations five turns down the road."

"No, Mr. Traveler, you are a man who prepares for ten turns down the road."

"We are at this situation now. This is what we face. Lady Aylen, look at me. Do not despair. Hold on to that determination to step across the gates of Atlantea."

"I do not even know what the city looks like." Lady Aylen had given in to her weeping.

"It is the same picture that you have had in your mind when you left your kingdom of Sirnegate. That has not changed."

She closed her eyes again.

"I will leave you with Gwyness. Stay here for as long as you need. I had it set up for your privacy."

"Do not tell anyone else," Lady Aylen pleaded.

"No one else knows but the three of us."

Traveler stood and slowly left the two women alone. Gwyness got up from her stool and ran to Aylen to embrace her. Lady Aylen wept more loudly.

"I do not want to die," she cried.

As Traveler marched through the camp, with his dog, men greeted him with smiles.

"Mr. Traveler, thank you so much for last night's tales," Nirgund said. He stood with Pangolin and the other Cut-Throats doing little more than nothing. "It should be a recurring event, sir."

"I will keep it in mind."

"And what we talked about."

"That too."

"Thank you, sir."

"Mr. Traveler, we never did learn what your two questions were to those fae."

"Another time, Mr. Pangolin. Gather your personal gear as if you were going to battle."

"Battle?"

"We leave immediately. There is less time than we need, or that I thought we had. You will be gone for a day or more. Task your men to function in your absence. Meet me at my tent when you are done."

"What has changed that has lit a fire under you to finally move at a quicker pace?"

"Maybe nothing. Maybe a lot. I do not mean to speak in riddles. I simply do not know for sure. However, I prefer to prepare for the worst at all times. People live longer when they do."

"No argument from me. Nirgund, you will be in charge. I-wulf, you will be his second."

"Is the camp in any danger, sir?" Nirgund asked.

"No, but keep a solid sentry around the entire camp. Talk to Hobbs and enlist the new youths as well."

"Those youths," Pangolin began. "What are they? They can see and hear farther than any person."

"They are half-elves, but do not speak of it until they are comfortable with their place within the camp. I will talk to Hobbs and the king while you get ready."

"Mr. Traveler, I am a berserker warrior, never without my armor or my weapon on my back. I am ready for battle always. I need nothing else. I'll follow you to Mr. Hobbs and we can leave."

Traveler smiled. "Then, let us find some fae warriors for you to command."

◆◆◆

Pangolin thought of himself as a traveler, too, having been to six of the Seven Empires. However, it was minor compared to the travels of their caravan master. From the sound of Traveler's stories the night before, Traveler had also crossed into all the magical lands and even explored another world. Their caravan master was indeed a unique individual.

The berserker did not speak much if the conversation had little to do with battle or defense. But had he been given to constant talk, he would have been speechless now. He sat on the back of Traveler's animal, overcome by the view. The animal had transformed into a gigantic flying creature with matted blackish fur. Its enormous bat wings flapped. Traveler sat on the animal's neck, several feet ahead of him, hooded, his magical sword strapped to his back. Pangolin had no clue what creature the dog had become. In Faë-Land, he was becoming aware of the fact that people and beasts often were not one thing but a combination of many different things.

They had been flying some hours, and they had long since left the green wooded areas surrounding their caravan's camp. The lands Pangolin watched from high above were barren and rocky. Finally, he spotted what looked to be civilization. As they approached, he watched the looming structure of the city and wondered why it seemed so large despite their distance from it. He realized why when he was able to make out the people in front of its walls. It was not a normal city. It was a giant city. The people were giants!

They set down. Pangolin had not even had time to look before the animal reverted back to his dog form.

"This, Mr. Pangolin, is the city of Khury."

"The giant city of Khury."

"As a fearless warrior of battle, I do not have to worry about your sensibilities being shocked, so I will skip the descriptions. Let us see some giants."

"From little people to big people."

"Very big people, and mean."

The entrance to Khury had to be at least a hundred feet high, the walls as thick as fifty feet. Clustered on either side of the path into the city were dirty, dusty fifteen-foot giants in armored chestplates, wearing shoulder, elbow, and thigh shields. Animal-hide togas covered their hairy chests and legs. Each of them had a spiked club or sword in one hand, which rested on the ground.

"Who goes there? Two little men in our lands."

"Where do we find the Antaeans?" Traveler yelled, not to be rude but because it was the only way for the giants to hear him.

"What business do you have with the Antaeans?"

"You are not Antaean, so it is no business of yours."

The giants turned away from them.

"They lose interest fast," Pangolin said.

"It is because they do not feel we can pay them for information."

"Can we?"

"We can, but our coins are too small."

"Too bad we cannot magically enlarge them."

"Yes, we do need a good sorcerer. We shall explore. We can find the giants we seek without guidance."

Like the fae villages, where the people were human-sized and every size down to that of a mouse, here, the giants ranged from heights of twenty feet, lumbering along with thunderous footsteps, to giants of about ten feet. Some were in perfect shape, with firm muscles. Others were moving mounds of blubber. Some had very wide bodies, and others were normally proportioned. However, they all were dressed as some type of warrior, and none were without a weapon.

With such a diversity of size, the establishments of the city were either outdoors or were large enough so the larger possible giants could enter, which Pangolin estimated had to be at least fifty feet. It all seemed strange to him—unlike any kind of city he had ever seen.

"Khury is a common city for the giants. They come here from far and wide for business with other giant races."

"You said you had delayed our initial visit for a reason."

"Yes. There is a contest I feel you should enter."

"Contest?"

"It will go a long way toward earning you respect among the giants. They are very much a warrior class. Respect and loyalty are foundational with them, and it comes from battle and fighting skill and courage."

"Then, I like these giants."

"If you gain their respect, they will talk to us. Otherwise, we are nothing but little people, and they have no interest in little people."

As they walked through the streets, an occasional giant noticed them, but Pangolin was struck by how completely disinterested the populace was in their presence. The streets were crowded and the market busy. Of course, Pangolin was especially interested in the weaponry being sold and those common to the giants they passed.

"Are giants only a warrior race?"

"The vast majority of the giant races are warriors. However, some of their races have quite diverse occupations. The giants we seek, called the Antaeans, are such a race. They have great warriors, but their home city is filled with citizens who work in other occupations. I think that is them up ahead."

They had been walking for some time down the same main street from the main gate. Like every other main street Pangolin had encountered in his travels in the Lands of Man, it was the center of all activity. Khury was no different. The giants ahead of them, who gathered around another weapons market—the city seemed to have an overrepresentation of such markets—were twelve feet tall and dressed in shining silver armor, including helmets that left their eyes, noses, and mouths free. Wrapped around their waists were belts with skulls for buckles.

"You there!" Traveler called to them.

The giants looked down at them with only marginal interest, then turned away. Pangolin watched the dog grow in size as it transformed into a gray lion as tall as the giants. It roared at them. Pangolin laughed. That got their attention.

"You there!" Traveler said again, as the "lion" growled.

"Is this your magic or is it a shape-shifter?" one of the Antaean giants asked.

"Its kind is a natural shape-shifter," Traveler answered.

"Then remove the beast from the city before its soldiers do so for you."

"Before we do, where is your king?"

"Why do you want to know about our king?"

"I know he is here, and I have a proposition for him. I wish to enter one of my colleagues in the Erymanthian Games."

"You have a giant among your group."

"No, my colleague here wishes to enter."

The response was not meant as a joke, but the giants began to laugh so wildly they almost fell to the ground. Pangolin, in fact, had to step back from them in case that did happen.

"Little man, that was a good jest. We have not had such a good laugh in a long time. You had your fun; now take your demon from the city."

"My dog is not a demon, and it was not a jest. In fact, take me to your king and let us wager on it."

"Wager?" The giants ceased their laughter and paid close attention. "What kind of wager?"

"A wager with money. Money for all of you."

"We do not take the dust you little people call money."

"Not little people money. Coins as large as your hand."

"You have no such coins, little man."

Traveler reached for a pouch on a cord around his neck. He opened it and struggled. Out popped a coin larger than a shield. With all his strength, he threw it. The giant snatched it from the air. He put the golden coin in his mouth and bit down on it. Then all the giants looked at it. They glanced at each other with smiles, nodding.

"Okay, little man. You are of interest after all."

Pangolin realized the city had more than one entrance. At a side gate, a group of other Antaean giants were gathered, and commotion filled the air. The giants they had met led them outside the wall to a camp with even more of the giants. As they followed, the dog reverted back to its usual form.

They did not need to be told or guess as to who the king was. He was a giant who wore a helmet more ornate than all the rest—crowned with sharp, fearsome horns pointing to the sky. His beard was also thicker and longer than the others. He watched Traveler and Pangolin as they were led to him.

"King, we have some little folk who wish an audience," one of the giants said.

"Why would I want to speak with little folk? Who are you?" their king asked.

"I am Traveler, king. My colleague here is Pangolin."

"Why do I care to know this?" the king asked them with a frown.

"Are not the Erymanthian Games about to begin?"

"They have already begun, little man. What of it?"

"My colleague here will enter as well."

Again, the giants burst into roaring laughter.

"The Games are not for jesting, little man."

"Mr. Pangolin is a berserker."

"Your supposed human warriors with the magical fire of rage within them for strength may be impressive in your lands, but not in ours."

"I have a wager then," Traveler said.

"This is why we brought them, king," a giant said.

"If my colleague, Mr. Pangolin, can complete the Games successfully to the end, then you will hear my proposal. If he finishes above your men, you will say yes."

The king laughed. "Say yes to what, little man?"

"Mr. Pangolin must finish the Games first."

"He will not even survive."

"Then, there is no risk to you."

"You think you are clever, little man, but you are not. I know what you are doing, but enter the Games. I could not care less."

Pangolin asked Traveler in a whisper, "Do you want to tell me what you are volunteering me for? And what does he mean, he knows what your cleverness is?"

"You must race across the barren lands from Khury to the single mountain, called Black Tooth. A pack of Erymanthian Boars will do everything to stop you from reaching the mountain, including kill you."

"I have heard the fable. Giant boars."

"Much more than giant, but you will see."

"Why does he think it is a ploy?"

"He thinks my plan is to use our small stature to circumvent the boars. But the boars are not dumb animals, quite the opposite."

"Why are you so convinced I can succeed?"

"The giant king can see your unique earth-like magical armor, but he cannot see your magical axe-mace on your back."

Pangolin smiled. "How do I begin?"

The entire giant camp marched to the start of the Games. Dozens of other giant camps were already there. In the distance, Pangolin saw clouds of dust all around. Beyond that stood an upside-down pyramid of a mountain, not especially huge, but of wonder because it looked like it should not be able to stand with its skinny tip touching the earth and its much larger plateaued top hanging in the sky.

Pangolin heard the screams and sounds of battle.

The Antaean king walked to them. "Little man, the rules of the Games are simple. Run. Stop when you get to Black Tooth, walk up the steps to join all the other competitors inside, and relax until you are summoned. Oh, and don't get killed by the boars."

Pangolin reached over his shoulder and grabbed his axe-mace from his back. "Tell me when to begin."

"I just did."

Pangolin smiled, then let out a yell that every giant around could hear. He barreled forward. At this point, the giants of all the other camps took notice.

"That is no average berserker human. Little man, are you going to succeed in tricking me?" the king asked Traveler.

"Not me, king, him!"

Pangolin's eyes were a bloodshot red, but he saw clearly before him, as he ran to Black Tooth. Unconscious and dead bodies of giants littered the barren space between city and mountain. He was unconcerned, but then he had never seen a real Erymanthian Boar before. Traveler was right—it was much more than a giant boar. The first beast stood in his path, watching him with blank red eyes.

However, that was not what made the giant beast so formidable. Its head, its hooves, and the ridges along its back and protruding from most of its body were bony, jagged, blood-stained tusks. The beast charged.

It was a good effort, but Pangolin easily stepped out of its way. The beast tumbled over itself trying to stop. The boar was far from alone—and if Pangolin were a lesser man, his courage would have vanished at what he saw. From the clouds of dust came at least a dozen of the giant boars. Pangolin might have been able to dodge a few but not all. He quickly changed his tactic, running into the center of the boars.

"I may have spoken too soon, little man," the king of the Antaean giants said to Traveler. The crowd watching the berserker's charge in the distance had grown from the camps outside Khury's walls to spectators rushing out of the city, having heard of the challenging human. "Why not tell me what you were going to ask anyway? I am curious, especially since I won't have to grant it."

"My caravan travels to Atlantea."

"A human caravan."

"A joint human and fae caravan, king. My desire is to have giants of Antaea accompany our master-at-arms, Mr. Pangolin there, as its vanguard. We travel through Titan's Trail: the lands of the sprites and fairies, the lands of the elves, and beyond, straight through to the fabled city of Atlantea. Your men could secure riches for your kingdom, whatever you could carry—and Antaean giants are known to be able to carry quite a *Herculean* load."

The king laughed at him. "I will ignore the insolence of your wordplay, little man. It is too bad your man will not make it, as it could have been a profitable alliance for us both."

They all heard an animal scream. The giants went quiet and still. One of the Erymanthian Boars sailed into the air, straight up, then crashed back towards the earth. Another beast cried out; it spun end over end, sailing away from where it had been struck, disappearing into the dust clouds. Another beast cried out. No one could see a body; not until they heard squealing did they realize the beast was falling from the sky towards them.

"Move!" a giant of another camp yelled as the beast crashed to the ground and tumbled at the giants, barely missing them.

In the distance, they heard the stampede: all the Erymanthian Boars fleeing the man, Pangolin, for dear life. They heard the human yell again. A giant peered through a telescope.

"He is at the steps of Black Tooth."

The Antaean king looked down at a smiling Traveler. "You did trick me, little man. His weapon is magic too. I do not like tricksters."

"Riches, king. As much as your men can carry. Humans cannot make the journey alone. Giants cannot make the journey alone. But humans, giants, and other fae can."

"You have elves?"

"We do."

"I hate elves, but we would need them to get through Faë-Land Major without incident. Okay, little trickster. Leave your berserker with us. If he can impress me with his warrior abilities and skill, which for giants means drinking ability and conversation, I will agree to this alliance. Our kingdom's coffers could use the money. My coffers could use the money. 'The only good kings are rich kings.' That is what my wife nags me with every day. What is your name, little trickster?"

"Traveler."

"Yes, Trickster Traveler. Maybe when I am a rich king, I will become a wise king, too, and not let little men trick me."

"Or elves," Traveler interjected.

"Yes, you can leave now. You will not use my own hatred of elves to trick me for a second time in the same day, little man." He gestured to his men. "Get this trickster away from me. And gag his mouth so he cannot say anything more."

CHAPTER SEVEN

The Goblin City of Damdread

Traveler returned to the Titan's Caravan camp upon the same giant white hawk with multicolored wings and head as he had when they first crossed into the magical lands. Maybe the shape-shifting dog enjoyed the form.

One of the half-elf men spotted him in the sky first. When they landed, every man was on his feet to greet them.

"Welcome back, sir," Hobbs said.

"Thank you, Mr. Hobbs."

"Mr. Traveler, you have returned," King Aereth said. "Where is our master-at-arms?"

"Sire, he is negotiating the addition of new fae men to our caravan."

"Very good."

"Did anything of interest happen in my absence?" Traveler asked Hobbs.

"Constant fae passing by the camp, sir. We seem to be very popular with the people here."

"They have never seen humans before."

"Lady Aylen said she wanted to see you as soon as you returned, sir."

"Yes."

"Mr. Traveler, is something wrong?"

"No, sire. I will speak to her now. I have much to do. Mr. Pangolin will be gone for a day or two. I want us prepared to leave when he returns."

Traveler was happy to see the lizard minders along the flanks of the camp, and their lizards of many colors were visibly larger. At the women's tent was Gwyness, who looked troubled. The female half-elves stood around her.

"Maiden Gwyness."

"She is in that tent," Gwyness responded.

Traveler turned and walked to the secluded tent farther away from the activity of the camp. Inside, Lady Aylen paced back and forth. She stopped when he entered.

"Lady Aylen."

She wrung her hands and composed herself. "Mr. Traveler, I do not want to wait. I cannot wait. I want to get on with it. As a healer, can you not hasten the process?"

"Incite the transformation?"

"Yes. I cannot bear it an instant longer. I want it over. Whatever happens, I want it over with."

"To increase the magic within your body is actually quite easy to accomplish."

"I thought so. We have not been eating the food of these lands."

"Not yet."

"How much do I need to consume?"

"Return to your tent. I will see to it."

"Thank you."

♦♦♦

Hobbs waited for Traveler at his tent.

"How are our fae humans, Mr. Hobbs?"

"Very well, sir."

Traveler noticed Lady Aylen return from the secluded tent.

"Sir, now that you have returned, I will have the noon meal served."

"Good." Traveler entered his tent, and his dog trotted in after him.

Hobbs saw the leadership gathering outside, eager to speak with their caravan master privately. Estus and Nirgund, especially. King Aereth noticed the somber expression on Gwyness's face and looked concerned.

"Everyone, I will have the meals served. Gather around. Mr. Nirgund, join us." Hobbs motioned to one of the camp men to immediately light a fire. The fae humans had already begun preparing meals. Many large black pots filled with water hung over their own campfires.

Three-quarters of an hour later, the meals were ready. The leadership, including Nirgund, sat around the fire at the royals' tents, but no one spoke. Lady Aylen stared at the ground, silent. The princess always either led the conversation or was an active participant, but not today. They all knew something troubled her greatly.

Traveler appeared with a large, slender glass pitcher. "Lady Aylen, for you." He handed it to her. "Ambrosian spring water. Have a glass or two with your meal."

Estus raised a hand. "Mr. Traveler, before the meal is served, a word?"

"Mr. Estus, I hope it has nothing to do with the väki."

"No, sir."

Traveler waved him on. The two men walked away from the group to talk.

Lady Aylen stared at the pitcher. She put it to her lips.

"I will fetch a glass for you, m'lady," one of the female half-elves said.

Lady Aylen began to drink. They all watched her tilt her head back as she drank the entire pitcher. When done, she dropped it to the ground and sat with a distant stare.

Gwyness watched her. "Why did you do that? Mr. Traveler said to drink a glass or two, not the whole thing."

The maidservant jumped to her feet in shock. King Aereth, too, stood.

Lady Aylen's eyes disappeared. In their place were two translucent, empty eyeballs—filling with water. Everyone looked around as water rose from the ground around them, up to their feet, past their feet, and put out their campfire. Lady Aylen began shaking.

"Mr. Traveler!" Gwyness yelled.

Their caravan master ran back to them just as the princess fell to the soaked ground, convulsing.

"Give me your belt, sire!" he yelled.

The king quickly ripped it from his waist and threw it to Traveler. The caravan master stuffed one end into Lady Aylen's mouth then wrapped the rest around her head. She was crushing it with her teeth, the violence of her fit growing. Traveler lifted her up into his arms; his dog appeared and transformed into a humanoid eagle-beast. He grabbed them both, and shot into the sky, the force of his wings almost knocking all those nearby off their feet. The trio disappeared.

Hobbs remembered the time when they were under siege by the wizard of the Four Kings. The current panic of the camp was close because no one knew what was happening. Hobbs could do little to allay their fears because he, too, knew nothing.

"He's back!" one of the male half-elves said. Hobbs made a mental note that it was always the half-elves who saw the approach of outsiders, even ahead of the Cut-Throats.

Traveler returned with the dog at his side. The leadership moved to him first, Gwyness at the lead. He held up a hand and looked at her.

"She is fine," he said calmly. "She rests and will remain resting through the night."

"Mr. Traveler, what is wrong with Lady Aylen?" King Aereth asked.

"Gwyness, you can tell everyone now."

"No, Mr. Traveler. You can do so better than I. I am too upset."

"Lady Aylen is an elf, sire."

The news surprised most of the camp. "That is why she is so fast and strong," Nirgund remarked.

"The same thing that happened to all of you when you first entered the magical lands is now upon the princess. However, it is far graver because, though born an elf, she has never been in these lands. She has never been exposed to the magic that is an essential part of any fae."

"Will she die, Mr. Traveler?" the king asked pointedly.

"I will monitor her, sire. That is all I can do. She is a strong woman, but it is a very dangerous time for her. Time will tell."

"We lost Mr. Pangolin, and now the princess," someone said.

"We have not lost anyone," Traveler scolded. "Mr. Pangolin is on a mission to hire fae for our caravan. The princess is temporarily ill. There is no need for gossip, because those are the facts."

"Sir, I will get everyone back to work," Hobbs said.

"Yes, please do. I will speak more tomorrow. Mr. Nirgund, please walk with me."

Hobbs dispersed the men as the leadership watched Traveler lead Nirgund back towards the royal tents.

"I am very sorry, sir. I did not mean anything by my comments."

"Mr. Nirgund, I do not even know what you said. Get your cloak and your weapon. We leave immediately."

"Leave, sir?"

"Oh, I misunderstood. I thought you wanted an animal, but you changed your mind."

Nirgund ran from him, holding back his joy.

The cold normally didn't bother Nirgund, but even with his head and body wrapped in his cloak, he was shivering. He looked at the beast the dog had turned into—some kind of bat-like monstrosity. Traveler sat at its neck. He looked over the edge; it was a long, long way to fall to a blackened land.

The warrior was happy to have his feet touch the earth. He looked up to see that the dog had turned into a large, shaggy humanoid. Was it some type of bear or wolf or ape?

"We are in the outpost city of Damdread," Traveler said as he fixed his hood upon his head.

"Why is it so unnaturally cold in these lands?"

"We are in the lands of the goblins."

"Goblins, sir. Aren't they an evil race?"

"Some would say so, but it is more complicated than that. They are the mortal enemies of the elves and fairies, and tolerated by most sprites. As humans, we should never turn our backs to them."

"Why are we dealing with them, sir?"

"We are dealing with one particular half-goblin. That is all. Keep your halberd in your hand and be ready to kill. Say nothing, and follow me closely."

The city was a dark, wretched hole of a place. It was the complete opposite of the fae villages—dreary, uninviting, dark, and smelly. The streets were lined with people of all heights, with green or gray skin, and long ears and noses. Nirgund noticed other races, too, that looked like humanoid lizards, wolves, and furry beasts he could not name.

The wall around the city was in disrepair, and Traveler led them through a crumbled section to a caravan of wagons. It was an outdoor traveling market. Traveler walked straight to one man in particular.

"You!" the man said. As Nirgund neared, he saw that the man's face had a greenish tinge, and he had one horn sprouting from his head. The half-goblin was average height but was built like an ox. Scratches, cuts, and welts covered his arms.

"What do you have?" Traveler asked.

They followed the half-goblin around to the back of a wagon and stepped up into it. For a moment, Nirgund was startled because he stepped up, too, and suddenly found himself in an open, wooded field with goblin brutes everywhere, whips in their hands. There were cages of animals and steeds; small groups inspected them. Most of the cages contained giant wolves; others had dark winged creatures.

The half-goblin led them to a cage all by itself.

"Only a human would want such useless animals," he grunted.

In the cage was a pack of what Nirgund initially thought were wolf-hounds, but then he looked closer. One of the dogs lunged at him, throwing itself at the bars of the cage, viciously barking. The beasts had long tails of tangled hair, but it was their forelegs that were of note—leathery and ending in the talons of an eagle.

"I thought there was only one," Traveler said.

"One, two, a dozen. All the same. Take your one."

"What will happen to the rest?"

"Meat for goblin warriors or their mounts. What else?"

"They seem to be well bonded as a pack," Traveler said.

"That's how they protected themselves from their master."

"You mean his cruelty," Traveler said.

"What you call cruelty."

The alpha hound barked at Nirgund again and tried to claw at him through the bars.

"Stop!" Nirgund yelled.

The beast stopped and watched him with caution. The other hounds of the pack were equally frozen.

The half-goblin chuckled. "A human who can show a strong hand to a hound of our lands. I think they like you, human. Their previous master was a goblin...or was it an orc? Got himself killed, and he deserved it. No real goblin or orc would keep such useless creatures. Human, these beasts used to be popular with the kings of your lands a time ago. But then they all wanted beasts that could fly. I'll sell them as a pack, or none at all."

"I paid you to hold onto them," Traveler reminded the half-goblin.

"And you will pay to take them off my hands. Hurry up, and let us conclude our business. I don't want anyone to know I've done business with humans."

"I will purchase the pack."

"Good."

"What are they called, sir?" Nirgund asked.

"Alphyns, human. The wolf-hound creatures are called alphyns. How will you transport them?" the half-goblin asked Traveler.

Traveler revealed a magic pouch in his hand.

"There better be money in that pocket-realm too. And I do not accept human or elfin coinage."

CHAPTER EIGHT

City of Fae-Wick

Gwyness sat alone at the fire, deep in sadness.

"You should eat, mistress," a half-elfess said to her, but Gwyness didn't answer.

The female half-elves now wore braided hairstyles that were dignified and covered their pointed ears.

A light-blue lizard, a bit larger than a full-size dog, scurried nearby. Its movement caught Gwyness's attention.

"I hated lizards in my own lands. I hate them here. Why do we need them?"

The lizard peered out from the camp at something. Gwyness noticed that all the lizards were looking out, and she stood. The female half-elves came out of the tent and watched too.

"What are they looking at?" Gwyness asked nervously, watching the pack behavior of the lizards. They were looking at something beyond the camp.

"They can see invisible things."

"What are they seeing now?"

"It could be anything. If it draws near, the lizards will attack."

The lizards settled back down and began to act as normal.

"Traveler returns," someone whispered.

"Traveler is back!" a man in the camp yelled out.

King Aereth exited his tent. Gwyness did not wait and rushed to Traveler. The caravan master saw the question in her eyes. "There is nothing new to report, maiden. I came from her resting place. It will be a few days before I have a clear understanding of her state."

"Cannot anything be done? You restored King Aereth with your tonics."

"She is being restored, naturally and slowly. She should not have drunk the entire pitcher like that."

"I knew she should not have. She was angry."

"It will be fine, Gwyness. She just needs time."

"Mr. Traveler, we were informed that you whisked Mr. Nirgund away last night and all our Cut-Throats before dawn. Even I am concerned," King Aereth said.

"Sire, all is moving forward. Mr. Hobbs!"

The steward appeared from among the men. "Yes, sir."

"Please bring Mr. Estus."

Hobbs acknowledged him and ran back the other way.

"We will have a meeting."

"Yes, Mr. Traveler. So much is happening."

The leadership—those who were left—assembled in the king's tent. Traveler allowed Hobbs to open up the tent so the camp could hear as well. Thousands encircled the tent.

"I will be quick, but do ask your questions. First, Lady Aylen rests. No need to ask me about her. I will inform you of her progress when there is something that needs to be said. We cannot delay though. We move forward, and she will re-join us when she is well."

"So she will be well again?" Gwyness asked.

"You have known her longer than anyone here. Do you think Lady Aylen will dare let us set foot in Faë-Land Major without her?"

It was the first time in a long time that the maidservant managed a smile.

"Mr. Hobbs."

"Yes, sir."

"You will become the keeper of the circle. It is an art that you will master, and the new circle I obtained is of more powerful magic than the current one. The instruction will be short, but its proper use will be paramount to the safety of the caravan. Many invisible things are moving around us. Those outside the new circle will not be able to hear our words; we will appear only as illusionary forms, so they will not be able to read our lips."

"Read lips?" Quillen was surprised.

"This circle doesn't require the user to be a magician, sir?"

"Not at all. They are made by sorcerers to be sold at market to those not of magic. It has been that way for ages."

"Mr. Traveler, will the lizards still be able to see invisible things from within the new circle?" Gwyness asked.

"Yes, and we will be able to see out clearly. Mr. Estus, please equip the men with the weapons from our hoard, and the women. Everyone will also wear battle gear at all times. You all might as well get used to it."

"Are we still a caravan and not an army, Mr. Traveler?" the king asked.

"We are, but no one will take us seriously if we are not dressed so. We must still add new fae to our party, and we must attract them to join our caravan.

"Mr. Hobbs, you will also oversee the change to the new food for the lizards. Yes, men. It means the lizards will grow to their normal size faster.

"As for the others. Mr. Pangolin will return in a day or so with, I hope, new fae members. Mr. Nirgund will rejoin the party with new fae hounds and take his place as the royal guard."

"Royal guard?" the king asked.

"Nirgund?" a man asked incredulously. "Our Nirgund, sir? Nirgund the Mad?"

Traveler spoke over the laughter. "Yes, our Nirgund. Also, the Cut-Throats will rejoin the party with their own animals."

"Animals?" Quillen asked.

"The Cut-Throats have animals, sir?" a man asked.

"What kind of animals, sir?"

"Animals that can battle. Men, we have a lot of work to complete. I know you are curious, but let us accomplish our tasks and be ready for departure to our first fae city. It will be unlike anything you can imagine. If we impress the people of that city, we will have fae asking to join us. It is better to receive offers than to beg for them. We cannot be the latter. And no sorcerer or sorceress, which it is essential that we hire, will join any caravan led by humans that is anything less than impressive."

"The men will be ready, sir," Hobbs said, loudly and defiantly.

The men responded with cheers.

Gwyness had an awful night. She could barely sleep, tossing and turning. Her mind was preoccupied with Lady Aylen. But there was nothing to be done. She did not know when she finally drifted off to sleep. Something hit her bare face, and she opened her eyes.

She screamed. The female half-elves sleeping on the floor jumped up. It was one of the lizards, and they chased it out of the women's tent.

"Lizards!" Gwyness yelled. She threw open the entrance flap to watch the fae reptile.

"Sorry, mistress. We thought it was secure."

"Has the lizard doubled in size?"

"It has grown, yes."

"How big do they get?"

"We have seen them as long as thirty feet and as tall as ten feet."

"That is tremendous. Will these grow that large?"

"I do not believe so, mistress. The largest of these lizards would be too much for us to handle on such a long journey. Larger than a horse would make more sense."

"I hope so. I am not fond of even tiny lizards."

In his magic book, Quillen sketched more from his recollection and wrote in the details. This was his early dawn routine before he began his duties. At night, all he wanted to do was sleep.

He looked up from the book and glanced around the camp. Another man sitting at his fire looked at him.

"Do you feel that?" Quillen asked. "Is the ground shaking?"

After a few moments, it became clear that something large was approaching the camp.

"It's Mr. Pangolin!" one of the half-elves yelled out.

Men ran to where he had been seen. Quillen reached the spot, and his mouth dropped open. Pangolin strolled to them, but he was not alone. Six ten-foot giants, each with even longer war hammers resting on his shoulder, followed him in two lines.

Traveler appeared with his dog. He greeted their master-at-arms with a firm forearm shake and a smile.

"Welcome to Titan's Caravan," Traveler greeted the giants.

They all nodded. One of the giants handed Traveler a rolled-up parchment. "For the king or queen of your caravan." The caravan master had to bear-hug the giant paper, which was almost as tall as he was. Hobbs quickly gestured to half a dozen men, who grabbed it for him, all of them holding it up from either end.

"By decree of the Giant King of Antaea, you have the kingdom's most able and fearless giant warriors as a royal escort to the Titan's Caravan."

"It is our honor," Traveler responded.

"Our king expects you to get us to our destination," one giant challenged. "We have many riches to acquire. Much more than would satisfy your men."

The men had encircled them, smiling and in awe.

"With you at Mr. Pangolin's side, we will arrive there, indeed. Mr. Pangolin, our Antaean giant warriors are in your charge. I leave it to you to get them settled in."

"Very good, Mr. Traveler. I will."

"Hungry?" he asked the giants.

The giants looked at each other, as if confused by his question.

"Always."

The camp laughed.

"We will see to that as well."

"Follow me, men." Pangolin led the giants into the camp. Traveler and the dog walked with them.

"This is even better than we had hoped," Traveler said.

"Whatever your conversation was with their king, it greatly helped put him in an agreeable frame of mind. He was going to send only two, but I played on his great dislike of elves: 'The elfin caravans we will encounter will have a giant or two. But when they see what we have, every elfin king will ask from what kingdoms those giants hail.' I suggested he would secure a place for his kingdom in the halls of Atlantea. Not to mention, I repeated the vast riches he would obtain."

Traveler laughed. "You learn quickly."

"It was not difficult for me to learn of the giant-elf animosity. They spoke about it all the time. Will it be a problem with those in our camp?"

"No, not at all. Our caravan is led by humans. We can have as many elves as we wish."

"Good."

"Now that we know what we have, do you agree to put four with you on point and two at the rear with the Cut-Throats?"

"Yes, a sound strategy."

"I took them out yesterday to get the chamroshes. I took Mr. Nirgund out the night before to get his animal. Instead, he will have a pack of them—alphyns."

"What are these beasts?"

"Chamroshes are hounds with the heads and wings of eagles. You think your Cut-Throats were formidable before, but with a pack of flying chamroshes at their sides, they will be able to battle any fae or beast. Alphyns are a type of reptilian hound with eagle-taloned forearms and legs. Nirgund, too, will be a formidable royal guard for the king and the women."

"What would you have done if the two of us had not met in tragic circumstances but so fortuitously? Would you have entered the Erymanthian Games yourself?"

"Oh, no. I would have simply hired a pair of Antaeans at Arion's Spear, the main fae city on the Trail. However, since we did meet, I saw an opportunity for our caravan that could not be ignored. At every chance, it is better to have our fae members offer to join us rather than for us to hire them with money. We saw how disastrous that turned out for Lady Aylen when we first encountered the Kings' Caravan. Someone can always offer more money if that is all they value."

"How is Lady Aylen?"

"She is...recovering. I will know more in the days to come."

"Will it delay us?"

"No, we will not wait. Once the lizards have grown a bit more, Mr. Estus will armor them up, and we will depart."

"So the Cut-Throats and Nirgund are here?"

"Each in their own pocket, training with their animals."

"Good. How many days?"

"Three at most. I will try for two."

The berserker nodded.

With the giants added to the caravan, Hobbs had to redraw the circle to accommodate them in a new section of the camp. The fae-human cooks kept the food coming. The giants devoured every chunk of food and every barrel of water or ale put in front of them.

Pangolin noticed Elman, the half-elf.

"Yes, Mr. Elman."

The half-elf drew closer. "Mr. Pangolin. I wanted to ask your permission."

"Permission? For what?"

"I would like to change my duties and join you and the giants at point."

"You?"

"My senses can be an asset. I am also a hunter and tracker by training."

"Well, the senses of you and your people are impressive. Hunter and tracker too?"

"Yes, I can read the signs of most land-based animals, including fae. I can read the trees, too, for signs of birds and aerial fae."

"What about fighting? I was told your people do not want to use elfin weapons."

"No, sir, we will. Unfortunately, I am not an archer. None of us are, but I am good with the sword and ax. I can choose one and carry a shield. I am fast and will not let you down."

"The vanguard of a caravan is the most dangerous duty of all."

"Yes, but it is also the most important. We guide the caravan and lead it away from danger."

Pangolin nodded. "Okay, Mr. Elman, I will speak with Mr. Hobbs. However, that will mean you will camp with us. Can you handle loud warrior humans and giants?"

"I can, sir."

"It is settled. I will speak with Hobbs."

Not only did Hobbs keep a tent separate from the royals, but he preferred to keep the tent in the center of the camp so that all could confidentially bring any issue to his attention. And he constantly made rounds through the camp.

"We have giants, Mr. Hobbs," a smiling man said to him.

"Mr. Hobbs, our caravan is unstoppable," another declared.

How could the men not be excited? Even now, as the giants sat or lay in their corner of the camp, their forms and voices loomed over all. This was when Hobbs enjoyed his job the most. Moving through the camp and seeing smiling faces, hearing prideful words—the Titan's Caravan was becoming more than anything any of them could have imagined.

The upbeat mood ended. The shrieks of eagles rang through the camp and Hobbs saw the fear in the men's faces—the hippogriffs of the Four Kings!

Hobbs heard laughter and saw Traveler with Pangolin near the giants, who were now standing. He ran to the gathering and saw the Cut-Throats had returned.

"What are those?" Hobbs asked with surprise.

The gang of warriors, berserker and otherwise, had fantastic beasts on leashes—hounds with eagle heads and eagle wings sprouting from their backs.

"The beasts are called chamroshes, Mr. Hobbs," Traveler answered.

"Are all of Mr. Pangolin's warriors to receive the beasts, sir?"

"Oh, no. Not even his warriors could handle such a number. One hundred of his fiercest Cut-Throats received a chamrosh. That is more than enough. Like the lizards, they attack and defend as a pack. The rest of Mr. Pangolin's warriors are fitted with goblin armor and weapons."

"You said, sir, that elves would think us in league with their arch-enemies the goblins if we used any goblin metal."

"Yes, but I have changed my mind. There have been increased sightings of goblin war parties. I want us to be able to avoid any confrontations with elves or goblins. If all it will take for goblin marauders to let us be is for them to see some of our warriors in goblin armor, we will gladly show it to them."

"Very well, sir. I will tell the men we have...chamroshes, then, and not hippogriffs."

"I apologize. I did not mean to frighten them with bad memories of the past. Have them take turns seeing the beasts themselves."

"Yes, sir. I will."

"Why did you pick these particular beasts?" Pangolin asked Traveler.

"They hate hippogriffs, for one."

Hobbs had the leadership gathered for the night meal. Estus arrived exhausted; he had been working hard each day for weeks, outfitting men and beasts with armor and weapons, and from the soot on his arms, it included much metalworking. King Aereth had continued drilling the heavy teams with their giant catapults and crossbows. They had become quite proficient at hitting targets from as far away as a mile. Gwyness and the female half-elves had also practiced their fighting and weapons skills. The maidservant didn't care for the drills, but the female half-elves enjoyed every second of them.

Traveler sat at the fire, facing them all, with the dog lying next to him. "Mr. Pangolin," Traveler began as their master-at-arms arrived, "Mr. Nirgund will rejoin the camp tomorrow."

"Good. How many beasts did you say he has?"

"A pack of thirteen."

Quillen ran to the fire, overhearing them. "Mr. Nirgund has fae beasts too? What kind?"

"Alphyns. A kind of wolf-hound with eagle talons for feet."

The young man smiled. "I will not need to go anywhere for my book of fantastic beasts, Mr. Traveler. They will all be in our caravan."

"Mr. Traveler, are we still on schedule to leave in a day?" the king asked.

"Should we leave tomorrow? Mr. Estus has finished his tasks with his men ahead of schedule."

Everyone looked at each other.

"Yes," Pangolin answered. "Why not at dawn?"

"Oh, please, Mr. Pangolin," Estus said. "Give my men and me a day to recover. The pocket we work in can get as hot as the sun with all the work we do. A much needed day of rest for us in the fresh outdoor air of the camp."

"Yes, you will have your one day, Mr. Estus. You deserve it. Mr. Pangolin, how is Mr. Elman doing?"

"I was skeptical at first," Pangolin answered. "He is a quiet man, but he has presented himself well. We have done several drills, and his fighting skills are quite good. Even the giants like him. He will be fine for our vanguard."

"Good."

"What about Lady Aylen, Mr. Traveler?" Gwyness asked.

The question quieted everyone. Traveler paused for a moment. Gwyness grew fearful again.

"Lady Aylen has gotten through the worst of it."

Gwyness was visibly relieved, along with everyone else.

"What does that mean, Mr. Traveler? Is she out of danger?"

"She is out of most of the danger. The physical danger is behind her, though I must keep watch over her progress."

"Why?"

"She has a fever, but that is normal. It is the body coping with the changes. I am not worried by it."

"Why can't she stay here, in the women's tent? We can care for her."

"No, she must stay where she is. She has quite a list of personal tasks to complete. She must learn to walk again—"

"Walk again?" Gwyness interrupted.

"Yes. If you had the legs of a two-foot fowl one day and those of a nine-foot horse the next, you would need to learn to walk again. Everything about her physical being is stronger and faster. She must adjust to her increased sight. We all know how exceptional the sight is of our half-elf members. Hers is even more exceptional. Then there is the hearing, which will be the greatest of her physical challenges. She must learn how to not hear things. It is a skill elves learn as infants. She is burdened with having to master it as an adult."

"Is it difficult?" Gwyness asked.

"Not difficult but time-consuming. We both know that our princess is not the most patient of people."

"No, she is not."

"Once she masters all that. She can rejoin us."

"What about the other matter you mentioned?" Gwyness asked.

"Exactly why she will need to rejoin us. For you to watch over her until she is fully past all her challenges."

"How optimistic are you, Mr. Traveler?" King Aereth asked. "Truthfully."

"Very. She is not patient, but she is also quite stubborn. I will use her stubbornness against her impatience. The notion that the caravan will journey across Faë-Land without her is a powerful incentive. She will make it through."

The leadership's mood lightened.

"I will keep all of you updated."

"Mr. Traveler, can you tell us about the fae city Fae-Wick, then?" the king asked.

"I could, but honestly, I am not sure I have the words to do so effectively, even after visiting it half a dozen times. Every time I was in...awe."

Their weaponsmaster, Mr. Estus, said he wanted a day of rest, but instead, he was still fitting men in new fae armor. Gwyness had resisted but was finally cornered.

"Maiden Gwyness, elfin armor is the lightest and most comfortable steel you will ever feel," he had told her.

King Aereth was also fitted. They stood in his tent, looking at themselves in a tall mirror that Gwyness did not know he had.

"I do not like it," she said.

"It fits you perfectly," King Aereth said.

"Yours looks regal, sire. On me, I feel I am a pretend warrior somehow."

He chuckled. "It is to protect you from harm, young lady."

She noticed that one of the half-elf females at the entrance, clad in her own armor, was petting a dog.

"I did not know Mr. Traveler's dog allowed anyone to touch him."

"This is not Mr. Traveler's dog, mistress."

Gwyness neared the animal and saw its eagle-taloned forearms and hind legs. "Oh, my. What is that?"

"It is an alphyn, mistress."

"Mr. Nirgund is back then," King Aereth declared.

The king moved to the entrance, and the reptile-dog hybrid sprinted away. Gwyness joined him. Immediately, they saw Nirgund surrounded by men in the distance. The giants towered above them.

The new fae hounds had almost jet-black fur and knotted tails. A ridge of knotted fur ran along their backs. In their jumping and playing with one another, Gwyness noticed that their underbellies were those of lizards. A pair of the hounds approached the royals, sniffed them, and ran off.

"We have passed their inspection," the king said to Gwyness.

"Their eyes are unusual, too, sire."

"Yes, almost like fire. I wonder...I once heard that they can breathe fire."

"Breathe fire? Sire, that must be a fable."

He laughed. "We stand in a camp of giants, fantastic beasts, and gnome-like men. What is fable and fact, indeed?"

"Mr. Tyfer and Mr. Oeric," Traveler called out as he approached the lead fae-human men. They were hard at work with the camp's now-increased cooking duties.

"Yes, sir," they said.

"I have a new duty to ask of you."

"Yes, sir."

"Your culinary skills are impressive, but I think we will find some fae cooks to add to the camp, especially now that we have six giants to feed as well. I have in mind, though, a more pressing duty that I think you both would be better suited for."

"However we can be of service, Mr. Traveler," Tyfer said.

"Mr. Hobbs."

"Yes, sir?" Oeric asked.

"He needs his own guards, sir," Tyfer guessed.

"Yes. Mr. Hobbs is an exceptional steward, well-liked by the men. He is lousy at personal security."

The men laughed. "Yes, sir. We will take care of him, sir," Tyfer said.

"See Mr. Estus to be properly fitted, and you will be Mr. Hobbs's personal guards. The king has his, Lady Aylen hers, and now Mr. Hobbs. My mind can be at ease."

"We depart in the morning, sir?" Oeric asked.

"At dawn."

"Very good, sir."

♦♦♦

"Mr. Elman," Traveler greeted as he approached the camp of male half-elves. The lads sat or reclined, quietly drinking broth. "Is it true?"

Elman stood to his feet. "Is what true, sir?"

"You can speak without words to each other."

Elman smiled. "Did you hear that, sir?"

"I was told that years ago, when I was in the magical lands. I was never told how or which elves possessed the talent. Do half-elves possess it too?"

"Not all, sir, and it must be taught at infancy."

"Master Tane taught you all."

"He did, sir."

"My dog can transform into creatures that hear such mind-talking. But that is not why I am here. You have joined Mr. Pangolin's vanguard. The female half-elves will be Lady Aylen's royal guards. That leaves the rest of your party."

The ten half-elf men got to their feet and joined them.

"I had been in a caravan years ago, and they had a group of mercenaries who always stayed together but were never stationed in any one part of the caravan. They moved through it freely. Their purpose was to go where the danger was and to deal with it. That is the role I want you men to fulfill."

They all nodded.

"Mercenaries, sir," one said, smiling.

"Yes, like a mercenary force, one that can speak to each other without words. See Mr. Estus and ask him to equip you with the special weapons we found. However, do not tell Mr. Elman here."

"What?" Elman exclaimed.

The other half-elves laughed at him.

Dawn.

There were men who had joined the caravan as far back as Hopeshire, and some after the attack at Ironwood. Some had been part of Lady Aylen's original party going back a year at Sirnegate. However, most of the men felt this was the real first day of their Titan's Caravan. Today was when it officially began. Most of the men had barely gotten a wink of sleep the night before; their eager anticipation and nervousness was too great.

Hobbs wore an armored chestplate and a helmet that was more of a metal hat. With his blue cloak, fine trousers, and new leather boots, he looked every bit the noble of his past Theogar Royal House days. His two bodyguards stood nearby, armored and armed with sheathed swords at their sides. "The men are ready, sir," Hobbs said to Traveler.

Traveler wore his black hooded cloak; a broadsword was strapped to his back. His clothes and gloves were of black-and-brown leather.

"Thank you, Mr. Hobbs. Sire, the honor is yours."

"Thank you, Mr. Traveler."

King Aereth, dressed in noble lavender, his gold crown upon his head, raised his hand and gestured onward to a watching Pangolin, who acknowledged him with his own forward gesture to the giants behind. Titan's Caravan was on the march.

The king did not want to wear his crown. He felt it pretentious on a long trek, but Traveler had convinced him that having a visibly identifiable royal would be to their great advantage. Gwyness marched, dressed in black, including her flowing cloak. The female half-elves walked behind her in white elfin armor, five with elfin spears, two in the rear with fine crossbows. Nirgund, now the royal guard, marched behind them with his pack of alphyns trotting around. The men followed in four columns—lizard and lizard minders on the flanks, and the other two lines in between. Two giants and the Cut-Throats, with their hyperactive chamroshes, made up the rear guard.

Traveler walked with the king. The dog was in its common form, but its size was larger, almost that of a horse. Ahead, Pangolin, with Mr. Elman at his side, led the four giants in the vanguard of the caravan— also known as the "tip of the spear." The giants' armor and war hammers were of the highest quality dwarvin steel.

♦♦♦

The march was quiet. Traveler could feel the men's nervousness.

"Mr. Hobbs."

The steward quickened his pace. "Yes, sir."

"Where are our Brothers Brimm?"

"The musicians, sir?"

"Yes, I forgot about them."

"They have been on cooking duty."

"That is fine, but tell them that they are now free to make their music. Have them play some tunes on our march to Fae-Wick."

"Seriously, sir?"

"I did not hire them for simple amusement. Their music will save us from much grief, especially once we reach the heart of the land of the fairies. Also, dark fae do not play music, so it will be a signal to all parties that we are benevolent."

"Yes, sir. I will see to it."

"Lady Aylen and I wondered why you secured those musicians," the king said.

Not too much later, three of the musicians began playing their flutes. Among the men, a relaxed state replaced their anxious mood.

The vanguard must have seen it first, but once the front of the column came upon the creature, Gwyness was sickened. On the side of the road, in the wooded area, was a humanoid beast—a man's blotched body, wearing trousers alone, with hooves for feet and the head of a sickly brown horse. The creature stared at them.

"No!" it yelled.

Traveler had not taken his eyes from it as they passed. He glanced back, and the dog kept a sharp eye on it.

"Ignore it," Traveler said under his breath.

"What was that, Mr. Traveler?" Gwyness asked.

"An ipotane. Half-horse, half-humanoid."

"That is a disgusting beast. Why is it there?"

"I imagine to watch for us."

"Watch for us, Mr. Traveler?" the king asked.

"No need for concern, sire."

None of the men knew how long they had marched, only that it had been hours. Then the vanguard stopped, and the king gave the signal for the rest of the caravan to cease its march. Traveler made his way with his dog to the waiting vanguard—Pangolin, Elman, and the giants. He looked out into the distance.

"That, men and women, is the fantastic city of Fae-Wick," he said.

King Aereth and his men, Gwyness and the female half-elves, Hobbs and his guards had joined them, all in awe.

"Let all the men move up to see, Hobbs," Traveler said.

Fae-Wick was a castle like nothing they had ever seen or could have imagined. The main castle, made of shimmering ivory rock, floated in the air. Walls connected its four towers; the end towers were shorter than the center towers, which were twice their height. The main entrance, in the exact center of the wall, was shaped like the open mouth of a crowned humanoid head. On either side of the mouth were slits where sparkling white water spilled outward and down about one hundred feet into a moat of mist. Before the mouth-shaped entrance was a floating, winding, unattached white drawbridge path.

The sky above Fae-Wick, for as far as could be seen, was filled with flying things—griffins, flying horses, flying unicorns, giant birds, and other fae creatures they had never seen wild in play. All around the castle was a cloud that looked like fireflies, but Traveler told the caravan that they were not fireflies at all. They were fairies.

The castle itself was not the largest they had ever seen, but they knew that was an illusion. Traveler told them that it was far more vast inside—its own pocket-realm. On the ground before it were other parties moving about, too far away—at least for the humans—to make out the races. Some of the parties flew flags high. The caravan even saw a few other giants amongst them.

Traveler pointed. "Mr. Hobbs, set up camp there, and remain in charge. Mr. Pangolin, you will come with me. Choose your men. Sire, Maiden Gwyness, you both will also accompany me with your guards."

Quillen waved his hands so Traveler could see. "Yes, yes, Mr. Quillen, you too. But only because you are the official chronicler of the Titan's Caravan."

"I am? Oh, I am!"

"We go to Fae-Wick."

CHAPTER NINE

Fairy Sisters

"Make your circle, Mr. Hobbs," Traveler told him.

It was a phrase they all knew they would become quite accustomed to in the days and months ahead. Their steward was not completely comfortable with the prospect of using magic as a nonmagical practitioner, but it was a prime responsibility. The circle was more than that. It was a dome—a dome to protect the very lives of the camp.

"Mr. Traveler," Gwyness began. Traveler turned his attention to her. "If I could, I would like to remain in the camp with our female guards. I feel...I do not think I can enjoy its sights without Lady Aylen being there too."

"I understand."

Hobbs took what looked like a wand, so common an artifice from fables told in their lands, and drew a circle in the air several times. In the blink of an eye, the circle took form around the entire camp. The men created the perimeter by standing at various points, roughly in the shape of an actual circle. The magical circle barrier appeared around them. Then, no one but the members of the camp could enter or exit. Outsiders had to be invited in.

"Mr. Traveler, I see that some of the parties outside the city bear the flags of their kingdoms. Do we need such for ours?" King Aereth asked.

"You have a valid point, sire, especially when we get to Faë-Land Major."

"Yes, the elfin kingdoms do observe the practice of only recognizing a party under a flag."

"Then, sire, I leave it to you to design the flag of Titan's Caravan. Mr. Hobbs will be more than willing to assign the laborers, experts in cloth and sewing, to create it. In fact, you could draw it, and we could hire a sprite or fairy to sew it instantly."

"Oh, very good. Let me give it more thought, Mr. Traveler."

"And remember, sire, we do have our own artist extraordinaire should you need advice."

"Yes, young Mr. Quillen."

The lad heard his name and snapped out of his gawking at Fae-Wick's castle. "Huh? Yes? I heard my name."

As they quickly prepared, Pangolin pulled one of the other berserkers aside.

"I-wulf, we have not had the chance to speak of it before, and you already know. You are officially in charge of the Cut-Throats."

"Yes, Mr. Pangolin," he said, smiling.

"Mister? I cannot say I like all these titles all the time. We are warriors, but I suppose the protocol is expected in this structure."

"I cannot say I ever would have guessed Nirgund's decision. We thought all he wanted was his own fae animal. We did not know it was to sell out, put on fluffy clothes, and take on the role of a royal."

Pangolin laughed. "I will tell him what you said."

"And tell him my animal can fly."

"But he has a dozen of his. No, Mr. Nirgund is right. It is easy to forget things. We have focused on perimeter security and the vanguard, but internal security is sometimes even more important. We've both been in many a party where one did not know who to thrust one's blade into, because the enemies were in front of you and behind."

"Yes, well, Mr. Pangolin, I will command the Cut-Throats as ably as you did or Mr. Nirgund would have. Your hands are more than filled with the task of managing the giants."

"Yes, indeed."

The two of them returned to the giants and Cut-Throats. "Grakdar and Barg, with me," Pangolin yelled. "Arteus, Aronir, Alceir, and Alebar, keep the men safe."

The giants who remained grunted their acknowledgment as the other two lumbered forward.

The dog changed its form again, keeping most of its dog features, but now had six legs, bulbous fly-like eyes, and gigantic patterned moth wings folded and running down its back.

Pangolin led their party in with an Antaean giant on each side. He did not like it at all. Elves and other fae stood on either side of the white soil path they followed to Fae-Wick's main entrance. Most of the elves seemed to be part of their own caravan, armored with swords at their waists. Their physical appearance was the same—dark hair, porcelain skin, and green eyes with a hint of yellow. Their clothing suggested they came from some mountainous domain. Pangolin could not tell if they were curious, or watching them for other wicked purposes. Regardless, their expressions were not friendly at all. The elves were especially angered by the sight of the giants, and the giants glared back at them.

Other parties, including two with their own giants, were moving on. Once they passed the staring elves, it was as if the land itself parted for them alone to make their way to the main entrance of Fae-Wick.

Everyone moved away from them. Pangolin did not like it, but the giants were unconcerned, so he pressed on without a word.

Traveler and the rest of the party closely followed Pangolin's vanguard. Without Hobbs, he gave to Quillen the duty of seeing that tasks were completed. He handed Quillen a paper list.

"After this, you will secure your place in the hearts of the men."

"Sir?" Quillen asked Traveler. "What am I buying?"

"New sleeping gear for the men. We will be on the Trail for a year. The men should be comfortable."

"Giant's slipper. What is that, sir?" Quillen asked, looking at the list.

"You will see. Take your men, and get the supplies."

"Do I need money, sir?"

"In these lands, the goods are brought to the camp. Besides, there are a lot of thieves in Faë-Land. And you, Mr. Quillen, would be a temptation too great for any to pass up. They would be off with our money long before you even knew to look. Remember, thieves here are often invisible."

"Oh, we should have taken a lizard with us, then."

"No, Mr. Quillen, you must keep a hold of your belongings."

Just ahead of Pangolin and his giants, Quillen moved with his fifty men, servants, and laborers of the camp, but they were armored and dressed to look like warriors. King Aereth was amused by how well Nirgund's new fae hounds behaved, following close around them as a pack. The king noticed that none of the animals ever responded to Traveler's dog, no matter what form it took.

"You and I, sire, will focus on heavy weapons and projectiles. Once merchants know we are here and that we are spending good money, they will seek us out. Then we'll get all our food supplies."

"Yes, Mr. Traveler, we have many mouths to feed—many very, very large mouths to feed. In fact, I meant to ask you. Do fae not hunt for food as in our lands?"

"They do, but the hunting fields are not near Titan's Trail. They are quite a distance, and here, it is advisable to avoid it. As humans, it is always tricky to know what and when to hunt. Here, stags and fowl may talk. They may be a fairy or sprite shape-shifter or may be an honored animal, and its killing will only bring the wrath of their master, their whole clan, an entire kingdom, or even the entire race. No, let us just purchase our food, carry it with us, and be done with it. Much simpler and free of peril."

King Aereth nodded. "Yes, I cannot agree more."

Quillen was beside himself with excitement. He was almost running to get to the floating white drawbridge at the mouth-entrance of the castle. But he gazed out of the mist moat and up at the falling waterfall. Clearly, magic caused the falling water to contain the mist into the circle below the structure. But where did the bulk of the water go? he thought. It was as if the waterfall disappeared into the earth itself.

Besides the mist, there was a cloud of fairies in constant motion encircling the castle. Quillen felt overwhelmed because there was too much to see, and now regretted his decision to take Hobbs's place to be in charge of the men. One could not record fantastic sights in their magic book if they could not stop to do so. His eyes were again pleasantly stunned by the real griffins, giant birds, and flying horses above their heads.

Someone cleared their throat loudly. Quillen looked to see the men in his charge, Pangolin, and the giants all waiting on him.

"Oh, sorry," he said, as he began moving forward through the mist to step onto the white drawbridge path.

The path wound like a snake up the entire hundred feet, but the walk was not tiring, and there was no sensation of rising elevation. Quillen wondered if it might be another magical illusion—that the castle was not floating at all and that they were all walking along the ground.

However, when they passed through the mouth-entrance of the giant crowned head of rock—a being that looked like a humanoid insect with large eyes—across the wall, and into the castle, they were in another realm.

They had visited many markets in their own lands and had been to the modest ones of the fae villages before. However, this was beyond them all. It was not only a market street of every kind of merchant imaginable. It was market street upon market street stacked on top of each other into the sky. Each level above ground was not floating, but only after staring for a while did they understand how it was accomplished. It was one giant multilevel structure inside, but the wall facing them was gone so all could see into the levels.

People spilled out on the main street and every other above. Unlike in the fae villages, which were filled with rustic folk in casual dress, here the people were in noble and professional attire. The colors of fabric were not as varied. Those in armor and carrying weapons were more the norm than the exception. They knew of elves and, from Traveler's accounts, knew that those halflings and little folk that looked very much like humans and wore colored hats were sprites. Fairies were often insect-like in some way, but there were also birdlike, reptile-like, amphibian-like, and even plant-like races.

"Fae-Wick is a city of fairies," Traveler said. "They build their structures like bees and ants. Many levels, rooms, and compartments. Always very busy."

"Very easy for a human to get lost," Pangolin said.

"No, Mr. Quillen will not get lost because he will stick to his task at hand with his men and not go exploring."

Quillen smirked and proceeded forward slowly as the men laughed. "Yes, Mr. Traveler."

"Sire, you can wait here for a moment. I wish to check something, then we will spend time in the fae-weaponsmiths section of the market."

"Very good."

Traveler disappeared into the crowds of fae, sprites, and elves.

"The dog is gone," Pangolin remarked.

King Aereth looked around and realized he was correct. "So, Mr. Pangolin, what is your task with your giant men?"

"We will wait here, sire. There is far too much activity here for my liking."

"I know what you mean," Nirgund said, keeping a watchful eye on his alphyns. The fae dogs were calm but watched everyone passing around them.

"The interior of this castle is another realm. See how the sky extends beyond the walls? But that is not the sky we saw when we approached," King Aereth said to them.

"And there are no animals flying in the sky inside this realm," Pangolin added. "Very interesting, these pocket-realms."

"Mr. Traveler has given me the task of designing the flag of Titan's Caravan. Any thoughts, Mr. Pangolin?"

"The fae flags seem to be very similar to what we humans have. A single animal or beast as its standard."

"Yes, but what animal or beast? We have so many, and Mr. Traveler says we will have more. Maybe, since we are Titan's Caravan, the flag should feature one of the ancient titans. Perhaps even the Maker of All Mountains, who legend says created Titan's Trail by simply dragging his Star Slayer sword along the surface of the world."

Pangolin smiled. "I like it, sire."

"How about a dragon, king?" one of the giants suggested. "They are extinct like the ancient titans, but I like dragons."

"Dragons convey war, in my mind. As Mr. Traveler said, we are a caravan, not an army. We need a symbol that is neutral, but conveys strength to any and all who see it. I would think, as a giant, you would have great respect for the titans."

"Perhaps, king, you can put a few tiny dragons on the flag, with a bit of fire coming from their tiny mouths."

King Aereth and Pangolin laughed.

"I like dragons," the giant said again.

"He has drawings and trinkets and other collectibles everywhere in his personal dwelling in Khury," the other giant added as he patted his comrade on the back.

"I had dragon toys as an infant. My favorite. I like dragons."

"You would not say that if they were still alive in our world," the giant Grakdar said to Barg.

"Hunted to extinction, you mean. By those elves."

"By all ancient fae. I do not like elves either, but it was not them alone. And had it not been done, this would be a scorched world of dragons with not a single fae, human, fowl, beast, or insect to be found."

King Aereth smiled with amusement at the exchange between the two giants, brothers-in-arms, when his eyes caught sight of a strange hooded man in the crowd. The king's smile disappeared as he took greater stock of the approaching stranger and felt a wave of intense fear over the man. On either side of the man's mouth were holes, but it was his black eyes that terrified King Aereth. The man lunged forward, and his mouth opened. The words he spoke were of a tongue they had never heard before. The sound was more than words, though—it was like hearing a rumbling within one's own mind.

Pangolin screamed in agony and fell to the ground. The berserker writhed on the ground, shrinking in size, and began flailing his arms and legs. The giants grabbed their throats as if suffocating and fell to their knees.

The king's eyes widened, seeing what the evil sorcerer could not. The point of a bony spear punctured through his forehead, and the man's words ceased. Traveler ran up behind the sorcerer and sliced off his head with one stroke of his sword.

From above, the dog—its form below its waist that of a spider made of bone with spear-like legs—dropped to the ground and leapt in front of Traveler to shield him. The caravan master threw a ball of electrified blue light at the decapitated head. The head burst into flames.

One of the giants recovered quickly and got to his feet, enraged. He raised his war hammer, yelling, and swung his war hammer, crushing the sorcerer's head with thundering force. The aftermath was not blood and matter but a strange black ooze. His giant comrade also recovered and smashed the man's decapitated body with his war hammer.

Traveler ran to Pangolin, who was still in a fit on the ground.

A dark-hooded and cloaked elf appeared from the crowd, raised his hand, and spoke an elfin spell. Pangolin began to calm down and his shaking stopped entirely—the pain was gone. His size began to return to normal.

"I reversed the dark magic," the pale elfin sorcerer said. "I expect to be compensated."

Traveler stood to his feet, reached into his cloak, and threw a pouch to the elf. It jingled when he caught it. The elf held it to an ear and nodded with satisfaction. He turned and disappeared back into the crowd of onlookers.

A fae guard appeared from thin air, aiming a magical bow and arrow at Traveler. More fae archers appeared, dressed in crimson with tall hats of a curved design, their bows seemed to be made of gold and the arrows of pure white light. They all had slit eyes, more like an insect, and large translucent fly-like wings sprouting from their backs. In moments, dozens of the archers surrounded Traveler's group.

Another fae appeared before them. He was not an archer; he was their commander. Before he could speak, Traveler angrily approached him.

"Fae-Wick is supposed to be a sanctuary to all!" he yelled.

"It is—"

"But here, within your walls, my men were attacked by a malevolent wizard that is not supposed to exist within these lands, let alone within a city. How could the likes of a spell-talker enter the guarded city of Fae-Wick? Imps, pixies, gremlins cannot attain entry, but a spell-talker can. A wizard creature that could kill every last fae in Fae-Wick's realm with a spoken word!"

"We do not know—"

"I am not interested in your lies or excuses!" Traveler turned to the giants. "Carry Mr. Pangolin back to our camp!"

"I can walk on my own." Pangolin began to walk but immediately felt light-headed and fell to one knee. One of the giants grabbed him by the arm.

"Mr. Nirgund, find Mr. Quillen and his men immediately. We are leaving!" The royal guardsman ran off with his fae hounds.

"There is no need—" The crimson fae leader tried to talk again. He had already gestured for the archers to lower their bows.

"I am not interested in anything you have to say. I have been to Fae-Wick many times in my youth. It was a city of order and safety. I see now that its reputation is a distant memory and that its security has been turned over to hobgoblins and other scoundrels."

The fae commander turned red, offended. He tried to speak, but Traveler turned from him and led the giants, with Pangolin and King Aereth, back to the entrance.

◆◆◆

"Outrageous!" Traveler yelled as he stormed back to their camp.

Already, Hobbs, Gwyness, and Estus waited within for their return. One of the half-elves spotted him coming down the floating white drawbridge. Traveler and the dog crossed the circle threshold first, then King Aereth and Nirgund, Quillen, and his men. The giants then lumbered in with Mr. Pangolin.

"Mr. Traveler." One of the male half-elves pointed.

A female humanoid descended from the sky out of thin air, dressed in white, with large translucent, fly-like wings sprouting from her back. Her face was like a human except for her pure-white hair and large black eyes.

"May I enter?" she asked, once she landed on the ground before them.

Traveler nodded, and she stepped across the circle. She saw Pangolin and raised her right hand. A ball of white light came from it and disappeared. Pangolin was enveloped in a glow, and they watched as Pangolin stood tall and clenched his fists. His eyes turned bloodshot for an instant—he was fully restored.

More fairies appeared, dressed identically as the female. A male stepped into the camp. He threw a pouch of coins to Traveler.

"No need to have paid for a service not properly performed," the male fairy said.

Traveler said nothing, as he returned the pouch to his cloak pocket.

"I am the administrator of Fae-Wick," the male fairy said.

"I am its chief sorceress," the female fairy said. "Your human berserker is as he was a decade of your years earlier."

"You made me younger?" Pangolin asked.

"I restored you and more," she answered.

"Human Traveler, I wish to officially apologize on behalf of the city of Fae-Wick. The attack was a gross violation of the trust of the sanctum of our city that we have built over many millennia. Those responsible for this evil breach will be found and punished."

"If they have not already escaped," Traveler interjected.

"Perhaps so. But we are very good at hunting evildoers."

"How would the likes of a spell-talker get into your city?"

"Another must have cast a spell on him so that he would not appear as he was until he entered and prepared to attack," the female fairy replied. "The matter will be dealt with. I can promise you that. It is not just Fae-Wick's reputation in the balance but my own."

"Human Traveler, we do not wish for you to leave our city or these lands with this incident in your mind. We will assign royal escorts for any and all parties you allow back into our city. Also, I have taken the liberty of having three of our master merchants at your disposal to see that you acquire any and all supplies you need."

King Aereth looked at Traveler and stepped forward. "That, sir, is more than adequate."

"Yes, thank you," Traveler said. "We will stay and conclude our business."

"That is good. Thank you for the honor to serve," the fae administrator said as he nodded.

"Also, you do not need to trek back to the city," the fairy sorceress said. "I will make a cloud available for your use."

Everyone looked at her with confusion except Mr. Traveler and the giants. "Did she say...cloud?" Quillen asked.

One of the giants pointed up at the sky. They all looked. One of the clouds above them began to descend.

Pangolin refused to remain behind. This time, Gwyness, with her female half-elf guards, accompanied the party back to Fae-Wick. However, now they stood on a cloud with the fae administrator and sorceress at the head, and dozens of royal escorts on the cloud around.

Quillen laughed to himself as he watched the cloud fly across the air, directly to the mouth entrance where many more insect-winged royal guards hovered, in wait. The cloud dissipated, and their feet touched solid ground.

"Thank you, administrator," King Aereth said again.

The fairy nodded, and so did the sorceress as they moved on, but all the royal escorts remained.

If Pangolin was uncomfortable before, he was doubly so now as they had the attention of every fairy, sprite, and elf in the markets. Who were those humans worthy of a royal escort through the city of Fae-Wick? None of them needed to understand the fae languages being spoken to know that was the question being asked among the crowds.

"Mr. Quillen, speak with the merchant master and have all our supplies brought immediately to our camp."

"Yes, Mr. Traveler."

"Is it safe for me to explore, Mr. Traveler?" Gwyness asked.

"Yes, it is. Please, do so. The city will give you escorts."

"Our task, Mr. Traveler?" the king asked.

"Is now a simple matter, sire. A merchant master can have what we seek brought to us as well. I will leave you to it."

"Are you leaving us again, Mr. Traveler?" the king asked.

"Only to equip our healing tent properly, sire, especially after what just occurred."

"Speaking of which, Mr. Traveler, is this not a place for us to acquire our caravan's healer?"

"If I could suggest." One of the fae escorts stepped forward. "There is a human healer within the city seeking a position."

"There, Mr. Traveler. Yes, please, how do we speak to him?"

"I will have someone bring him here." The fae escort motioned to another.

"Who are you?" a high-pitched voiced asked.

A fairy barely two feet tall stood next to them. At her side was an even smaller fairy girl. The taller one had two antennae poking out from her short golden hair, translucent insect wings emerging from her back, and she wore a muted ivory frock. The smaller one differed in dress only in that she also wore a brown half-jacket whose texture resembled that of a woolly caterpillar.

"I am Traveler."

"Why do you have royal fairy guards attend you?"

"We are special."

"But you are human."

"I am."

"Humans are not special in these lands."

"You are correct." Traveler moved the men away, ignoring the taller female fairy further. "Have the healer see King Aereth here," Traveler said to the fae escort, who nodded.

"We know who you are," the same high-pitched voice said. This time the bigger fairy girl was hovering above the ground. "You are Traveler's Caravan."

"Titan's Caravan," Traveler corrected.

"Traveler's Caravan and you are Traveler. We want to join Traveler's Caravan."

"Why?" Again, Traveler moved the men away from the two fairy girls.

King Aereth was trying not to laugh. "Is there something we should know, Mr. Traveler?"

"We have work to do, sire."

"We want to join Traveler's Caravan!" The high-pitched voice was back.

"No," Traveler said.

"Why?"

"You didn't tell me why."

"Because—because we want to join Traveler's Caravan."

"That is not an answer."

"We want to join Traveler's Caravan because we want to go to the Kingdom of Atlantea."

"Why?"

"Because we always wanted to go there."

"That is not a reason. It is a dangerous journey, and if we did reach Atlantea, you would be alone."

"No, we would not be alone. Atlantea has fairies."

"They are no fairies there."

"Yes there are. They are part of the royal court."

"Since when?"

"Since a long time."

"What does that have to do with you?"

"We would not be alone in Atlantea. Other fairies are there."

"Why not join an elfin caravan?"

"Yuck!" the fairies yelled. The giants began to chuckle. "We do not like them."

"Join a sprite caravan."

"Yuck! There are no sprite caravans. They do not go to Atlantea. We want to join Traveler's Caravan."

"What will you do to help our caravan succeed in its journey?"

"We can do magic and talk to the birds and animals along the Trail to tell us if any evil is around."

"That is a good reason."

The fairies smiled.

"But fairies like to make mischief."

"No, we don't."

"And cast spells on humans."

"No, we won't!"

"So, if you join our caravan, you must promise three things. One. Follow all the rules of the caravan, like all its humans, sprites, elves, and giants."

"We know Traveler's Caravan has sprites and elves. And we can see the big dumb giants there."

"Hey!" the giants yelled.

"Two. You will never cast spells on anyone in the caravan—ever!"

The fairies frowned.

"Three. You will leave the caravan for no less than six hours each day to play and not return until you have done so."

The fairies began to laugh.

"Yes, to all the rules. We can join Traveler's Caravan?"

"Yes."

The fairies cried out in joy, their arms raised in the air.

"But don't come to the caravan until we leave."

"Yes. We will be there."

The fairies turned into balls of light and flew away.

Everyone laughed except Pangolin. "We are taking on children now, Mr. Traveler?" he asked.

"Mr. Pangolin, even the smallest one there is older than you, me, and the king combined."

Pangolin made a face, still not pleased, but let it go.

"I am going to speak for Lady Aylen. Let us do our work so we can set out," Traveler said.

CHAPTER TEN

Gresham the Healer

It was the way of things outside any major city of consequence. Thieves and ne'er-do-wells loitered outside the main gate looking for victims. But here at Fae-Wick, it was different. They were known. Traveler was pestered by fae after fae claiming to be a sorcerer of some note.

"I am the most powerful sorcerer in these parts, from Magica itself. I am both conjurer and oracle. And I only charge a modest price," a man in a silver hooded cloak announced as they stepped off the white drawbridge path.

The dog barked ferociously and gave chase. The man transformed into a cackling imp and flew away.

Traveler moved through the market, the hood of his cloak covering his head. A giant humanoid beast of thick woolly fur walked alongside him. Both of them felt the presence. The caravan master stopped, turned, and locked his eyes on the lone woman watching him.

She was taller than average. Her clothing, including her cloak, was all black, and she wore necklaces of brown stones. Her hands were clasped together in front of her, as she stepped forward slowly.

"Good day, sir."

"Good day," Traveler answered.

"I understand that you are the leader of the human caravan en route to the Kingdom of Atlantea through Titan's Trail."

"You are well-informed."

"It is common knowledge in the lands."

"Yes, I have not yet decided if I like that fact."

"Are you still taking on new members?"

"I am."

"I wish to join your caravan."

"In what capacity?"

"Sentry, guard, or fighter."

"Why would you join a human caravan? Many elfin caravans pass through these lands, even flying ones."

"My race does not...mix with elves."

"My caravan has an elf."

"Your caravan is run by humans."

"We have half-elves."

"Half-elves are...humans."

Traveler smiled. "Where is your party?"

"I travel alone."

Traveler was now suspicious. "Alone? Fae do not travel alone."

"I am not dark fae. I am simply alone, seeking a good caravan to join in my own journey."

"Humans though? My kind is not regarded well in these lands."

"Humans are weak and pathetic. However, you and your party are not most humans. No one in these lands can remember when they last saw a human caravan such as yours. Led by humans, not elves, but including giants and sprites. I will never see such a caravan again in my life, so I seek to join."

"If you were part of a larger party, I would not hesitate, but a single fae…"

"I am not a predator of humans or from the Nether-lands if that is what you fear."

"What is the name of your people?"

The woman hesitated. "We are called…fae-blood."

Traveler thought for a moment. "I believe I have heard of your people. A very private people."

The woman nodded. "Yes, we are."

"However, from what I remember, your people never travel alone."

The woman sighed. "I cannot explain my circumstances further. What must I do to secure a place on your caravan? I suspect an offer of money would be rejected."

"We have money."

"What does your caravan need?"

"What any caravan can never have enough of—magic."

"I will find you a good magician and seek you out again."

"Sorcerer?"

"Yes, my people still use the word 'magician,' but others do not."

"In my lands, the word refers to one who engages in the illusion of magic."

"I am sorry. I will find you a sorcerer."

"One who knows your people well."

"Yes, and who knows me." The female fae said nothing more and walked away.

The woman looked like a human female. Her brown hair hung down her back in a single braid. Her skin was fair. She was indistinguishable from a human in every way, but Traveler knew she was not. Maybe they would see her again, maybe not.

◆◆◆

It took nearly two hours for Traveler to conclude his shopping in the markets. He was aware that many eyes watched him and his dog shape-shifter at all times. He saw the looks and heard the whispers. He had purposely dismissed the Fae-Wick royal escort, but they still watched his movements from a distance.

As they neared the main entrance of the city, a crowd waited for them. The humanoid fae were short compared to most humans, all about five feet in height. They were deerlike in appearance—large eyes, a black deer nose, and cloven feet. Most prominent was their large, deerlike ears that were in constant motion. They all wore the same light-brown tunics and darker brown trousers. Fifteen of the deerlike fae moved towards Traveler and his humanoid dog as a pack.

Traveler smiled. "Good day."

"Good day," one said in a high-pitched voice. "You are the human leader of the human-fae caravan journeying through Titan's Trail to the kingdom of Atlantea."

"Yes, I hear it is common knowledge in these lands."

"Yes, it is. My party wishes to offer its services as archers to your caravan and join in your journey to the legendary kingdom."

"What are your people called?"

"We are rusines."

"Related to satyrs and fauns."

"Yes, our races are related and allies."

"I know of your people."

The rusines smiled at him. "Then you will accept us in your caravan."

"No." Traveler shook his head. "Rusines are archers, but I need archers who do not simply hit a target. They must be able to kill a target or take it down. Rusines are not known for that; your race does not have the strength of, say, elfin or centaur archers, who are considered the best in Faë-Land.

"Also, rusines are a good people, but they are a nervous people. This is a very dangerous journey. Your people run from danger, which is not a criticism. It is your nature. There will be times on this caravan where we will need to stand our ground and fight, no matter the cost. That is not your nature, and I have seen in the past what becomes of rusines who try to fight that nature. Your bodies collapse in a nervous fit. No, I cannot do that to you, any of you. I am too compassionate a human to subject you to that kind of danger. I am sorry."

The rusines, with sad eyes and lowered heads, slowly walked past him. Traveler was also sad that he had to disappoint them, but the caravan had to be comprised of those who could fight any danger. Everyone on the caravan had to be a fighter, including the cook and cleaner.

◆◆◆

King Aereth led the new man back to the camp. Nirgund and his alphyns followed.

"Your animals are very well-behaved. Very unusual for pack animals of their ferocity," the man said. He was an Avalonian and a stout man with strong hands, a mustache, and balding brown hair. He looked more like a bare-knuckle bruiser than a healer, but the king was pleased with his presentation.

"True, but they have also always had a reputation for obedience with the right master," Nirgund said.

"And that undoubtedly is you."

"Mr. Gresham, as soon as our Mr. Traveler returns, I will have you meet with him."

"I look forward to it, sire."

"You should know, Mr. Gresham, that our caravan master was a healer himself and, by our most recent observations, remains a very gifted one."

"I do not envy you," Nirgund said to the new man.

They returned to the busy camp, made even busier by a myriad of merchants gathered around them from Fae-Wick. The royal escorts remained, and two giants stood watch from within the circle. The lizard minders remained on alert at the circle too.

Men were accepting bags, boxes, barrels, and whole wagons of supplies. Hobbs directed the work, while Quillen recorded what they received in a book.

"What is this?" Hobbs asked a fae merchant, a being with six arms.

"Only the best spices, sir."

"We have plenty of herbs, seeds, roots, fruits, and vegetables. We even have fruit and vegetable trees alive and well in a pocket. Why do we need spices?"

"Seasoning for the soul, sir."

"Mr. Tyfer," Hobbs turned to his guard to ask, "should we take this on?"

"Oh yes, Mr. Hobbs. How do you think we have made our food taste so heavenly?"

"That is all you have to say then. Spices it is."

Pangolin and the Cut-Throats, with the other four giants, took on the weapons supplies under the direction of Estus.

"Do you know what all this is?" I-wulf asked, unloading the seemingly endless number of crates from wagons.

"Enough armaments to fend off an army for months," Estus replied.

"I hope so, after all this work."

Pangolin neared the giants and asked, "What of these fairy children we have taken on?"

The giants laughed. "Children?" one asked.

"Mr. Pangolin, we are fortunate to have fairies amongst us. They were not telling tales. All of Faë-Land is a network of nature. Fairies speak to that nature, and nature—birds, animals of the land and sky, fish, insects, trees—speaks back to them."

"Trees and insects speak to them?"

"You have noticed yourself the ever-watchful eyes of the animals and birds. They do talk. Mr. Pangolin, when you and Mr. Traveler first came to Khury, we already knew of you. We knew of you from when you first crossed into Faë-Land."

"That was weeks ago."

"The animals and flora saw you. They told the fairies. The fairies told everyone else."

"Here is my question though. If there was a battle between giants and fairies, who would win?"

"Mr. Pangolin, they would!"

"I do not understand."

Pangolin saw the giant beckoning to someone. The berserker turned to see Traveler and his dog returning.

"Yes? Let me guess. Mr. Pangolin is still displeased with our two fairy members."

"Not displeased, Mr. Traveler. They are children. Whether they are older than any man in the camp does not change the fact that they are children. Can they cope with this journey? We have asked the same questions about Mr. Quillen and the other lads."

"Fair enough."

"He asked us, 'if there was a battle between giants and fairies, who would win?'" one of the giants repeated.

"The fairies would, Mr. Pangolin. You have not yet witnessed the full power of fairydom. You may be under the mistaken notion that Faë-Land Minor is, in fact, minor when compared to Faë-Land Major. Actually, that is a mistranslation. Minor means 'first' in this case; the first of the lands of fae to be set upon from the Lands of Man. 'Major' really means 'next.' Faë-Land Minor is actually a much larger region than all of Faë-Land Major. Mr. Pangolin, you have been to the deserts of Gondwana and Laurasia."

"And Oceania."

"Yes. In a battle between a large desert mammal, no matter how ferocious, and millions and millions of fire ants, who wins in the end? Who can be killed by millions and millions of poisonous bites and flees to escape? There is a sight that will strike fear in the soul of any giant or elf or sprite—a fairy-storm. Mr. Pangolin, even my dog flees when he sees that."

"Understand now, Mr. Pangolin?" one of the giants asked.

"I do, maybe."

"The fairies may be children and look adorable to us," Traveler said, "but they could, if they set their minds to it, kill either one of us or any of the giants. They are tiny, but remember, like sprites—and unlike giants—they can change their size at will."

"I did not know that," Pangolin said.

"Our Mr. Traveler is a treasure trove of knowledge of these lands." King Aereth stood listening with the new man, while Nirgund stood nearby. "Mr. Traveler, this is our new healer, Mr. Gresham."

"Good to meet you, sir." Gresham shook Traveler's hand. "I hear I have very big shoes to fill, but I think I will manage."

"Healer, you say. What specialty or specialties?"

"Specialties, sir?"

"Herbalist? Potions? Tree medicines? Earthen remedies? Curing fevers? Sewing a battle-torn body back together?"

"I reckon I have done all of the above, sir. I began as a boy. My father and all the men before him, as well as most of the women I descend from, were healers of some sort. Not magical, of the sciences."

"How did you get to Fae-Wick, Mr. Gresham?"

"I accepted a contract from a caravan from Goodmound's Castle a year ago. I thought it would give me the experience within the magical lands that I could then use to secure a position on the King's Caravan. Well, that caravan was not as organized and well financed as I was led to believe. It fell apart as soon as we crossed into Faë-Land. I saw no reason to go back, so I stayed here to work. I carved out a nice living and built a reputation here."

"And you still desire to go to Atlantea?"

"Most assuredly, sir. What man from our lands could do without a king's treasure? I would use my wealth to return to Avalonia, and use the knowledge I have gained here as a healer to create a teaching academy for healing sciences."

"Admirable," Traveler said. "Welcome then, Mr. Gresham. See Mr. Hobbs to get settled into camp. Are you alone?"

"Yes, I am, sir."

"What happened to the rest of your party?"

"Scattered to the winds, sir."

"They left you alone here in Fae-Wick."

"Yes, they did."

"How large was your original caravan?"

"Two thousand men, sir, mostly warriors and a sorcerer."

"What kingdom?"

"Not sure, sir."

"No royals?"

"I do not believe so, from what I can recall, sir. I was lucky to find them when I did."

"Well, go find Mr. Hobbs, then."

"Thank you, sir. Sire."

The new healer left them and hurried to Hobbs, who was still directing the incoming supplies into the camp.

"Well, Mr. Traveler?" King Aereth asked.

"He is lying, of course. But where are the lies and where are the truths? I do not know."

"Then, he should not be allowed in," Pangolin challenged.

"No, the king is right. We need a healer. Also, he is human, so I do not have the same concerns about him traveling alone as I would about a fae. If he can fulfill our role, then he stays. Mr. Pangolin, you know well that men lying about their circumstances about how they came on any caravan is nothing new or unusual."

"What if they threw him out of their caravan?" Pangolin asked.

"True, and we shall find that out before we depart. If not him, then another. We must fill all our roles so we can set out as soon as possible."

"They are called 'giant-slippers,'" Quillen told them.

When night fell, he and some of the fae humans passed out the new bedding to the men. The giant-slippers did look like their name, or a giant jester's shoe, that opened in the top for the man to slide into. Most of the men gladly accepted them, cushions and quilts covering all contained. Inside it was like sleeping in a giant bed of feathers.

For the Cut-Throats, half-elves, and fae humans, they preferred the new feather beds—mattresses of giant felt with quilt covers. King Aereth and Gwyness received new platform trussing beds. Nirgund asked for and got a new giant fur blanket to wrap himself for sleep.

The giants were already asleep, and Pangolin sat at his campfire.

"Mr. Pangolin." Traveler neared him with his dog. "You look unsettled."

Pangolin paused before speaking. "I am simply thinking about that...spell-talker."

"None of us are invincible."

"Yes, but I never imagined I would encounter an adversary who could stand before me and merely speak words to cause my death. Is that what he could have done?"

"Yes. You, then the giants, then the rest of us there, I imagine. Now you understand why archers are so important to us. Some sorcerers are too dangerous to be anywhere near us. However, this particular evil sorcerer was much more. No fae civilization allows them to even set foot on their lands."

"Spell-talkers, you said. What manner of sorcerer are they? When the giants crushed him, there was no blood but a foul black ooze."

"They are demons."

"Demons?" Pangolin stood to his feet. "There are demons walking about in these lands?"

"There should be no such creatures in these lands. Follow me to a meeting."

Traveler led the berserker to a new large tent in the camp. When they entered, it too was larger inside than appeared on the outside—another pocket-realm. Inside was King Aereth, Nirgund, I-wulf, Estus, Gwyness, and Hobbs, who closed the entrance securely.

"This is a special night meeting. I have already informed Lady Aylen."

"How is she, Mr. Traveler?" Gwyness asked.

"Much better. She is progressing nicely. So, I did mention a new fact to Mr. Pangolin. I'll tell you as well, but do not share this with the camp. I do not want to alarm them. The creature that attacked Mr. Pangolin was no ordinary wizard or evil sorcerer or warlock, whichever term you prefer. It was a demon. They come from a realm outside of Faë-Land. At any sighting of them, hunters are called to find and destroy them. They are so dangerous that races have destroyed all life within a region to exterminate them from this realm."

"Demons walk these lands, Mr. Traveler?"

"Demons have walked our lands, too, Maiden Gwyness. There are whole orders in all the races that watch for them, fight them, and hunt them, if need be. In the magical lands, all life watches for certain creatures of evil that should not be there—and here."

"Besides demons, what other creatures, Mr. Traveler?"

"Basilisks, gorgons, lycanthropes, undead creatures. All these creatures are extremely rare. Gwyness, do not worry yourself. Again, all life of Faë-Land watches for them and actually protects our own lands from these creatures."

"It is hard not to worry, Mr. Traveler. A demon that can kill you with a word, a creature that can turn you to stone with a look, creatures that can take your soul and turn you into an evil creature yourself," Gwyness challenged.

"Perhaps, Mr. Traveler, Maiden Gwyness should have been spared this meeting," the king said.

"No, sire. I disagree. Maiden Gwyness has her own stories to tell us one night."

"What do you mean, Mr. Traveler?" she asked.

"We can save the conversation for a later time—when Lady Aylen has recovered. Returning to the spell-talker, he not only managed to move through the lands of the fairies but to enter a fairy city unseen. I do not believe that to be a random occurrence any more than its attack on us. It was deliberate."

The speculation concerned them all.

"Who?" Pangolin asked.

"Allies of the Four Kings, perhaps. Others we have offended somehow. Maybe they do not like humans. It is hard to know for sure, but to do this is no small matter. Very powerful forces would have to be involved. It is all the more reason for us to secure all our men and supplies and be on our way. As guide, I know of more than a few ways to obscure our movement along the Trail from those wishing to do us harm."

"Do we not care to know why or who for sure, sir?" Nirgund asked.

"There is no time to do so. If the fairies do find out who is behind this act, they will let us know. They will inform everyone.

"Also, some of you asked me what my two questions were to Browncrown of the tree-folk who visited us with the nisse. I asked him about making an introduction to a race that is allied with his, called the leshy. I will attempt to hire them for our caravan, as I believe we need more security of a magical nature than we had anticipated. But that was not my chief question. I asked them to make contact, on our behalf, with elfin caravans in Faë-Land Major. It is the far more dangerous leg of our journey, and if we can have interested parties awaiting our arrival, then the time saved will be invaluable."

"We need them?" Pangolin asked.

"For every leg of our journey, we want the people of its lands to help us move forward. We don't need them, but I doubt we would make it without them. They would have far more sorcerers than we would have. This is also why I have tasked King Aereth to learn all their royal customs and noble protocols."

"Why would they need us, then, sir?" I-wulf asked.

"We are humans. Humans did not try to invade the kingdom of Atlantea ages ago. If you have not realized it, fae live a long time, and they have even longer memories."

"So what you said is true. The Atlanteans like humans."

"Yes. They can get in with us. Getting in without us humans, is doubtful."

"That disgusting creature we saw—that half-human, half-horse creature—was it in league with this spell-talker or the people behind it?" Gwyness asked.

"I do not know, but they would not have required a sole scout. Finding us would be easy. Getting a spell-talker, getting it into a guarded fairy city, is a far, far different matter. And it was waiting for us."

"Did you see it beforehand?" the king asked. "You and your dog did excuse yourselves before the attack."

"My dog felt a strange energy. We left to find out where it was from. The energy was of pure dark magic."

"It can sense that?" Gwyness asked.

"Only sometimes. My dog is not magic. His powers are not magical but are native to his species."

"Then we must also acquire our own sorcerer," King Aereth added.

"We must all be on guard at all times, but our caravan will move ahead without delay the moment we secure all our fae members, including at least one sorcerer."

"Mr. Traveler, there were many in Fae-Wick," the king said.

"Sire, none of those were real sorcerers. Pranksters are common. You would not know what to look for, but I do."

"Maybe we need more than one sorcerer," Gwyness said fearfully.

"We need at least one, then we can set out. The fairies have magic, the väki, and we have magical weapons. Once our caravan continues through the Trail, we should add other parties that will each have a sorcerer. That will suffice."

"How many others do we need, Mr. Traveler?" the king asked.

"We are almost complete there, sire. It will not be long now."

"Are we waiting for Lady Aylen to fully recover, Mr. Traveler?" Gwyness asked.

"I think that would be best, but again, she is progressing nicely, so there should be no added delay. The physical part is almost behind her."

"So the ultimate message is for us to be on guard," Pangolin said.

"Yes. The ultimate message for the entire journey."

"Then, we may also need a better night watch," Pangolin said, "especially now that Mr. Quillen has given out these fluffy giant-slippers to the men. Nothing will rouse them in the night."

"Yes, I have already hired the fae for that role, and hopefully we will have the leshy. That is all for the time being. We do not need any other special meetings on this. Our regular night meetings of the leadership will continue, and include Mr. Quillen. Like Mr. Hobbs, he is an important representative for the men in the meetings."

"Do we have a new healer too?" Gwyness asked, looking around.

"We do, indeed, Maiden Gwyness," King Aereth said. "His name is Mr. Gresham."

"We hope we have a new healer," Traveler interjected.

Traveler sat at his table in his tent, a fairy candle on the corner. He was not surprised when Hobbs appeared at the entrance, and already knew the reason.

"Sir," Hobbs called out.

"Yes, Hobbs. Is someone there to see me named Gwyness?"

Hobbs half-chuckled.

"Send her in."

"Yes, sir."

Gwyness entered the tent, and Traveler gave her his full attention from his chair.

"When is Lady Aylen returning to the camp, Mr. Traveler?" she asked directly.

"When she is ready and not before."

"She must be with us. If she is past most of the danger of her change, why can't she return? Why does she stay away? I can help her recover. Why is she treating us in this manner?"

"Gwyness, this is not anything against you. It is not personal. She will recover fully, learn her new abilities, and regain her confidence. She will return soon."

Gwyness's eyes teared up. "It is as if she no longer has confidence in me."

"Gwyness, that is nonsense. Nothing could be further from the truth." Traveler stood from his chair and moved closer. "She can hear you," he said in almost a whisper.

"Pardon?"

"She can hear you."

"She can hear me? Lady Aylen? Now?"

"She is an elf, Gwyness. She can hear. She knows you want her to return, and she will."

The revelation stunned Gwyness. She did not know what to do but composed herself.

"Thank you, Mr. Traveler, for confiding in me."

Traveler smiled. "Have a good night, Maiden Gwyness."

♦♦♦

As he typically did, Hobbs woke before dawn, got himself ready, and began his rounds. This morning, the men did not automatically awake at his passing; he had to yank them out of their new fae bedding.

"I hope this does not become the routine, or I will have Mr. Quillen take your new bedding away and return the old."

The steward reached Mr. Quillen, who was so wrapped up in his giant-slipper and blankets, that all that was visible was part of his forehead.

"Mr. Quillen, get up this instant! You will accompany me in waking the men."

There was a loud sigh, and the lad slowly sat up, appearing from under his covering.

Traveler had his own morning routine these days. He sat at a table in his tent, with something warm to drink and his maps spread out in front of him. The dog stood watch and rose onto its four legs.

"Mr. Traveler, sir." Hobbs appeared at the entrance. "Something is happening outside Fae-Wick."

The men stood gawking at what they could see. Traveler had his sword strapped to his back, and he peered through a telescope.

"Mr. Hobbs, have Mr. Gresham join me." Traveler ran out of the circle, the dog following.

Pangolin motioned to two of the giants, and they ran after their caravan master. "Mr. Elman, come too. You can be an additional sentry."

The half-elf bolted from the camp after them.

Soldiers of an elfin party filled the fields around Fae-Wick.

"It was a goblin army of thousands," they heard one elfin warrior yell in conversation to a fairy royal guard.

Traveler surveyed the wounded and dead. There were not enough healers to go around. He turned and saw Gresham moving to him. Traveler motioned to him to move quicker.

"Yes, sir," Gresham said, almost out of breath.

"Move through these men and see what service you can provide."

"Service, sir? These are elves, not humans."

"They are men returning from battle, some wounded, some near death. You are a healer. Heal, Mr. Gresham."

Gresham walked among the elves with great discomfort. He stopped at one elf, all alone, who was bleeding badly. Gresham froze in place. Traveler pushed him away and knelt at the elf's side. The caravan master pulled out his entire healer's bag from his cloak—it came from a magical pouch—and examined the wound.

"I will attend to your wound," Traveler said.

The elf opened his eyes and nodded slowly.

◆◆◆

Pangolin and the giants stood guard over Traveler as he worked, moving quickly through the wounded elves sprawled everywhere. At one point, Traveler properly bandaged an elfin warrior while an elfin healer did the same for another nearby.

Elman and the dog watched over them too. Fairies flew down from Fae-Wick and also assisted with healing duties and transporting elves to the city, picking them up and flying away.

Gresham followed and, from a distance, watched Traveler work but stayed close enough that he could see clearly. Pangolin shot their new healer a disgusted look many times. King Aereth appeared with his guard and the fae hounds, a disappointed expression on his face.

When done, Traveler stood and put his healer's bag back into the magical pouch in his cloak. A group of elfin knights approached them.

"You there, human," one of them said. Traveler waited for them.

They stood before him, unsure how to react or what to say.

"In human lands, the custom is to say 'thank you,'" Traveler said.

"Thank you."

"You are welcome, but I did not do it for you. I did it for them."

"A healer of elves and humans."

"Many races."

"You are quite fortunate, human. There is a rumor that your caravan is allied with the goblins."

"Who would spread such an obvious lie?"

"Do you not have men in goblin armor, bearing goblin weapons?"

"Our caravan is on a long journey through Titan's Trail, and we may encounter goblins or hobgoblins. If all we must do to avoid a battle with either is display our goblin armor-clad warriors, then we will."

"What of the rumor that you visited Damdread to conspire with the goblins?" the other elf asked.

"The fact you know of my visit to Damdread tells me that other parties are very keen on discrediting our caravan, probably the same parties involved in the spell-talker sent to kill us."

"Spell-talker? Here?" the elves asked, shocked.

"Our visit to Damdread was to see a half-goblin. A half-goblin whom I dealt with years ago. He is a trader, and that is all I did. See our pack of fae hounds? That was what our visit was about. To purchase a pack of animals abused by goblins and give them a new home and master, free of cruelty and the company of goblins. I do not need to justify myself to you. I do not, and have never, conspired with goblins. I recognize them as a vile race, however, they have never hunted me. I cannot say the same of elves."

"Why would elves hunt you?" they asked.

"Perhaps they did not want me to reveal to other elfin races that they were plundering and enslaving the shape-shifting animals of other worlds."

The elves suddenly lost their interest in talking.

"You have a safe journey through Titan's Trail, human. Thank you for your care of our warriors."

The group of elves walked back the way they came.

"Well, Mr. Traveler, that was quite the conversation," King Aereth said.

"Gresham!" Traveler yelled. "Go back to Fae-Wick!"

Traveler walked back to camp, not even looking at the man, with the dog following.

Traveler was back at his tent, busy with his maps, when he heard Hobbs's voice.

"Yes, Hobbs."

Hobbs appeared. "I do not mean to disturb you, sir."

King Aereth stepped in, too. "Mr. Traveler, a word."

"Sire, what can I do for you?"

"The man, Gresham."

"Is not a healer we can use, sire."

"Mr. Traveler, the man did not perform. That is clear, but he is a healer. I questioned him myself, and I have hired quite a few in my time. He froze under the color of battle. This is inexcusable but not unforgivable. It has happened to warriors. Why would we not think of it happening to healers?"

"Why are you taking up this man's cause, sire?"

"He confided in me. His caravan did cast him out for losing his nerve. He has been a healer in battle for many years. One day, he simply lost his nerve. He assured me that he will regain his confidence."

"Sire, under the stress of this journey, and especially knowing about the new threats we have to face, why would he regain his confidence? Do we not need a man who can perform his duties?"

"We do, Mr. Traveler." King Aereth motioned, and Gresham appeared in the tent.

"Sir, I apologize for my behavior. I explained the full facts to the king here. All I ask is to be given another chance. I am a healer, a good healer. I simply lost my way, but I know I can regain my footing. This is a long journey, and all men in the caravan must live up to their responsibilities. I know that already. The next time I do not, cast me off at the nearest village."

"Why should you get such a second chance, Mr. Gresham? What if those men were our men?"

"I took the liberty of writing out in detail all the procedures you performed on the elves." Gresham revealed a notebook from behind his back. "I have commented on each, where I agreed, and where I differed with my alternative procedures, along with my reasoning."

King Aereth took the notebook and handed it to Traveler.

"I will review it."

"Thank you, sir."

"Mr. Hobbs, have him wait in the camp."

"Yes, sir." The steward led Gresham from the tent.

"Please, Mr. Traveler, we need a healer who is not you. If you are satisfied with his notes, under your supervision, though he may never be as gifted as you, he could, with determination, come close. You must focus all your energies on your duties as caravan master. Others must take up the healing duties."

"I will review the notes immediately, sire."

"I read them myself. I cannot say I have any true idea of what he is saying, but you will know."

"If he cannot do the job—"

"No need to worry, Mr. Traveler. He would be cast off without hesitation."

CHAPTER ELEVEN

Tree Shepherds

King Aereth sat with Traveler in his tent as Hobbs recited the list of supplies.

"The amount of supplies seems excessive, Mr. Traveler," the king said.

"Actually, sire, we may still not have enough," Hobbs answered. "The giants and lizards will consume most of our total food supply."

"Will there not be opportunities to replenish our supplies along the way, Mr. Traveler?"

"There will be, sire, but I want us to have the flexibility to completely bypass a city or town if necessary. I would like us to have at least enough supplies for our caravan to make it halfway through Faë-Land Major."

One of the female half-elves appeared at the entrance. "Mr. Traveler, you have an animal visitor," she said.

"Animal visitor?" the king asked with a smile.

The three men exited the tent and walked to where the half-elf pointed. Beyond the circle in the fields was a green dog.

"What is that, Mr. Traveler?" It was Quillen's voice. He ran to them with his magic book and writing instrument.

"It is called a cù-sìth," Traveler answered.

"Aye, a fairy dog." Nirgund watched it too, as did his alphyns with curiosity.

"Yes."

The fairy dog was as large as a small horse and had a shaggy coat of dark green. The rest of its body was light green in color, except for its pointy dark-green ears and long curled tail.

"Is it a bad omen for us, Mr. Traveler?" Nirgund asked.

"Oh, Mr. Nirgund you are from the Gaeli lands of Avalonia."

"I am."

"No, the opposite." Traveler turned to the king. "Sire, please accompany me on a walk."

"Walk, Mr. Traveler? Where to?"

"We are being summoned by the leshies. Mr. Nirgund, you will remain here"

They followed the green fairy dog through the fields. Traveler led, while his dog walked beside King Aereth a few paces behind.

"Are leshies considered sprites or fairies, Mr. Traveler?"

"Fairies, sire. Though some would say they are among the original earth elementals."

"Is this the meeting you were waiting for?"

"Yes, sire. Browncrown, the tree-folk king, said he would make the introduction. It is up to us to convince the leshy leaders. Despite their rustic appearance, they are every bit a monarchical society as are the elves. If they speak with another royal, even human, it is to our advantage."

"How are we faring, Mr. Traveler? We have supplies, but I sense we do not have what we need in manpower, yet."

"We are close, sire. Fae-Wick's merchant masters have also helped with the inquiries. By nightfall, we will have quite a few new fae members."

"Archers?"

"Both archers and sorcerers are the most sought after by every party, and they know it. I have increased our price. We are fortunate because every one is interested in our caravan. If this meeting is successful, those standing on the sidelines will join."

"I would also be remiss if I did not ask."

"Sire, Lady Aylen is moving about now."

King Aereth stopped and stared. He smiled. "Will she return soon?"

"I am working on it, but you know that she is a very proud woman. She will not return until she is ready."

"This is excellent news, Mr. Traveler. Does Maiden Gwyness know?"

"I have kept her informed, too, sire. I told her to keep it to herself for the time being."

The cù-sìth moved at a carefree pace. Fae-Wick and its beautiful waterfalls were still visible in the distance, but then the fairy dog turned direction and vanished.

"Let us step through, sire."

They found themselves in a pocket-realm thick with vegetation, giant leaves and trees towering into the clouds. The cù-sìth stood at the side of five very tall male fae in green robes. However, there were many more of the fairy dogs, with birds and squirrels resting on each of them.

"Approach," the center leshy directed.

They all had white skin. Their hair and full beards were living grass and vines. With bright green eyes, they watched Traveler and the king. As they neared, King Aereth noticed they all had hooves for feet.

"You are the one called Traveler?"

"I am. And this is King Aereth of Helm Earldom in our lands."

"A king?" The leshies bowed their heads slightly, and King Aereth returned the gesture.

"King Browncrown brought you to our attention. What is your request?"

"We lead a caravan to the kingdom of Atlantea."

"All know who you are and your destination."

"Directly, I request a party of Tree Shepherds to escort us to Atlantea."

"You know of Tree Shepherds?"

"I do."

"You know too much for a human. You lived in our lands, we are told."

"I did."

"From your shape-shifter, you lived elsewhere too. Why should we grant your request? We are not the elves or giants. Like humans, they wish to spread their presence far beyond their lands. We are content with our own lands. We have no desire to be anywhere else. And unlike all you younger races, we have no desire for treasure. Nature is the only treasure we covet."

"It would be to establish a presence in Atlantea on behalf of your kingdom. If, as you say, elves, giants, sprites, and fairies, do so, why not the leshy?"

"Fairydom has no presence in Atlantea."

"But they do."

"Who told you this?"

"Fairies. Two of them have joined our caravan."

The leshies spoke amongst themselves in a strange language of bird song, whistles, and gusts of wind.

"Giants and sprites. Elves and you humans. We will confer with the fairies. If they do have a presence in Atlantea, we will send Tree Shepherds to your caravan before sundown."

"Thank you," Traveler said. "We are glad that Browncrown made the introduction."

"It was not because of Browncrown that we agreed to meet you. We asked the trees to tell us about your group since you have been in our lands. Humans are not highly regarded in our lands. You have killed no sacred animals, cut down no sacred trees. You treat your own animal well and with affection; all the animals are treated so within your group. We already knew of you when Browncrown spoke to us. He and his people, and the nisse, spoke highly of your stories. If we do send Tree Shepherds to your group, we expect to hear many good stories in your camp. Leshies can be quite mischievous, even Tree Shepherds, without good stories."

"And music."

"Good. You do know fairy and leshy ways. You both can return to your group. It was nice to meet you, royal Traveler and royal Aereth."

The men nodded. Traveler led them back out the portal of the pocket-realm.

"Is there something more I should know?" King Aereth asked as they walked back to camp. "Mr. Hobbs always suspected you were a noble. But these fae called you a royal."

Traveler held back a smile. "I am nothing more than a common-born in our lands."

King Aereth laughed. "I am onto you, sir. But what status did you attain in these magical lands."

"Sire, you are becoming far too clever. I must limit our exposure to each other."

The king laughed.

It was as the leshies had said. The caravan would have its answer before the sun set, and that answer was for all to see. The half-elves spotted the first of four moving trees approaching the camp. The roots of each tree crawled along the ground faster than a trotting horse. In each tree, sitting on a large branch, was a white-skinned, green-bearded, hooded, and robed leshy.

A smiling Traveler walked out from the circle to greet them. The branches of the trees set the fae onto the field, and they walked to him.

"Master Traveler," greeted the tallest one. They were all over six feet, and each carried in his right hand an even taller, thicker wooden staff, curved at the top. "I am Greenwig. This is Mossberry, Thornbeard, and Little Root, our youngest."

"I have seen a Tree Shepherd with a herd of dozens of trees, and I have heard they can have a herd of hundreds, but more than one Tree Shepherd at a time?"

"It is not uncommon for there to be hundreds of us congregated at one time in our lands. I will be in the center of your camp. Mossberry and Thornbeard will be at either end from me. Little Root will maintain our hidden realm with our soul tree."

"This is our steward, Mr. Hobbs. Simply instruct him as to the space you need or any other needs."

"Thank you, Master Traveler."

CHAPTER TWELVE

Hoofed Fae Archers

Near the royals' and Traveler's tents was one tree. Immediately, Nirgund's alphyns took to it and were quite content with sitting or lying on its branches to watch, from above, the men within or beyond the camp. Since the fae hounds would not come down, Nirgund relented and joined them. Soon, he enjoyed the vantage point himself. Elman also climbed into the tree and made his way to the top, shielded by trees and leaves. At his new height, he could see much farther.

At the other end of camp, the chamroshes also loved their crawling tree. The griffin-like animals flew into the tree to watch the surroundings but also played and sharpened their claws on the bark. The giants quickly dubbed it the "beast tree." With its war-flock of hundreds of animals, it was quite a curious, and fearsome, sight to behold. The Cut-Throats kept watch on them but from a comfortable distance, not under the tree.

In the center of the camp was the largest and widest crawling tree. It towered far above both trees and its branches and foliage hung over the camp like a shield. Pangolin had already surveyed the view and could look out across the fields to Fae-Wick and see its people and visitors watching. He was glad they had more fae protection for the camp, but displeased at the greater scrutiny from outsiders.

Traveler approached their master-at-arms with Hobbs. "Mr. Pangolin," he said.

"Please tell me, Mr. Traveler, that we'll set out soon. I feel our feet will become roots and will never leave this patch of ground. In fact, we share a camp where the trees do pull their roots from the earth to move."

"I have gotten word of two new parties seeking to join us, and I have already hired three other parties. Tonight, we will also receive our fae steeds for the royals and Maiden Gwyness. So, gentlemen, we leave tomorrow at dawn."

"Yes!" Pangolin said with glee.

"What will be our first destination, sir?" Hobbs asked.

"The fae city of Arion's Spear. I need both of you to impress upon your men that Arion's Spear is not Fae-Wick. The attack of the spell-talker aside, the people of Fae-Wick are fairies and sprites, people of trade. Arion's Spear is of elves, giants, satyrs, centaurs, and other humanoid fae who are by no means friendly. It is a city of warriors, knights, sorcerers, and killers. It is the first fae city on the path of Titan's Trail. What I am trying to say is that it is a very dangerous city. There will be many threatened by the sight of a human-fae caravan."

"Threatened how? What would they do?" Pangolin asked.

"There will be many, many other caravans there. Every one of their caravan masters is eager to have only the best join them, and is not eager to compete for those people. The advantage we have, that many will not, is we do not need a guide. We know how to get to Atlantea. There is little they can do to us, but we must remain on guard."

"There are other destinations, sir?"

"Yes, to the lands of the dwarves, the Nether-Lands, many other destinations, even those outside Faë-Land. Prepare your men."

"What of Lady Aylen, sir?" Hobbs asked.

"I will see if I can coax her to join us."

Hobbs and Pangolin smiled.

Traveler made his way to Gresham's healing tent. The man sat on the ground, studying a medical book, one of many in his possession. The caravan master stood at the entrance, and Gresham jumped up at seeing him.

"I am here to return your notes, Mr. Gresham." Traveler handed the notes back to him.

"Your opinion, Mr. Traveler?"

"Mr. Gresham, the issue is not the quality of your medical knowledge as proven by your notes. Can you perform under the chaos of battle, the stress of a long day, the pressure of men standing inches from you, begging you to save their comrade?"

"Yes,sir. That is always the only question. I will do more than my best. All I can do is apologize again for what occurred before. You and the king have given me another chance, and I will not let you down."

"Not us, Mr. Gresham. The men."

"Of course, sir."

"I will leave you to your work." Traveler left without another word.

Traveler saw them on his own as he walked back to his tent. The dog was watching them too. A herd of hoofed fae walked to the camp. Nirgund had jumped down from the first tree to find him, but immediately saw Traveler approaching.

The caravan master walked with his dog, through the lizard minders and their lizards at the perimeter, . This time a couple of half-elves stood nearby as guards.

Three types of hoofed fae were before them. The largest were deerlike—nose, ears, and eyes. Huge antlers sprouted from their skulls. They were dressed as warriors with shiny greenish metal breastplate armor, chainmail sleeves, and trousers made of a material thicker and much tougher than leather. The bows they bore were what commanded Traveler's attention. Long bows as tall as these antlered deerlike fae—over six feet, smooth, immaculately polished, and of a white wood.

"Beautiful craftsmanship," Traveler said to the lead antlered fae.

He smiled.

"May we help you?" Traveler asked.

"You are in alliance with the leshy."

"We are. They have joined our caravan."

"We are the elaphine. I am Strag."

"I have heard of your people, but have never seen you directly."

"Our cousins here are the cervid." He motioned to the second group of hooved fae who were not as large—of normal human height—and had no antlers, but small horns, one above each brow. They were dressed in dark brown with turtle-shell-like breastplate armor and carried shorter, dark wooden bows.

"You already know our other cousins, the rusines."

It was the same small hooved fae that Traveler had met in Fae-Wick and had declined their offer to join.

"We had already joined another caravan, but when we heard this morning that leshy had joined you, we spoke. It was decided that we would change our decision and ask to join your caravan. We hear you still do not have archers."

"No, we do not. Strangely, they have all disappeared from the city."

The fae were smiling or laughing. "Not strange, human. People know you want them, so they are keeping them from you."

"Oh, that is a shame. We must move onto the next fae city and hire ours there."

"No," the elaphine leader said, near panic. "We can be your archers."

"Are you real archers? As good as elves or centaurs?"

The elaphine archers snickered as a group. "Elves and centaurs may be among the best known fae archers, but they are hardly the only ones in the lands of fae who can make that claim and prove it. We can do anything they can."

"You go to Atlantea?"

"We do."

Traveler scanned the group to get a count.

"If you accept us, you accept all of us."

"You will mind the rusines?"

"Yes, of course."

"What is the role of the cervids?"

"We protect our camp," one of the cervids replied.

"We do the primary fighting," the elaphine leader said. "And the rusines manage the camp. We set out without thinking about the servants we needed. Our rusine cousins will do that. The three of us are now one party."

"If you join, you must assign archers for the vanguard."

The pack looked at Pangolin, who stood with his arms folded, and two of the giants nearby.

"The vanguard is led by Mr. Pangolin, four giants, and a half-elf."

"We will assign a dozen archers to the vanguard."

Traveler nodded. "The rest of your archers will protect the camp. So, I will give you the center tree for your camp."

Immediately, the faces of the hoofed fae lit up, even the stern elaphine archer-warriors. The rusines started giggling.

"Is that acceptable?"

"It is, human." The elaphine reached out his hand. "We accept."

"Good. Mr. Hobbs—no, actually, Mr. Pangolin, these fae will fall under your purview as warriors. Mr. Pangolin will get your party settled into the camp."

The elaphine leader nodded. The entire herd of fae turned their attention to the berserker.

Pangolin gestured to them, and they followed him to the massive center tree.

"We have archers, Mr. Traveler," King Aereth exclaimed.

"Was that true, Mr. Traveler?" Nirgund asked. "That the city was hiding archers from us?"

Traveler nodded.

"It's like Ironwood all over again, sir."

"It's not treachery this time, Mr. Nirgund. It's jealousy. Human-fae caravans are extremely rare."

"Your caravan was a human-fae party when you were last in Faë-Land, Mr. Traveler."

"It was, sire. Humans and elves, but led by elves. Ours includes giants and many other fae. Soon we'll have pechs and brownies."

"Brownies?" Gwyness had joined them.

"What are pechs, sir?" Quillen asked, sneaking away from his duties to see the hoofed fae.

CHAPTER THIRTEEN
More Sprites

Hobbs began his morning rounds as normal, just after dawn. Each morning the lizards were a bit bigger. He stood with his hands on his hips. The lizard minders were all still asleep in their new giant-slippers. The lizards seemed to have doubled in size again. Each night, a lizard minder dug a shallow pit in the ground, created a fire, and filled the pit with rocks. It was prepared in such a way that the fire burned throughout the night, and the rocks emitted steady heat. These heat pits were what the lizards craved, though the air was not cold, even at night. The lizards stayed in the pits or nearby.

Hobbs estimated that each lizard, in its individual colors of blues, yellows, greens, and oranges, was now nearing fifteen feet long, not including its long tail, and four to five feet tall. Their eyes blinked and tongues flickered every so often. He did not envy Estus's task of refitting their growing necks with leash collars and the prospect of armoring each reptile. No wonder their weaponsmaster, normally a jovial and gregarious man, was rarely seen these days.

◆◆◆

Seven hundred fifty hoofed fae joined Titan's Caravan, five hundred of which were the archer-warrior elaphine fae.

"Is five hundred archers enough?" the Cut-Throat leader, I-wulf, asked.

"Five hundred fae archers are equivalent to two thousand human archers," Traveler answered. "Since we never had more than a thousand archers, we have double of what we had."

At the entrance, the dog rose to his feet. One of the male half-elves appeared. "Mr. Traveler, they are here."

Two columns of fae marched to them, singing and whistling. One column they were very familiar with as humans. Brownies: halfling, old men with short, curly dark hair and wearing brown pointed conical caps and clothes.

In the other column was a different kind of halfling. They wore dark caps, had wild, bushy eyebrows—the far ends pointing up—big noses, and even bigger forearms bulging from their tunics. Brownies wore brown; these other halflings wore off-white tunics and dark trousers and boots.

"Gentlemen, the brownies will be our night watch and workers; they sleep during the day. The pech will be both day bearers and, King Aereth, if the time arises, help with the heavy weapons. They have the strength of a giant. I will turn in early so that I can greet the other fae members of our night watch who will arrive after nightfall. We will leave at dawn as planned."

"Who will oversee the brownies, sir?" Hobbs asked.

"I will put them under your charge, and the pechs as well, when they are in the role of bearer or laborer. Sire, the pechs will be under your charge in battle. They will be transporting the heavy weapons from now on. The weapons are of little use to us tucked away in a pocket with Mr. Estus."

"Dawn," Pangolin said with a smile.

"Dawn," King Aereth repeated.

"Dawn," Traveler said. "When both of you awake, there will be even more members of our caravan."

CHAPTER FOURTEEN

Darklings

All the men had heard the stories of brownies, the little men who lived in human houses and aided with chores. Apparently, they could be hired to do the same for caravans. Once the sun fell for the day, they would appear from their pocket, singing and chatting with one another. By the time they appeared, the men would have all the night campfires going. However, the brownies were especially accomplished fire-lighters and would add many long torches throughout the camp. They, too, would make their own rounds through the camp in small groups. Traveler told the men that he didn't know exactly how many had joined the camp, likely around five hundred, the same number of pechs. The pechs were busy in the day, with Mr. Estus. Brownies ran the functions at night, ensuring the men, and especially the giants, kept a clean and orderly camp while all others slept.

Earlier, Traveler had introduced them to the pechs. The cousin races spent hours individually greeting every other member. It was very amusing for the men to watch. Then, Traveler took them into a pocket to meet the väki, which took all but five minutes. The väki never changed their frowns, and the always-smiling brownies did nothing but frown themselves.

However, their first night within Titan's Caravan the brownies were furious, but not because of the väki.

"What are they doing here?"

Traveler knew better than to interrupt the little men. They sneered, glared, and shouted insults. Gwyness had awoken and exited the women's tent to see what the commotion was about. The female half-elves followed; all the woman had wrapped themselves in robes. They saw Mr. Traveler with the brownies on one side and a group of other things on the other. It appeared to be a group of rabbit-like humanoids with black fur, and of shorter and lesser stature than the brownies. Their eyes flickered in the light of the moon.

"They are evil creatures," a brownie yelled.

"They are not, and you know it. There are good and bad, just like other fae."

"Human, do you not know the true nature of phookas? They feast on human blood and human flesh in the night," another brownie said.

"Do they feast on human blood or human flesh? Which is it, because it can't be both."

"Well, they feast on the flesh but do not mind the blood."

"I cannot believe that respectable brownies are reciting human superstition tales to me. I am human. I have heard the tales."

The phookas cackled.

"They are related to the trolls."

"They are not."

"They are nothing but demons of the fae."

The phookas cackled again in unison.

"These phookas may be mischievous tricksters—"

"Violent shape-shifters!" a brownie challenged.

"The leshy are shape-shifters. The väki are. Fairies are. My dog is. The phooka stay."

Traveler turned and looked at the black fae with a cross expression. "You are not helping your position by laughing at them."

"Why are they in the form of rabbits?" another brownie asked, annoyed. "Take the form of a demon goat or vampire cat, as you should."

Traveler had to hold both groups away from each other. "You both are worse than humans or elves."

Both groups were offended and backed away, giving him dirty looks.

"You are both the night protectors of this camp. The brownies are inside to protect the men in camp. Phookas patrol the outer perimeter of the circle. It is a tremendous responsibility. We have already been attacked by a spell-talker."

"Spell-talker?" a phooka asked.

"Spell-talker?" a brownie repeated.

"Can you keep the night camp safe? The day camp will keep you safe with their lives. Will you keep them safe at night with your lives? If this is a task too overwhelming, you must leave the camp now, and I will find others."

The brownies looked at each other. They grudgingly nodded. "We can do the task," one of the brownies said. "But they must stay away from us."

"Good. The väki are the guardians of the weapons and supplies. The brownies, the guardians of the men. The phookas, the guardians of the circle at night."

"Brownies are only good for sweeping and washing up." The phooka riled up the brownies again.

"He is making mischief," Traveler said to the brownies. "They are doing to you what they always like doing." He looked back at the phookas and pointed at them. "I am not like other humans or these brownies. You will not distract me! What is your answer? Guard or go?"

One of the phookas grew in height and, with a smile, said, "Stay."

"Meaning what? What will be your function?"

"But we like the other name better."

"The name I gave you when I was younger."

"Yes!"

"What will be the function of the darklings of Titan's Caravan, then?"

"We will guard the Caravan of Traveler from all forces of evil." He laughed, and the other phookas joined in.

"You are to play no pranks against any human, fae, or animal of this caravan. No pranks, no damaging, no mischief. There will be plenty to amuse yourselves with along the Trail, but never anything in this circle."

The phookas cackled.

"Yes, Master Traveler. We will obey."

"You will. I hold you to it, just like the fairies who have joined the caravan. I told them the same. Follow the rules, or we will cast you off."

"We will obey."

"Good. Now shake hands on it, like humans do."

The brownies and phookas made loud sounds of disgust. They walked away from each other, and from Traveler.

Gwyness stared up at the ceiling of the tent. The female half-elves were fast asleep already, but she could not quiet her restlessness. Her eyes slowly looked to the nearest corner. Before they had taken on the half-elves, the women's tent would be well lit, even at night. Now, all they would leave lit was a single hanging candle from the center of the tent. It created plenty of corners for shadows. Gwyness was convinced that something else was stirring in their tent. Had one of the new phooka shape-shifters crawled into the tent to frighten her with an evil prank—or worse?

Her eyes adjusted to where she had focused them. A figure stood in the shadows.

"Gwyness." She heard the whisper and abruptly sat up in her trussing bed.

"Lady Aylen?" she asked, keeping her voice low.

A hooded cloak fully covered the figure, but Gwyness knew it was the princess.

"I am sorry, Gwyness, that I did not come sooner."

"It is fine, m'lady. You are here. How are you?"

"I am better, better than yesterday, and tomorrow, I will be better than today. I cannot express in words what I have been experiencing. I know now how the caterpillar feels in its transformation."

"But you are now the butterfly." Gwyness was crying but smiling.

"Yes, I am. All these years of growing up, Gwyness, I thought I was an elf. Mr. Traveler was right to frighten me, to get my mind in the proper place. I was nowhere near, in body or mind, being an elf. I have no words for it."

"But you can return now. I can help you."

"Yes, it was cruel of me to stay away so long. But our caravan begins its journey anew."

"Yes, at dawn. Have you seen all the new fae in our caravan?"

"Yes, it is very impressive what Mr. Traveler has helped us assemble."

"He did say that nothing would keep our caravan from moving ahead."

"And he was right."

"Will you set out with us tomorrow? Please say yes. Everyone wants to see you. They all ask about you daily."

"Yes, so my ears tell me. I will see. If I am feeling strong and in good spirits, I will. Mr. Traveler told me that he has a surprise for me if I show myself tomorrow."

"Surprise? What is it?"

"Mr. Traveler. He is as mischievous as any fae. He would not tell me."

"Then you must join us."

"I am tempted. I cannot deny it. Well, Gwyness, you get your sleep."

"I will now that I know you will be returning."

"Yes."

Gwyness lying back down but then abruptly sat back up. Lady Aylen had vanished into the shadows of the tent.

CHAPTER FIFTEEN

Fenodyree and the Kirin Steeds

Hobbs had the leadership assembled in the royal tent for a special breakfast meeting. Final preparations had to be made before the caravan officially set out. However, it was Mr. Quillen who had taken over, sitting in his corner.

"But they called them vampires, Mr. Traveler," Quillen challenged, with a look of worry.

"Mr. Quillen, fae do call other fae names too, out of spite, just like humans."

"But vampire? Aren't there real vampires though, sir?"

"Yes, and vampire beasts and vampire birds."

"Mr. Traveler, please do not give our young scribe any additional material for his active imagination," the king cautioned.

"We are not going to encounter any vampires, so put it out of your mind, Mr. Quillen," Traveler said in a loud tone. "Phookas are fae shape-shifters that are always in the form of some humanoid or animal, always black. The bad ones are violent and dangerous. Those are not the ones in our camp. The good ones, and they do exist, are given to mischief and harmless pranks, no different than the fairies."

"They have other names, too, sir," Nirgund said.

"Yes, Mr. Nirgund, our Gaeli expert of fantastic beasts. Pooka, puca, and other derivations. Are you in competition with Mr. Quillen?"

The berserker laughed, as did the group. "Oh, no, sir. Mr. Quillen has nothing to fear from me."

"Refer to them as darklings. They are the night protectors of Titan's Caravan."

"How do you know these creatures, Mr. Traveler?" Gwyness asked.

"I saved one of them, many years ago. It took the form of a vicious fox, and I did not know what it was initially. It revealed its true self only much later. I spent time with his clan."

"What was that like?" Nirgund asked nervously.

"It was a memorable experience, but gave me a good insight into their race and many others, like fairies. They are mischief-makers."

"What animals do they change into, Mr. Traveler?" Quillen asked.

"Dogs, foxes, wolves, cats, horses, goats, rabbits, birds. I am sure much more, as they choose forms to frighten and shock. They are especially fond of changing into distorted versions of those animals or a combination of more than one. And changing into humanoid forms with animal features. Again, they are here to keep us all safe at night. If any beast of the night attacks us, you will see their full vengeful power and be thankful we have them. Otherwise, we would have to run out into the night to do battle. We cannot see in the dark. They can."

"Why would the brownies say those things about them, then, Mr. Traveler?"

"Mr. Quillen! They don't like each other. Their races are not allies. It is no different than giants and elves, or fairies and väki."

"Well, no one likes the väki," Quillen quipped.

"Well, I do not like them, Mr. Traveler, these darklings," Gwyness announced. "They look like a wicked-minded group of beings. How many of them are in the camp?"

"The benevolent members of their race can be quite helpful, and are only dangerous to evil beasts and beings. All we must do is curb their mischievous nature, and they will be fine. And to answer the question, fifty of them. We can manage that many. More than that, no one can manage. They become worse than gremlins and imps."

"Mr. Traveler," Quillen began, "actually, I realized that no one likes the väki, except for you." The lad smiled.

"Are we supposed to be having a meeting, Mr. Hobbs?" Traveler asked.

Hobbs was still laughing along with the group. "Yes, sir, we are."

"Then take charge of your understudy so we can be done with it, and get on our way."

"Hear! Hear!" Pangolin, Nirgund, and I-wulf yelled.

The dawn meeting was over. Pangolin took charge of his men for the vanguard, and they formed up ahead of the camp. Hobbs attended to the rest of the men, forming them up in columns, with the lizard minders and their now-giant lizards on the flanks. The rest of the leadership, save Estus, formed up behind the vanguard.

"Mr. Traveler, should we include Mr. Gresham in the leadership?" the king asked.

"Mr. Traveler!" one of the men in camp yelled.

"Yes, sire, as soon as he proves himself."

The man in armor reached them.

"What is it, man?"

"Sir, there are..."

"What?"

"These hairy...halfling men standing outside the circle."

"Good. The fenodyree. Bring them around to us."

"Yes, sir."

"Hairy men, Mr. Traveler?" Gwyness asked.

Traveler chuckled. "Lady Aylen, your presence is requested."

Gwyness's mouth dropped open. The king looked at Nirgund with a smile. Quillen, standing right behind them, lit up with joy. He bolted away to get Hobbs.

The same men appeared with four hairy halflings. The fae had human faces, but every other part of them was covered with thick brown fur.

"What are those?" Pangolin asked. "They have fur like a buffalo."

"Buffalo?" Quillen had returned.

"A bison," Pangolin replied.

"Oh."

Traveler walked to the fenodyree. "Welcome." All four of them nodded. "Are the merchants here?"

One of them pointed beyond; Traveler and everyone turned to look.

From a portal emerged a long golden wagon, pulled by two riders on large griffins. The beasts stopped and roared. The faces of the riders were completely covered by the hoods of their cloaks, but their arms holding the reins of the griffins looked reptilian.

Traveler looked up, and everyone saw two balls of light descend from the sky. When they were above the ground, they changed into the two giggling fairy sisters.

"Lady Aylen," Traveler said aloud. "If you do not come to choose your surprise, King Aereth and Gwyness will have their steeds, and you will be walking."

"Look!" Quillen pointed at the center tree of the camp.

A hooded figure approached them. All the men watched the "new" Lady Aylen walk to the front of the caravan. She wore her same royal attire as they had seen before, but two war tridents were strapped to her back. Her hood covered her head, but it did nothing to obstruct her two long elfin ears that jutted out. Her skin had a radiant glow, with a tinge of blue. Her eyes had always been blue but now had a greater intensity.

"Princess!" Quillen yelled. "You—you—you are an elf!"

"Yes, Mr. Quillen. I am."

"I want to be an elf!"

Lady Aylen smiled, then began to laugh.

"Lady Aylen, we are so glad to have you back with us," King Aereth said.

"Thank you, sire."

Hobbs, Pangolin, and Nirgund also warmly greeted her. Gwyness gave her a long hug.

"Royals, Maiden Gwyness, let us choose your steeds," Traveler said.

"Are we choosing among griffins, Mr. Traveler?" the king asked as he led them to the back of the magic wagon.

"Originally, that was the plan, but Lady Aylen made me change my thinking."

"Me, Mr. Traveler? How did I change your thinking?"

"Rather than give you and Maiden Gwyness one set of animals, sire, and the princess another, I inquired about ones more versatile than griffins."

The back of the wagon was open, and they walked up a gangplank into another pocket-realm. It was a strange field of long yellow grass and an alternating blue and red sky. All through the fields, horse-like animals were roaming.

"They are called kirins. They are from lands very far away from us—fae and magical animals far different from here. Unlike griffins, as powerful as they are, kirins can also swim. I had planned to get griffins for the king and Gwyness, and a unicorn for the princess."

"A unicorn, Mr. Traveler? I would have liked that."

"Unicorns are beautiful beasts, too, princess, but they do not like to be without others of their kind, or at least flying horses. They definitely do not like to swim. You need a steed that can move about in water as easily as on land."

"What are these kirins, Mr. Traveler?"

"There are many species of them. They are commonly called dragon-horses."

A strange bald man dressed in a brown patterned robe floated to them.

"Show my three friends their animal companions," Traveler said to him.

"Are we choosing from among them, Mr. Traveler?" Gwyness asked.

"No, the seer has already chosen the ones you would have."

"Chosen for us, Mr. Traveler?" the king asked.

"Chosen the ones you chose."

"But we have never been here before, Mr. Traveler," Gwyness said.

"Gwyness, Mr. Traveler is telling us that this seer has read our minds or dreams and chosen the very beasts we would have chosen for ourselves," Lady Aylen said.

"The beasts must also accept you," Traveler added.

The entire field of dragon-horses disappeared except for three.

"Go meet your kirin," Traveler directed.

King Aereth approached his steed with its golden fur and scales. It was the most beautiful animal he had ever seen, and the animal never took its eyes off of his. It was horse-like, with very powerful muscles and a thick mane of hair but with cloven hooves and its head was dragonlike, or what he would have thought an ancient dragon head would look like. He ran his hand along the beast's mane, and it closed its eyes for a moment.

Lady Aylen's dragon-horse was similar, but its fur and scales were a lucent blue. Its head was adorned with a single horn, like a unicorn, and around its nose and mouth were long whiskers like a catfish.

"I do have a unicorn," she said to herself.

Gwyness's dragon-horse was larger than the others, though Gwyness had a stature smaller than either the king or the princess. Her beast was of black fur and scales. Its head was adorned with full antlers and, unlike the other animals, had a tail not unlike a lion. She nervously approached it. When she touched its forehead, it closed its eyes then playfully nudged her with its head, careful not to touch her with its antlers.

"We can go," Traveler said. "The kirin will follow you."

"How do we care for them, Mr. Traveler?" Gwyness asked.

"The fenodyree will mind them most of the time. They are as strong as the pech. They are also much like brownies; they like to keep their surroundings tidy and orderly, and enjoy the work of outdoors. They are very good with benevolent animals. A perfect role for them in the caravan. They will have their own pocket-realm. However, you must spend time with your steeds daily."

Traveler led them out of the pocket, with the kirins following.

Traveler's dog had not entered the pocket. It waited for them outside, the four fenodyree nearby. The caravan master directed the shaggy fae to take charge of the kirins. The splendor of the dragon-horses amazed everyone. None had ever seen their kind before.

"Mr. Traveler, how do you know the traders of these…kirins?" King Aereth asked.

"I met them in my travels. I sent word of our needs. There are people in these lands who can communicate through magic with those in other realms."

"Do we have our sorcerers yet, Mr. Traveler?" Lady Aylen asked. King Aereth and Gwyness stifled their laughter. "What?"

"Lady Aylen, it is as if you have never been gone," the king replied.

"My seclusion is over, and I am as anxious as Mr. Pangolin, the Cut-Throats, and the giants to move on. Caravans must move, or they are not caravans."

"We do need sorcerers, but with the leshies, our two fairies, and the magical weapons and instruments we have been collecting, we can address the matter along the way."

"I agree," Lady Aylen said.

"So do I," Pangolin said from his post nearby.

"Then, it is settled. We are ready to set out to the fae city of Arion's Spear."

"The Titan's Caravan marches," King Aereth declared. "Mr. Hobbs, get the new flags, and let us show the men our official caravan standard."

CHAPTER SIXTEEN
The City of Arion's Spear

Hobbs stood tall with pride, gazing across humans, sprites, giants, fantastical beasts of land and air, crawling trees, and even the pair of fairies—Titan's Caravan. It was beyond anything he could have imagined those months ago in that Hopeshire tavern, in the Lands of Man, when he became the first man Traveler hired to set out on the year-long trek to the legendary kingdom of Atlantea.

They marched in four columns. The outside flanks were the lizard minders and their giant lizards. Both men and reptiles, thanks to the busy work of Estus and his team, were fully armored. Traveler cautioned Estus that the lizards were still growing though, so the work of forging lizard armor was far from over. The two center columns were of not just humans, each equipped with fae gold and silver polearms, but also the pech, the brawny, big-nosed sprite halflings with wild eyebrows, carrying large dwarvin spiked shields and, in their other arm, any elfin weapon of their choice. Also in the center columns were the human domestics, servants, and laborers towards the front, with pull carts and one of the crawling trees in the center, with all the hoofed fae archers and servants following. The other two crawling trees were at each end. In the rear, were all the Cut-Throat warriors and their chamroshes, flanked by an Antaean giant each. Mingling through the columns was also the roving team of male half-elf warriors.

At point, Pangolin's vanguard consisted of himself, Mr. Elman, four of the giants, and two dozen of the elaphine archer-hunters. Behind them, at the front of the columns, were the royals: King Aereth, with his royal guard of Mr. Nirgund the berserke, and the reptilian fae hounds, as well as Lady Aylen and Maiden Gwyness, with their female half-elf royal guards. They decided not to ride the dragon-horse kirins but have them walk along. Hobbs followed behind them at the head of the columns, with his two bodyguards, Mr. Tyfer and Mr. Oeric. Traveler and his dog led the caravan behind Pangolin's vanguard. Also in the caravan among, the men, a couple of the Brothers Brimm musicians played flutes.

The new flags of Titan's Caravan flew high! Six men carried the standards—poles twelve feet in height. The white flags featured an iconic representation of the Titan, the Maker of all Mountains, and seven points of light to represent the seven points along Titan's Trail.

When they first met, Traveler had told Hobbs that humans alone could not get to Atlantea, even with complete knowledge of the path and a shape-shifting animal. Their caravan master had said they needed elves and other fae. They had that and more. Traveler said that their caravan must be impressive not only to them but to any fae warrior, sorcerer, or royal. They were—nearly six thousand in all.

Hobbs glanced at the young Quillen walking beside him. The lad had a perpetual smile on his face. Tyfer and Oeric noticed and laughed.

"Keep your eyes forward, lad. In this caravan, you are liable to walk right into a man, fae, beast, or moving tree," Tyfer joked.

"Lad, you must be in Nirvana. You need never set foot outside the camp to fill your magic book with magical beasts and the people of these lands," Oeric added. "We have it all."

◆ ◆ ◆

Traveler's dog had settled on a larger form, but close to the appearance they all were accustomed to. Traveler quietly led the front of the columns.

"I hear something," Lady Aylen said, more speaking to herself. "Voices, many, many voices." Her elfin ears were moving on their own.

Traveler noticed that the vanguard had stopped and the giants were looking back at them.

"Is something wrong, Mr. Traveler?" the king asked.

"We are about to have visitors," Traveler answered. There was no joy in his voice.

The caravan stopped, and what at first seemed like a swarm of fireflies appeared around them.

"From your expression, Mr. Traveler, unwelcome visitors?" the king asked.

"We shall see, sire."

"What are they, Mr. Traveler?" Gwyness asked.

"We are about to meet fairies, the real ones, but not from our childhood fables. It will either be a professional encounter or a potentially deadly one, but by no means friendly either way."

Traveler, with his dog, neared the stationary vanguard; others followed. The look on the faces of the giants echoed Traveler's concern. The swarm of fireflies encircling the caravan grew in vast numbers, first like a wall and then like a dome over all of them. Then the fireflies transformed to their true forms: tiny flying fairies, females with flapping translucent wings, antennas sprouting from their foreheads, frocks made of leaves or grass. Their squinting eyes looked cold, and they all had pointed razor-edged spears. The air grew black and thick with their increasing numbers.

The entire swarm surrounded the caravan.

"This is a fairy-storm," one of the giants said to Pangolin. "Do you understand now?"

Pangolin glanced back at Traveler. "How does one battle this?" he asked.

Traveler shook his head. "For us, there are two ways—magic or words. I think the latter is best."

Their caravan master stepped forward, as if he were going to walk right into the black swarm, but halted.

"Stop!" he yelled. His dog sat near him, unconcerned. Both man and animal had no look of fear, unlike the rest of the caravan.

The swirling swarm did stop, and the fairies hung in the air. Dozens of human-sized female fairies flew out of the swarm and set down before him. Their skin was pale, almost transparent. Their silvery hair was very short, and they had the same forehead antennae and translucent wings. However, these six-foot-tall fairies were much more insect-like, with slits for eyes and two sets of arms.

"You are the human who kidnapped our kind!" one of the fairies yelled.

Traveler was unmoved by the intensity of her voice, which echoed through the caravan. "Silence your mouth, and let us be. This is open land and you have no claim to it. Move out of our way. I am in no mood for fairy foolishness."

Shock came over the faces of the fairies. *How dare this human speak to us in this manner!*

"Human, I will fly down your gullet and—"

"Silence your mouth!" Traveler interrupted. "Mr. Hobbs, where is that pouch of pixie dust? It works on wayward fairies too."

One of the fairies stepped to him, her face red with rage. "Human, you will show the respect we are due!"

"Why? You surround us without cause—"

"Not without cause! You kidnapped our kind!"

"Whom did we kidnap?"

"Two fairy children!"

"What are you talking about? The only fairies that are part of our caravan are from Fae-Wick. There are no others."

"Human, they are the fairies to which we are referring!"

Traveler shot her a dirty look. "Wildglow and Sunpetal! Come here this instant!"

Two fireflies flew out of one of the pull carts. The barely two-foot-tall fairy and her sister, half her size, stood near Traveler. For most in the caravan, it was the first time the fairy sisters were seen. Quillen drew closer to get a better look. The taller one had two antennae poking out from her short blondish hair, translucent insect wings from her back. She was wearing a muted ivory frock. The smaller one only differed in dress in that she also had on a brown half-jacket that had the texture of a woolly caterpillar.

"Are these your people?" Traveler asked the fairy sisters.

"No," the taller one answered quickly.

"Wildglow!" one of the tall fairies shouted.

"Wildglow, what did I tell you and your sister?" Traveler asked. "As a member of this caravan, you must follow all the rules. Is telling lies following the rules?"

Both fairy girls looked all around. "No," Wildglow finally answered.

"Are these your people?"

"Yes, but we can do what we want."

Traveler looked at the fairies. "Are these the two fairies you were referring to? Wildglow and Sunpetal, members of our caravan?"

"How can two fairy children be members of your caravan?"

"We are not children!" Wildglow yelled.

"They asked. I accepted," Traveler answered the fairy leader derisively. "They are treated no differently than any other human or fae member of our caravan."

The fairies were quiet and then looked at each other. "What other fae?" one asked.

"Come and see." Traveler gestured and led the nearly two dozen tall fairies into the caravan.

He gave them a full tour from the front to the rear. They were visibly pleased to be greeted by the four Tree Shepherds and the brownies, who spilled out of a pocket-realm—its entrance was a bag on one of the pull carts—to meet them as well. They returned to the front, and the tall fairies stopped at Lady Aylen.

"A water elf," one said.

"What is the name of your kingdom?" another asked.

"I am a princess of the kingdom of Sirnegate."

"What is the name of your elfin kingdom?"

Lady Aylen sighed, not knowing how to answer.

"Her kingdom was lost," Traveler answered. "It happened in her infancy."

The tall fairies were satisfied.

"Who will protect our fairy-sister children on this journey?" one asked Traveler.

"You have seen our defensive means. If there is danger we cannot manage, they will be put into the pocket-realm with the väki to be under their protection."

"You have väki here?"

"Which clan?"

"The tulen väki."

"The väki of fire."

"Yes. Do you wish to meet them too?"

The fairies snarled. "No, we do not."

"We are satisfied with your measures, but why would a human accept fairy children? We have known humans to attempt to drown themselves to get away from fairy children."

"They behave, play for at least six hours a day, and cast no spells on anyone or anything in the caravan. They have both followed the rules, so they are equal members of the caravan."

The two fairy sisters giggled and crossed their arms in front of their chests, taunting the tall fairies.

"Do you have any other inquiries?" Traveler asked.

"No."

"Where did you hear the ridiculous story that they were kidnapped?"

"We were mistaken," one of the tall fairies said. "You can proceed. However, their mother may visit you along your path to check their progress."

"We are not going back!" Wildglow yelled.

"If your mother wishes it!"

"No!" both sisters yelled.

"We are going on the caravan to Atlantea!" Wildglow added. "We are not going back! No one can make us."

One of the tall fairies drew closer to Traveler. "Keep them safe. They are only children."

"We are older than all these humans!" Wildglow yelled.

"Everything is older than the humans," one of the tall fairies snapped back.

Traveler looked at the fairy sisters and put a single finger in front of his lips to gesture, *Silence!*

Traveler began again. "I have interacted with fairies before, and the four Tree Shepherds are far more knowledgeable than I."

"Yes, we know of Greenwig. He is an able Tree Shepherd leader."

"Then our two fairies here will be fine. Other fae, three crawling trees, the rainbow lizards, alphyns...there is much to occupy them within the caravan, not to mention the surroundings of the Trail itself. They will join the fairies in Atlantea when we arrive."

The tall fairies nodded in unison, satisfied.

"Yes. Good journey, Master Traveler and to your Titan's Caravan."

The fairy leaders jumped into the air and flew away. All the fairies around them turned back into balls of light and followed. They were gone.

"My word," King Aereth said aloud, still as overwhelmed as the caravan.

Pangolin looked up at his Antaean giant comrades. "I understand now."

"Yes. We have never heard of any of the races making war on the fairies. You have seen with your own eyes as to why. That fairy-storm was one of the smaller and tamer ones. They can blanket an entire region and turn day into night with their numbers," Grakdar said to him.

"It is no different than in our lands," Traveler said. "Even the largest and most vicious mammal there will run from a swarm of locusts. Mammals always view themselves as the top of all flora and fauna, but the number of insects eclipses all other life on the world by many, many million-fold. Fairydom is the equivalent of the insects of this realm."

"I was fascinated by insects when I was a boy," Pangolin said. "I have always viewed them as warlike as men, but without the burdens of emotion. A fairy-storm. I see why my Antaean comrades were ill at ease."

"If such a fairy-storm attacked with its full fury, few of us would survive the encounter," Grakdar added.

"We were never in any real danger," Traveler said to them. "Fairies are benevolent, as is our caravan. We did nothing that would arouse their wrath. Someone has been spreading lies about us, but it has all been settled."

"Should we be concerned about the false tales being spread about the caravan, Mr. Traveler?" the king asked.

"No, sire. Now the truth will be spread about us far and wide, coming from no less than fairy warriors. It will work in our great favor and build our reputation as we continue along the Trail."

♦ ♦ ♦

Lady Aylen's eyes caught sight of it for the first time. A large lime-green bullfrog watching them from a distance behind a tree in the woods. She could sense no malevolence from it, so she ignored it.

♦ ♦ ♦

"Ripped to pieces by fairies." Nirgund chuckled to himself as the caravan continued its march. The vanguard was about a half mile ahead of the front of the columns. Hobbs and Quillen walked beside him, following the royals and Gwyness, with Traveler in the lead.

"Mr. Traveler, how many different types of fairies are there?" Quillen asked from his side.

"Don't trouble, Mr. Traveler," Hobbs scolded. "You have time to pester him with questions at the noon meal or at night."

"It is fine, Mr. Hobbs. I can answer. Mr. Quillen, there are more species of fairies than you can imagine. All the elves, sprites, dwarves, and giant races combined make up but a tenth of the total of fae. Fairies make up most of the majority. Most a human eye will never see, and we'll never know of their race."

"Why is that, Mr. Traveler?"

"They do not interact with outsiders—ever."

Traveler glanced over at Lady Aylen. "You are very quiet, princess."

"I am in a quiet mood, Mr. Traveler."

"What are your ears picking up? Not the men in the caravan or the vanguard. Around us, ahead, our flanks. Just...listen."

Lady Aylen closed her eyes, but her expression was of pain and discomfort.

"You are still blocking out sounds, princess. You must not do that, or you will never attain your full elfin-hearing potential. At day's end, I want you to sit quietly, eyes closed, and listen. You need not do anything more. It is no different than being human. We do it all the time. We listen and naturally tune out things we are not interested in, and we can also focus in on what we wish. You must simply relearn how. But not by blocking out everything."

"I am not very comfortable with these hearing exercises of yours, Mr. Traveler."

"The exercises are not about hearing, princess, but of focus. There is a major difference between blocking out your new hearing abilities and allowing them to hear all that there is to hear in the background while you function as normal."

"I did hear the fairies."

"No, you heard voices. You should have heard much more than that and much sooner. Princess, you are too self-conscious about your ears. You are an elf. Elves have pointed ears. Have pride in them, not shame."

Lady Aylen sighed.

"Shall we change the subject?" he asked.

"Yes, please, Mr. Traveler."

"How about your magical abilities?"

"I have none, Mr. Traveler."

Traveler flashed a smirk at her.

"Lady Aylen can do magic, Mr. Traveler?" Gwyness asked.

"You all saw it."

"Saw what, Mr. Traveler?" Gwyness asked.

"What did you see when Lady Aylen had her fit after drinking the pitcher of ambrosian nectar? When she fell to the ground?"

"The water?" Gwyness realized.

"What water?" Lady Aylen asked.

"You are not just a water elf, princess. You may possess water-enchanting powers as well—elemental or summoning. I will have more exercises for you so we can find out."

"I tire of the exercises, Mr. Traveler."

"They will end when you have mastered them. I would rather you be vexed with me than be challenged by one of your own kind. There will be a lot of elves in Arion's Spear. You will see how uncharitable elves can be when they are suspicious of an elf they think not to be a real one."

"Why would they be suspicious of me?"

"You are too human."

Lady Aylen laughed. Gwyness and the female half-elves joined in.

"I do not see that as a detriment at all, Mr. Traveler," King Aereth said.

"We have visitors," Nirgund called out. He moved ahead of the king to stand with Traveler. His dozen alphyn hounds watched as intently as Traveler did at the approaching riders in the distance.

The two riders were mounted upon large red unicorns. They stopped, then turned and galloped away.

"Red unicorns," Quillen said aloud. "I thought they could only be white. And these look ferocious."

"What was that about?" Pangolin asked Traveler when he reached them.

"Curiosity, or let us assume so. Do you know the rider's kind?" Traveler asked the giants, his head turned up.

"There are a few types of elves that are fond of red battle unicorns. Some good, some not," Grakdar answered.

"Mr. Pangolin, we proceed, then."

Traveler had done his best to prepare the men beforehand. He spoke of the city the night before to the leadership, especially so that

Hobbs could spread the word upon the start of the new day. Traveler noticed the female half-elves laughing to themselves as he did. They stayed with the princess and Gwyness, as Nirgund kept the king within his sights. He knew why they laughed. Nothing he could say would prepare them.

The fae city of Arion's Spear appeared close by but was still a two hour's march away. They could see it as they started down into the wide-open valley before it. Its namesake was a mammoth white rock statue of a horse on its hind legs, reaching for the heavens; a golden spear wound around its body and pointed upward. The horse was not an ipotane but reminded Gwyness and some of the men of the creature because the horse statue's body was more human than animal. The entire structure was worthy of the titans themselves; it was as large as the castle walls beside it.

Titan's Caravan was far from alone in the wooded valley. Camps of elves, sprites, and other fae littered the vast expanse to the large castle entrance. As they neared, all fae eyes were on them—some curious, others shocked, others contemptuous.

What caught their eye above all was the fae caravan that was departing from the city—a flying caravan. Seemingly hundreds of elves on flying horses and flying unicorns, elves on griffins pulling winged wagons of supplies and people. There were even flying fae archers on their flanks.

"Are they off to Atlantea, too, Mr. Traveler?" Nirgund asked.

"More likely to the lands of the dwarves."

All the men had a picture of what elves looked like even before they had seen their own Lady Aylen. However, unlike her and the accounts of fables, most of these elves appeared anything but regal. These elves were more uncouth than the väki—with scarred and pockmarked faces, chewing who knew what herbs, spitting, and unkempt. Closer to the city, the fae looked to be more of noble and royal stock, but their knights and warriors were more deadly looking; their glowing weapons were pure magic or forged from it.

"Mr. Pangolin," Traveler began. Their master-at-arms turned and walked back to him to hear. "Find a place for us to set up camp. It will not be easy, but see what you can manage."

He nodded and returned to the vanguard.

Traveler moved close to the royals and the front party. "We must go into the city."

"Must we, Mr. Traveler?" Lady Aylen asked.

"We have all our supplies save one thing: the most current maps of the Trail. The smaller the group, the better for us. King Aereth, you will remain in the camp."

"Sir, I would like to accompany you this time," Hobbs said.

Traveler nodded. "Then you will, but your guards can remain. Lady Aylen, you will accompany me too."

"Then my team."

"Gwyness, yes. Your guards will remain."

"And why is that, Mr. Traveler?"

"You know why, princess. Let us be quick about this. Mr. Pangolin and two of the giants will escort us. We will wait until we have secured our campsite."

"There are so many people outside the city," Gwyness remarked.

"Worse than when we were back on Caravan Row," Hobbs added.

"Why are they giving us such dirty looks, Mr. Traveler?" Gwyness asked.

"Ignore them. We will get what we need in the city and go. I do not like being in such close quarters, in what should be a wide-open field."

"Why are so many people out here, Mr. Traveler?" King Aereth asked.

"This is caravan season for the fae, sire. This is when caravans travel to and from every corner of Faë-Land for trade."

"So the Four Kings were not arbitrary in their selection of the time of year for their caravan."

"No, they were not, sire. It was all planned. You could say it is like a giant caravan throughout all the realms. But it also increases our danger, not lessens it, as long as we stay amongst everyone else. We must set off on our own as soon as possible."

◆◆◆

Pangolin had enlisted several of their fae members to find a suitable spot for their camp, but it was the fairy sisters who found it on their own. The pair appeared out of thin air, giggling and pointing.

I-wulf did not like the crowds of elves and other fae gathered in the woods any more than Pangolin, and had his Cut-Throats stand among the nervous lizard minders as the camp was set. Pangolin also left two of the Antaeans and most of his vanguard archers with them.

Traveler pulled up his hood to cover his head and led them into the city of Arion's Spear. Lady Aylen's face revealed her discomfort. Gwyness kept a roving eye on the crowds around them. Hobbs kept close to Traveler, always half-running to keep up. Pangolin, the giants, and two of the elaphine deerlike archer-warriors followed on either side of him.

"What are your senses telling you?" Pangolin asked one of them.

"This is a mistake, and we sense danger. But our senses are always sensing danger. We are elaphine."

"This lot seems especially disagreeable," Pangolin said.

"We are humans unlike any they have ever seen. More of equals than helpless animals," Traveler said to him. "And we command a caravan of humans and fae."

"Despite what occurred in Fae-Wick, I much prefer that city than this one."

They finally crossed the city walls and into the open market square. It, too, overflowed with elves and other fae, worse than outside.

"What kind of elf are you?" an elf shouted at Lady Aylen. His face was wrinkled, and he looked like he was drunk from his reddened eyes and red nose.

Traveler waved the elf away as he led them away from him.

"We will not be long—" Traveler began.

"You!"

As they turned to see who was addressing them, Hobbs gasped. A spear ripped through his chest, the tip protruding from his back. Gwyness screamed as their steward began to fall.

Traveler ignored everything around him and grabbed Hobbs before he crashed to the ground.

"None of you belong here," a white-haired elf said, strolling to them with a smirk.

Pangolin already had his axe-mace in his hand and was about to attack.

"Mr. Pangolin, we must get Hobbs back to camp now! Leave him be!"

"Yes, human. Listen to your human," the elf said mockingly. "Leave me be."

Pangolin returned his weapon to the back of his armor. "Lift him!" he yelled to one of the giants.

The two giants had their war hammers ready for battle too. Grakdar threw his weapon to his comrade giant and picked up Hobbs.

"Run!" Traveler said.

"Giants do not run!" Grakdar yelled back.

Traveler had already started for the main entrance. Grakdar followed with extra long strides, Gwyness at his side, crying. Aronir, the other giant, was behind him.

Pangolin looked at Lady Aylen who stood like a statue, her eyes locked on the elf.

"If you were a real elf," the white-haired elf said, "you might have caught the spear before we killed your human." He glared at Pangolin and said, "You humans think you are great because you have a few lumbering, clumsy oaf giants and a handful of lowly sprites that you can travel the lands of fae. Go back to your own worthless lands, human."

Pangolin noticed other dark-haired elves approaching in the same royal dress, silver-blue tops, dark-crimson trousers, and snake-scale boots.

"Lady Aylen, we must go!"

He looked for Traveler's dog, but it was nowhere to be seen.

"If you cannot handle a single elf with a javelin, human, you should not be in our lands. There are far greater beasts than me here. Yes, go back to your own worthless lands."

Lady Aylen seemed to be in a trance. He reached her and pulled her towards the entrance. She came to her senses and walked, but it was as if she did not know what had happened—void of emotion and dazed.

Pangolin glanced back to see six more elves. The white-haired one who was speaking waved him goodbye.

Grakdar stumbled through the camp, the men in panic, Gwyness screaming. The giant reached the healing tent, where Gresham waited. A look of shock came over his face.

"What happened?" Gresham asked.

Their steward's body was still impaled by the elfin spear. Blood was all over him and Gwyness too.

"What do I do?" the giant asked.

"In here!" Gresham yelled, then realized the giant was far too large for the tent. "No, give him here! Help me!"

The giant rested Hobbs's body in their new healer's arms. Other men helped carry him in. No bed was set up in the empty tent, only a large bag in the corner. Gresham directed them to set him down on the ground on his side.

Gwyness rushed inside. "Help him!"

"Where's Mr. Traveler?" Gresham asked.

"You're the healer! Help him!" she yelled.

Gresham jumped up, grabbed his healer's bag, and returned to the ground at Hobbs's unconscious body. "We will remove the spear, but you must apply pressure to the openings," he said to the men.

Traveler stepped into the tent, not with his own healer's bag but with a purple bag. "Do as he says," Traveler yelled to the two men assisting. "No, the other end so you can pull the spear cleanly from the body."

"Press down firm, man!" Gresham said to the first man. "And you too!" Gresham grabbed the spear from the second man and threw it away into another corner of the tent.

"Hold your hands over the wounds, but shift Mr. Hobbs to his back," Traveler directed as he opened the bag.

Immediately, there was a bright glow. A pure-white bird, three feet in height, rose from the magical bag. Its wings rose high above its head. Feathers jutted back from its crest. The bird landed on Hobbs's chest, flapping wildly, then stopped. It touched him with its beak, and in moments, Hobbs began to glow bright too. The blood flew to his body from outside the tent—from Grakdar's clothes—Gresham, Gwyness, the two men at Hobbs's side, still holding his open wounds. The blood flew to his body and disappeared. The man holding the top of Hobbs's chest lifted his hand. The wound and blood were gone.

Hobbs made a noise.

"Mr. Hobbs?" Gwyness yelled.

Hobbs's head moved to the side, his eyes dancing beneath his closed eyelids.

"You are alive, Mr. Hobbs!" Gwyness dropped to the ground, smiling. She wanted to grab him.

"Mr. Gresham, I will leave Mr. Hobbs in your care," Traveler said. He stood and held the magical white bird down on the ground.

Gresham rose to his feet in both joy and astonishment. "Yes, sir. Is that the animal I have heard of in fables?"

"The caladrius bird, yes," Traveler answered. "Little Root!"

The youngest of their Tree Shepherds stepped into the healing tent. "Master Traveler," he greeted.

"Please attend to our magical fowl and friend, here. He will be more at ease with you and your comrades than me."

The leshy raised his right arm, and the caladrius bird flew to it without instruction. "We will put it in our soul tree. It will be safe in our pocket-realm."

"Thank you, Little Root."

"We did not know you had such a beautiful animal."

"No, but I think you should be its keeper for the rest of the journey. It takes to you instinctively." Traveler folded the purple bag up and handed it to Gresham.

The leshy smiled as he looked upon the bird. "It does."

With that, Traveler the healer was gone. His entire demeanor switched from compassion to darkness as he marched from the tent.

News spread quickly among the men that Hobbs's life had been saved by Traveler using a bird of magic, just as their caravan master marched past them all to his tent. Pangolin had gotten Lady Aylen back to the camp and left her with the female half-elves to be near the healing tent. He knew the look on Traveler's face well. He had seen it before—when they were back in the Lands of Man against marauders and ogres. Pangolin glanced up at the giants. They looked back and nodded. The giants looked at the elaphine archer-warriors, who looked amongst themselves and nodded.

Traveler emerged from his tent, not with his magical sword but with an elfin curly dagger in each hand. The dog trotted behind him; its mouth had a distinct wicked grin. Traveler already had a naturally brisk pace when he walked, though he slowed down for the sake of the caravan march. Now, he moved at almost a running pace back to the fae city.

Pangolin pulled his axe-mace from his back and marched after them, giants and elaphines behind him.

"We know what is about to happen next," one of the giants said. All six of them were following Pangolin.

The crowds of elves and fae on the way to the city also sensed what was about to happen. They snickered, smiled, and laughed. They all thought the human caravan master would soon be dead and said so to him in English and their own tongues.

Inside the fae city's walls, the white-haired elf waited in the middle of the merchant road for Traveler.

"Where's your sword, human? I thought with your man dead, you'd return with your magical sword I've heard of. Do you really suppose you can hurt me, in the least way, with two little daggers in your hands?"

Traveler had ignored every word from the grinning elf as he marched up to him.

"Humans cannot touch elves in battle! Let me show you!"

The elf's appearance wavered. He was one place, then another, and then behind Traveler. He screamed! Traveler had lunged inexplicably not at where the elf was, but spun around as the elf rematerialized right into a dagger strike to the gut. Traveler sliced off both tips of the elf's ears; the elf screamed again and grabbed them. Traveler plunged the daggers together into the elf's chest and cut down to his groin. Then, with both daggers, he sliced his throat open, almost severing the elf's head cleanly off.

Arion's Spear was a massive city, filled with crowds of fae. Everyone watched, frozen where they stood, not a word spoken by any. Pangolin could feel the shock in the air, from his giant comrades, too, as the elf's innards spilled from his gut, blood sprayed from his neck, and his body collapsed to the ground.

Pangolin expected Traveler to turn around and march back to camp, but that was not what happened.

The rage welled up in the other six elves, still shaken at what just occurred. Traveler did not wait; he marched to all of them. The sole swordsman, the tallest of them, yelled, drew his sword from his side, and charged. Traveler caught the blade of the sword in a crossed-dagger move and it fell to the ground. Traveler plunged a dagger into each of the elf's feet, straight through his scaly boots; the elfin swordsman screamed. From the ground, Traveler sliced the elf's Achilles tendons and thighs, thrust one dagger into his groin, thrust the other into his belly, and in a move none could imagine, kicked up with all his might, and the tip of his own boot connected with the elf's forehead. When the caravan master lowered his leg, it revealed a dagger tip. The elf was dead, with his mouth wide open. Traveler let his body fall to the ground as he got back to his feet.

One of the other elves went mad, and a magical spear appeared in his hand. A bony spear exploded through the elf's skull, obliterating his head. The dog stood before them, but its tail was a long grayish tubular mass with another bony projectile protruding from the tip. Its eyes were pure black and glistened.

More screams rang out as Traveler attacked the remaining elves. Pangolin now knew that Traveler had set his mind not only to kill the chief elf who had almost killed Hobbs but all seven of them. The elves did not know what they had unleashed in the human, who they never would have known lived and trained in Faë-Land. Traveler killed another by plunging both daggers into the elf's skull, ducked to avoid the lunges of the two others, and snap-kicked another elf with the dagger in his boot. The elf was still alive, but he could not stop the blood loss from his neck and dropped to his knees before falling over.

The two remaining elves were almost in tears and glared at Traveler. The elves yelled, their own daggers raised high, and charged. To Pangolin's eyes, the elves were moving in and out of vision, but Traveler fought both of them with brilliance. A human was not supposed to be able to do what he was doing against an elf, let alone two. However, Pangolin could see it in Traveler's eyes; the man was tiring, and he was slowing down under the blistering lighting-quick dagger attacks by both elves. Then Pangolin glanced at the dog. The dog was not readying to attack. In fact, its monstrous tail was gone. The animal was as relaxed as could be.

The city gasped. Pangolin quickly looked back at the fight. Traveler had been bluffing. He was waiting until he could kill both elves with one move, and he did. The heads of both elves were together and Traveler pulled out his daggers as the bodies dropped to the ground.

Traveler flicked off the blood from the blades as he started to the main entrance. The dog trotted after him. Pangolin noticed his giants and archer comrades were frozen in shock. He was about to speak up when he heard commotion from within the city.

"Oh no," one of the giants said.

The riders were elfin knights in shining white armor on black unicorn warhorses. They were elves of both pure-white and jet-black flowing hair. They gazed upon the carnage of bodies and stopped their steeds in horror.

"Who did this?" one yelled as he jumped down from his black unicorn. He ran to the body of the elf with hair as white as his own. The elf stood, his eyes locked on Traveler.

"You killed him," he said in a whisper, but everyone in the merchant row heard him clearly.

"Yes, I did. He tried to kill my friend, and now he is food for the worms, the elfin bastard with goblin blood."

"You killed my brother."

"Oh, then you must have goblin blood too."

The elfin eyes went white with rage. Suddenly, the elf was at the side of his steed and drew his broadsword, a magnificent blade that glowed.

"Ramil!" another elf from a unicorn mount yelled. "You must not engage this human!"

Ramil ignored him. The other elf leapt down to the ground to stop him. Ramil swung his arm, and the other elf was magically picked up and thrown over the adjacent building, disappearing. He turned his enraged white eyes to Traveler. "I will kill you and then everyone in your pathetic camp, human."

Traveler yelled out, startling everyone. He dropped his elfin daggers to the ground. Through the air came a sheathed sword, which flew into Traveler's outstretched hand. Pangolin, alone, recognized it immediately. The caravan master unsheathed it, threw the covering to the ground, and marched to the elfin knight.

"Yes, human. Let us see how you fare against the Elfin War Prince of Raindark and my sword of swords!"

Traveler swung his sword. The elfin knight thought he would simply block the move. Traveler cut the elf—through his sword—in half at the waist with a swing to one side, then removed his head with a swing back.

The elfin knights dismounted their unicorns to stare upon their dead prince on the ground. One yelled out in agony.

The other elf who had been thrown over the building returned, running so fast as to be barely seen. He dropped to his knees. "You! No human can do this! No human can do what you did! What dark magic did you enlist to steal the sword you wield?"

"Steal, did I?" Traveler walked to him. "Do you wish to take it from me?"

"You thief!"

"Here, take the sword you claim does not belong to me, and cut me down." Traveler tossed the blade to the elf, who snatched it from the air.

The elf screamed louder than any of the previous elves. His sword arm was engulfed by an intense ghostly flame. As his arm burned away, the rest of his body was consumed by fire. The sword fell to the ground, and soon so did the elf's corpse.

Traveler reached down and grabbed his sword.

"Does anyone else wish to challenge me?" he yelled to all.

No one moved or spoke.

The crowds of elves and fae parted to give Traveler and his dog, a wide path as they left the city. The moment Pangolin and his men crossed the threshold of Arion's Spear after him, an explosion of chatter began in different languages and dialects.

Traveler and the dog crossed back into the camp then disappeared from sight. Pangolin sent his giants to their personal camp and the elaphines to their tree camp to rest, while he stood quietly. The leadership gathered in front of the royals' tents around him.

"Mr. Hobbs?" Pangolin asked.

"He remains under Mr. Gresham's observation in the healing tent," King Aereth answered.

All the men, from wherever they stood or sat, waited quietly to hear what had transpired.

"What happened, Mr. Pangolin?" the king finally asked.

"Did Mr. Traveler avenge Mr. Hobbs?" Gwyness asked.

"He did," the berserker answered. "He did."

"We take it much more happened though," I-wulf said from amongst the other Cut-Throats.

"I am usually not a man who has trouble speaking. When we joined this caravan those months ago, it was not only for the honor and skill he showed as healer to our battle fallen, but chiefly, for his skill as a fighter. What we saw in that fae city was far beyond what he did against the marauders when we were in Ironwood in our lands or the attack of the ogres at Last Keep. Mr. Traveler killed seven elves with nothing more than daggers."

"Seven elves?" I-wulf asked. "You mean the dog shape-shifter helped him."

Pangolin shook his head. "The dog killed only one. Mr. Traveler killed the one who almost killed Hobbs, and six more. Then he killed an elfin knight with his sword. You can say his sword killed a final one. Nine dead in all."

"Mr. Traveler's sword," Lady Aylen spoke up.

"It flew through the air to his hand, and Mr. Traveler cut one elf, along with his sword, in half with that blade. Then a final one made the fatal mistake of accusing Mr. Traveler of stealing it. The elf burst into flames when Mr. Traveler threw it into the elf's hand."

"Burst into flames," Gwyness repeated.

"So, Mr. Traveler's sword can cut elfin metal in half." It was Mr. Estus, who had been scarcely seen.

"Did you doubt it?" Pangolin asked.

"Not really, but I was not sure. He also showed me goblin and dwarvin blade fragments. So it is all true."

"His dog is not from this world. Maybe neither is his sword," King Aereth noted.

"How did he kill them?" Gwyness asked. "The ones who attacked Mr. Hobbs."

"Viciously, maiden. Mr. Traveler killed them more viciously than I would have. I now realize that a gifted healer who becomes a gifted swordsman would be the most vicious fighter of all. He would know exactly where on the body to strike to inflict the most amount of pain and damage with the least amount of effort. That is what Mr. Traveler did to those elves." He looked at Lady Aylen. "I am glad you were not there to see it, m'lady."

She cast her eyes to the ground. "Where is Mr. Traveler now?"

"Maybe it is best if we let Mr. Traveler have his time alone," Estus said.

"I agree," Pangolin said. "We must keep everyone in the camp within the circle."

"Yes, Mr. Pangolin. It would be unwise for any of us to venture out under these circumstances," the king said. "Do we believe there will be any attempt at retaliation? The behavior that was described, to kill a man for no reason, it is not the behavior of elves. They are a very moralistic people, with religious mores, codes of honor and duty, kingdoms ruled by monarchies, even the worst of which is benevolent by our standards. But I was not there."

"They were royals, sire. A prince, no less."

"In Mr. Traveler's absence, we defer to your judgment in these matters, Mr. Pangolin."

"We must increase the guards for what remains of the day and through the night. Where are those...phookas, pookas, whatever they are called?"

"Darklings," Nirgund added.

As soon as Pangolin closed his mouth, one of them appeared.

"You summoned?" The darkling had a long, gaunt humanoid frame with a raven's head and grinning mouth. Several of his fellow phookas appeared behind him.

Gwyness, especially, found the sprites disgusting. And they knew it.

"Start your watch immediately," Pangolin directed.

"Are we taking orders from you and not Master Traveler?" the darkling asked.

"You are taking orders from anyone in leadership. Mr. Traveler just killed seven elves, and I suspect he is in a very, very dark mood. Should I find him and tell him you are not following my instructions?"

"Killed elves?"

"We heard you say it was especially vicious," another said.

"We heard the elf's inner body parts poured out on the ground. We haven't had elf innards for a meal in some time. Not as good as human though."

Gwyness made a loud sound of disgust.

The darklings cackled in unison.

"You do not fool me, pranksters. Mr. Traveler told me all about you. You say things for shock. Go to your watch. You wish to shock people. Shock those who try to enter our camp and do us harm. Amuse yourselves that way."

"I wish Master Traveler didn't tell you that we are really angels." The darkling was now in the form of an adorable humanoid cat with big sad eyes. "How can we frighten if people know we aren't evil?"

"Go!" Pangolin yelled.

They glanced at Gwyness as they transformed into hounds with lionlike manes and lion tails. They ran off as a pack.

"I hate those things!" Gwyness said. "I want them out of the camp. They are evil."

"No, maiden. They are here to protect us from evil," Pangolin said.

"Yes, Gwyness," Lady Aylen said softly. "They are not evil. I would sense it if they were."

Gwyness calmed herself.

"Do you think we will have trouble tonight, Mr. Pangolin?" the king asked.

"We must expect it every night, sire. But especially tonight."

No one knew where Traveler was except for the deerlike fae—the elaphines, cervids and rusines. Traveler was at the very top of the center crawling tree, shielded by its branches and leaves. However, Traveler could look out across the valley, peering occasionally through a telescope that had accompanied him on every journey to the magical lands since he was a boy. The dog had changed into a part-baboon, part-spider-monkey creature and sat on a branch next to him.

The telescope was magical, so Traveler could see at night as well as day. Dusk was upon them, and he watched the darklings run around the perimeter, playing chase with each other and watching for intruders. The brownies had awakened and were making their own rounds through the camp. All the other fae were asleep, and the humans would be soon.

"Why are you up here?" The larger fairy sister flew in the air not far from him. Her smaller sister hovered next to her, smiling, with fluttering wings.

"I am not sure I can tell you. I do not think you and your sister can keep a secret."

"We can keep secrets!" the older sister said.

"I am hiding. But you cannot tell anyone."

"We can do that."

"Good. You both should go to sleep too. We have a long day tomorrow."

"Did you do something bad in the city today?"

"No. Who said that?"

"People said you did something bad there."

"Did I do something bad? Or did an elf do something bad to Mr. Hobbs, and I fixed them?"

"Yes, they killed Mr. Hobbs. But you brought him back to life with the caladrius. You could have called us. We have healing powers too."

"I know, but you were out playing."

"Yes, we were."

"Go sleep, then. There will be plenty of opportunities to talk tomorrow."

The fairy sisters became fireflies and flew away.

CHAPTER SEVENTEEN
Fae-Blood and Drows

The moon was full and high when Traveler was summoned from his treetop perch. The brownies had found his hiding place too. He neared the perimeter where both brownie and darklings—in the appearance of shadow brownies—stood, waiting.

Traveler saw the same fae woman who had approached them back in Fae-Wick. Her skin was fair, her clothing, including her cloak, all black, and she wore a necklace of brown stones.

"I never expected to see you again," he said.

"I did say I would return when I found a sorceress for your caravan. I have."

"Where is she, then? I see only you."

"I will take you into town."

"I am sure you heard what transpired earlier today."

"You know that I do not care for elves, so what transpired earlier today is of no interest to me. My interest remains in getting to Atlantea through the Trail in a caravan not commanded by elves."

"Or weak, pathetic humans."

"Them too."

"Is this sorceress also alone?"

"No, she is with her own party."

"You want me to follow you, in the middle of the night, into Arion's Spear."

"No. Arion's Spear is a city for commerce and outsiders. Residents and the more modest convene in the towns around the city. We will go to one of those towns. If you can kill high elfin knights with daggers and your dog can transform into one-hundred-foot monsters that can destroy entire castles, I don't imagine you have much to worry about. Shall we go?"

The quaint, secluded villages in the shadows of Arion's Spear's city wall reminded Traveler of similar towns of the Green Glens and Hopeshire in their own lands. There were no warriors on these quiet dirt roads, only common workers.

The fae woman led Traveler, the dog, and three brownies. They stopped at a tavern hall. The brownies stood outside as she led Traveler and the dog inside and immediately to a private room at the back. Fae establishments often had secret rooms, both physical and pocket-realms.

As Traveler stepped into the darkened room, he saw a group of hooded figures seated around a large, square table.

"Why is it so dark in here?" Traveler asked. "Are we in a dreary epic fantasy tale told at the campfire?"

The dog's eyes grew large and beamed bright lights on all of them. The people shielded themselves from the rays.

Traveler looked at the fae woman. "Drows?"

She held up her hand to calm him.

The wall torches in the room magically grew brighter, and he could see all clearly. They removed their hoods—drows. Drows were a separate elfin race with dark-bluish skin and most often white hair, though sometimes they could have dark hair. Their white eyes often had brightly colored irises. Sometimes their eyes glowed with their colors. These drows all had white hair and purple eyes. All were men except for one.

"You did not tell me you were taking me to meet with drows," Traveler said to the fae woman.

"Do you not need a sorceress for your caravan?" the drow woman asked.

"I will ask you the same question I asked her: Why would you want to join a caravan run by humans?"

The group of them laughed.

"Did I say something funny?"

"You are not mere humans," one of the drows said.

"We've heard of your caravan for months. One of your humans knocking about no less than giant-killing Erymanthian Boars at the Erymanthian Games. Today you kill six elfin knights, two elfin princes, and your shape-shifter another."

"You do know you are the heir apparent to an elfin kingdom?" the drowess asked.

"I will not be accepting."

"If it were any other who said that, I would say they were lying, but you speak the truth."

"I am a caravan master, and our caravan will continue through Titan's Trail to Atlantea without delay. I will not be taking on any drows."

"Why not?" one of the drows asked. He had the bearing of the group's leader. "We can see in your eyes that you have no ill will towards our race."

"We already have a caravan where everyone hates the phookas. No one cares for the väki. But drows? I will have a full-out insurrection.

Why do you keep your normal appearance? I know drows can appear as other elves, if they wish."

"That is not true. Elves, or drows, are not shape-shifters like your animal."

"Drows who will not hide their appearance to others. If I remember, there is a drow clan that feels such magic an offense to drow kind itself, even going so far as to wage war on those drow that do." He looked at them. "D'Shar?"

None of the drows spoke.

"You, human, have too much knowledge in your head, and not all of it is correct," a drow finally said.

Traveler looked at the fae woman. "No, I will not take D'Shar into the caravan. We would have a real war."

"We are not D'Shar!" the drowess said.

"I did not hear any of you deny it."

"Human, there are many clans and kingdoms of the drows, as with all elfin kind. We do not have time to instruct you in the history of our people over thousands of millennia. It is far more complex than you throwing out a word you know nothing of, which you heard through gossip."

The fae woman stepped between them and looked at Traveler. "All we ask is for you to allow us to join your caravan. That is all. You will have a sorceress at your command, my sword, and theirs to defend the caravan. We will follow the rules as anyone else in your caravan. When we are not engaged in our duties, we will stay in our own camps and trouble no one."

"She is right," the drow leader said. "All else is irrelevant. A caravan is an alliance of parties to combine their knowledge and strength to reach their destination as a whole in safety. You do not have to agree with every aspect of a member of your alliance. You said so yourself. You are already doing so now. Humans, elves, half-elves, sprites, giants...we hear you even have fairies. Your caravan has them all. You need a magical fighter. We have one. Do you want her services?"

Traveler's expression was not one of happiness. He reached into his cloak and pulled out a palm-sized wooden box. The drows looked at each other.

"Do you know what that is?" the drowess asked.

"You do not really believe I am going to take your word that you are a sorceress."

"Why not? I could see you from here through second sight, you sitting up in your moving tree in your camp," she said.

"As impressive as you might think that is, we need a sorceress who can fight and not just see people sleeping in trees or a mouse in the distance. Take the box, go outside, open it, close it, and then bring it back to me."

"Do you have any idea how dangerous that box is?"

"Why should I? I am not a sorcerer."

"Where did you get a Pandora box?"

"I cannot recall. Maybe there will be a clue to the answer when you open the box."

He tossed it to her, and she caught it. She gave him a look but stormed out of the room with it.

"Human, I hope you are not endangering her."

"My name is Traveler, not 'human,' drow."

He smirked. "My name is Dr'as."

Traveler looked at the fae woman. "What is your name?"

"Are you convinced she will be successful?"

"You seem to be."

"I am...Ursi."

"Why did you hesitate?"

She watched him without answering.

"You are a fae-blood of the bear clans. Why are you so secretive about that?"

"We are private people."

The door opened. Immediately they heard heavy breathing. The drowess walked to Traveler with an angry face. She was drenched, and one of her hands was locked in a contorted death grip.

"What happened?" the drow leader yelled. He took her hand and tried to pry open her fingers, back to normalcy. "What did you do to her?"

She placed the dripping wet box into his hand. "I completed the task."

"What is your name?" Traveler asked her.

"Dr'amal."

"Dr'amal, you will be the caravan's sorceress. Dr'as, what is your intention? Allowing you in the caravan is not the same as being accepted."

"She will be in your main camp. The rest of us will follow alongside."

"I prefer if you follow to the rear. Our rearguard are called the Cut-Throats. They are human berserkers and warriors, a very rough-and-tumble group. You establish yourselves with them, and you will do well within the caravan. Giants do not like elves."

"They do not like drows, either, but not as bad as elves," Dr'as said.

"Good. It is settled. The women will join our women's tent—"

"If I could have my own tent—" Ursi said.

"I would need my own tent, as well," Dr'amal said. "I am a sorceress. I carry things that could be dangerous to others."

Traveler sighed. "Are we all agreed then?"

The drows and the fae-blood acknowledged with nods.

"Our steward is asleep, so I will have our brownies settle you all into the camp."

"But the brownies—" Dr'as began.

"Yes, yes, long before the age of man, drows and brownies waged war. And today, drows and sprites remain adversaries. Then change your form to look like standard elves, so they won't know. We will sort all this out tomorrow."

CHAPTER EIGHTEEN

Titan's Step

When dawn arrived, not a single elfin or fae caravan remained in the valley.

"Where did they all go?" a man asked.

"When did they go?" another asked.

Pangolin, Elman, the giants, and the archers maintained a constant vigil on the fae city. They saw no one stirring outside its walls.

"Traveler is back!" a man called out.

Hobbs stopped at the entrance to his tent. "Sir." He stepped inside.

Traveler stood at his table. He set down his cup. "Good morning, Hobbs," he greeted with a smile.

"Good morning, sir. The leadership has been waiting for you."

"How are you, Hobbs?"

"I am doing well, sir."

"No. How are you?"

Hobbs looked down. Sadness covered his face. "I can still feel the spear coming through my chest." He touched the spot. "I can still feel the pain, I mean, the shock of it."

"Mr. Hobbs, you can have more time for recovery."

"No." Hobbs snapped to attention. "No, sir. I have my duties. I can recover on my own time."

"You don't have time for much."

"That little time is plenty for me. I will not neglect my duties. Coming back from the dead is not an excuse."

"Hobbs, I do not want your mind to dwell on that. Maiden Gwyness is especially fixed on such things, but you mustn't think of it as coming back from the dead. You were dying and the caladrius bird restored you. You did not come back from the dead, because you were not dead. You were brought back to life. There is a difference. You are not some undead beast. Never think that, because it is not true."

"Brought back to life, sir."

"Exactly. It was a shock, but it is over. There was no possible way I would let our steward leave us. The men rely on you. I rely on you."

"Thank you, sir."

"I will join the front. Oh, we have new members of the caravan."

"We do, sir?"

"We have a sorceress."

"Oh, good, sir."

A single figure emerged from the castle entrance on horseback. It was a black flying horse, and it flew close to the wooded fields before stopping a hundred feet away. The man was a tall, thin elf. He approached with a feathered quill and parchment in his hands. A look of deep distress was on his face.

"Good day," he said to Pangolin and his men. "May I speak to the king of your caravan?"

King Aereth appeared with his guard and the alphyn hounds. The king saw fear in the man's face, despite his forced smile.

"Yes?"

"Good day, king. I am from the city. I wish to speak and personally extend my deepest apologies for the events of yesterday."

"An elf killed one of our men for no cause," Pangolin said, "or thought he did."

The man swallowed hard. "Yes, and he paid for his offense with his life, and so did all those responsible."

"How can I help you, sir?" King Aereth asked.

"This is both a delicate matter and a serious one. One of the men was the crown prince to a major elfin kingdom. Because he took part in the ignoble treachery and died in battle, his royal seat was forfeited to the one who killed him in noble battle. However, that person, those for just cause, is a human and—"

"And what, sir?" the king asked.

"King, you can understand the situation. If this human were to claim that crown, it would inflame its kingdom to war. It would engulf the entire region in war. Many would die."

"Your elf with no honor kills our man, and gets himself killed, and you talk to us about war," Pangolin snapped.

The king put a hand on Pangolin's shoulder to calm him.

"I have no words, sir."

"Is it common for your city dwellers to greet visitors with a spear through the chest?"

"No, sir. It is unheard of."

"Then why did they do it?"

"We do not know, sir."

"That is your answer? You have no answer?" Pangolin asked.

"What is it that you ask?" the king asked the elf.

"Please, king, if you could speak with your man, Traveler, and have him relinquish his claim to the seat in writing. I have the royal papers here. We could set all this right. Please—"

The elf saw Traveler nearing the perimeter with his dog. They turned to watch him too. Traveler joined them, glaring at the elf.

"Good day, Master Traveler."

Traveler ignored the elf. "He has a proposal, Mr. Traveler," King Aereth said.

"What is that in your hands?" Traveler asked.

"It is the royal papers for you to sign and relinquish claim to the royal seat of the elfin kingdom of Raindark."

Traveler stepped to the man, scaring the elf, to grab the paper. He signed it and handed it back to the elf.

"We came to your wretched city for a map. A map! We were met by a pack of elves. One threw a spear into the chest of one of our men for no cause whatsoever. Any kingdom that breeds such elves is a kingdom of such dishonor and lowliness that it should never be recognized by the lands of humans, fae, or any other realm. You tell its king that I expect never to see him or any of his kind ever again for the rest of my life or the lives of humankind. If we should, I will send my dog, or my descendants will send his descendants to that kingdom. It will take the form of a beast the size of the sun, and it will burn the skin from the bones of every man, woman, and child within that place and turn to dust. Is that clear?"

The elf swallowed. "Yes."

"As for Arion's Spear, I will never set foot on these lands again. The last time I was here, I was quite young, and it was a horrid place then too. I will never return. And I will tell everyone never to come here either. It may have been a noble city once, a long time ago, but no more and never again."

"I am truly sorry for the events of yesterday, sir. We will make available all the maps you need for your journey. I also wish you to know that Raindark will face severe repercussions. This matter is far from over for them. They will never set foot in our city again. I hope you can one day forgive us because we had no hand in their evil deeds."

"But they have their royal seat back, so your task is done."

"I was appointed to this task, sir. I did not volunteer. You have graciously returned their seat out of the compassion of your heart, but they have none to take it. Their king is elderly and near his end days, and you killed the royal heirs and possible noble successors. The kingdom is no more. What your compassion has allowed is for a quiet and orderly transition of power. None of that would have happened with a human as head of their royal court. It will occur. You, sir, have done the honorable thing, and I wholly agree with you that it is for a very dishonorable kingdom and court."

"Yes."

"Thank you, sir." The elf lifted the parchment. "Many people will live because of your forgiveness. Do know that we will spread the word and make sure all that we have influence over will treat you and your caravan with due respect."

"Thank you, sir," King Aereth said.

The distress in the elf's face was gone, the burden from his shoulders lifted. He nodded, smiled, and turned to walk back to his flying horse.

"And thank you, too, Mr. Traveler," King Aereth said.

"No need, sire. We came here so our Titan's Caravan could complete its fantastic journey to the fabled kingdom of Atlantea for treasure and adventure. Hopefully, now we can do so and not be pulled into any more battles, treachery, scandals, or—no offense, sire—affairs of royal politics and intrigue."

"No offense taken, Mr. Traveler. I never dealt with it personally. I simply delegated that tedious burden to others."

"That is why the men and I get along so well with you, sire."

The king laughed.

Traveler glanced at Lady Aylen. "Maiden Gwyness, did I not tell you the princess would recover in time to hear me say the following? Mr. Pangolin, we set out in half an hour."

The berserker said triumphantly, "Yes, sir."

◆◆◆

Traveler stood in his tent with an open chest, examining the contents. The elfin administrator had the maps delivered promptly. The dog kept poking his head in the container, ensuring only papers were within.

"Sir."Traveler heard Hobbs's voice.

"Come in, or send them in."

Lady Aylen entered. The dog looked up at her, eyes squinting.

"Well, I am a full elf now," she said to the dog.

"So, Mr. Traveler, you were a royal yourself but gave it all up out of principle."

"Princess, it is that kind of camp. Commoners to royal all rubbing shoulders here. However, I will leave royalty to you and the king. I have no interest. I am busy enough with my other endeavors. How can I help, princess? Are you feeling well? I will continue to pester you until you master your exercises."

"Yes, Mr. Traveler. Your exercises."

"For your benefit, princess, not mine."

"I came to say, Mr. Traveler—I have not had a chance to say—"

"Yes?"

"Thank you. I cannot say I am a good patient. But I can say that I could not have had a better healer through my ordeal. I do not think I would have survived without your aid and guidance."

"You are a strong woman, princess, whether as a human or an elf. You would have survived."

"It is kind of you to say, but I am not so sure. There were days in the pocket when the only thing that kept me going was waiting until you appeared the next day. I am not one to rely on anyone. Gwyness can tell you that. But I was able to rely on you."

"I learned early in my days that healing is much more than the physical work of attending to fevers, sores, and wounds. Healing science includes the mind and the soul. Even more paramount to the healing arts is simple compassion."

"Yes. If our Mr. Gresham can attain a fraction of your skill, he will be a great healer indeed. Thank you, Mr. Traveler. I wanted to say it personally."

"Yes, princess. You are quite welcome."

She put a hand on his arm and looked into his eyes with a smile.

They heard yelling from outside.

"Now, what is it?" Traveler cried out as they ran from the tent.

Pangolin held at bay all six enraged Antaean giants, a pack of yelling hoofed fae, all the brownies, and all the pech. Two of the three crawling trees had closed in, with the angry fairy sisters hovering above. In the center of the chaos were the drows, their sorceress in the center.

"What is happening here?" Traveler yelled.

"There are demonic elves within our camp!" a brownie yelled.

"Drows are not demonic and not from the Nether-Lands, and you know that!"

Traveler put his body between the drows and the other fae. He noticed that the fae-blood woman and the darklings stood with the drows.

"Why have you brought them here?" one of the giants asked.

"Listen, all of you! The caravan needs its own sorcerer or sorceress. As of today, we have one. I am not interested in ancient rivalries or hatreds."

"They were on the dark side!" another giant yelled.

"In this great war, it was the fairies versus the elves?"

"Yes, and the drows fought on the side of the fairies."

"And the sprites sided with the elves?"

"Yes."

"This is about elves?"

"Yes, we don't like elves," one of the giants said. "No offense to the princess."

"None taken," Lady Aylen said.

"Or you half-elves."

"We are human," Elman said.

"But the giants have never fought the drows," Traveler began again with a straight face.

"We have fought elves."

"But not drows?"

"Yes, drows. They are elves."

"But the drows and elves are ancient enemies, bitter enemies after many wars."

"No!" fae yelled.

"Oh, the war between the fae, sprites, and giants."

"Yes!"

Traveler folded his arms and stared at them. The giants, sprites, and fairies looked at each other.

"When will the new war between your races begin? The men, human men, do need some diversion. We can all watch from the side with cups of ale as you pummel each other."

"No, we're talking about the other war," a brownie challenged.

"The other war? Oh, my mistake. Which ancient one was this? There are so many."

"The War of Light and Darkness."

"Oh, that one, yes. Where drows fought on the side of the light and the night elves fought on the side of the darkness?"

"No! Drows and night elves are—"

"Are what? Are not the same race. Were there not dark fae on the side of the darkness—fairies, sprites, and other elves? Oh, there were drow, but clans on both sides."

"How do you know it wasn't their clan?" a pech asked, pointing at the drows.

"I don't, but obviously neither do you! When I traveled in Faë-Land as a boy, do you know how many times I heard fae make jokes about us warring humans? You all are worse than us. This is Titan's Caravan, and it is made of many races, races that dislike each other, and races that outright hate each other. None of that matters. We have work to do! Anyone who doesn't like it can leave. If I don't care our sorceress is a drow, then neither should you, and I don't think any of you will be complaining if she happens to save your disagreeable lives with her magic. Fae? Humbug! I am going to start calling the men and half-elves fae, and you, humans. Go back to work humans!"

Grunts, groans, and other sounds of displeasure rumbled as the fae returned to their individual camps. The two trees crawled back to their posts, while the two fairies turned into fireflies and flew away.

King Aereth looked at Traveler and chuckled. A smiling Gwyness patted Hobbs on the back.

"I am so sorry, sir," Hobbs said. "One of the drows was coming to speak with you, disguised as a human, magically that is. One of the fae saw him, snapped his finger, and the drow appeared as normal. The fae came at him. The other drows appeared around him. The whole camp—"

"It is all settled, Mr. Hobbs. No harm was done. I have full confidence in your steward abilities to manage all the many disparate factions within our camp and to keep them from strangling each other. Wait until we have other fae parties join our caravan. Then life will become interesting."

"My life is interesting enough, sir."

"Yes it is, Mr. Hobbs. You can find that drow who wanted to speak with me."

"Yes, sir."

Hobbs gestured the drow leader, Dr'as, to enter Traveler's tent. The dog sat in the corner, watching him closely. All elves, including drows, instinctively tried to connect with any animal they saw, but this never worked on the dog. Dr'as returned his attention to Traveler.

"Thank you for calming the others."

"It seems today is the day for me to receive thanks from all kinds of elves. I did it out of principle, not necessarily for you."

"Of course."

"Mr. Hobbs said you had been on your way to see me."

"Yes. I was told that in the city of Fae-Wick you encountered a spell-talker."

"We did. I killed it before it was able to do its evil."

"What are your theories regarding it? They are not fae."

"What are they then?"

"The word makes us bristle since it is often incorrectly attributed to us, though not true. Spell-talkers are demons."

"How do you know?"

"My people—"

"You mean the D'Shar."

"My people have much experience fighting practitioners of dark magic, which also has included demons."

"That gate to their realm is guarded by all the races of fae."

"Which does not mean a few cannot slip through."

"Do your people have special knowledge of demons?"

"No. The knowledge we possess is no different than the fairies, sylphs, and high elves. We do, however, have experience with spell-talkers. These demons are servants of others. If its goal was to kill your party, then it was sent there to do so."

"Then, I have no suitable theories."

"Is there anyone that your party encountered along the way, who would have such power? Such beasts cannot be summoned recklessly and commanded by anyone."

"There was one, no, actually four, but they no longer live."

"I bring this to your attention because some in my group feel that the Raindark elves did not single out your steward to kill at random or out of malice for your human-fae caravan. Rather, it was for other motives. Motives that I do not know."

"Are you concerned?"

"I am, and so should you be. Since you say there is no one out there who harbors ill will towards you, we are in the shadow of an unknown enemy on this journey. That is more cause for concern. "

"Then we will all be on guard, as we should be."

"Yes. Thank you for seeing me. You are the first human I ever met that knew the difference between drows and night elves."

"One of my many unfortunate encounters in the past."

"How did it end?"

"The drows and I won. The night elves did not."

Dr'as smiled. "Have a good night, Master—no—you humans say… Mr. Traveler."

"Good night, Mr. Dr'as."

The work of the past weeks had been brutal on Estus. The lizards were still growing and it was his task, along with some seven hundred fifty men, to make the reptiles the equivalent of a living wall. They had their own pocket, as did the väki, Tree Shepherds, fenodyree and kirins, and the one maintained by the Cut-Throats for training. In

Estus's pocket was a magical furnace with their own smithy for him to do all the caravan's forging and metalworking.

Often, he and the men remained after work in a make-shift camp, and slept when they could. The men were sleeping as he was, but something woke him. He was lying on his stomach, and he lifted his head to look around. Their realm was a small castle that only housed the furnace and smithy, encircled by water, and a vast plain of golden grass. Quillen had tried to get them to take giant slippers, but they so often did without a bath before they crashed to the ground to sleep that they did not want to dirty the new bedding.

Estus lay his head down again, but it bothered him that he could not determine what woke him. When he slept, he did not get up, and he was not a man aroused by loud noises. What could it be? He lifted his head and looked around the camp of men again. He saw nothing strange about the men. There was no other presence in the realm he could see. None of the fae could get into their realm to play pranks on them. He was about to lay his head down again but instead sat up properly. He had to figure it out. This was the magical lands. Traveler had told him many times: If he sensed something was amiss, find out what it was; even humans had uncanny senses, and it could be a matter of life and death. But he felt sleepy.

There was a noise! He looked up to see a large lime-green bullfrog in the distance. It croaked again. Estus gasped as he realized the magic bracelet Traveler had given him many months ago was glowing red and vibrating.

Estus burst out of the invisible entrance to the realm. It was dark outside but well lit by torches. The men were sleeping, but as he ran to Traveler's tent, he noticed there were no sentries. The lizards were asleep over their heat pits. He ran into Traveler's tent. Immediately he stopped and saw the dog was floating in a kind of opaque sphere.

Inside the sphere, the dog seemed to be violently shape-shifting into all kinds of forms.

"Mr. Traveler!" Estus grabbed Traveler from his bed. "Wake up!" He shook him, then again more vigorously. Estus let him fall to the ground and ran to his healer's bag. "I have seen you use this before, Mr. Traveler." He ran to the caravan master and put the tip of a tiny bottle under the nostril. Traveler's eyes opened.

Estus closed the top of the bottle, set it on the ground, and began shaking Traveler again. "Mr. Traveler!"

Traveler shook his head. He grabbed Estus's tunic and looked at the man, then at the glowing red bracelet. Traveler jumped to his feet, seeing the dog in the floating sphere.

"Hit the sphere with the bracelet!" Traveler yelled as he ran from the tent.

Estus got up and did so. The sphere exploded as it disappeared, knocking the weaponsmaster to the ground. Estus heard a strange yell, and as he looked up, his eyes widened. The dog was in a strange alien form that he had never seen before—a round mass.

Traveler entered the women's tent. He reached the female half-elves in the center, all sleeping close on their mats under blankets. He grabbed their wrists and then under their necks. He listened to their breathing. He jumped to do the same for Lady Aylen on her trussing bed. Estus ran in.

"Check Maiden Gwyness! Wake her!"

"Maiden Gwyness!" Estus grabbed her shoulders. She awoke immediately, and screamed. "No, it's me." He let her go, and they watched Traveler run from the tent.

"What is—"

"Something is very wrong," Estus said to her.

Traveler returned to the tent with his hands cupped together in front of him. He walked around the female half-elves and set on the ground what looked to be a pile of wet leaves. Traveler ran from the tent again.

"What is happening?" Gwyness asked.

Traveler returned with his healer's bag and two black pots.

"Get up!" he yelled at Gwyness. "Estus, I need a fire under both of these pots now. Gwyness, I need them both filled to the top with water. Put one pot at the feet of the half-elves, the other at the end above their heads, but keep it away from the pile I left there."

Traveler dumped out his bag on the ground as Estus and Gwyness worked quickly.

"You light the fire! I'll get the water." Estus ran from the tent as Gwyness gathered tinder from the tent supplies and in quick time had fires aglow at both ends. Estus returned with the pots, water sloshing around in both.

"Wait!" Gwyness said, grabbing a metal fire stand to set over the fires at each end.

The second Estus set the pots down, Traveler threw yellow powder into each. The pots were instantly boiling, and clouds of yellow smoke erupted from them.

"Gwyness, get the princess out of her bed and into the smoke. Estus, I need every pot you can get, and as you get them, kick one of the human men to wake them and help you. Run!"

Gwyness struggled to drag Lady Aylen from her bed and to the ground, but she did it. As she pulled Lady Aylen to the smoke, which began filling the tent, she glanced at the pile of wet leaves. They began to change and become more humanoid.

"Gwyness!" Traveler called. "Leave them! I need you to run outside and wake the men. Do whatever you must to do, but get those men in here!"

Gwyness ran, almost crashing into a returning Estus, who held a pot of water in each hand.

"I have them, sir."

"Get a fire under them."

Estus worked in a corner. The water had just begun to boil when Traveler threw powder into each, and clouds of yellow smoke erupted.

"Take one and set it in the female drow's tent, then the second in the other fae woman's tent, then bring King Aereth in here."

Estus ran from the tent. Hobbs appeared, then Quillen.

"I need pots or containers filled with water! Go!"

The two men ran.

Traveler frantically mixed his powders. Estus appeared, helping the king inside the tent.

"I'm awake," the king said to Estus. The weaponsmaster left again.

"Sire, I need you to fetch Mr. Gresham, his healing bag, and all our healing supplies. He will know."

The king ran from the tent. Men entered with buckets of water.

"Those will do!" Traveler tossed in powder, which erupted. "Take those to the camp with the giants, and get them over a fire. Hurry! I need more men!"

More men did arrive, a stream of them, and Traveler sent them to the camp of the giants, the camp of the male half-elves, the pocket with the väki, the brownies, who were sprawled around the general camp, the darklings, who were still in their pocket, the pocket of the Tree Shepherds, and the camp of the drows. In the pocket of the kirin, the fenodyree were asleep and under the dark spell, but the dragon-horses were not, and the hairy fae were soon restored.

Gresham and the king had arrived to help Traveler mix his powder. Every pot, bucket, bowl, and cup was used to blanket the entire camp, including the giant fae lizards, the alphyns, and the chamroshes. Under the magical dome of the circle, the yellow smoke permeated every inch.

The female half-elves were revived and sat quietly, as did Lady Aylen. The pile of leaves was actually both of the fairy sisters, who were fully awake but dreary eyed, and they were without wings. Traveler could see their curiosity, so he picked them up and set them on the table to watch him work.

Dr'amal, the drow sorceress, walked into the tent. She stood over Traveler, who continued working. He now directed the men to toss fresh powder into the water of every container in the camp.

"What is this called, this use of healing powders?" she asked.

"We are saved once again by Mr. Traveler and his vapors," Lady Aylen said.

"It has many names but was taught to me under the names of *arbularyo*, *kulam*and *pagkukulam*. Magic of the earth, herbs, and candles," he answered.

"The use of nonmagic means to counteract the effects of dark magic," Dr'amal said. She looked at Gresham. "Do you know of this?"

Gresham shook his head. "I may have the title, but Mr. Traveler is the true healer of this caravan."

"No, Mr. Gresham. You are the healer, and you will earn your title, even if you must study all day."

"I am happy to do so, Mr. Traveler, and I will."

"I know of no fae healers who know of this healing art," Dr'amal said. "Was it taught to you by fae?"

"Human sorcerers."

Dr'as and a few other drows entered the tent. The drow leader looked at Traveler and the king. "Do we talk now or in the morning?"

"In the morning," Traveler answered.

"No one will dare sleep now," Dr'amal said.

"True, but after I clean up the mess, I plan to. We can talk after I get a proper rest."

"Mr. Traveler, where is your dog?" Lady Aylen asked.

"He is quite upset, so I thought it best to keep him away from everyone until he calms himself."

◆◆◆

Lady Aylen stood outside the women's tent, staring out past the perimeter into the woods. Her eyes caught sight of it again in the distance: the large lime-green bullfrog. It hopped away into the woods.

◆◆◆

The leadership was meeting—but not in the king's tent, outside in the open, and not just the humans, all the fae leaders. The men of the camp would be able to observe from their places, seated in the camp.

"What happened?" Traveler asked their sorceress.

Her eyes looked more human; the purple of her irises was muted. "It was a deliberate magical attack of tremendous power. The purpose was to kill all those not human within the camp."

Greenwig spoke, the other Tree Shepherds stood beside him. "We will magically enhance the circle that your man Hobbs creates. What was done last night will never be repeated. Our protective circle will be as three."

"Can we sense such a thing before it were to happen?" King Aereth asked.

"No," Dr'amal replied.

"How far away was the spell cast?" Traveler asked.

"We do not know," she answered.

"Do we know anything about the spell-caster?"

"No, other than what has been said."

"That is not an acceptable answer," Pangolin said. "All our fae members were almost killed, and we know nothing of those responsible."

"We were incapacitated as well, or I would have been able to cast a spell to find out."

"How were you roused, Mr. Traveler?" Lady Aylen asked.

"I put a special bracelet on Mr. Estus to shield him from dark magic and warn of any in his vicinity. He woke me."

"So, again, Mr. Traveler was our salvation. If he had not had the foresight to fit Mr. Estus with a magical bracelet, and if he was not skilled in his vapors, we would all be dead."

"All the fae would be dead," Dr'amal corrected.

"Leaving the humans alone," Lady Aylen said. "Is a trap waiting for us?"

"I cast a spell to fly the entire region, and there is nothing," Dr'amal said.

"We have spoken to all the trees and animals in this area, and nothing awaits us of an evil nature," Greenwig said.

"The fairies also flew across the area and saw nothing," Traveler added.

"Is that all? There is nothing more to be done?" Pangolin asked.

"I must concur with Mr. Pangolin," King Aereth said. "This is not acceptable. Fae-Wick, Arion's Spear, and now an attack last night."

"What kind of wizard or wizardess could do this?" Traveler asked, looking at the fae.

"I suspect more than one," Dr'amal said.

"Why?" Traveler asked.

"A feeling. Your vapors dissipated the power of the magic, but my sense of it was that the magic that attacked the elves and half-elves was different from the attack on the giants then the fairies then the sprites, in general, and the fae animals. Also, your dog was enclosed in a sphere but was not asleep."

"Multiple wizards."

"We are a camp of not just humans but fae," Lady Aylen said with annoyance. "Fae that can do magic, and we cannot find out who attacked us? That strikes me as pathetic. A non-magic human is doing all the magic of the camp for fae and sorceresses alike."

"We were all in a death-sleep, princess," Dr'mal countered. "All us fae, including you. And our Mr. Traveler is no ordinary nonmagic human, but I take your point."

"We will convene amongst ourselves all the magic-practicing fae," Greenwig said to Lady Aylen. "No other magic attack will be able to cross the circle of our camp again, no matter how powerful the spell."

"Convene? A human meeting?" Traveler asked, with a grin.

"We fae have never understood why you humans must meet at a set time to talk when you can simply talk. It must be a peculiarity of your short-lived race. We will convene, and our circle will never be breached again."

"Also, if Mr. Traveler can devise a method of boiling herbs to act as a magic spell, we should all strive to be equally creative," Dr'amal added.

"Good. Action and what sounds like the beginning of a plan," Lady Aylen said.

"Multiple wizards. What does that mean to you, Mr. Traveler?" The king saw the look in their caravan master's face.

"Sire, there is nothing to do at the moment. Suspicions are all we have."

"Are we saying the Four Kings are alive?" Lady Aylen asked directly.

"The Four Kings are dead," Traveler said.

"You seem quite sure, Mr. Traveler. Their allies, then, in this land?"

"Perhaps, sire. I do not know."

"The Four Kings?" the drow leader asked.

"The Xenhelmians," the drow sorceress said to him. "You are quite certain of their death?"

"I was the one responsible for their inglorious end."

"You know of them?" King Aereth asked the drows.

"We do, king," the drow leader said.

"We must set out," Traveler interjected to end the line of conversation. "I want to put as much distance between Arion's Spear and us as possible. In the next fae towns and cities, we will begin taking on other parties. We can stand here all day, wondering and talking about the Four Kings, or we can go. We have a caravan, they do not. Our journey is not even halfway done, and with or without them, there is still much danger.

"Mr. Pangolin, get your vanguard ready. Dr'amal, you will walk with Mr. Hobbs and his guards."

"Ursi will be my guard," the drowess said.

Traveler glanced at the fae-blood. "Everyone else already knows their place. Mr. I-wulf, you will have the further benefit of a team of drow archers for the rearguard."

"Yes, Mr. Traveler."

Traveler looked out at the men. "Yes, many in our caravan could have died last night. It won't be the last time. However, we can stop and turn back now."

"Absolutely not, Mr. Traveler!" Lady Aylen yelled.

The men's laughter had changed the mood, and with the playing of music by the Brothers Brimm, both human and fae were back in good spirits as they marched.

"Mr. Traveler, what is our next stop? And will we have our full caravan before then?" King Aereth asked.

"Sire, whoever wishes to join us can do so as we move. We will stop once before Titan's Step." Traveler saw the smile on Lady Aylen's face. "Yes, princess, the second official marker on our journey."

"Do we have to be concerned about those who do not officially join following us, Mr. Traveler?" the king asked.

"No, sire. After we set off from Titan's Step, we enter the Dark Forest—not to be confused with the dark forest in our lands. The Dark

Forest here in the magical lands is a far different thing. If you are not part of a moving caravan, there is no way to follow behind without being separated."

"Are there any beasts in this forest, Mr. Traveler?" Gwyness asked.

"In this one, only those in your mind."

"Where is your dog, Mr. Traveler?" Lady Aylen asked.

Traveler smiled. "He is right here with us, princess."

She instinctively knew where to look. Traveler had what appeared to be a furry garment around his neck. She saw a tiny eye watching her and grinned.

The valley of Arion's Spear was made of open fields, but beyond were thick green woodlands on either side of a wide dirt road that could accommodate a marching force of ten columns across. They were a caravan of four columns.

Pangolin held up an arm, and the caravan slowed to a stop. As Traveler moved to the vanguard, the master-at-arms carefully watched the approaching party, as did the giants and archers.

"What do you see, Mr. Elman?" he asked.

"Humanoid fae warriors, Mr. Pangolin. Well armed, light armaments, and facial tattoos."

"Good. We reached you before anyone else," the lead warrior said. The large, bald man was tall and wide. His face was lionlike, with whiskers but human ears on the side. Tattooed symbols adorned his forehead and the side of each eye.

All the men with him were animal-like in some way: cat-like, reptilian, and boar-like with tusks.

"I did not know there were fae berserkers," Pangolin said to him.

The warriors noticed Pangolin's tattoos—symbols down each cheek. "A human berserker." The lion-like warrior reached out and patted him on the shoulder. "What manner of armor is that? It is earthlike but stronger than any human metal, and of magic." All the warriors admired Pangolin's earthy armor, which was more like the scales of some kind of snake, and his matching helmet. "Very impressive. We are not impressed by your giants. We have seen Antaeans before. Their power is in their bodies not their armor. Your power is in both."

"Your armor can do the job."

"True, but the dwarvin metal we prefer is so common looking. It suits us well that we have a fellow berserker leading your caravan."

"Our guide is Mr. Traveler, here."

"Yes." Every fae berserker turned their eyes to him. "Everyone in these lands has heard of you and your shape-shifter. But you, human, seem to be the more dangerous one of the pair."

"How can we help you?" Pangolin asked.

"I am Hax, and my band of berserkers wishes to join your caravan. Provided you can answer one question satisfactorily."

"What question is that?"

"Do you actually know how to get to Atlantea?"

The men laughed. "We do," Pangolin replied.

"Good. Then if we are acceptable, we will take our place and follow."

"We have a man named Hobbs," Traveler began. "He will visit and make sure you know our rules."

"Rules. We are berserker warriors, but we will follow them nonetheless. I cannot see them being more than follow when you move and stop when you do."

"And never touch my dog," Traveler added.

The fae berserkers laughed. "We knew already. And don't touch his master either." The men laughed louder. "We heard how you gutted those elves."

Now, both human and fae berserker warriors made up the rear of the caravan as it continued on. They all would have plenty of stories to trade as they marched.

◆◆◆

The kirin steeds remained in their pocket-realm. The sensitive animals did not want to come out, and Traveler saw no reason to force them. The royals and Gwyness walked at the front of the column. Nirgund's alphyns playfully trotted around them all. The female half-elves and Nirgund followed them.

"This is quite unusual," Dr'amal said to get Lady Aylen's and Gwyness's attention. She walked just behind them.

"Where is your guard?" Lady Aylen asked her.

"Oh, I sent her to find one of the phookas."

"The darklings." Gwyness made a disgusted face. Dr'amal laughed.

"Maiden Gwyness, you must not mind them. If you do, they will do everything they can to shock you. It is in their nature to do so. I was saying, princess, that it is quite unusual for a caravan such as this to have so many women among its ranks."

"It cannot be all that unusual," Lady Aylen said. "Are not the fairies a matriarchal race? They have warriors."

"Oh yes, all of their races and clans. Merfolk, nymphs, many elfin and drow kingdoms too, like my own clan. Sprites and giants are exclusively patriarchal. However, it is not common when the party is a mix of many races."

"Titan's Caravan is unique," Lady Aylen said.

"It is indeed."

"I am not sure I understand one thing about fae. I always thought sprites were fairies, but these sprites are little people and grumpy old men," Gwyness said.

"Sprites used to be part of fairydom and elves. That was very long ago," Dr'amal said.

Ursi, the fae-blood woman, returned. Hopping behind her was one of the darklings; three others appeared behind him. Their appearance startled the alphyns who growled, and kept their eyes on them. The darklings were in the form of halfling, humanoid black rabbits.

Dr'amal glanced at them. "I know you creatures better than you know yourselves. We were all attacked by dark magic last night. You may be 'nice' phookas, but you are phookas. Phookas never let an attack go unanswered. What do you have for me?"

"We know not what you mean, sorceress," one of the darklings said as he hopped along.

"Stop with the lies. My drows heard you plotting. The half-elves may not know your tongue, but we do. What do you have?"

Lady Aylen, Gwyness, and others were intently watching the mischievous shape-shifting darklings.

"Master Traveler's magic powder saved us because it absorbed the dark magic into itself."

"And?"

"We simply swallowed the powder to use for our own spell." The darklings cackled in unison.

"Give it here!" Dr'amal reached out her hand to the one speaking. "I can create a far more powerful spell than your lot."

"Can you, sorceress?"

"What spell were you making? A seeker spell?"

"Yes, sorceress."

"Those who cast this spell are too powerful for that. They will safeguard against it. You are being too fae in your response, too predictable. Perhaps a poison and seeker spell combined, in the form of a spider, no, a snake."

The darklings began jumping up and down in a frenzy.

"What are you all talking about?" Gwyness asked.

"Give it here!"

They started jumping, and one of the darklings waddled over to her hand and vomited out a clump of saliva and yellow powder.

Gwyness turned her head away in disgust. Everyone else made sounds of revulsion.

Traveler had been walking back from the vanguard with King Aereth. The king could not believe what he was seeing. Traveler watched their sorceress with squinted eyes.

"Ah, Mr. Traveler. Your people are right. More can be done about the magic attack from last night."

"Please, whatever you and the darklings are about to do, do so out of sight of the men. And, Dr'amal, since I do know how the drows are a vengeful race, if the choice is between revealing our attackers or killing them, please choose the former. That is more valuable to us."

"I will endeavor to do the former first, and then the latter." She smiled and walked away disappearing into thin air.

The cackling, hopping darklings also disappeared, but all could still hear their words: "Snakes and spiders! Snakes and spiders!"

Everyone looked at Traveler, even the animals.

He held up his hands. "I swear they are not malevolent. And even if they are, they are on our side."

Quillen had ran to one of the general carts being pulled by a pech to get his magic book from his things. He returned to the front as the little bearded men with bright red conical caps waited on the side to file in behind the new fae berserkers who had joined the caravan.

"Gnomes, Mr. Traveler?" he asked.

"Yes, Mr. Quillen."

The lad was so happy.

"Mr. Quillen, you have your duties to attend to," Hobbs said. "Put that book away. You can do your sketches and writings at the end of your work day."

Quillen groaned and dragged himself back to his cart.

"How many parties do you think will join us, Mr. Traveler?" King Aereth asked.

"Could be several, sire. Once we get to Titan's Step, we will see what we have before we set out."

"So, Mr. Traveler, we will make night camp once more?" Lady Aylen asked.

"Think of it, princess, as when we set out across Titan's Bridge. There is a good time, bad time, and best time to cross. We should start at dawn. By now, every fae who has been observing us and deciding whether to join will make their final decision today. These gnomes who joined us actually came across us back in Fae-Wick. They have been following us in secret to be sure."

"How long will it take us to get through this Dark Forest?" Lady Aylen asked.

Traveler hesitated in his answer.

"Mr. Traveler, enough. We do not want to hear something like 'three days or three weeks.' A simple answer will suffice."

King Aereth chuckled. "Yes, caravan master. What is the answer?"

"It should take us about seven days."

"There, Mr. Traveler, that was not a difficult answer at all."

"But—"

"No buts."

"But the Dark Forest is an enchanted forest. Its environment affects human and fae in different ways."

"What does that mean, Mr. Traveler?" Gwyness asked.

"Why cannot things be simple, Mr. Traveler?" Lady Aylen asked.

"We are not in the land of simple, princess. Think of the Dark Forest as Titan's Bridge, the Mist Mires, and the Howling Mountains all in one. The enchantment is to make you see things, hear things, and feel the presence of things that are not there. As we move through, after a time, there will be no outside sunlight at all. Some humans in perpetual dark do not behave at their best, and it is even worse for fae, especially fae of light. Most of our fae are not the brownies or darklings."

"We will have plenty of torches around us then," Gwyness said.

"That we shall."

◆◆◆

Gresham marched alone in the center of the caravan. His eyes took notice of the colorful fae lizards who he was certain were much larger today than yesterday.

"Mr. Gresham, sir."

Two men drew near. They were among the fae humans of the caravan.

"Yes, gentlemen, how can I help?"

"We have a favor to ask, sir."

"Yes, what is it?"

"Those of us humans, who have spent some years in Faë-Land have a...morbid fear of these particular lands."

"Your names are—"

"Tyfer and he is Oeric, sir, but all in our group are afraid. If you could devise a plan to have Mr. Hobbs assign us to another task until we arrive at the Dark Forest...maybe, assist Mr. Estus in his small-realm. We are not avoiding our duties, sir. We just wish to be elsewhere for the moment."

"What are you afraid of, man?"

"We are in lands that are thick with fairies and nymphs. They revel in enchanting human men and making them act against their will."

"Surely, man, we are all protected from that."

"Sir, we would feel at ease if we are nowhere in their presence," Tyfer said.

"Sir, when I was bewitched by one of them, I was a young man. When I was finally released, twenty of my years were gone." Oeric was on the verge of tears.

"Leave it to me," Gresham said. "I will handle the situation."

"Please do not let Mr. Hobbs know," Tyfer pleaded. "We are good at our duties, sir."

"And well respected by the men. Leave it to me."

Hobbs moved through the marching men, handing out pouches. His guards, Tyfer and Oeric, held a basket of them, following.

"Pixie dust, Mr. Hobbs?" one man asked as he took the pouch. All the men were amused.

"Yes, man, we will soon cross into the fields where they are fond of assaulting passersby to rob them of their possessions. Mr. Traveler said they like to fly down a man's ear canal, straight into his belly."

"Yikes! Ear into the belly!"

"Mr. Hobbs, a man's ear does not go into his belly."

Hobbs grinned at him, and the men began to laugh.

"Mr. Hobbs."

The steward turned to see their new healer approach. "Yes, Mr. Gresham."

"If I could borrow your two men, Mr. Hobbs, when you complete your task. I need the expertise of our men who have lived among the fae for my own tasks for the day. If that would be acceptable."

Hobbs glanced at them. The two men tried to hide it, but it was clear they were anxious for him to agree. "Yes, Mr. Gresham. Mr. Tyfer and Oeric will join you and the others. I am sure Mr. Nirgund and his fae hounds can stand in for my personal protection."

"Thank you, Mr. Hobbs," Tyfer said, smiling.

"Thank you, Mr. Hobbs," Oeric added.

Quillen was especially unrestrained as the caravan marched. All around them were black flies, but the insects never crossed over the flanks on either side of the giant fae lizards and hovered no closer than fifteen feet above their heads. The lad had used his telescope to look at them and after that became obsessed with them.

"They are not flies," he said.

"We know that, Mr. Quillen," Gwyness said.

"Mr. Quillen, one day your curiosity will get you whisked away by beast or being," Lady Aylen warned.

He flashed a smile, then put his pixie dust pouch in his mouth to pull his magic book from his pocket. At that very moment, a swarm of black flies was upon him. "No!" he cried.

They were no longer black flies but tiny winged men with childlike faces, pointy ears, green pointed hats, in green outfits. They tried to steal his magic book. Quillen managed to grab it as three pixies attempted to fly away with it.

Men began throwing their dust at them. In the blink of an eye, the pixies were gone. Pixies were flying into the caravan from everywhere but when met with a face full of dust, they also disappeared. Men then began jumping up in the air to throw their pixie dust high up to get at the black flies above their heads.

"What would have happened if we did not have this pixie dust, Mr. Traveler?" Gwyness asked.

"The pixies would have robbed us of everything."

"Do we not have the magic of our fae to protect us, Mr. Traveler?"

"You do, princess. Notice that not a single pixie came near you. They only went after the humans, and if we had any horses, they would all been upon them. Pixies are not evil. They're mischievous—annoying but harmless. They like to play with animals, especially horses. They also like music, dancing, and their favorite is to pester humans. The stealing is for mischief, not to steal."

"Mr. Traveler, where are these other fae villages? We saw them in the distance when we set out, but they are not here now that we march by," the king inquired.

"Sire, the villages are all around us. They are invisible. The residents are hiding the towns from us. Not out of malice or spite. They are just shy. Anyone in their towns who wishes to join us will simply come out on the road to inquire."

Lady Aylen began to laugh. "They can hide their towns from our sight. Sire, that is a bit of magic we could use in our lands. So many visiting princes, princesses, dukes, and duchesses. The endless boredom of parades and ceremonies. If we could just magically hide our castles from them, none of my sleep would be disturbed."

◆◆◆

The princess directed their attention to the vanguard up front. The caravan slowed to a stop again.

"What are those beautiful beasts?" Lady Aylen asked. They were all taken with the steeds of the three riders galloping to them.

"Peacock unicorns," Traveler replied. "But you all have beautiful beasts too."

The royals and Gwyness turned to see that their kirins were standing behind them.

King Aereth stroked the side of his dragon-horse with its golden fur and scales, and then its mane around its neck. Lady Aylen stared into the eyes of her unicorn-like dragon-horse, with its lucent blue fur and scales. She touched its long catfish-like whiskers before mounting the beast. Gwyness remained nervous about her pure-black dragon-horse with its large antlers. She still wondered why Traveler had chosen this one for her.

Traveler sat on his own beast. The dog had joined them and had taken the form of a hippogriff-like animal with a wolf-dog head instead of an eagle. They all trotted out to join Pangolin and his vanguard.

The three elves had reached them. Their unicorns were bright-blue with yellow-green horns and flowing peacock-feathered tails. The elfin female riders were clearly of royalty, clothed in white dress outfits, with white-gold bands around their foreheads.

"Good day," the center elfess greeted Traveler and the royals.

"Good day," King Aereth responded for all.

"What magnificent beasts," she said. "I used to see their like in the picture book my sisters and I would read. What are they called again?"

"Kirins," Aereth responded.

"Yes. I believe they have other names too. You can see the intelligence in their eyes. Equal to unicorns in that respect."

"At least you are not lumbering around on griffins like so many other humans," said another elfess. "So many humans fail to realize that the beasts were bred to guard treasures, castles, and land, not prance around like feeble horses."

"Yes, other humans mistake them for majestic beasts when, in fact, they are noisy creatures that appear more noble than they are. Well, we have heard so much about you. When we were told you were nearby, we had to ride out to see for ourselves. The Traveler's Caravan!"

The elfesses laughed.

"Titan's Caravan," Traveler corrected.

"Oh, look how modest he is," the lead elfess said. "No, Mr. Traveler. The caravan bears your name because, without you, there would be none."

"Did you really kill those Raindark elfin brutes with a simple pair of daggers?" another asked with a fetching smile.

"Arion's Spear is going to great effort to spread rumors that it was not Raindark at all, but a rogue party of elves that had gone mad, and you were defending your party and others from them. However, we have our own reliable eyes within their walls and heard the truth."

"You are not the average human at all. And as we can see, you have assembled far from the average caravan for a human."

"Most humans never make it past Fae-Wick," one elfess said.

"Most humans never make it past Titan's Bridge," said the other.

"You are quite the specimen, Mr. Traveler...for a human."

"I try my best."

The three elfesses laughed again. "You have accomplished much more than that. Magic sword. Other-worldly shape-shifting steed. You are like a magical human. Is your shape-shifting companion from the world we think it is?"

"I don't know what world that may be. How many moons?"

"And he is clever," the lead elf said to her sisters. "Humans, from our experience, tend to be of very low intelligence, like giants and sprites."

Pangolin was tempted to look up but did not. He did, however, hear the giants muttering under their breath. He saw the elaphine archer-warriors grinning, completely ignoring her insults.

"If I were you," she continued, "I would be *very* careful as you move through the land of elves. Take special care to avoid all celestial elves. Those star elves used to be very fond of their shape-shifting pets, but one day, as the story goes, some boy with one of those shape-shifter creatures as his own companion landed on that world, led a revolt of all those creatures, and drove away all the star elves."

"They did say that the boy was a human."

"Yes, but it was far too long ago to have been Mr. Traveler. He is still a human, and humans live far too short a time to be good for any extended period of amusement. What a shame. We have satisfied our curiosity and met the Traveler's Caravan that many stories are being told about by fae far and wide."

"Before you leave us," Traveler began, "maybe there is something you can give me."

The three elfesses laughed. "Be careful, Mr. Traveler. I am still an elfin princess of the highest birth."

"Do you have a reader by any chance? I know your attendants are nearby."

"Reader?" the lead elfess asked. "You mean for elfin children?"

"Yes."

"My, that is a strange request. Are you planning on learning elfish too, Mr. Traveler?"

"I already do."

The three elfesses gave him a confused look, then their eyes turned to Lady Aylen. They burst out laughing.

"Yes, Mr. Traveler, we shall."

The elfess yelled out something in another tongue. In moments, an elfin knight in golden armor appeared out of thin air on a flying white unicorn. He stopped near her and handed her a simple leather-bound book. She looked at it, grinning.

"I have not seen one of these in ages. My youngest niece began using it when she was a few days old, but that was many years ago. Here, Mr. Traveler," she said as she reached out to hand it to them. "You can begin your own instruction of another elfin child."

Lady Aylen bit her tongue to contain her humiliation.

"Thank you, princess," he said to the new elfess.

"Enjoy your great journey, Mr. Traveler," she said. "Maybe we will meet again in Atlantea, should you ever arrive."

The other elfesses laughed under their breath as they turned their unicorns around. The three sprinted away, with their elfin knight flying after them, and disappeared.

Traveler handed Lady Aylen the book, but she did not take it.

"Princess, I am going to say the same thing to you that I have said to Maiden Gwyness about the darklings: Do not take them seriously.

They behave the way they do to get a rise out of you. If you take no offense by it, they will stop."

Lady Aylen grabbed the book. "Another exercise, Mr. Traveler?"

"Not an exercise, princess. A mandate. When we get to Faë-Land Major, you will be able to speak elfish, or at the very least understand it. Otherwise, you will put us all in danger."

"Why would that be?"

"They will think you are a changeling or goblin masquerading as an elf. It is quite serious, princess."

"Changeling?" Gwyness asked.

"Trows and trolls. Doppelgangers. Witches."

"She will become quite proficient, Mr. Traveler. Leave it to me." Gwyness took the book from Lady Aylen. "I will keep it," she said to her lady.

♦♦♦

The pixies hung above the caravan, but it no longer drew near. However, as they marched, the men saw young barefoot women in sheer dresses appear from the woods. The women were beautiful with long hair—yellow, golden, black—down to their ankles. They looked human, but not only did each have an angelic glow, the human men felt a powerful attraction.

Traveler glanced back at their steward then at Nirgund and King Aereth. "Princess, keep a keen eye on the king. Maiden Gwyness, watch Mr. Nirgund and Mr. Hobbs. Where's Mr. Quillen?"

"I'm here, Mr. Traveler!"

"Come here, and walk next to me."

The lad joined his side. "What's wrong, Mr. Traveler?"

"I want to keep you close at hand."

"What are they, Mr. Traveler, these half-naked women walking about?"

"Lady Aylen," King Aereth said with a chuckle. "The women are not that."

"Nymphs, princess."

King Aereth's expression changed to one of worry. "Oh."

"Yes, sire, 'oh.'"

"The land-bound version of sirens."

"Yes, sire. They do not have a siren's raw power of entrancing, but they do not need to sing, only beckon from afar."

"Well, as long as we don't have to encounter sirens too."

"Unfortunately, sire, we will but that is another story. We are not even out of Faë-Land Minor yet, let alone across Faë-Land Major. We will be prepared for that, as we are prepared now."

"I hope so, Mr. Traveler, if our men don't run away with these women here," Lady Aylen said. "Will your special herbal necklaces protect them?"

"Yes, princess. Mr. Hobbs replaced all the men's herb necklaces a couple of days ago. Isn't that so, Mr. Hobbs?"

"Yes, sir."

"Mr. Hobbs, you don't look so well."

Hobbs was touching a part of his necklace above his breastplate. "I have noticed that all our fae humans are nowhere to be seen."

"Yes, Mr. Hobbs, they are helping Mr. Gresham with his...thing?"

Hobbs laughed. "Thing, sir?"

"Yes, his task 'thing.' You should have asked to join too."

"No, thank you, sir."

"Mr. Traveler," King Aereth called out to get his attention.

The nymphs had encircled the marching caravan with smiles and gestures to the men. Traveler raised his hand. The pech switched places with the lizard minders to be on the outside flanks. All four of the Tree Shepherds appeared and joined the front of the columns. Both the center and rear crawling trees spread out their leaved branches to create a protective mesh over the entire marching caravan.

There were audible groans from the nymphs as they all strolled away—some floating through the air—to disappear into the woods. The Tree Shepherds waved to one of the nymphs in the trees who wore a crown of rainbow flowers. She smiled, waved back, and disappeared.

"Thank you, Greenwig," Traveler said.

The Tree Shepherd leader nodded and led his comrades back through the columns to the center of the caravan.

"This is far too much excitement for me, Mr. Traveler," Lady Aylen joked. "I am still an elfin child, so I may need a nap soon."

They laughed.

"The women were tree nymphs then, Mr. Traveler," Gwyness guessed.

"Yes, dryads. Though, since we did not see where specifically they came from, they could have been napaeae, nymphs of wooded valleys; oreads, mountain nymphs, there is a range hidden from our eyes to our left; or hamadryads, who live in the trees themselves—though doubtful in this case.

"We will come across their races again as we travel, both water nymphs and the cloud nymphs in Atlantea. Ah, it looks as if we have passed another key test. Men and women, Titan's Caravan will begin taking on its fae parties."

◆◆◆

Suddenly, they could see the fae villages nestled in the woods on either side of the dirt path. A group of fifteen reached them first, all men in black attire and cloaks. They looked human in every way except for a tint of yellow in their brown eyes.

"Good day," the lead man greeted them.

Traveler had moved to the vanguard, and his dog returned to its "normal" form. "How may we help you?"

"We would like to join your caravan. We can pay for the privilege."

"What do you have?"

The man produced a bag. Traveler took it and saw that it was filled with both coins and gems.

"What race might you be?"

"We are fae-blood."

"Mr. Quillen!"

The lad joined them with his book.

"You are smiling, Mr. Quillen. Do you already know what I am going to instruct?"

"Make a record of everyone joining our caravan, Mr. Traveler."

"Good, lad. Take two pech with you and direct our new fae-bloods to their post. Remain with the rear guard, and we will send new ones to you."

"Yes, sir."

The next group was a party of wild woodland elf-like sprites, halflings, who bore red spears twice their size. They were a fairly large party of three hundred.

Then came more gnomes. One party wore purple conical caps and were visibly younger than the gnomes that had joined days before. With them was a group of ram-horned gnomoids—spearmen, archers, axemen. They had bulky upper bodies. There were more than fifty of them combined.

Endless smaller parties of humanoid animal men joined them: frogmen, lizard men, squirrel-like men, fae that looked like raccoons, possums, foxes, rabbits, birds, and mice. They came with their own steeds and guard animals: giant crabs minded by the frogmen, giant turtles ridden by the possum men, giant porcupines used as guard animals by the raccoon men. Some of the birdmen had large jackalopes (rabbits with antlers, as big as hounds), while other birdmen had enfields (animals with the head of a fox, forelegs like an eagle, and the hindquarters and tail of a wolf). There were also giant ducks and cranes. One surly mole-looking fae had a giant carnivorous moose as his companion. Combined, the animal-men parties were several hundred in number.

There were also more fae humans, over a hundred fifty, but they were definitely warriors and traveled with their own brood of tiny owl griffins—the size of a small dog, with the head of an owl instead of an eagle, and the wings of an owl. Traveler noted they were traveling mercenaries that most often worked for royal elfin houses.

The largest party to join them were the fauns. The caravan had stopped to speak with them without distraction. There were a few hundred of them with a large contingent of archers and bearers carrying large packs of supplies.

"Fauns and satyr are very similar, but they are not the same race," Traveler told Quillen, who made his way back to the front, eager with anticipation. "Before you ask, observe, and you tell me what you think the difference to be."

The leader of the fauns was shorter than an average man, but he was made taller by his large, curving ram horns sprouting from his head. His goatee and the hair under his nose—not quite a mustache— were graying.

All the fauns had pointed ears, legs of goats, and cloven hooves. The others had goat horns sprouting above their eyes. They were cloaked in half-robes of green forest colors. All were men, except for a single fauness that Traveler suspected was the leader's daughter.

"Are you a sorceress or healer?" he asked her.

"I am both healer and spell-caster of my flock."

"What do you offer to join the caravan?" Traveler asked the leader.

"I suppose you would want another magical weapon to add to your collection," the leader said in an annoyed tone.

Traveler looked at the fauness again. "What natural items do you carry in your healer's bag?"

"You would not know what any of them are. You are a swordsman."

"Let us see what you have." Traveler turned to Hobbs. "Have a table brought to us."

One of the pech retrieved a table from a cart. Traveler dumped out the contents of her healer's pouch. Like most fae magical pouches, it was larger on the inside than it appeared on the outside. Traveler sifted through the herbs, roots, seeds, leaves, and cloves. He picked up one and passed it under his nose.

"You have mandrake? I do not see it here."

"What kind of swordsman are you who knows of medicines?"

"A swordsman who began as a healer when he was a boy."

"Why did you change?" the faun leader asked.

"I grew tired of healing the wounded and near-dead beings sent to me. I decided to take a more direct approach in preventing any more from being sent to me in the first place."

The faun laughed.

"We will take payment in mandrake."

"Do you know how to use it? It can kill."

"I have used it before. It is one of the few items missing from my own healing bag. Having a supply from you will save us from having to stop in any city along the Trail for it."

"You are still the healer?" the fauness asked.

"No, the king, here, has forbidden me from practicing. I am simply in reserve."

"Do not blame me, Mr. Traveler," King Aereth said playfully. "We all feel guide, caravan master, and swordsman are more than enough duties for you."

"I will give you a supply," the fauness said.

"Good. It is settled. You are accepted into our caravan," Traveler said.

Titan's caravan had accepted all parties, both large and small, that had waited to do so. On the horizon, they saw the ridge of the Dark Forest. At least a few hours remained in the day, but Traveler instructed Hobbs and Pangolin to set up camp.

◆◆◆

When dusk was upon them, Hobbs summoned the leadership to gather in the king's tent.

Traveler stepped out of his own tent and immediately noticed a heated exchange between the fae woman, Ursi, and the new fae-blood men who had joined. They noticed him and quieted down, but he marched to them anyway.

"What is happening here?" he asked.

"We did not know you had another member of our kind in your caravan," one of the men said.

"Is that a problem?"

"Not at all," he said with a false smile.

"What is your clan?" Traveler asked him.

"We...are fae-blood."

"You are wolf clan. She is bear clan. That means you will be plotting against each other, and I cannot allow that—"

"No," Ursi interrupted. "There will be no problems at all. I will stay in my place. They will stay in theirs beyond the rearguard. We will have no contact with each other."

"Is that true, or are you simply telling me that?"

"I do not lie," she said.

"We will have no contact with each other," the fae-blood said, and then led his pack away, heading to their personal camp.

Traveler sighed. Ursi left him, returning to her tent.

♦♦♦

"So the fae leaders of our main camp will never join us?" King Aereth asked.

"No, sire. In fact, none of the fae we bring on the caravan will ever want to attend our night meetings. Such gatherings are a very human thing. Fae regard human meetings as silly. You heard the leshy."

"Will I grow to think so, too, Mr. Traveler?" Lady Aylen asked.

"No, princess, you were raised human from birth. Your view will always be human. No way to change that, no matter how elfin you become. Well, we humans and elf will hold our silly meeting."

Pangolin sat with I-wulf and Nirgund, stroking his alphyns. The hounds inspected person and tent. King Aereth, Lady Aylen and Gwyness sat on another side. Hobbs and Quillen sat next to Traveler to form an almost-triangle formation.

"Not even our drow sorceress?" Lady Aylen asked.

"Not even her. How do we feel about the new parties to the caravan?"

"Excited!" Quillen answered, getting laughs.

"A more productive assessment, please, Mr. Quillen."

"We have more warriors," Pangolin answered. "Fae berserkers, human mercenaries with owl griffins."

"Those are such delightful beasts," Gwyness said. "We should have some."

"They are not pets, Maiden Gwyness. Those delightful beasts can rip a human to shreds, just like their larger, eagle counterparts. Go on, Mr. Pangolin."

"The fae-blood men, I suspect, are good warriors too."

"The wooded elves do not look fearsome, but an elfin archer is an elfin archer," I-wulf said. "And the fauns too. They look to be fearsome archers like our own deerlikes."

"Deerlikes, Mr. I-wulf?" Traveler asked. "The fae term is deer-folk, deer-people, or even hoofed fae. Our specific archer-warriors are called elaphines."

"And all those animal-like fae with their giant animals," Nirgund added. "That is an army right there."

"All the others are passengers," Pangolin said.

"The horned gnomoids are fighters, too, and the gnomes can do magic—simple, but sometimes that is all that is required," Traveler said.

"I like those squirrel men," Quillen said.

"Squirrel men. Why?" Traveler asked.

"They look cuddly. I had a squirrel once that I took care of as a boy."

The group laughed. "Mr. Quillen, they are not squirrels or pets, and you are still a boy," Traveler said to him. "How often do I have to say that all fae can be deadly? Those squirrel men have claws as sharp as any dagger. The same goes for their incisors. They can rip apart any of our exposed flesh. Do you see how fast they move? They are warriors. Be on guard with all fae, especially since you are determined to speak with all of them for your bestiary book."

"Mr. Traveler, what is the difference between fauns and satyrs?" Quillen asked. "Are they not the same?"

"Satyrs are far more aggressive and war-like. We will come across them when we reach Centaurian Fields. Fauns are peaceful by nature, though the ram-horned ones can fight as forcefully as any satyr."

"I must say, Mr. Traveler, that we could not be more pleased with the caravan. What are our numbers now?" the king asked.

"More than eleven thousand?" Pangolin asked, looking at Quillen.

The lad nodded. "Probably closer to twelve thousand."

The king looked at Lady Aylen. "More than what we had when we left our lands, but now nearly half are fae."

"Yes, very impressive," Lady Aylen said. "Are we lacking in anything, Mr. Traveler, that prevents us from continuing on to our final destination without delay?"

"Nothing at all, princess. Tomorrow at dawn, I will consult our maps. Then we move on to the Dark Forest. From there, we move to the Flying Forest and onto Centaurian Fields, marking the threshold of the Trail from Faë-Land Minor to Faë-Land Major."

Traveler turned to their weaponsmaster. "Mr. Estus, you have been laboring in obscurity of late, though your work has been of paramount importance. Tell everyone what you and your men have been doing besides armoring our ever-growing giant lizards."

"Thank you, Mr. Traveler. Over the past several days, we have also been collecting sunlight in preparation for entering this Dark Forest. Mr. Traveler had me acquire a huge supply of small clear orbs back in Fae-Wick. They are magically constructed. One simply opens them up in the sun and closes them, capturing the sunlight itself within them. We will have their use, as needed, for the entire length of our march within this Dark Forest."

"Very good, Mr. Estus. I think that our silly human meeting can come to an end. However, before it does, I want to impress upon all of you, as the leadership, the following principles you must never forget. Our great steward does so with the men."

"Yes, Hobbs. Hear! Hear!"

"I do so with you. On the caravan, be aware of your surroundings at all times. Being in the circle, under the branches of a crawling tree, or standing next to a sorceress does not free you of that rule. Notice everything, even the smallest things. If something seems strange or out of place, no matter how small, tell someone. That is how we stay alive and keep the men of the caravan alive.

"Everyone, get a good night's rest. We leave at dawn for the next leg of our journey."

♦♦♦

Lady Aylen rose before dawn, relaxed and refreshed. She was finally learning to sleep through the night with her enhanced elfin hearing and senses. Gwyness and the female half-elves had already gotten up and were ready. This morning they were hurrying her to follow.

All the men were ready and waiting, in armor, with weapons, animals ready to go. Again, the colored fae lizards looked even bigger. They were all large enough for a man to comfortably ride.

Outside the circle, they saw what the men were watching. The new fae were crowded around Traveler. Their caravan master was crouched on an open patch of ground with one of his maps opened, taking up an eight-foot-by-eight-foot space. Traveler studied it carefully as he took notes in a small notebook.

The two fairy sisters stood on the map itself with their tiny sizes of less than a foot, watching him work. All around it were the fae party leaders. Greenwig stood to one corner while the brownies and the darklings—in the form of black gerbils—sat around one edge with a group of rusines in the middle. The other deerlike fae of cervids and elaphine watched behind them. All the gnomes and gnomoids sat around the other edges, with the woodland elf-like sprites. Pech, a single fenodyree, fae berserkers, fae human mercenaries, fae-bloods, and all the animal men stood around.

On the side where Traveler crouched stood the drows, Pangolin, I-wulf, Nirgund, and Ursi. Hobbs and Quillen were also at a corner with Elman and the male half-elves. Lady Aylen and Gwyness moved to the front where Traveler crouched and King Aereth stood. He smiled when he saw them. The only fae missing were the giants, who were all on sentry duty.

"Are they all watching to make sure you know where we are going, Mr. Traveler?" Lady Aylen asked.

"Something like that, princess."

"What—Mr. Traveler, the map is...things are moving on the map," Gwyness said.

"Yes, it's a magical map. It changes with every second."

"Look! There we are! Traveler's Caravan." She pointed at the map and caused laughter.

"Are we not Titan's Caravan?" Lady Aylen asked.

"Yes, an easy error to correct, princess. You can do so now."

Lady Aylen and Gwyness looked at each other. "How?" Gwyness asked.

Traveler looked up and pointed at a bird in a nearby tree. "Tell the bird, and it will tell its friends. They will tell fairies and so on. The map will change when the lands know."

The women laughed. "That cannot be true, Mr. Traveler," Lady Aylen said.

"Try it."

Gwyness stood on her tiptoes. "Bird, it is Titan's Caravan, not Traveler's Caravan!"

The bird instantly flew away.

"There, all I did was scare it away." Gwyness saw it the same time as the princess. The name of their caravan changed on the map.

"That cannot be!" she shouted.

Everyone laughed.

"That is why I must consult the map daily, often many times a day. Being a guide in Faë-Land is a far more complex matter than in our native lands. Everything can change. Remember, there are towns, even cities, that can disappear into pockets. The map can also show us of any beasts nearby."

"Beasts?" Gwyness looked at the map carefully. The tiniest fairy on the map pointed at something, and Gwyness bowed down a bit to see it. "Troll!"

"We do not have to worry about him. Trolls do not move during the day, but it was sighted there last night. We will be long gone before it wakes."

"Can you see other parties too?" Pangolin asked.

"Yes, no matter how small. All I need is a magnifying glass, and the map will tell me if they are good or evil. With all this changing information, I will chart our path through the Trail every step of the way. Though, you can see that there is scarce information on the Dark Forest. That is because there are no eyes in there, so I will be going by my own previous experience and instinct."

"Seven or eight days is it, Mr. Traveler?" the king asked.

"If we move straight through." Traveler stood. He looked at the brownies and darklings. "Your two races will be relied on by the other fae, as only you will be unaffected by the long absence of daylight." Traveler pointed at the darklings. "And do not take advantage and try to make mischief against them either."

The shape-shifters cackled. Their gerbil bodies became more humanlike so they could clap their hands.

Traveler looked at Dr'amal. "Since fae do not convene for meetings, we can share information now. Will your seeker spell work and reveal who attacked us with the death-sleep spell?"

"I believe it will, but it will take a little time."

"Spiders and snakes!" the darklings cackled.

"Are drows adversely affected by the deep darkness of the forest like other day fae too?"

"We will be fine," she replied.

"What of your humans?" one of the animal men asked. "You are known to be scared of bumps in the night." The fae laughed.

Traveler smiled. "Do not worry about our humans. We will see to them and our animals. You fae see to each other and your animals. Shall we all cross the Dark Forest?"

CHAPTER NINETEEN
The Dark Forest

The change in terrain across the threshold into the Dark Forest was quite stark. Within a couple of steps, wooded green forest and fields became thick weeded ground.

"A recurring theme with these lands is that barriers are magically created to separate lands and keep out people," Lady Aylen said to Traveler.

"Very good, Lady Aylen," King Aereth said. "I was thinking the same. The unnaturalness of the design."

"You are correct, princess. The Lands Between were created to keep fae out of our lands; humans were not civilized back then, not much more than nomadic animals, so no thought was given to the reverse. The Dark Forest was created later to separate the lands of the fairies from the lands of the elves after their war, as well as to separate the lands of land nymphs from the hoofed fae of fauns, satyrs, and centaurs."

"Mr. Traveler, I want to ask again, since we are about to enter. Are there any creatures within it?" Gwyness asked.

"You're thinking of the stories of giant spiders and snakes?" Traveler asked, with a smile.

"Yes."

"Wrong forest, Maiden Gwyness. That will be the other forest we have to pass through—the Giant Forest. But do not worry yourself. We will be well prepared. Here, in the Dark Forest, the enemy is the darkness."

Traveler had told them this was one of three magical forests they would pass on Titan's Trail, and one of them was the Giant Forest. But the black trees of the Dark Forest were giant enough. Pangolin and his vanguard entered first. Elman's enhanced sight and the enhanced hearing of the elaphine archer-warriors were immediately nullified, a fact reflected in their faces. Looking up, they could not see the tops of the trees. The only thing above them was blackness, with intermittent holes where sunlight peeked through.

The path ahead was well lit, and all could see the sunlight through the black trees, but they also knew as they ventured deeper into the Forest that the darkness would grow. After the vanguard came the lead column, all on foot, of Traveler, the royals, their guards, and the drow sorceress. Hobbs and Quillen followed, with Ursi. The main body of men, in four columns, marched after. Then came all the fae parties, some in columns, like the gnomes, but most walked along as an uncoordinated mass.

Some thought that the magic of the forest would make them see or hear things, but there was nothing of significance. After a while, the lack of any bird or animal sounds and the absence of wind through the trees and brush had been completely forgotten. A calm sense of security settled in over the caravan, so much so that the men and parties began having casual conversations as they marched.

For the first time, the two fairy sisters could not leave the caravan during the day to explore and play. They were restless and irritable; it would only be a matter of time before they started causing trouble.

One of the Tree Shepherds came for them and escorted them into their pocket-realm to play magical games to divert their attention. Very few beings had the patience to deal with two wayward fairies. Fortunately, leshies were among them.

With time, the men too began to bore. There was nothing to see: darkness above, black trees on the sides, with no life, and their never-shortening path.

"Sir, can we have the musicians play music?" Hobbs asked Traveler.

Their caravan master thought for a moment and nodded. "I do not see any harm in it. As long as they stay alert."

"Yes, sir. It will help greatly."

"Will we be stopping soon, Mr. Traveler?" Lady Aylen asked.

"Another hour and we will make a quick stop then continue on."

"Eight days within this forest, Mr. Traveler?" King Aereth sighed. "It is already quite tedious."

"Sire, there will be days in the future when the men will look upon this brief respite with fond memories."

The music from the Brothers Brimm helped lighten the atmosphere greatly. Previously, only two men had played, but this time half a dozen of them moved through the caravan, playing flutes, fiddles and psalteries—a cross between a guitar and a harp.

The caravan stopped, and the fae humans made and served food to the men. In three-quarters of an hour, they were back on the march. In better spirits with food in their bellies and the musicians entertaining them, the next half of their march did not seem quite as long. Traveler gave the signal to Hobbs for night camp to be set.

"Mr. Traveler!" Lady Aylen called out.

"No need, m'lady," one of the female half-elves said as all seven of them, kept a sleeping Gwyness from falling to the ground.

"What is wrong with her?" Lady Aylen asked. She looked at their faces. "What is wrong with all of you? You look like you want to collapse too. Set her down, and then all of you get to bed."

Lady Aylen looked around. Men were on the ground sleeping—Hobbs, Quillen, even King Aereth. Normally, the quartering staff would be quickly setting up the royals' and Traveler's tents, but they were all fast asleep.

She ran farther and gasped at the sight of all the lizard minders sprawled out on the ground. The pechs were all laughing. She turned to look the other way and saw the elaphine archer-warriors dragging Pangolin and Elman to her.

"Oh no. Not Mr. Pangolin, too. Mr. Elman? He's only half-human. Where are the giants?"

"Sleeping too," one of them replied.

"So this enchantment affects humans and giants. There you are."

Traveler walked to her, the dog at his side, leading a contingent of brownies. The brownies spread out around them—setting up the tents, picking up humans from the ground, arranging their bedding, and then putting them to bed. Hobbs had drilled the men so that they were able to light a torch or build a campfire in seconds, but none were better than these sprites. The brownies had the entire camp fully illuminated in seconds, merely snapping their fingers to light long torches or ground campfires in bright flames.

"The brownies will put all the humans to sleep, princess."

She also noticed Nirgund on the ground with all the alphyn reptilian hounds stationed around him, ensuring none drew near. However, a brownie stepped over them and lifted the royal guardsman to put him to bed, too, with the animals following.

"Why are you not affected, Mr. Traveler?"

"I am immune because I have been in the lands before. So are all the fae humans."

"The giants. Why are they affected?"

"Unlucky them. The enchantment regards them as human too. Or, more likely, it regards humans as tiny giants."

Lady Aylen smiled. "This place."

"Well, princess, you have exercises to occupy your time."

She scoffed. "I wish I were human then, so I could escape your pestering."

For her, it was the complete opposite. Lady Aylen could not sleep at all. In her tent, Gwyness and the female half-elves were deep in slumber. Lady Aylen took out the elfin reader and opened the book from her trussing bed. The page she opened was blank, but then words appeared. They were not of any human language. The book talked. She jumped, immediately closing it.

"I do not like talking animals or talking books!"

After a few moments, she opened it again. It was the same page of words. The book began talking again.

"Repeat," it said in English.

She laughed out loud. "You speak my language too. This is too much." She closed the book again. "This is too much embarrassment for me. Mr. Traveler speaks elvish, and now a magic book."

Lady Aylen lay awake on her bed and just stared at the top of the tent.

"Good, you are awake, princess." She heard Traveler's voice and turned.

Traveler entered with a tray of large glasses and a pitcher of water.

"Oh no. Not a pitcher of water again. The last time you did this trick, you turned me into an elf."

He laughed. "No, princess, that is not what happened, but if you wish to say it, I will not stop you. However, you will not be drinking anything. Another exercise for you. If you cannot sleep, you can work."

"What time is it?"

"We are a couple hours from dawn."

"I haven't slept a wink! Is this how it will be in this forest, Mr. Traveler?"

"No," he answered seriously. "Actually, the longer we stay, the more things will reverse."

"I knew it would be something unpleasant. Fae will be sleeping fools, and the humans will become sleepless zombies."

"Something like that."

"What is this fine exercise, Mr. Traveler?"

"Did you learn any elvish today, princess?"

"I do not like talking animals or talking books."

"Have you met any talking animals?"

"Yes, once, in Sirnegate. A traveling wizard visited our kingdom. He had a talking black cat. I did not like it. Reminds me a lot of your dog, but thankfully he cannot talk."

Traveler set the tray down on the ground and then began setting up the glasses. He put one in the center, two on one side, spaced out, and the other two on the opposite side. He filled each glass to the rim.

"Sit there, princess," he said as he pointed to a spot in front of the center glass.

"Mr. Traveler, I am not properly dressed. Now that I think of it, you did enter the women's tent unannounced."

"All your humans were sleeping. Sit there, princess."

"What am I about to do, Mr. Traveler?"

"You will sit there, eyes closed, and think of nothing but water. That is all. It is an exercise to clear your mind of all thoughts. No concerns, fears, or emotions. There should only be a void of serenity in your mind. If you are tempted to think of anything, think of the clear water in any one of these glasses."

"How long am I to do this pointless exercise, Mr. Traveler?"

"As long as you can."

She sat on the ground in her nightclothes, sighed, glanced at each of the glasses, then closed her eyes. "You humans are a very strange lot with your meetings and exercises."

Traveler chuckled. "Yes, princess."

As she sat quietly with her eyes closed, she had no concept of the passage of time. She did feel at total peace. Her ears picked up a sound. As her eyes opened, she was drenched with water.

"Ah!" she shouted, jumping to her feet.

Gwyness was lying on her side in her bed, smiling. The female half-elves sat huddled together in a corner, giggling.

"Who threw water at me? Why are you all looking at me and laughing? Who threw the water?"

"No one, m'lady," Gwyness replied.

"Someone did!"

"Well, then, you did."

"Gwyness, what are you talking about?"

"You truly do not know?"

"Gwyness! Know what?"

"The water. It was floating in the air."

"What do you mean?"

"The water from the glasses was floating in the air, spinning around, joining and separating, rising and falling. You were giving quite the performance, m'lady."

Lady Aylen looked at her with disbelief. All the glasses of water were empty.

"Floating? I did? What does that mean?"

"You are a water elemental, m'lady," one of the female half-elves answered. "You can control water."

◆◆◆

Quillen thought he had outsmarted the forest's enchantment. It was the third day, and the moment he saw Traveler give the signal for night camp to be set, he began running in place, waving his hands around and chanting to himself. The fairies appeared around him, laughing hysterically.

"We know what you are doing!" the largest fairy sister, Wildglow, said, fluttering near his face.

Quillen had caught the attention of the pech, who roared with laughter.

"We admire your effort, human, but it won't work," one of the brownies said, who appeared with his comrades.

Quillen continued his madness but felt himself slowing down. Then the darklings appeared in the form of thin, smiling humanoid cats with long, spiderlike arms and legs. They mimicked Quillen's movements, cackling and dancing in a ring around him.

"Snakes and spiders, spiders and snakes!" they sang.

The boy ignored them, focused with all his might on his task.

"There he goes," a brownie said.

Quillen collapsed, fast asleep, into an outstretched arm of a brownie. Other brownies chased the darklings out of the main camp back to the perimeter circle.

Every other human, save Traveler and the fae humans, had already succumbed to their enchanted sleep.

Quillen was put into his giant-slipper and covered by two brownies.

"It was a good effort, sir." Tyfer and Oeric had stepped up to take over Hobbs's night camp oversight until the caravan came out of the Dark Forest. "What was it like for you, sir, when you were last here?" Tyfer asked Traveler.

"Enchanted sleeping for four days. None for the final four days. I was miserable."

"As a healer, I am sure you tried quite a few concoctions to beat the enchantment, sir," Oeric said.

"I tried everything," Traveler said with a laugh. "Nothing worked. An elfin overseer told me that if demi-Titans could not beat it, what chance did I have? But they let me try."

"We all had to try, sir, at least once," Tyfer said.

◆◆◆

The fourth day was when things turned. The two fairy sisters walked to the royals' and Traveler's tents, droopy-eyed and yawning incessantly. The older one moved as if she were intoxicated; the young sister clung to her side.

It was the first night in the Dark Forest the human men remained awake and were able to eat a meal at nighttime. They sat at their campfires with warm meals and liquids to drink. Hobbs, from his seat outside the king's tent, saw the two fairy sisters drop down to the ground. He immediately rose to his feet.

As the brownies moved through the camp in their duties, Hobbs grabbed a spare blanket from one of the nearby pull carts. He walked to the fairies and gently covered them with the blanket.

The high-pitched scream that erupted shook everyone. Even the giants stirred from their sleep. Traveler ran out from his tent.

Hobbs stood in shock and looked down at the fairies. The two of them looked up at him with large eyes of shock and fear, their little mouths open. "I did nothing," Hobbs said when Traveler reached them.

Traveler noticed the blanket in his hands.

"All I did was try to put a blanket on them, sir. They were lying right in the middle of the ground. It was cold."

Traveler sighed. He sat on the ground in front of the fairies. "Mr. Hobbs was not doing anything wrong. In the world of humans, adults see children and they want to keep them safe. He thought of you as children, and when he saw you sleeping, he wanted to keep you safe from the cold. Humans use blankets for that. They cover them to keep them warm and safe. In the world of fairies, you only cover people when they are dead. He did not know that. Customs in the world of humans are different from the world of fairies. In the world of humans, we do not cover our dead above ground. Come, let me show you."

Traveler rose and led the two fairies to the women's tent. They shot dirty looks at Hobbs as they passed. Inside the tent, Traveler pointed at Gwyness, who was already in her bed, though wide awake.

"See, Maiden Gwyness is a human, and she is covered by a blanket. The half-elves here all have blankets for when they sleep." The female half-elves all sat on the ground and had been in the middle of a conversation. "Over there, Lady Aylen was raised human and she has multiple blankets."

That was of interest to the fairies. They flew over to her and carefully looked at her trussing bed. Sunpetal even touched the blanket.

"Mr. Hobbs meant nothing by his action. He is a good man and takes the safety of the caravan and all in it seriously, including its two fairies."

They were convinced and marched back to Traveler.

"You can go back to sleep. No one will disturb you."

The fairies left the tent. They looked around with squinted eyes but did not see Hobbs. With that, they returned to their spot to sleep.

"Is Mr. Hobbs in trouble, Mr. Traveler?" Lady Aylen asked.

"He is fine. The fairies will soon forget it ever happened."

"Poor, Mr. Hobbs," Gwyness said. "That scream was loud enough to wake the forest."

"Mr. Hobbs must sleep with one eye open for a while. The fairies are after him," Lady Aylen joked.

"I will find him and let him know, contrary to rumors, he is fine."

◆◆◆

All the light was gone. They were marching in a black void. The parties that joined the caravan all had their own magical light sources, but it was the magical light orbs that Estus and his men had distributed through the main caravan that were their salvation. Men fastened the orbs to their bodies or to the top of a torches. For the vanguard, the giants had necklaces of them, the elaphines attached them to their antlers, and Pangolin carried two torches with them to light their way.

The effect was still unsettling. It was as if they were walking through a path bridge within the deep void of the heavens. No music was played, and no one talked. The animals were especially nervous, having to be constantly calmed and reassured by their handlers. The day was a living nightmare for both human and fae.

By the time night fell—only Traveler and the fae knew when— even the perpetually cheerful brownies were not in a good mood. The darklings did not even appear. Humans sat in their small camps, staring off into space. Fae fidgeted in their small camps. Some were physically shaking. Others looked as though they were at the very edge of sanity.

Nirgund brought Traveler to the king's tent. King Aereth and Lady Aylen waited with Pangolin and Hobbs.

"Yes, sire," Traveler said.

"We have a problem, Mr. Traveler."

"The men are not going to make it through the night," Lady Aylen said. "I am convinced of it."

"I am particularly concerned about the fae, sir," Hobbs said. "They seem to be worse off than our human men. And our human men are not doing well at all. None of them will sleep tonight."

"Mr. Traveler, I have never seen the giants in the state they are in," Pangolin said. "They seem...frightened. Those deerlike fae, it is as if they will stampede, they are so spooked."

"Leave it to me," Traveler said and left the tent; his dog followed.

"Where is our drow sorceress?" Lady Aylen asked. "In fact, I have not seen her for a couple of days, nor that other fae woman."

"The entire caravan is going mad," Pangolin noted.

The royals looked at him nervously.

"Follow me." Traveler fetched them all from the king's tent.

They followed, and one moment they were in the darkness, the next they were standing in the breezy, warm air of a sunny environment: blue skies, vast green pastures, rivers, and waterfalls. It was a pocket-realm they had never seen before. Inside were most of the men, smiling and laughing. The lizard minders let their giant lizards roam free. Nirgund ran with the alphyns. The three crawling trees had gathered together where the leshies and deer-like fae relaxed. The Cut-Throats let their chamroshes play in the branches of the trees. All six of the giants were in the lake, still in their full armor, splashing water at each other.

Traveler led in the other parties of the caravan. The fenodyrees appeared, leading in the three kirins. Each dragon-horse instinctively walked to the royals and Gwyness. Hobbs helped bring in the rest of the caravan, including all the brownies, the darklings—taking the forms of ravens to fly high in the skies—and the drows.

"Thank you, Mr. Traveler," the king said to their caravan master when he neared them with the dog.

"Not at all, sire."

"We were not going to make it, were we?" the king asked.

"No, sire. The negative effects of the forest progressed faster than I experienced in the past. Normally, this occurs by the sixth or seventh day. But it does not matter. We will recover here."

"But we must leave again, Mr. Traveler. Go back out into the terrible darkness," Gwyness said.

"Yes."

"How long would we last then?"

Traveler smiled. "You have noticed two groups have not been affected at all by this. Myself, a few of our own fae humans, and the fae human mercenaries. We all were here before but are now immune to its effects. Maiden Gwyness, you and everyone here in the pocket are now also immune."

"Yes, we heard the fae human mercenaries say they were in the Great Forest but on a different path," King Aereth said.

"Yes, sire. There are many, many paths. Parties take the paths they need, depending on the destination. You can emerge on a path going deeper into the fairy lands. A path comes out on a great ocean where you can seek passage on fae ships to far-off lands, which our fae human mercenary friends are familiar with. Or there is the longer path we will travel to get to Faë-Land Major quicker than any other."

"Immune? Completely?"

"Completely. When we leave, we will march through without any issues at all. Out we will emerge to behold the Flying Forest."

Gwyness smiled.

"We are so fortunate to have the perfect guide who knows all," Lady Aylen said.

"Not perfect, princess. I have had problems like any other who has ventured into the magical lands. I am no different than either of you. I demand not perfection but competence. The former is impossible, the latter is essential. The knowledge I possess came at great cost and sacrifice, most of which I would not wish on my worst enemy. I became the man I am because I had to. Most people do not change. They simply complain or surrender. I did neither. I accepted the challenges and persevered because I would never surrender. Even this journey for me, as you all have gathered, is not for wealth, but to complete the Trail on my own terms. The Dark Forest was one of those horrible experiences I came through."

"How did you survive the last time, Mr. Traveler? Did your party have a pocket-realm?" Gwyness asked.

"No, we did not. All we could do was huddle around a magical fire and endure the suffering until it passed. We had been in the Forest for seven days already. We would not emerge whole for another seven days because we moved so slowly."

"My goodness," Lady Aylen said.

"Yes. None of us recovered from the aftereffects for another few months. But we did recover. And that was a long time ago. Enough of the past. Enjoy your respite in this new pocket-realm, courtesy of the winged sylphs of Emusias."

They stayed all the next day within the pocket-realm. Most did not want to leave, but they did. As Traveler had told them, they were forever immune to the powers of the Dark Forest. It got darker and colder, but they persevered with their magic orbs of sunlight. Then it stopped the following day. It was as if the Forest surrendered. As they marched, more daylight shone from above through ever-growing gaps in the foliage. The black trees around them became brown trees. The dark, hard path became sandy and ivory in color.

"Mr. Elman, are we nearing the end?" Pangolin asked.

"Yes, I think we are—" The half-elf stopped. They all saw giant shadows moving across the top of the tree covering.

"Antaeans, can you see what is in the sky from your vantage?" Pangolin asked, looking up at the giants behind him. "Are we about to do battle with giant flying creatures waiting for the caravan?"

"We cannot see clearly, but we do not think the shadows are from anything living," said one giant.

"Do none of you know what lies beyond the Dark Forest?"

"Faë-Land is far more massive an expanse than your own human lands," another giant said. "We have never traveled to these lands before. We know the same rumors that you have heard. We have never heard of any fantastic beasts of the air, dangerous or otherwise."

Pangolin grabbed the massive axe-mace from his back as they neared the end of the outer edge of the Dark Forest. The elaphine archer-warriors readied themselves with their arrows and longbows.

Traveler was suddenly standing next to them.

"Gentlemen, behold the Flying Forest."

CHAPTER TWENTY

The Flying Forest and Beyond

Stepping out of the forest, they moved from a place of dread to a land of wonder. The giants, too, had never seen anything so breathtaking. The elaphines were all smiles. Elman was frozen in amazement. Pangolin, who prided himself on hiding "weaker" emotions, stared with his mouth hanging open.

The moving shadows that they imagined were giant flying creatures in the sky were actually giant floating trees, twenty feet or more in the air. The greenish trees were contained on their own islands of brush-covered earth. As far as they could see were floating tree islands with floating rocks and boulders swaying in the air around them.

Through the clouds above the floating fields of island trees was a sight even more astounding—a massive, flowing, crystal-clear river. Birds were both diving into the river and flying out of it in large flocks. They could not see where the floating river originated or where it went, but it traveled for long distances on either side.

On the ground, the ivory sand continued to what looked to be a distant mountain ridge.

"The Centaurian Fields are over that ridgeline," Traveler told them.

"How long of a march?" Pangolin asked.

"More than a day, almost two. The sand ends at a wide chasm. On the other side is the mountain ridge. We do not want to cross on land."

"Another bottomless chasm like the one of Titan's Bridge?"

"This one is not empty, though. The chasm is a gateway to the lands of the plant people and is filled with dangerous plant creatures. However, we need not concern ourselves with them. We will not be going that way."

Traveler gestured to Hobbs, who was already nearing them.

"Hobbs, we are going to rest here for the day."

"Yes, sir. I will have the men set up camp immediately."

"Well, Hobbs, yes and no."

"Sir?"

"Gather the men."

Nearly seven thousand was their number, not including their animals. Hobbs gathered them around Traveler and the vanguard. The leadership were in the front. The other parties of the caravan kept a short distance back to watch too.

Traveler raised a hand. "Men, we have made it through the Dark Forest and now stand at the Flying Forest."

The men broke out in applause.

"We will rest here, but we will not be resting *here*." Traveler pointed up at the floating trees. "We will make camp up there."

Everyone watched him. They heard the other parties laughing from behind them.

"Impossible," I-wulf said to him.

"Impossible, Mr. I-wulf?"

"Yes, sir. Unless you plan to have your animal turn into some flying beast and carry each man up there."

"I am sorry to hear you express such a defeatist opinion. Mr. Hobbs, gather all the cooks and servants. We will set up our own camp up there on the tree islands. Where will you go?"

"With you, sir."

"Good. Then we go up; the rest of the men can remain here."

Traveler walked the supplies in the carts. Estus stood near one of the weapons carts and watched as Traveler opened it then dug through its contents. He found a large bow and, after a while, found the rope he wanted.

"Mr. Traveler, I can find you a proper bow. We have some very beautiful ones."

"No, Mr. Estus. I do not want anyone to say that I could only accomplish my task at hand with magical weapons or those forged by magical weapons. A simple human-made longbow and old rope are all I require."

Traveler had his men, which included the fae humans, tie ends of the different rope together. When satisfied with their work product, he wound it up and rested it over his neck. From the ground, on his back, he used his feet and legs to brace his longbow. One end of the rope had already been fastened to his single arrow with a long hook at the end.

"Mr. Traveler, you are accomplished in many things, but there is no chance you can make that shot," one giant said. "Pangolin could but not you. No offense."

"None taken, Mr. Alebar."

Traveler aimed the bow then yelled out, "Men!"

The largest and strongest of his cooks and servants, including Tyfer and Oeric, ran up to him and grabbed the end of the arrow. Traveler let his grip go and rested his arms to prop his body up as he extended his legs as far as they could go.

"One, two, three, fire!"

The men let the arrow fly. Up it went, and everyone watched it hit its mark. Traveler pulled the rope; the hook caught on a sturdy branch above. The men applauded. Traveler got to his feet, and his team helped him put another pile of rope around his neck. With that, Traveler began to climb, mostly with arm strength alone, then he used his legs for the remainder.

"Are you going to say he won't make it?" Pangolin asked I-wulf.

"My seer days are over," the fellow berserker answered.

Traveler did make it. Hobbs ran to the rope and tied a brown bag to the end. No one knew what was inside. Traveler pulled it up as everyone watched.

The entire caravan watched and waited.

"Our Mr. Traveler is a performer too," Lady Aylen said.

Traveler threw something down. It was a full rope ladder. The fae humans started up two at a time, each with their own bag of supplies. Hobbs was the last man to climb, and when he reached the top, the rope ladder was pulled up. They all saw Traveler wave at them and disappear. The dog, now with large eagle-like wings, flew up to the same tree island and disappeared too.

"What is happening?" Gwyness asked with a laugh. "What are they going to do?"

People stood there, looking up, as they talked. One of the giants noticed the flames of a fire. Their fae members sniffed the air.

"Food!" someone yelled.

The giants looked at each other, then started walking away from the caravan.

"Where are you going?" Pangolin asked them.

They dismissed him with a gesture. They were dozens of feet away when they stopped. Everyone watched with amazement as one giant picked up another comrade and, with a loud yell, squatted down a bit, then threw him into the air to land on one of the tree islands. The other two did the same. Of the remaining three on the ground, one threw one comrade and then another, leaving only one giant on the ground. It was Barg.

Barg ran to the caravan—or for a giant, meant walk very briskly—to get his war hammer. He, too, found some rope from a pull-cart to tie around it, and he easily threw it up to his comrades. Two of them pulled him up the entire twenty feet with ease.

The men applauded again. Pangolin looked at the Cut-Throats.

"This is so far from being acceptable. The cooks and servants are up there. The giants are up there. And here we remain."

"Oh, look," one of the Cut-Throats said.

The giggling fairy sisters flew past them all to the tree islands.

"Men! We're going up!" Pangolin announced. The Cut-Throats, including Nirgund, acknowledged him.

At that moment, two of the crawling trees approached, filled with smiling elaphines, cervids, rusines, and the Tree Shepherds. The trees grew, extending up to the tree islands.

"Go up!" Nirgund yelled out, and the alphyns ran up the tree for the top.

The pechs did the same as the giants. They picked one another up and literally threw each other the entire twenty feet to the top.

"This is embarrassing," I-wulf said. "We are going to be the last to arrive."

"Sire," Lady Aylen called out.

Their three kirins were standing behind them all.

"I assume they plan to get us up there too," the king said.

"Are you not coming?" Lady Aylen asked their fenodyree minders.

The fae shook his head "no."

She looked at her female half-elf guards. "You all also look like you wish to remain on the ground."

"We will ensure everything is secure here, m'lady. Then we will join you and Maiden Gwyness."

"Very good."

Lady Aylen, King Aereth, and Gwyness mounted the dragon-horses. They were in the air as the magical beasts galloped—flying without wings—to the tree islands. All three of them were without words as the animals touched down on the floating earth.

"Ah, royals cannot go without food for long." A joking Traveler approached them.

"Is this another exercise, Mr. Traveler?" Lady Aylen asked as she dismounted.

"Speaking of which, princess, I will have another one for you soon."

"Oh, please, no."

"You all should look at this while you can." Traveler peered over the edge of their tree island.

The royals and Gwyness joined him. The giant fae lizards, moving as a pack, created a living horizontal bridge as men and lizards ran up, grabbing any part of lizard armor they could.

"How is that possible, Mr. Traveler?" Gwyness asked, not believing what she was seeing.

"That is how they fight too—as a unit," Traveler said. "Mr. Estus and I have been drilling them."

The lizards reached about fifteen feet up when they began jumping onto the tree island, with several men tightly holding each. Gwyness did not know how, but the entire mass of lizards pulled itself onto the tree islands.

"Magic, Maiden Gwyness," Traveler said.

"I begin to understand their value, Mr. Traveler, when you said they would be our living wall," King Aereth said.

"Poor Mr. Pangolin," Lady Aylen said. "He and the Cut-Throats will be the last men standing."

"We will simply make sure there is plenty of food left for them."

"What of the drows and brownies, that fae-blood woman and those horrible darklings you like so much? And the väki, the friendliest fae in the world?" Lady Aylen asked.

"They will all remain on the ground, with Mr. Estus in charge."

"Oh, Mr. Estus," King Aereth said. "He will not join us?"

"The other parties will not join us up here, but we are still a caravan. Mr. Estus will maintain our ground presence. I did this exercise for the men, for morale."

"We do not see enough of Mr. Estus," Lady Aylen said. "You have been working him too hard, Mr. Traveler."

"The lizards are almost grown to their full size, so that work will soon be over."

"Still growing, Mr. Traveler? They are large enough," Gwyness said.

"And what of Mr. Gresham?" the king asked. "I take it he is down below too. He has been working hard to establish a good rapport with the men."

"Yes, Hobbs told me, sire. I will bring him up. Oh, watch out."

Arrows on ropes landed on the edge.

Lady Aylen laughed. "Here comes Pangolin and the Cut-Throats, finally."

Hobbs made his rounds through the camp in a way he had never done before. The tree islands were large but not large enough to accommodate the entire caravan, so camps were scattered across a dozen. Not a man comfortable with heights, especially twenty feet up in the air, he moved from one tree island to the next by nearing the edge and jumping. A good steward did what he had to do to get the job done.

Traveler landed on a now-massive winged dog to bring Gresham and the female half-elves to the tree island with the royal tents.

"Hello, Mr. Gresham," Hobbs greeted him. "See Mr. Tyfer, there, for your meal."

"Thank you, Mr. Hobbs."

Hobbs neared the royal tents to greet the female half-elves. "Ladies, you will double for the king's royal guard, as Mr. Nirgund decided to rejoin his former Cut-Throat comrades in today's act of solidarity. He now lies exhausted with them in an adjoining camp."

Suddenly, a ball of blankets hit the steward in the head. He was immediately startled, but when he heard the high-pitched laughter of the unseen fairies, he smiled.

The royals, Gwyness, and the half-elves laughed.

"I guess they have not forgotten yet," Hobbs said.

One of the female half-elves approached Traveler, who was about to step in and say something. "Sir, you have a visitor in the ground camp."

Traveler set down on his giant flying wolf-dog. Estus waited with several armed men in what was a smaller, more modest ground camp.

"Mr Estus, how goes the night?" Traveler dismounted his animal.

"No problems, sir. Your visitor awaits."

"No brownies?"

"They flew up to the floating tree camps. I did not know brownies could fly."

"Most sprites can."

"Over there, sir," Estus said as he pointed.

A single fairy stood near the entrance to the Dark Forest. Traveler neared her, recognizing her form and dress similar to the fairies they encountered in the fairy-storm. She was a six-foot-tall female fairy with pale translucent skin, gaunt features, forehead antennae, insect-like slits for eyes, and two sets of arms. Her cloaked robe was a muted gray.

"Good day," he said.

She greeted him with a nod. "We did not expect you to get this far. What will be your path when you set out?"

"Not across the chasm, if that is what you are asking. Titan's Caravan will not be disturbing the plant people."

"You know of them?"

"Yes."

"Of their guardians?"

"I have heard of their plant creatures but have not had the pleasure. I am a human who has no desire to encounter every single magical creature in these lands. Reading about them is sufficient for me."

"A wise position. I hear they have added carnivorous flowers to their collection. The entire area has deadly mushrooms and weeds and strangling vines many miles long."

"All the more reason to simply float above them all."

"Good, you do know. The two fairies with your caravan are my daughters."

"I suspected as much."

"I have hundreds of children, but they are my youngest and my favorite. They are not bored with life and suspicious of all outsiders as I am. They are still eager for adventure outside our lands. I can barely remember those traits in myself—it was so long ago.

"My fairy sisters were impressed with your caravan. You made wise use of your time in our lands and learned much. The haltijas, brownies, and leshies—good races to have on such a journey. Good use of animals, as well."

"I am glad you approve."

"No, you are not, but I am glad my tiny daughters are not in the company of the more common, weakling species of humans. Are you going to Atlantea for untold riches?"

"No, I am not."

"Are you one of those humans who undertakes the journey to a destination simply because it is there?"

"Something like that."

"I believe you. I can see it in your eyes. No lust for wealth or power. I would have taken my daughters away this moment if I did. You set out tomorrow?"

"At dawn."

"Very good."

"I get the impression you want to tell me or ask me something."

"Because I do. You have come to the attention of many, many people. It is not simply the novelty of such a caravan being led by humans and comprised of fairies, sprites, giants, and elves.

"There has been some debate about whether you are really human. You have a calmness about our lands and its people that is very uncharacteristic of any human we have ever encountered. To oversee fairies, tulen väki, phookas of the night, and sprites of day, fae-bloods of warring clans, drows, all in the same caravan—such varying races. We couldn't do that. I couldn't, nor would I want to. I can't even get my two daughters to do what I say. But you have managed them well. Some thought you might be a sprite or fae wizard appearing as a human. Others said you were something as dark as a changeling. But we came to realize you were just a human, a very unique one. Hopefully, you will return to your lands one day to breed and raise other humans like yourself."

Traveler laughed. "Individual humans do not personally have hundreds of offspring. Not even I have that ability or energy. Nor do our women. Human women birth a single child at a time, in rare instances twins or triplets, and the birthing process takes humans several months."

"Yes, short-lived, limited reproductive abilities, monogamous mores. How your race made it this far in history is a mystery to all. Despite that, your race expands like a slow-growing fungus across your realm."

"Yes. Fae always find great new ways to describe my people."

"I am sure your people have their own descriptions of my people."

"My people have never seen the realms of your people. They have seen but a single or few fairies in the wind or flora. I have seen your true realm."

"How would you describe it?"

"My description of it is the same as elves, sprites, and giants: terrifying. But your realm is not meant for others; it is meant for fairies alone."

"And we both venture out into the realms of others. Sadly, I believe one day our realms will be forever closed to each other. But we have observed you and your camp—all of high character."

"Thank you. What is it then? What people have we come to the attention of?"

"Very powerful people, dangerous people are interested in you."

"We are a caravan heading to Atlantea. We are not interested in anyone else—kingdom or individual. If left alone, we will slip through the lands without incident."

"There are those in fairydom who are interested in your caravan and its destination."

"Why?"

"They wish to involve you in their own conflicts, to their advantage."

"Then, they will be disappointed because we will not oblige them."

"Yes, I see that too."

"May I ask what is going on in Faë-Land? What has happened? I have been consulting my maps. There are goblin war parties about.

Sightings of creatures I have never heard of. I have a contingent of half-elves in our caravan, raised under the care of a human but within elfin lands, being cast out simply because they are half-elves."

"Why are you surprised? You are the cause of it."

"Me? How am I the cause of it?"

"Did you not destroy the army of the Xenhelmians in our land?"

"I did, and if they had not tried to murder us multiple times and had taken us to Atlantea under their banner, they would still be alive."

"Do not misunderstand me. My faction within fairydom is privately overjoyed about what you did."

"Your faction? And others?"

"You are not a fool. You already know the Xenhelmians could not have had their Kings' Caravan for twenty human years, built a massive city on our lands, and assembled their own army without the complicity of fae—very powerful fae."

"They were also stockpiling fae weapons, including goblin and others of dark metal I am not knowledgeable of?"

"We suspected."

"Also, his army was not only an army of men. It was also an army of war wizards."

"What do you believe his intentions were?"

"I believed his intentions were to use what he had acquired, assembled, and stolen from Faë-Land to make war and seize all the Lands of Man. But I am not so certain, now that I speak with you."

"Why do you say that?"

"You did not see the war wizards and battle elves he assembled."

"Battle elves? He had an elfin army?"

"Yes. And we both know elves would not follow a human king in any conquest of human lands. However, they might form an alliance to use such an army in the Lands of Fae."

The fairy closed her eyes, deep in thought. Traveler watched her quietly and waited. She opened her eyes.

"Yes. We know."

"You know?" Traveler asked with surprise. "You have eyes in our lands too?"

"You know we do. However, we did not know about the elves. What of the female elf in your own caravan?"

"She was raised human."

"What of the drows?"

"They despised the Xenhelmians more than I did."

"Yes, the drows did speak out against it at the time, all their clans. Can I say anything that would make you abandon your journey?"

Traveler smirked. "Nothing at all. Nothing in this world or any other could make us turn back."

"I knew that would be your answer, so I will tell you what I came to tell you. *The Four Kings are alive.*"

Traveler felt as if his heart skipped a beat. He looked at his dog, which had been sitting quietly to the side.

"How do you know this?"

"The network of fairies is vast. We know. The only reason you have not seen them for yourself is because they are rescuing one of the sons from the Nether-Lands. How did you manage to send one of them there? By portal?"

"No, my dog transformed into a giant beast and threw him through the air."

"I see. They are hunting you."

"If they are alive, then I would expect revenge from them."

"But you are not truly surprised. You already knew in your being that they lived, but you said to others they were, indeed, dead. Why?"

"I have a fae charm. One can ask it a single question; it knows all and never lies. I asked it if King Oughtred was dead. It said yes."

"Curious. I know of the charm you speak."

"Someone in our caravan said it was if we walked in their shadow. I assumed that the danger was from the agents of Xenhelm."

"Yes, they have already sent many agents after your caravan."

"The half-elves told me they had encountered an army of elves inquiring about us, weeks before they joined us. They had the sense they were hunting us. Well, this also explains the spell-talker and other confrontations."

"Spell-talker?"

"Yes."

"If you stand before me, it must be dead. The heavens must favor you."

"Or we were lucky."

"What other unexplained confrontations have you encountered?"

"Needed archers pulled from our reach, an elfin attack at one fae-city, vicious rumors told to your people to get them to attack us."

She smiled. "They knew it was not true, but you handled yourself well. Our fairy-storms intimidate most."

"What do you know? What can the network of fairies tell us?"

"There are rumors that they have dispatched a war-pack of gnolls after you."

"What kind of gnolls? Dog, wolf, or hyena?"

"Giant hyena."

"Worse than wolf gnolls."

"Some have said so."

"Where are they?"

"No one knows, but some believe they may ambush you at Titan's Arch."

"The Xenhelmians seem to have taken a special interest in our caravan from the start."

"Do not flatter yourself. They have destroyed others. You, however, have caused them more destruction than anyone has ever inflicted, human or fae."

"There is something more, though."

"I am unable to speak of it directly. I must be very careful in how I conduct myself. A delicate balance must be maintained. Knowing now that elves are involved gives me more pause for discretion. I will tell you this: there may be people secretly in league with the Xenhelmians to destroy your caravan, but there are also those who are secretly in league with you. They wish to destroy the Xenhelmians and all their allies."

"Fae allies."

"Yes."

"How do we know which is which?"

"You will know. They are also working in the shadows on your behalf."

"I have never liked shadows. I thought fae didn't either."

"I know you are not naive, Master Traveler. All the real work of principalities happens in the shadows. Fae or human, it is all the same."

She reached into her robes. For the first time, Traveler saw the translucent, insect-like wings on her back, stretching from behind the shoulder down to her feet. In her hand was a glowing piece of paper.

Traveler accepted it. "What is this?"

"Titan's Caravan is traveling under the official banner of giants. Now it will also be under the official banner of the fairies. It will help you once you reach the land of the elves. There, you will face more danger than you ever have so far on your journey."

"I do wish you could tell me more. I have done all that I know to keep my caravan and its people safe. However, if we must do battle with a gnoll war-pack, and undoubtedly have other Xenhelmian agents in wait for us, I would like a better picture of things. I know why the Four Kings seek revenge now, but why did they seek murder before? Was it simply because we were possible rivals, or was it personal? I have always felt their murderous actions to destroy the entire caravan were intended to kill a specific person or persons."

"You, perhaps?"

"Maybe, definitely now, but not before. There are others with magical swords and shape-shifting companions. No. We have a human king who originally joined with three of his comrade kings and their three sorcerers—"

"Master Traveler, what is your elfess's name?"

"Lady Aylen."

"What kingdom is she from?"

"I do not know. She was raised in the human lands in the kingdom of Sirnegate."

"Her name is not Aylen. We believe it to be Faylen."

"And?"

"Ask her. And her companion. They both possess magic."

"Lady Aylen, yes. Her maidservant is a human with no magic, but she does possess a magical object."

"They are both magic and both born in the elfin lands."

"Why not tell me yourself?"

"I am a fairy queen, but I am not the Fairy Queen. I can say no more. Ask them."

Traveler was troubled but pressed no further.

"If any fairies approach your caravan to assist or join you, turn them away."

"Why would I do that?"

"Despite any appearance, they are the most savage of fairy warriors and have no interest in your caravan other than to use you for their own purposes. To use you against all humankind."

"If we are under the fairy banner, give us a swarm."

The fairy queen laughed. "You are quick, human. Give you command of a swarm?"

"No, of course not. Your daughters."

The fairy queen was caught off guard. Her eyes were no longer slits but large and humanlike. They darted around as she thought. Finally, she nodded.

"That would give you a plausible reason to deny their assistance," she said, "and my daughters would have an additional insect army to protect them. Yes, I will give them more than one swarm. They can nest among your giant lizards and the leshy crawling trees."

"Good. We are in agreement. What else can you share with me?"

"More, Master Traveler? You have received more than you deserve."

"What about when we arrive in Atlantea?"

"Are you sure you will get that far?"

"We will. Remember, I have been there before. Back then, I had no dog, no magical sword, and no caravan. We will."

"If you make it to Atlantea, if the Four Kings intervene with their unclean allies, all your unseen allies will be there too. I wish for your success, but I do not expect it."

"Expect it. You are a long-lived race, so it will be a long time for us. However, for you it should only be the time it takes to blink your eyes."

The fairy queen smiled.

◆◆◆

The fairy queen flew into the night sky and disappeared. All was quiet on the ground and in the island-tree camps above.

Estus waited at a campfire with a couple of sentries. The weaponsmaster stood.

"Mr. Estus, you did not have to wait up on my account."

"I felt I had to, sir. I forgot to tell you something about the magic attack—the death-sleep, I believe the fae call it."

"Yes. There is more? Because you were the one who saved us all, Mr. Estus."

"That may be true, but I may have had help."

"What do you mean?"

"When I was in the pocket, your magical bracelet did wake me, or I think it did. But that is not what really made me get up. There was frog in the pocket, a lime-green frog. It was croaking, and now that I have had time to reflect on it, I realize it was croaking to make me get up."

"Where did it go?"

"I did look afterward. It disappeared. In fact, you said nothing could get in our pocket."

"No, not physically. But—"

"I am sorry for not telling you earlier, sir. I do feel it helped us."

"Yes. I believe so too."

"That tall fairy woman, did she have information for us?"

"Quite a bit. I will share what I can at our next leadership meeting, but I do not want us to lose focus. I want us to get to Titan's Arch with urgency."

"Trouble, sir?"

"Always."

"Well, the work on the lizards will be done soon, so I will be able to work on my other weapons duties. We still have weapons in the hoard of unknown origin and ability."

"Yes, we may need to consult with a sage on the journey. However, Mr. Estus, if you ever see that frog again, find me. Wherever I am, find me immediately."

"Yes, sir."

At dawn, the men broke camp and scaled down from the floating tree islands to prepare to march. Hobbs led their healer into a tent set up specifically for the impromptu group meeting.

"Good morning, Mr. Gresham," Traveler said.

"Thank you, sir. I am honored to attend my first meeting of the leadership."

"Mr. Hobbs."

"I will find her."

The drow sorceress entered the tent before the steward could run out.

"Dr'amal," Traveler greeted her. She nodded. "I will get to it, since we must set out. Some of you already know I had a visitor last night. I spoke with a fairy queen."

"The mother of the two fairy sisters?" Dr'amal asked.

"Yes."

"So, we have fairy royalty amongst us too," the drowess said.

"I was wrong. The Four Kings are still alive," Traveler said directly.

The revelation drew gasps. Gresham looked at everyone, unaware. Hobbs made eye contact with him and gestured that they would speak after the meeting.

"They survived my attack with the dog," Traveler continued.

"You were certain that you had killed them," Pangolin said.

"On reflection, I was certain I had destroyed their armies and their new kingdom in the outer regions of Faë-Land. I witnessed both. I assumed they were dead because no others could have survived. I was wrong."

"But you already knew," Dr'amal said. "The fairy did not have to tell you. You knew."

"I had a suspicion."

"I suspect much more than that."

"True. Too many coincidences and strange occurrences. Too much strange behavior by fae strangers. However, since we set foot in the magical lands, everything I have done—the supplies acquired, the animals chosen, and the fae we brought into the main caravan—has been to prepare this caravan for anything and everything, including the possibility they were not dead."

"We have been under the shadow of the Four Kings all this time and remain so," King Aereth said.

"Yes, sire."

"What should we do, Mr. Traveler?" King Aereth asked.

"Now that it is confirmed that they are hunting us," Pangolin added.

"It all makes sense now," Lady Aylen said.

"There will also be those hunting them. We do not deal with this alone. That is what the fairy queen revealed to me. Sending a spell-talker into the fairy lands, into a fairy city, will not go unanswered by fairydom. I doubt the Four Kings had a direct hand in that, but whoever the intermediaries are, whether hired or bribed, they will receive the full wrath of the fairies and never be seen again. As I have explained before, fairies in real life are not the fairies of our fairy tales. They can kill quite effectively when they wish. And they will inform all the fae empires of the elves, sprites, giants, and even the distant dwarves. Those who were there might have seen a hole on either side of the warlock's face. That was to rivet shut its mandible straight through its skull. Only specific dark magic could release the restraint. No, we have some very powerful allies, albeit indirectly, on our side to find those behind it."

"We are being hunted by the Xenhelmians," Dr'amal said, more to herself than to any other.

"I notice that all fae refer to them as such. Do they have a status of respect and honor within your lands?"

"Not from drows." Dr'amal had an angry face.

"You were so sure they were dead, Mr. Traveler," Lady Aylen said. "But I did not believe it."

"Can we now say that the trouble we had in both Fae-Wick and Arion's Spear was their doing?" Pangolin asked.

"We assume that it is true."

"Then what now, Mr. Traveler?" King Aereth asked.

"Nothing, sire. I wanted you all to know. However, this does not change anything. We move forward. The fairy queen also revealed that, at some point, we might have to face a war-pack of gnolls."

"Gnolls?" Gwyness asked.

"Orcs are reptilian. Gnolls are mammalian. Dog, wolf, and hyena."

"Hyena?" Lady Aylen asked.

"Like a jackal," Pangolin said.

"War-pack?" Lady Aylen sighed loudly.

"But again, we are not alone in this. Also, Titan's Caravan, in addition to the giants, will be under the banner of fairydom. Our two fairies will have command of a swarm."

Dr'amal was visibly happy, almost clapping. No one else knew the significance.

"Think of it as a war-pack of magical butterflies. Like fairies, they can pick up a giant, block raining arrows, and much more," Traveler explained.

"Those two fairy children will command that?" Lady Aylen asked.

"Yes, and they will do fine. The Four Kings are in the Nether-Lands, lands far, far from us, and they are occupied with other matters. We will deal with all dangers, including their fae accomplices, but our journey continues. I do not want to delay. Oh, have any of you seen a green frog near the camp?"

"Yes, I have, Mr. Traveler. A bright-green bullfrog," Lady Aylen replied.

"If any of you see it again, you are to notify me immediately."

"Is it dangerous, Mr. Traveler?" Gwyness asked nervously. "From the Four Kings?"

"According to Mr. Estus, it may have actually saved our lives in the death-sleep attack on our caravan. But I must know for sure. Mr. Hobbs, nothing changes in terms of your duties. Mr. Pangolin and Mr. I-wulf, let your men know and find out all there is to know about gnolls. The fairy queen surmised they might try to ambush us at one of the points on the Trail, possibly Titan's Arch."

"But all someone has to do is look at one of these magical maps and see where we are at any time," Lady Aylen remarked.

"Yes, princess, but we will be able to see them too."

"We had such a pleasurable time here at the Flying Forest," Gwyness lamented, "until now."

"Yes, and you will always have those memories, Maiden Gwyness. Dr'amal, as the sorceress for the caravan, do you have anything to add?"

"No."

"You have the same evasive demeanor about the Xenhelmians as the fairy queen. Why is that?" Traveler asked, watching her closely.

"You are not a feeble human, Traveler. You are already wise to the possible reasons. Do we wish to involve ourselves in the machinations of the fae races and all their kingdoms and clans, or do we wish our caravan to continue on to its destination? My race, in particular, must be very cautious in these matters. We do not have the power we once did. We must remain in the shadows and stay silent. So should we all. We do not want to get involved in this."

"It would seem we are already involved in this," King Aereth said.

"No, king. We are not. You have been on the receiving end of a human madman king." Dr'amal paused, as if angry with herself. "I say too much already. We are not involved. If we were, it would involve all the powers of Faë-Land. I ask you the same question: Do we want our caravan to reach its destination of Atlantea, or do we want to get entangled in the matters of empires? This has gone on since before I was born, and if it was before I was born, it was before you were born. It will continue long after we are all dust."

"Well, obviously, we are here for Titan's Trail," King Aereth responded.

"Then, we must resist the temptation to speak of it again," Dr'amal advised. "There is nothing for us to do. If we are attacked, we defend ourselves. But that would be true whether it were Xenhelm agents or an attacking beast."

"I agree completely," Traveler said. "Others are involved. We must stay uninvolved, or we will never get to Atlantea."

"But will we be allowed to remain uninvolved?" Lady Aylen asked.

"The fairy queen said the same thing, princess. We must. She even cautioned me against other fairies who might try to involve us."

"How long will it take us to reach Faë-Land Major, then, Mr. Traveler?" the king asked.

"We will be there in a fortnight." Traveler returned his attention to the drowess. "Any progress on your seeker spell?"

"It was unsuccessful, and now we know why. But now that we know who, I may be able to try another method. Do you doubt my abilities?"

"I have not seen your abilities. None of us have. We have an adversary that uses multiple sorcerers for a single attack. I will ask you directly, Dr'amal. Are you able to be this caravan's sorceress?"

"I am."

"Good. Then I will leave you to it. Sire, I will meet with you and Mr. Estus tonight to review the new plans for our heavy weapons teams and prepare for any future gnoll attack. Lady Aylen and Maiden Gwyness, I will meet with both of you afterward."

"You speak as a general commanding an army, Mr. Traveler," Lady Aylen noted.

"It is merely the additional duties of a caravan master in the lands of fae, princess. It is what you and the king hired me for."

"Did we hire you, Mr. Traveler?" the king asked with a smile. "I thought the princess and I were along for the journey."

"Oh, no, sire. You hired me. You have simply forgotten. Well then, our meeting is over."

Lady Aylen and Gwyness glanced at each other as everyone filed out of the tent.

Quillen ran up to Traveler and the dog the moment they exited the tent. Hobbs glanced at the lad but was already directing men to break down the camp.

"Mr. Quillen," Traveler said as he turned. "What may I do for you?"

"Thanks, sir. I wanted to ask about the new fae parties."

"What about them?"

"Well, I have been talking to—or trying to talk to—all of them."

"For your magical book of fae people and fantastic beasts."

Quillen smiled. "Yes, sir. The gnomes are friendly enough, but all the others, the horned gnomes, too, do not talk to me."

"Mr. Quillen, you must stay clear of them. Remember, there are thousands, tens of thousands, millions of fae races. Most, we humans will never see. Most of those fae have also never seen a human, don't like humans, don't like other fae outside their own race. That is simply how it is. It is not personal."

"I should not talk with them?"

"Conduct your duties, and let them grow accustomed to you. If they wish to converse, they will let you know. If not, that is the way it is. You will still be able to sketch their likenesses in your book."

"Thanks, Mr. Traveler. I will do that."

The moment Quillen ran off to continue his duties, both fairy sisters flew in front of Traveler before he could move on.

"You met our mother!" the larger fairy sister announced.

"I did."

"Was she going to take us away?"

"She had planned to do so, but I convinced her not to."

"Yes! She told us. And she gave us swarms. We are fairy warriors now!"

The two sisters giggled hysterically.

"We need armor too!"

"Speak with the Tree Shepherds. They can help you create something."

"Yes, we will do that."

"Where are your swarms?"

"Where should we put them?" Wildglow asked.

"Not the crawling trees?" Traveler asked.

"We want to put them on the lizards!"

"Let us speak with Mr. Hobbs and Mr. Estus first. If it is the lizards, we would want to make their armor special so we can grow plants on it for your insects."

"Yes!"

"Keep them in the trees for now, until we know."

"Yes!"

The fairies flew up into the sky. Everyone gasped as millions of fae butterflies descended from the clouds. The swarms of colored insects divided, flew to one of the three crawling trees, and landed. The giggling fairy sisters appeared again and flew through the camp in search of the leshies.

♦♦♦

The arrival of the fairy swarms sparked excitement and chatter among the men. The main caravan formed up in its columns, while the secondary parties lined up behind them. Hax, the lionlike fae berserker, eager to set out, marched to the vanguard itself.

"Are we not moving forward?" he asked Pangolin.

"Mr. Traveler tells us that we will be traveling another way to the Centaurian Fields."

"Is his shape-shifter going to transform into a walking island to step across the chasm?"

"Maybe, I am as anxious to know the method as any here."

From the center of the caravan, the doorway to a pocket-realm opened, and Traveler appeared. He led the men inside. The realm was devoid of anything except for a massive sailing ship of dark brown wood constructed in a flatboat design, resting on the earthen ground. It had a foremast, mizzenmast, and mainmast with a crow's nest, all rising fifteen to twenty feet from the ship, and each with white sails. Unlike human ships, the outer edge of the ship was a battlement, much like that of a fortified castle.

"The craft does not have quarters, but there is plenty of space below for our provisions and supplies. The ship is designed for quick trips and is large enough for our entire caravan," Traveler told them.

"How did you know how big our full caravan would be, Mr. Traveler?"

"I didn't, sire. It's a magic ship built by sprites. It grows in size to accommodate your party. When done, it shrinks to fit in your pocket. You might have seen them in our lands, brought there as curiosities, the possessor not knowing what he had—ships in a bottle."

"Mr. Traveler, even I am amazed," the Cut-Throat leader remarked.

"I heard, Mr. I-wulf, you were a seaman in your day, or was it a pirate?"

"More like an involuntary passenger, Mr. Traveler, who learned sailing to pass the time. You are not going to do what I am thinking."

"Mr. I-wulf, we are going to get the entire caravan aboard. Then one of the crawling trees will set our pocket-realm on the flying river above. We will sail across the Flying Forest, over the Chasm of Flowers, to the end of the Flying River, and arrive at the edge of Centaurian Fields and its tall golden grass."

"How long did it take you to acquire one of these pocket-realms of surprises, Mr. Traveler?"

"I have been collecting them all my adult life. We now take advantage of them."

"Titan's Caravan has its own ship. I am amazed, Mr. Traveler, truly amazed."

The main party boarded the ship first and settled in the rear half. Lizard minders and giant lizards clustered in the center. The Tree Shepherds had the three crawling trees, now home to the fairy-sister swarms, clustered around the mainmast, with all the deerlike fae at their bases. The six giants sat at the very rear of the ship. The royals, their guards, and the leadership also took their places at the very rear of the ship, where the captain's steering cabin was manned by a proud I-wulf.

"You do know how to sail a ship?" Pangolin asked jokingly.

The rest of the men took places anywhere they wished. Some wanted a view directly from the side of the ship. Others, nervous about the prospect of being so far up in the sky, preferred to be close to the center of the ship. The other fae parties boarded and settled into the first half of the ship. Then pech pulled up the gangplank and secured the ship.

Traveler, his dog, and one of the Tree Shepherds were the only ones missing from the group.

"Can one of the crawling trees really lift us and set us that high in the sky?" Quillen asked.

"We are in a pocket-realm," Dr'amal said. "We can be set anywhere it wants to set us. And no, Quillen, this does not mean I or my fellow drows wish to be tormented by you for inclusion in your magic book of fae and fantastic beasts."

Quillen burst out laughing as the drowess smiled.

The entire ship rocked, startling the caravan.

"I agree with Mr. Quillen," Lady Aylen said. "How exactly is this going to be accomplished?"

"Look!" someone yelled.

The portal door was no longer of the plains below the Flying Forest; the view was rising. They saw flying boulders and rocks, then the floating tree islands up higher, then the magical floating river roared past. The portal door fell, and as soon as it touched the river's surface, the water rushed in.

Everyone cried out, but then the entire ship tilted forward and they all heard the splash of its contents. They were out of the portal and on the floating river. The portal doorway disappeared and there was Traveler, mounted on a giant flying wolf-dog. The Tree Shepherd, Little Root, stood on the animal too.

People in the caravan were startled again when the fourth crawling tree reached over one side of the ship like an advancing creature. However, all it did was crawl in and join the other trees at the mainmast. Traveler flew over the ship. Little Root jumped onto the mainmast and slid down to the base to join his fellow leshies. Traveler landed next to the captain's steering cabin, in front of the giants.

For those who were brave enough or excited enough to look over the sides, the view was magnificent. The ship raced along the currents of the floating river. In addition to the birds flying in and out of the waters, they could see the river's many unusual, multicolored fish. They could barely make out the tree islands, at least twenty feet below. Finally, they could see far down to the surface.

They had already crossed over the Chasm of Flowers, moving so fast they barely had time to look upon it. Below them were golden-yellow plains and nothing more. The sky was beautiful, and though it was daytime, high above they could make out distant moons.

What would have taken them well over a full day of marching, took them barely an hour to cross. The floating river descended and emptied into a giant lake. The ship dropped into it, splashing water on those along the side—the final part of their magical sailing trip to bring smiles and laughs from the men.

"Mr. I-wulf, steer to the coast," Traveler said.

It took no more than a quarter of an hour to do so. The main party disembarked then the other parties. Hobbs meticulously moved through the men to ensure every soul was accounted for, as he always did.

"We are ready, sir," he announced to Traveler.

Traveler made his way to the fauns at the rear of the full caravan. The leader, with his large curved ram's horns sprouting from his head, watched Traveler approach with the dog.

"Chief Ammon, since we have arrived in the Centaurian Fields, can you spare a few of your men to join our vanguard, at least until we come out of the Golden Sea?"

The faun nodded. "Yes, I will send four of my scouts."

Before the caravan was the sandy shore surrounding the lake, but thirty yards away was a wall of golden-yellow grass fifteen feet tall.

"The Golden Sea," one of the giants said to Pangolin.

"Is there anything in this 'sea'?" he asked.

"No. There is not supposed to be."

Pangolin did not like this answer. He noticed Traveler leading four fauns toward them. The fauns carried large scythes, but the blades were not metal; they were wood.

"Mr. Pangolin, the fauns know these lands better than any of us. They will lead us through the Golden Sea."

"I asked my giant friends if this 'sea' is free of creatures. His answer was not as certain as I would have liked."

"What did he say?"

"There is not supposed to be," the giant repeated.

Traveler smiled. "Mr. Pangolin, there is not supposed to be."

The tall golden-yellow sea of grass was cool to the touch and had a sweet smell. As they walked, the four fauns moved their wooden blades back and forth, not to scatter anything that might be hiding within but to make a path for the caravan. The men and parties marched quietly and steadily. Never was there a sense of other life or danger of any kind. The only negative thing one could say, especially the humans, was they had a growing desire, as the hours of marching passed, to just lie down and take a nap.

The caravan master had joined the vanguard. "Are all the faun clans allied with the centaurs and satyrs?" Traveler asked as they walked.

They had pushed through the Golden Sea and marched through normal golden plains to another set of mountains far in the distance. The four faun scouts rested their scythes on their shoulders as they walked.

"Yes, there has never been enmity between our races."

"Your clan is from here, but you ventured all the way to Arion's Spear."

"We could not join a caravan in our lands. If we wanted to find a suitable one not of elves, Arion's Spear is where we had to go."

"True. The ipotanes are in these lands."

"Far away. We do not interact with their kind at all."

"I see something!" Elman called out.

"I hear something!" one of the elaphine archer-warriors added.

Pangolin raised his arm to stop the vanguard and the main caravan behind them. Traveler looked at his dog, who was staring off into the distance at something. Both Traveler and Pangolin pulled out their telescopes to look. Elman, a couple of the elaphines, and one of the fauns did the same.

"Stampede!" Traveler yelled at the top of his lungs.

Stampede of what? Pangolin had been to other continental regions in the Lands of Man—not all Seven Empires, as Traveler had, but a few more than most men. He had seen stampedes of deer, elk, horses, bison, elephants, giraffe, lions, tigers, and wild dogs. He watched as the wild herd came into view, spanning across the entire horizon. At first, he thought it was humans or humanoids on horseback. It was not.

The giants pushed Pangolin behind them as they lined up, shoulder to shoulder. They removed the armored knee guards from their right legs and took a knee. Then each pressed a bare palm on the ground, and tucked his head in. Suddenly, the other two giants of the caravan joined them on each side and took an identical stance to create a wall.

Elman grabbed the berserker and moved him in, close behind the wall of giants. Traveler yelling at everyone to run in behind the giants as quickly as possible. The branches of the two crawling trees stretched out over the main caravan one way and over the rest of the caravan the other, as parties huddled together. Most of the animals of the camp were panicking, including the giant lizards. The lizard minders had to fight to restrain and calm them. The alphyns ran to Nirgund and pushed themselves to his body. He threw his cloak over them.

A wave of seemingly hundreds of seven-foot-tall centaurs was upon them!

The first of the stampede collided with the wall of giants. The fae with the upper bodies of men and the lower bodies and legs of horses tumbled over the giants and slid across the protective canopy of the crawling trees. The centaurs were bare-chested or wore sheer leaf-woven vests. Their long hair fell to their shoulders. Some had goatees. All had wide eyes of sheer terror.

Centaurs continued crashing into the giants, but all were not so lucky as to flip over them. Many were violently colliding and rendered unconscious by the impact. Their bodies piled up in front of the giant wall.

"When an Antaean giant touches the earth to stand firm, he becomes one with the world itself; no force can move him" is what Traveler had told them the very night the Antaeans joined their caravan.

"Archers! Fire to move the stampede from us! They will kill themselves!"

Traveler was tucked in close behind the Antaeans too. The elephine archer-warriors looked at each other, then aimed their bows in unison.

"Fire arrows!" the leader yelled.

They fired their arrows high up. In flashes of fire, the arrows fell to the ground in front of the barrier of giants. The fae archers continued. They were joined by brownies, who threw balls of magic light through the protection of the crawling tree branches out front. The magic light hit the ground, grew in size, and exploded in a flash.

Traveler was not satisfied. The stampede was too great, and the centaurs too crazed. Centaur after centaur was still crashing into the wall of giants and fallen centaurs in front of them.

Traveler yelled out. A roar followed. A serpentine creature shot out from the protection of the crawling trees and dove into the ground before the giants. The ground rumbled, then a crack opened up and widened. The continuing wave of the centaur stampede moved around the huddled caravan.

The waves of centaurs seemed unending, and the cloud of dust made visibility difficult, but it did stop.

"Mr. Pangolin!" Traveler yelled. "Dr'amal!"

Traveler came out from his protective spot to walk in front of the wall of giants. Pangolin stood with Traveler. The elaphine archers and the male half-elves with crossbows joined them.

"Have any of you seen that before?" Traveler asked. He looked at the fae, who shook their heads: "no."

King Aerth and Lady Aylen joined them with their guards. Dr'amal appeared.

"Have your people ever seen such a thing?" Traveler asked her.

The drowess shook her head.

"Is it over?" King Aereth asked.

"It was as if it would never end," Lady Aylen said.

"No, sire. We saw the stampede, but what caused it?"

Traveler's words made them all hold their breath. The caravan master kept his gaze fixed on the horizon.

"Was it fire?" Pangolin asked.

"Centaurs have no fear of fire. Did you see their eyes? That was wild panic and pure fear."

"I hear something," one of the elaphine archer-warriors said.

Elman grabbed his telescope from his clothes. "It cannot be!"

Traveler and the others grabbed their telescopes.

"What is it?" Lady Aylen asked.

Traveler put his telescope away as quickly as he could and grabbed his magic sword from his back. "Mr. Pangolin, archers!"

Pangolin grabbed his battle-axe from his back. "Archers, kill them!"

The centaurs that had knocked themselves unconscious against the wall of giants began to awaken. When they came to their senses, they sprinted off in terror after their people.

The next stampede spilled over the horizon, moving much faster. They saw the horns from a distance. Dozens of giant minotaurs charged as tall as the caravan's own Antaean giants!

The humans had heard of elfin archers. In the time it took a human archer to fire one arrow, an elfin archer could fire a dozen. Traveler had told them elves were not the only fae archers that could do so. Their elaphine fae archers rained down arrows on the closest minotaurs. Each arrow hit its mark, but not one of the beasts slowed. Traveler ran at them. Pangolin followed. The minotaurs screamed.

The first of the minotaur stampede was upon them—dozens rather than hundreds—but they were far more frightening now that they were closer. Their dual whitish horns—sharp, pointed or jagged—protruded from their heads, and they had large bull ears, and extremely muscular necks. Their forms were entirely covered with thick brown hair. The thick brown opaque nature of the nails on their humanoid hands made them look more like claws. Only a few were in loincloths. Most had no clothes at all. The beasts had putrid white eyes and were foaming at the mouth.

Traveler sliced off the arm of one in one stroke, but the minotaur was unaffected and tried to claw at him with the other arm. Traveler sliced it off too. The minotaur tried to bite off Traveler's head. Even when Traveler decapitated the creature, its armless and headless body continued forward.

Pangolin quickly learned that cutting the creatures did not stop them, so he bludgeoned them into the ground. But, even as he moved on, their crushed bodies kept crawling forward.

The realization came across Traveler's face. "Do not let any of the creatures touch you!" He stepped back to make sure all heard him. "Not even a scratch!"

The bulk of the minotaur stampede charged to the camp. Dr'amal raised both her hands and clapped them together. A shockwave of magic knocked the herd back to the horizon to start again. Other elaphine archers appeared, and they all began shooting fire arrows at the creatures. However, even as those they hit caught fire, the minotaurs kept advancing.

Lady Aylen joined the king with her war tridents. "They will not die!"

"Because they are already dead!" Traveler informed her.

The Cut-Throats, their chamroshes, pech, drows, human fae berserkers, and some of the animal men joined the front. The crawling trees enclosed all others in a circle of protective branches.

"Do not allow them to touch or scratch you!" Traveler yelled.

Boulders flew from the caravan, with King Aereth directing the heavy weapons teams. The catapults hit their targets, but most of the maimed or crippled minotaurs kept moving, crawling forward.

The serpentine dog shot out from the ground and transformed again. An orange phoenix, feathers glowing and flickering in flames, with wings more than fifteen feet wide, hovered in the sky above them. The caravan men had shielded their eyes and faces from its glowing heat. The phoenix shrieked, and a wave of tremendous heat stopped the minotaur stampede in its tracks. The creatures burned where they stood and disintegrated to dust.

The phoenix landed near his master and reverted back to his dog form. Traveler looked across the now-scorched field.

"Hobbs!" Traveler yelled.

The steward peeked out from the protective branch circle. "Yes, sir!"

"Have Mr. Gresham come out here and immediately check every human and fae for any cuts or scratches from these minotaurs!"

"Mr. Traveler!"

They all looked behind them to see new centaur warriors in full silver armor galloping toward them. Hundreds of them appeared, seven feet in height. All had pointed ears jutting out from the sides of their heads, very much like Lady Aylen and other elves. They were armed with halberds, tridents, and crossbows, except for one with a long blue-tipped spear. The lead centaur galloped to the front. He ignored them all. His eyes scanned the now-brown fields. As he walked back and forth, he yelled in another tongue to his fellow centaurs.

The faun leader came out of the caravan and walked to him with two faun warriors, followed by the fauness. The centaur saw them and galloped forward.

"I am Hycor of Centaur City."

"I am Ammon of Faunus."

"Who leads this caravan?"

"The human."

"Human? You travel with humans?"

"Humans, giants, elves, sprites, fairies, other fae."

"Yes, we have heard of this caravan. The one with a shape-shifter and the sword that cuts elfin rogues and their swords in half."

"Yes."

"May we ask what has occurred?" Traveler asked the centaur, stepping forward.

The centaur showed his disdain. "No. I speak with the fauns only."

"I would expect more consideration from you. We protected your people as well as our own."

"You protected your people and nothing more."

"You will not tell us what occurred."

"Are you not journeying to Atlantea? Do so, and be gone from our lands. Good journey, Ammon," the centaur said and galloped off, his centaur soldiers following.

"Pleasant people," Pangolin remarked.

"We will wait here for Gresham to work and for us to get our bearings," Traveler said.

Pangolin looked at his men. "Post sentries, immediately."

It was not even noon, but the decision was made to set up camp. The leadership assembled at a campfire outside the royal tents for meals to be served, but no one was hungry. They watched Traveler many yards away, to the side, yelling at the drowess. She was vigorously yelled back.

"Our Mr. Traveler was not satisfied with our sorceress," King Aereth said.

"I completely agree," Lady Aylen said. "She did nothing. Some sorceress she is. Magically pushing back those beasts so they could charge us again; it is not acceptable for one who is supposed to protect us."

"I cannot say we collectively did much better," Pangolin said. "We were becoming as panicked as those centaurs."

"What would have happened if the dog had not been able to turn into a phoenix and destroy them?" Gwyness asked. "What would have happened if one of us had been scratched by those minotaurs?"

No one had an answer for her.

Traveler walked back to them; the drowess stormed off into the main body of the caravan. He took a seat around the fire, next to his dog, who was lying with his belly on the ground.

"Are we going to need a new sorceress, Mr. Traveler?" Lady Aylen asked.

"No."

"Not a bold endorsement, Mr. Traveler," King Aereth said.

"I am not pleased, sire."

"Those centaurs were speaking in another tongue," Lady Aylen began. "My elfin reader, in addition to teaching me words in elvish, can tell me the meaning of words I hear. There was a word the centaurs kept saying that I honed in on. The book translated it. *Ghoul.*"

"Yes. The attacking minotaurs were already dead."

"How? How did they rise again?" Gwyness asked.

"Unknown, and none of this should exist in Faë-Land. Those centaur warriors are among many who will scour the lands to wipe them out."

"Spell-talkers and ghouls," Pangolin said as he sipped his tea.

"Yes, but there is nothing for us to do."

"And, Mr. Traveler, no one was bitten or scratched," Gresham spoke up.

"Good. Thank you, Mr. Gresham."

"What if someone had been, Mr. Traveler?" Lady Aylen asked. "Would they have turned into such a creature? What then? What would we have done?"

"Princess, unfortunately, my previous skill and experience as a healer cannot inform us. My only knowledge on this is that I have none. What I do know is not to take any risks with these creatures. The dark magic that drives them gives them many abilities, one of which may include turning victims into its evil race, or so the stories go."

"What now, Mr. Traveler?" Pangolin asked.

"Nothing. The centaurs were quite clear. It is not our concern. It is theirs."

"They were quite unfriendly about it," King Aereth said.

"Yes, sire, they were. Ammon, our faun chief, told me they sent an official edict to Titan's Caravan, in writing, delivered by arrow. We are to vacate these lands by morning and move on."

"My word," Lady Aylen remarked. "By arrow? They wish to be rude from a distance. Well, our excitement at entering these lands did not last long, not long at all."

"The heavy weapons teams worked quite well, Mr. Traveler. Do you agree?"

"Yes, they did, sire. If what they hit was not already dead, they would have been stopped in their tracks."

"Mr. Traveler, what creates ghouls?" Gwyness asked.

"There are many, many answers to that question, Maiden Gwyness. But it must wait for another time. But do know that fae are as unnerved about such creatures as humans. They are all magically preparing better means to defend against them, should that become necessary. I myself want to study our maps carefully through the night so we can go."

"Oh, yes, please do, Mr. Traveler," Gwyness said. "Do not mind me."

"Will these creatures show up on the map?" King Aereth asked.

"The first stampede of centaurs did, sire, as incredible as it was, but not the second herd of minotaurs that caused it."

"So the creatures could be camped nearby, and we would not know?" Pangolin asked.

"Stay in the circle, Mr. Pangolin. Always stay in the circle."

As night fell, Traveler continued visiting the leaders of the fae parties of the caravan. Hobbs accompanied him, listening closely to the questions the caravan master asked. The conversations were casual, but their purpose was serious. None had ever seen a centaur stampede, and more than a few noted that it was as if an entire city had emptied to escape the creatures. But also, like humans, ghouls had always been the stuff of dark legends; all had thought such a transformation in a minotaur was impossible.

"Mr. Quillen asked me if ghouls are not associated with grave sites?" Hobbs asked as they walked back to the main camp.

"They are, always. That is how they are found, or so I am told. I have no experience with them. The centaurs will find them."

One of the men ran to them. "Mr. Traveler, one of the sentries has spotted a small party nearby."

It was a party of humans, about seventeen men in all, in colorful clothes—like anyone living in the lands of fae—with bags and satchels. The men noticed them and smiled.

Pangolin stood with the human sentry. Nirgund also watched them but kept glancing at his alphyns, who stared at the passing party with low growls.

Traveler stepped forward with a big smile and waved his arms wildly. "Hello! How are you? Come on in!"

The party did the same—smiled widely and wildly waved back, but they kept on their path.

"What are your names?" Traveler yelled.

The men did not answer, only continued to smile and wave.

Pangolin and the others at the perimeter looked at Traveler, confused.

"Did they not hear you?" the human sentry asked.

Traveler turned to see the royals and Gwyness joining them along with others. His eyes moved to Gwyness.

"Maiden Gwyness, where is that amulet of yours?"

"Mr. Traveler?"

"Your amulet."

"In my things."

"Please fetch it immediately and return to this spot."

Gwyness shuddered but ran. Traveler turned his attention to the party that was now almost out of sight. Gwyness returned with a small box.

Traveler grabbed the box and opened it. "The amulet had a very faint glow, and then it disappeared altogether."

He looked up at Gwyness. The women looked at him with nervousness.

"Why were you not wearing your amulet?"

"I do not always wear it, Mr. Traveler. It bothers my neck sometimes, so I put it away."

"Mr. Hobbs, please get the faun leader."

"Yes, sir. Right away."

Traveler took the amulet and put its necklace around Gwyness's neck. "For the rest of this journey, you are not to remove that amulet from your neck."

They waited for Hobbs to return with the faun leader, accompanied by two other fauns and his daughter.

"Ammon," Traveler said as he pointed. "What lies in that direction?"

The faun leader squinted. "Many centaur villages. Beyond them is Centaur City."

During the stampede, the fae-blood woman had been conspicuously absent from the front columns, but she stood nearby now. Traveler noticed that the fae-blood men were standing nearby, too, on the other side. He marched to them with an angry face.

"Did you see those humans?" he asked.

Ursi walked up to him. "Please do not do what you are about to do. It is not our concern."

Traveler ignored her. "Were those men lycanthropes?"

The fae-blood men smiled. One said, "We have never encountered a lycanthrope. How would we know?"

"Wolves tend to know other wolves."

"We are fae of light. We do not know those of darkness."

The leadership had now gathered near him.

"Lycanthrope?" Gwyness asked with a look of fear.

"You have no proof of that," Ammon, the faun leader challenged. "Why say such a thing? I have walked this world a long time, longer than you could know, and never encountered such a dark beast."

"Did we not encounter minotaur ghouls today?"

Ammon did not respond.

"This is not our matter," Ursi said. "It is for the centaurs and satyrs. It is their lands."

"Why is this of so little importance to you?" Traveler asked her.

"It simply is not."

"I tire of all this secrecy among you fae."

"Mr. Traveler, what is it you want to do?" King Aereth asked.

"Nothing, sire. However, between Arion's Spear and here, we have encountered creatures that none have seen in ages. I think, sire, maybe that is the answer. This is not about us and never has been. It has been about keeping us, or anyone, from stumbling into and interfering with the many dark plans taking place in these lands.

"But, again, it is not for us to involve ourselves. Humans have problems in our own lands. We need not take on those of other realms. I will go into those centaur villages, and Centaur City if need be, and let them know what we saw. If they wish to dismiss me, that is their right, but they will be informed."

"Why would you do that, Mr. Traveler?" Pangolin asked.

"Because I must, Mr. Pangolin. It is my nature. The dog will fly us, so your wait should not be long. In fact, we will not wait. Mr. Pangolin, you and the king will move the caravan forward at dawn, even if we are not back. The path is clear to our to next stop. Ammon, will you send faun warriors to accompany me?"

"Why?"

"I thought your people were allies of the centaurs."

"We are, but they told us that none of this is our concern. We joined your caravan to get to Atlantea, not to involve ourselves in the affairs of other races."

"I will go without them then. And no, we are not getting involved in the affairs of other races. We are simply acting as all living things should toward other living things—informing them about extreme danger in their lands, danger they may be unaware of. You saw the faces of the centaur stampede. You saw how many they were. You saw the minotaur ghouls. Like you, I did not know fae creatures could become ghouls.

"And then there were those humans, who were not humans at all. I may not know what is truly happening around us, but I will conduct myself as I would expect others to act if all the circumstances were reversed and if this were the Lands of Man and unknown creatures were roaming our lands with defenseless towns nearby. Gwyness and princess, a word."

Traveler led the two women into one of the pocket-realms.

"Who are you?" Traveler asked immediately.

"What? What do you mean, Mr. Traveler?" Lady Aylen asked.

"Princess, that fairy queen knew of you, both of you. What is Faylen?"

A look of recognition came across the women's faces at the name.

"The fairy queen suggested that the Four Kings' fixation with us is because of the two of you. Lady Aylen, who are you? Tell me about the elfin kingdom where you were born."

"It was the kingdom of Faylen, but it was destroyed."

"By whom?"

"I do not know. Gwyness and I were taken from those lands to Sirnegate as infants. We had a governess, but she died when we were little children, so we never had a chance to learn the full story."

"Was your governess human?"

"We don't know. Maybe; we have no way to know now."

"The kingdom was destroyed by creatures," Gwyness said.

"You remember, then?" Traveler asked.

"I have a feeling about it. Flashes of memories."

"And you possess an amulet that reveals undead creatures."

"Yes."

"Gwyness, from that spell you cast, the magic-seeking spell, that took the form of an apparition."

"How would these fairies know anything about us?" Lady Aylen asked.

"If that fairy knows who you are, then other fae do too. Both of you have been dishonest from the beginning."

"Mr. Traveler, that is not true!" Lady Aylen yelled.

"You are not going to Atlantea for treasure. You go for other purposes that have to do with your former kingdom."

"Mr. Traveler, please do not think we are dishonest," Gwyness said.

"I am going to those centaur villages to tell them what we saw. I will return, and we can leave these lands as quickly as possible. The two of you are coming with me."

"What?" Lady Aylen asked.

"Us?" Gwyness asked.

"Mr. Traveler, I may be the last surviving royal of my elfin clan, maybe its entire kingdom. Gwyness does know more about undead creatures than she lets on. She knows how to kill them."

"From books only, though. I have never done so in real life. I am not even certain I could."

"You do know more, then."

"We know nothing, Mr. Traveler. We only know what our late governess left in our care. We have pieced together a narrative based on scribblings, distant memories, only fragments of facts—not the whole facts or the full history of what occurred."

"What you both know is still more than I know. I spent hours talking to the other fae parties. There is not one among them who has ever before seen these creatures of the dead. Stories of the supernatural may be common in our lands, but in the lands of fae, they are almost unheard of."

"But they exist," Gwyness said.

"The creatures are more likely to walk in our lands than here. That is what is so frightening to the fae. Few know the magic necessary to battle them. What you know, however little it is, could help. You both will come with me to warn the centaurs."

The women protested, but he ignored them.

"Then our caravan will move on to the lands of the elves," he continued. "There, being in the deadly shadow of these kings aside, we will face more extreme dangers. It is for that leg of the journey that I have endeavored these past months to prepare us. Ladies, we go."

Everyone waited for Traveler, Lady Aylen, and Gwyness to return. Already, the news of the strange human party had spread throughout a nervous caravan. So did all the many rumors. Were they really humans? Were they fiends? "Fiend" being the common fae term for the undead. Were they in the lands for some evil purpose? Had they completed some evil deed? Both human and fae wanted to know what the caravan would do next.

Still others wanted Titan's Caravan to move beyond it all to continue their journey to Atlantea.

"I will send warriors with him, if he so wishes," Ammon said aloud.

"Thank you," King Aereth said. "We must always remember that our caravan master still has the heart of a healer. He wishes no innocent to come to harm."

"Yes."

Quillen watched for Traveler's return too. He held his breath. He saw hiding in the golden grass the lime-green bullfrog.

The Fabled Quest Chronicles continues in Book Three: ***Comes the War Wizards' Wrath.***

THANK YOU FOR READING!

Dear Reader,

I hope you enjoyed *In the Shadow of the Kings*.

<u>Can You Write Me a Review?</u>

If you enjoyed *In the Shadow of the Kings (Fabled Quest Chronicles, Book 2)*, I'd greatly appreciate an honest review on one or more of the following sites:

Reviews are the best way for readers to discover good books. My writer's motto is simple: "Readers Rule!" Thanks so much.

Always writing,

Austin Dragon

CONTINUE THE ADVENTURE

<u>Get Your Next *Fabled Quest Chronicles* Books!</u>

- ***Through Titan's Trail*** *(Fabled Quest Chronicles, Book 1)*
- ***In the Shadow of the Kings*** *(Fabled Quest Chronicles, Book 2)*
- ***Comes the War Wizards' Wrath*** *(Fabled Quest Chronicles, Book 3)*

- ***Fabled Quest Chronicles Box Set*** *(Books 1-3)*

<u>Also by Austin Dragon</u>

See all my books in fantasy, science fiction, and horror: http://www.austindragon.com/books

Want to know when the next *Fabled Quest* novels come out? Sign up to my VIP Readers' Club! Click HERE to get started: http://www.austindragon.com/be_a_vip

Quillen's List of Races, Beasts, and Monsters of Myth and Magic

Alphyn - a fae wolf-hound with black fur and a knotted tail, a ridge of knotted fur along its back, a lizard-like underbellies, and eagle-like forelimbs. Alphyns are rumored to be able to spit fire.

Animal Men (Animaloids) - human-like fae that have the features of a specific animal. In Titan's Caravan, one animal men has the features of a lion, others are cat-like, another reptile, and another boar-like.

Antaean - members of the sub-race of giants regarded as great warriors, ranging in height from eight to twelve feet. Antaeans wear shining armor and helmets. Their greatest magical power is that when they directly touch the earth in a deliberative stance, no force in the world can move or harm them.

Brownies - halfling sprites who look like old men with short curly dark hair and wear brown pointed conical caps and clothes. These fae are nocturnal, coming out at night to do their daily chores. They make their homes in enclosed dwellings or traveling wagons.

Caladrius Bird - a pure-white bird able to take a person's sickness into itself and then fly away, dispersing the sickness and healing both itself and the sick person.

Centaur - one of the major races of fae who live in patriarchal societies. They are half-man, half-horse; having the torso of a man extending where the neck of a horse should be.

Cervid - one of the race of deer-folk, a hoofed fae of normal human height with small horns, one above each brow. As archers, they carry short dark wooden bows.

Chamrosh - a fae hound with an eagle head and bird wings sprouting from its back. They particularly hate hippogriffs.

Cù-sìth - the name means "fairy dog" and it is as large as a small horse with a shaggy, green coat. It has pointy green ears and a long curled tail. Some have a long tail rolled up in a coil on its back. Often, it has other animals such as birds and squirrels resting on its back. Forest fae, especially leshies, have them as watch dogs or guardians.

Deer-folk or Deer People - one of the races of fae who live in patriarchal or matriarchal rustic, nomadic societies. They are a pack society who live and travel as a group at all times. They are part of the hoofed-fae races, which includes fauns, satyrs, and centaurs.

Sub-Races of Deer-folk:

Cervid - a hoofed fae of normal human height with small horns, one above each brow. As archers, cervid carry short dark wooden bows.

Elaphine - the largest species of deer-like fae with deer noses, ears, eyes, and huge antlers sprouting from their heads. As warriors, they wear armor and chainmail. They carry long bows as tall as they stand—over six feet and made of smooth, immaculately polished white wood. They are fae archers as gifted as elves and centaurs.

Rusine - are deer-like in appearance—large eyes, a black deer nose, and cloven feet. These humanoid fae are short compared to most humans, no taller than five feet in height. Most prominent is their large deer-like ears that are in constant motion.

Darkling - the name given to the phooka by Traveler when he first encountered them in Faë-Land as a lad.

Phooka   -   also   known   as   pooka, púca,phouka,phooka,phooca,puca,orpúka. They are fae shape-shifters that always take the form of some humanoid animal or animal but always black in color. The malicious ones are violent and dangerous, taking the form of frightening black animals. The benevolent ones are given to mischief and harmless pranks, not unlike fairies, but they can be quite helpful and are only dangerous to evil beasts and beings. All phookas can take the form of dogs, foxes, wolves, cats, horses, goats, rabbits, birds, and much more to frighten and shock their enemies. They are especially fond of changing into distorted versions of those animals or a combination of more than one or changing into humanoid forms with animal features.

Drow - or dark elf (not to be confused with a night elf) is a member of an elfin sub-race characterized by dark bluish skin, most often white hair—though some have black hair, and their eyes often have irises of a bright color, such as blue or purple. Drows wear only dark colors like black, dark blues, and dark purples. The original Drow sub-race had separated from high elves due to embracing dark magic. Drows abandoned the practice long ago but remain enemies to all elves, and most fae.

Elaphine - the largest species of deer-like fae with deer noses, ears, eyes, and huge antlers sprouting from their heads. As warriors, they wear armor and chainmail. They carry long bows as tall as they stand—over six feet and made of smooth, immaculately polished white wood. They are fae archers as gifted as elves and centaurs.

Elf - one of the major races of fae and the one most resembling humans in appearance. They are humanoids characterized by pointed ears, taller than the average human, and slim in build. They have fair to porcelain-like skin—though there are sub-races with darker skin. Their eyes can be one of many different colors, depending on their sub-race and clan. Their senses, strength, and stamina are far superior to humans. As with many fae, they can make themselves invisible through magic in their natural environment, can move at extreme speed whether running or fighting—almost seeming jump from one point to another in the eyes of humans, and are very long lived. Along with centaurs, they are known as the top archers in Faë-Land. They fight with blade weapons never bludgeoning weapons, and bows, never crossbows.

Different sub-races of elves have additional physical and magical abilities.

<u>Sub-Races of Elves:</u>

<u>Drow</u> - or dark elf (not to be confused with a night elf) is a member of an elfin sub-race characterized by dark bluish skin, most often white hair—though some have black hair, and their eyes often have irises of a bright color, such as blue or purple. Drows wear only dark colors like black, dark blues, and dark purples. The original Drow sub-race had separated from high elves due to embracing dark magic. Drows abandoned the practice long ago but remain enemies to all elves, and most fae.

<u>High Elf</u> - one of the elfin sub-race of tall, regal elves, exceptionally beautiful/handsome in appearance. High elves consider themselves the most royal and highest of all elves. They dwell exclusively in highly advanced and magical cities.

<u>Woodland Elf</u> - an elfin sub-race known as the best trackers in the forests with strong societies built around hunting. They have eyesight more powerful than eagles and magically can see the "after-presence" of prey they are tracking. There are two main divisions: Rustic—who live in wooded lands of modest hamlets, and Hunter—who fashion themselves after high elves and live in large tree cities.

Enfield - a fae animal with the head of a fox, foreleg like an eagle, and the hindquarters and tail of a wolf. Domesticated ones are primarily used for hunting.

Erymanthian Boar - a giant monstrous boar with red, white, or black eyes. Protruding from most of its body, including its head and forelegs, are bony, jagged, blood-stained tusks. It also has a sharp bony ridge along its back.

Fae - the sentient and dominant humanoid species of the realm of magic known as Fäe-Land.

Fae-Blood - A member of a fae race rarely seen by humans who appear to be visibly indistinguishable from an average human. They wear black attire and colored stone necklaces. There are many clans named after a specific animal, such as bear, wolf, cat, chameleon, hawk, etc., and each clan has its own unique magical powers. As their name suggests, they are fae whose very blood is pure magic.

Fairy - one of the major races of fae who live in matriarchal societies governed by queens. Fairies are often insect-like, but there are also bird-like, reptile-like, amphibian-like, mollusk-like, snail-like, and plant-like races. They are shape-shifters able to take the form of other animals, such as smaller mammals, birds, or insects. Like sprites, their different sub-races and tribes have differing magical powers. Like many fae, they possess the ability of "sizing" wherein they can magically increase or shrink their size to defend themselves. Fairies live and work with animal companions, most often birds or insects.

Faun - one of the major sub-races of hoofed-fae who live in patriarchal, rural societies governed by kings and chiefs. Fauns and satyrs are very similar, but they are not the same race. Fauns are shorter than the average human, often with a goatee, and both male and female fauns wear tops. They are peaceful, reasoned, and congenial. They often act as guides.

<u>Sub-Races of Fauns:</u>

<u>Common</u> - have pointed ears, goat horns sprouting just above their eyes, legs of a goat, and cloven hooves.

<u>Grand</u> - have large curving ram's horns sprouting from their head and are above average human height.

Fenodyree - also fenoderee, are hairy sprite halflings, covered from head-to-toe in thick, woolly hair. Similar to brownies, they like outdoor work and can be very helpful performing arduous tasks. They are also fond of caring for livestock and animals.

<u>Flying Horse</u> - a horse with the wings of a giant bird and capable of flying. They can be of any color and different kinds have differing magical properties. They are also (incorrectly) called a pegasus by humans, but Pegasus was the name of a specific legendary flying horse.

<u>Ghoul</u> - an undead creature but, unlike a zombie, are intelligent and calculating. They are extremely strong and only special magic or physical force that can destroy their entire physical form at once can kill them. They can also turn another into a ghoul with physical contact, such as with a scratch or bite. Ghouls serve dark masters and "live" to commit acts of evil.

<u>Giant</u> - one of the major races of fae who live in patriarchal societies governed by kings and chiefs. The majority of the giant races are warriors, all possessing great strength, but others have kingdoms of diverse occupations. Giants can range in height from ten to one hundred feet.

<u>Sub-Races of Giants:</u>

<u>Antaeans</u> - members of the sub-race of giants regarded as great warriors, ranging in height from eight to twelve feet. Antaeans wear shining armor and helmets. Their greatest magical power is that when they directly touch the earth in a deliberative stance, no force in the world can move or harm them.

<u>Giant Animals</u> - domesticated ones are used as steeds, guard animals, or beasts of burden. Titan's Caravan includes giant crabs, giant turtles, giant porcupines, giant ducks, giant cranes, and a giant moose.

<u>Gnome</u> - fae halfling sprites known for their perpetual happy-go-lucky personality, amiability, and love of dancing, singing and music. They often have beards but not always. They often look older, but there are baby-faced clans. They always wear hats, though gnomes exclusively wear pointy, often red, conical hats.

<u>Gnomoid</u> - there are many races of sprites similar to gnomes, though not as good-natured. They also wear hats but not the pointy conical ones of gnomes.

<u>Griffin</u> - a fantastic beast with the body, tail, and hind legs of a lion and golden yellow fur. Its head and foreleg talons are that of a giant eagle. The animal is known for its echoing roar. Griffins are often used by fae as royal steeds or guardians of treasure. Like hippogriffs, they have a fondness for eating horses of the Lands of Man.

<u>Half-Elf</u> - humanoid with one elfin parent and one human parent. They have pointed ears but often not as pronounced as a full elf. They are far stronger than an average human and possess superior senses. Many often have the same magical abilities as their elfin lineage or to a lesser degree. They have a much longer life span than humans, and some have the ability to communicate telepathically with other half-elves, suggesting that elves, secretly, have the same ability.

<u>Half-Goblin</u> - one parent is goblin and the other human. They have pointed ears, green skin, and its goblin features vary: one or more horns, a large pointed noise, and a larger chin.

<u>Haltija</u> - a sub-race of sprites that guard, help, or protect something or somebody. Haltijas appear as frowning full-bearded halfling men with pointy hats. They are nocturnal sprites like brownies, coming out at night for their daily tasks. They are ill-tempered, rude, surly, and hate being talked to directly. They are also shape-shifters. A clan of haltijas is called a väki and there are many different clans in Faë-Land.

<u>Sub-Races of Haltija</u>:

<u>Tulen Väki</u> or väki of fire - the clan of haltijas who wear charred dark brown and orange fabric clothing. They are a race of guardians with the elemental magically ability to conjure and control fire and use warm air to heal or burn.

<u>Väki</u> - Besides the tulen väki or väki of fire there are also väki of specific trees, forests, mountains, water, precious metals or gems, underground lands, etc.

High Elf - one of the elfin sub-race of tall, regal elves exceptionally beautiful/handsome in appearance. They consider themselves the most royal and highest of all elves. They dwell exclusively in highly advanced and magical cities.

Hippogriff - a fantastic beast that has the hind half of a horse and the front half, including head and forelegs, of a giant eagle. It is known for its loud eagle shrieks. Like griffins, they have a fondness for eating horses of the Lands of Man.

Humanoid Animals

<u>Sub-Races of Humanoid Animals</u>:

Frog men, lizard men, squirrel men, raccoon men, possums, fox men, rabbit men, bird men, and mice men.

Imp - this dark fae is a small, gray, ugly humanoid creature, with bat-like wings, big ears, and tiny horns poking out above its eyebrows. Its skin is either stone-like or scaly. Imps are known for their destructive mischief against unsuspecting fae or humans. Their wild pranks are often a result of boredom rather than evil. When discovered or caught they are given to wild outbursts as they run or fly away. Imps can also be very territorial—bound to a specific region or love to hide in specific objects, especially magical objects. Though most of their pranks are harmless, they have been known to engage in more serious acts such as taking babies or small animals, leading people astray to their death, and starting fires. They are also shape-shifters, which they often take full advantage of in their pranks, and can turn invisible as they escape. Imps have been used as spies or agents for evil wizards.

Ipotane - a fae race of half-horse, half-humanoids. They have a man's body, hoofed feet, and the head of a horse, and they wear trousers alone. They are a semi-intelligent race similar to minotaurs and are not regarded as part of the hoofed fae races of fauns, satyrs, or centaurs.

Jackalope - a fae animal that is a rabbit with antlers. Domesticated, they are used as watch dogs and for hunting.

Kirin - also ki-rin or quilin. A fantastic beast from the magical lands beyond Faë-Land, and is often called a dragon-horse (though there is another magical beast by that name). These intelligent animals serve as companions, guardians, and protectors. They have varying characteristics of other animals to match their environments and varying magical abilities. They can fly, whether they have wings or not, and can swim or gallop under water.

They never harm benevolent life or pure souls, but they are swift and fierce to attack if threatened or to protect a defenseless or pure person threatened by a malicious thing. They are thought to be a symbol of luck, good omens, protection, prosperity, success, and longevity. They are also rumored to see future events before they happen.

Leshy - known as guardians of the forest, they are male fae with white skin and hair and full beards of living grass and vines. They have bright green eyes and hooved feet, and some have horns and tails. They areshape-shifters known for the ability to take the form of any animal or plant. They can shrink to the size of an insect or grow to the size of the tallest tree. They can imitate the voice of any human or humanoid, make the sound of any animal, and can scream horribly to frighten enemies. They often keep animals as companions, the favorite being a cù-sìth.

There are also dark leshies given to leading travelers astray, kidnapping, or making people sick.

<u>Tree Shepherds</u> - are leshies who control any number of magical, sentient trees—walking, crawling, or flying.

Lizard, Giant Fae - or giant rainbow lizard of fae. The lizards can be blue, yellow, green, or orange. They hatch from large melon-sized, leathery eggs and grow to over twenty feet long, not including the tail. Together, giant fae lizards walk, defend, and attack as a pack. They can magically see invisible fae beings and animals during the day, must have heat during the night to sleep, and have magical regenerative powers, including the ability to grow severed limbs. As they mature, they exhibit other magical powers based on their environment and keepers.

Merfolk or Merpeople - See Mermaid or Merman.

Mermaid - one of the major races of fae who live in matriarchal underwater cities governed by queens. They are beautiful female humanoids with a large fish tail instead of bipedal legs. Their skin is an almost luminescent light blue; they have long, flowing hair, and their eyes can either be similar to fish's or human's. The only clothing they wear are a type of brassiere—like cloth wrapped around their breast area several times.

Malevolent mermaids love storms and floods, and are present at shipwrecks and drownings. Also, like sirens they can lure and attract humans and other humanoids with their enchanted singing, often to crash sea-going vessels onto rocks. Benevolent ones can help victims of natural disasters at sea and have been known to fall in love with humans, giving up their fae life to live as a human.

Merman - Ugly male sea humanoids that look like a brown fish but with the head of a man—blue-green hair, unsightly teeth, and slits for eyes. They enjoy storms and being present at sinking ships. Despite their appearance, they can magically cure sickness and lift curses. Others are sages and oracles.

Minotaur - a race of semi-intelligent fae that are humanoid bulls. Minotaurs have sharp, pointed or jagged, dual horns protruding from their heads, large bull ears, and extremely muscular necks. They wear loincloths and sometimes use weapons such as axes, maces, and clubs.

Nisse - A sub-race of sprites who are very friendly and gregarious little people, knee-high, wearing bright green pointy hats as long as their bodies. They are never without a smile on their face. There are both men and women. The bearded men dress in standard dark tunics and trousers; the women dress in lighter colored dresses with their blond or brunette hair braided behind them. Other nisse wear red or orange hats too. They are believed to have shape-shifting abilities too.

Despite size, they have tremendous strength, like all sprites. Often they are protectors of farmlands, livestock, and animals. They are easily offended by rudeness, laziness, and the mistreatment of animals.

Nymph - one of the major races of fae who live in matriarchal societies. They are enchanting, beautiful women with long hair. They look human, but have an angelic glow. Human men are helpless to their powerful, magical attraction; fae men can also be susceptible to their enchantment.

Sub-Races of Nymphs:
Crinaeae - water nymphs of fountains
Dryads - nymphs of the trees
Hamadryads - nymphs that live in the trees themselves
Hydriades or ephydriades - water nymphs
Limnades or Limnatides - water nymphs of lakes
Naiads - water nymphs of fresh water
Napaeae - nymphs of wooded valleys
Oceanids - water nymphs of oceans
Pegaeae - water nymphs of springs
Potameides - water nymphs of rivers

Ogre - a carnivorous giant humanoid, often with large fanged teeth, and especially fond of human or humanoid flesh. It can be anywhere from eight to fifty feet or more. Many are deformed or misshapen with one or more heads, and oversized facial features or body parts, such as hands, arms, or heads. Its skin is often a sickly greenish or gray color. It wears animal hides or fur for clothing. The creature is a solitary hunter that roams its chosen territory. Along with trolls, ogres are not considered by fae as part of the fae race of giants.

Pech - halfling sprites with wild, bushy eyebrows—the far ends pointing up—have big noses, and even bigger forearms bulging from their tunics. They wear off-white tunics, dark trousers and boots, and dark caps. They are some of the strongest sprites in Faë-Land.

Pegasus - see Flying Horse.

Phooka - also known as pooka, púca,phouka,phooka,phooca,puca,orpúka. They are fae shape-shifters that always take the form of some humanoid animal or animal but always black in color. The malicious ones are violent and dangerous, taking the form of frightening black animals. The benevolent ones are given to mischief and harmless pranks, not unlike fairies, but they can be quite helpful and are only dangerous to evil beasts and beings. All phookas can take the form of dogs, foxes, wolves, cats, horses, goats, rabbits, birds, and much more to frighten and shock their enemies. They are especially fond of changing into distorted versions of those animals or a combination of more than one or changing into humanoid forms with animal features.

Pixy - a tiny sprite that appears as an insect-winged man with a child-like face and pointy ears, who wear a green pointed hat and a green outfit. They are prone to mischievous but harmless pranks. They like to play with animals, especially horses, music, gather in groups for dancing or horseplay, and their favorite pastime is to pester humans, which includes leading them astray and stealing children!

Rusine - are deer-like in appearance—large eyes, a black deer nose, and cloven feet. These humanoid fae are short compared to most humans, no taller than five feet in height. Most prominent is their large deer-like ears that are in constant motion.

Spell-Talker - a rare demon that looks like a pale human male with pure black eyes. On either side of its mouth are holes—used to magically lock its mouth closed by its master. It can kill any living thing by simply speaking words of dark magic over a steady but short period of time unless stopped.

Sprite - one of the major races of fae who live in patriarchal rural societies governed by kings, chiefs, or clan chiefs. Sprites are human-like halflings or smaller but like all sprites and fairies, they possess the ability of "sizing" wherein they can magically increase or shrink their size to defend themselves.

Tree People - A race of fae tree humanoids with bark for skin, wide eyes, and loosely foliated branches for hair. Known for their ancient wisdom and ability to speak with all fae flora and fauna.

Tree Shepherd - a special clan of leshies who control any number of magical, sentient trees—walking, crawling, or flying.

Tulen Väki or väki of fire - the clan of haltijas who wear charred brown and orange fabric clothing. They are a race of guardians with the elemental magically ability to conjure and control fire and use warm air to heal or burn.

Unicorn - a magical horse with a large single horn one to two feet long protruding from his forehead. They can be of any color and different kinds have differing magical properties; some are also winged and can fly. Unicorns are a favorite steed of elves and an animal companion to fairies.

Väki - a clan of haltijas. Besides the **tulen väki** or väki of fire there are also väki of specific trees, forests, mountains, water, precious metals or gems, underground lands, etc.

Woodland Elf - an elfin sub-race known as the best trackers in the forests with strong societies built around hunting. They have eyesight more powerful than eagles and magically can see the "after-presence" of prey they are tracking. There are two main divisions: Rustic—who live in wooded lands of modest hamlets, and Hunter—who fashion themselves after high elves and live in large tree cities.

ABOUT THE AUTHOR

Austin Dragon is author of the new epic fantasy adventure *Fabled Quest Chronicles*, the cyberpunk detective series, *Liquid Cool*, the *After Eden Series* (including the *After Eden: Tek-Fall* mini-series), and the *Sleepy Hollow Horrors*. He is a native New Yorker, but has called Los Angeles, California home for the last twenty years. Words to describe him, in no particular order: U.S. Army, English teacher, one-time resident of Paris, political junkie, movie buff, Fortune 500 corporate recruiter, renaissance man, dreamer.

He is currently working on new books and series in science fiction, fantasy, and classic horror!

Connect with Austin on social media at:

Website and blog: http://www.austindragon.com

Twitter: https://twitter.com/Austin_Dragon

Pinterest: http://www.pinterest.com/austindragon

Google+: https://google.com/+AustinDragonAuthor

Goodreads: https://www.goodreads.com/ADragon

<u>**Other books by Austin Dragon**</u>

See all my books at: http://www.austindragon.com/books